HISTORY OF THE POLK ADMINISTRATION.—By Lucien B. Chase, Member of the Twenty-ninth and Thirtieth Congress. 8vo., pp. 512. New York: George P. Putnam.

OPINIONS OF THE PRESS.

The administration of Mr. Polk is probably unsurpassed by any previous one, in the grandeur of its enterprises, or the brilliancy of their accomplishment. The conquest of Mexico, the acquisition of California, the settlement of the Northern Boundary, the adoption of a new Commercial system, the Reduction of Postage, and the opening of new and vast routes of postal communication, belong to a class of national measures, so wide, so far-reaching, and so weighty, that their progress attracted every eye, and their adoption touched every interest. It is for this reason that the influence of Mr. Polk's administration is so vast, so immeasurable, and even, as yet, so partially developed. Amid such gigantic operations, there were likewise mistakes and errors, which were serious, widely pervading, though never disastrous. To take up such a subject, and do justice to its merits, in a single volume, requires a comprehensiveness, and grasp of intellect, a condensation of thought, a force and energy of style, which belongs only to the most cultivated and talented writers. Highly as we have ever esteemed the abilities of the author of this interesting volume, we must confess that we were not prepared for such a successful and brilliant accomplishment of his great task as he has here presented to us.

The great measures of Mr. Polk's term; their nature and extent; the causes that led to their introduction; the embarrassments and obstructions that beset their progress; the difficulties that were vanquished, and the circumstances of success, that were even created by foresight and judgment; their successful achievement, with the strong approbation of the nation, are pourtrayed with a fullness, a discrimination, and a justness, which renders this work not only the most correct and best general history which we have of that period, but probably places it beyond the reach of a competitor. The statement of facts appears to be prepared with much care, as it regards their correctness; and for this the author possessed unusual advantages, as he was a distinguished member of Congress during the entire period. The work is remarkably free from partizan bias, and the errors of Mr. Polk are related without qualification or extenuation. It is also entirely free from anything like bitter, or party epithets, and the dignity of the historian is preserved throughout. As a historical work, in itself; as a history of a most important period in our national existence; as a collection even of some of the most interesting events in our career, delineated with much urbanity and graphic richness of style, this volume should be sought and obtained by every patriotic American citizen. —*Hunt's Merchants' Magazine.*

HISTORY OF THE POLK ADMINISTRATION.—It is an able defence of the Administration of Mr. Polk; abler, indeed, than the opponents of that administration, whether whigs or free-soilers, will probably be disposed to admit. . . . . . In the narration of events it is brief and clear; in its statement of facts accurate and guarded; and in that portion of it relating to the war with Mexico, it is succinct in narrative and apparently impartial. . . . . . Those parts of the work animated by a spirit of self-respect, in defence of his party—or those written, *con amore*, and, as it were, under the victorious banner of the Union, in praise of the gallantry of the army, and as a tribute of respect to its chivalrous leaders, are in our judgment highly creditable to their writer, and exceedingly interesting. These passages, brief, off-hand, and evidently penned without effort and without labor, are indeed as just as they are beautiful.—*Whig Correspondent of the Albany Argus.*

"Mr. Chase, a member of two Congresses, a personal friend of the President, and an intimate friend of Post-Master Cave Johnson, whose district he represented, has undertaken to write the history of that administration. He seems to us to have performed his task with impartiality, with clearness of style, and particularly with great power of argument. . . . . . Evidently there has been no effort spared on the part of the author to find the most reliable authorities for every statement, and he has consulted in his relation of the Mexican War, the Mexican account as well as our own. . . Mr. Chase censures as readily and as honestly as he praises, and his work, if we mistake not, will become authority upon all the points which it treats."—*New York Evening Mirror.*

"For the statesman and politician and those who devote much time to the political history of the day this volume possesses decided interest. The author was a member of Congress from the State of Tennessee during the whole of the Administration of President Polk, and enjoyed a large degree of intercourse with him. His position was therefore such as to put him in possession of various facilities and a mass of information relative to current political events accessible to but very few. These have been used with great discrimination in the production of the present 'History.' The remarkable events that crowded into the administration of Mr. Polk are narrated with perspicuity and vigor, and so arranged as to prove invaluable for reference."—*Buffalo Courier.*

"The History of the Polk Administration—one of the most eventful and memorable in the history of the government—has been written by a distinguished member of Congress through Mr. Polk's entire term, the Hon. Lucien B. Chase. We have it before us in a large quarto form, from the press of Putnam, of New York. It is an interesting and able review of the policy and measures of the late administration, of the Mexican War, and the great questions in agitation during that period, with sketches of Mr. Polk's career, and of the cabinet—which it will be found useful to consult, now, and in the future."—*Albany Argus.*

"This work opens with a view of the contest that resulted in the election of Mr. Polk, and then proceeds to a consideration of the various questions that came up in Congress during his administration. A large portion of the volume is occupied with the Mexican war, and the narrative is clear, interesting, and impartial. The reader will not only find here a detail of the brilliant progress of the American armies, but a good view of the rise of the whole Texas question. This history occupies seven of the twelve chapters of the book. Three other prominent questions occupy a proper degree of attention, and are treated much in the same way—namely, a concise detail given of their origin and progress—and those are the tariff, the internal improvement, and the slavery questions. These are presented with great fulness and ability.

* * * * * * *

This volume is a valuable addition to our political history. It contains facts gathered with care and much research, which the politician will find to be most convenient and useful, and which the general reader will find to be reliable. The author, though a member of the democratic party, and though in the main a defender of Mr. Polk's administration, is no blind eulogist. He does not hesitate to blame as well as praise. The reader will find here written in a friendly hand, and yet in an impartial manner, a good history of the remarkable events that will make Mr. Polk's administration stand out forever in our annals. The work is handsomely got up—no small recommendation—and is as creditable to the scholarship as it is to the patriotism of its author."—*Boston Post.*

ENGLISH SERFDOM

AND

AMERICAN SLAVERY:

OR,

OURSELVES—AS OTHERS SEE US.

BY LUCIEN B. CHASE,

AUTHOR OF

"THE HISTORY OF THE POLK ADMINISTRATION."

"The celebrated saying of Sir Richard Fletcher, uttered more than two hundred years ago, 'Let me write the *ballads* for a people, and I care not who make the *laws*,' might be transposed by saying—Let me write the *fictions* for a people, and I care not who make the *speeches*."—NATIONAL INTELLIGENCER.

"Now step I forth to whip hypocrisy."—SHAKESPEARE.

NEW YORK:

H. LONG & BROTHER,

42 ANN-STREET.

TO THE

ARISTOCRATIC LADIES OF GREAT BRITAIN

IS DEDICATED THIS WORK,

Wherein the author portrays the graceful equanimity with which they regard the horrible condition of the *substratum* of English society. Credit is also very properly given them for discovering fascinations in the sooty progeny of Ham—that excellent gentleman, and especial favorite of the Almighty—which may vainly be looked for in their own vulgar race: fascinations that have aroused the admiration of England's too susceptible Dames, and awakened the slumbering goodness of her benevolent politicians, to such a painful degree, that they are disqualified for a performance of those charitable obligations, which are imposed upon them, to ameliorate the condition of English Serfdom.

PREFACE.

THE world is indebted to the philanthropic ladies and gentlemen, who frequent Almacks, and lead London fashion, for several remarkable improvements upon the example set by the Redeemer. Their sensibilities are so much affected by the presence of suffering, that they take especial care to avoid it. At the same time they discreetly compromise with conscience by an ostentatious bestowal of alms upon distant, and, *therefore*, more worthy objects.

Our Saviour did not avail himself of an expedient which commends itself to persons of less goodness, but greater tact. With him, charity began at home; with them, a commencement there, would preclude the hope of its ever reaching far enough to swell into *notoriety;* especially where it has so many objects to relieve, as can be found upon every square acre of the British empire. And hence, the folly of making the attempt. Again, Jesus taught humility. Now humility sits very uncomfortably upon a proud man, or woman either, and hence, it is much more agreeable for them to asseverate their own purity, and the sinfulness of the "rest of mankind." They have made a decided improvement upon the teachings of the Saviour, in this regard; for they graciously condescend to point out, and with commendable precision, wherein other nations, and especially the slavery-loving people of the United States, are far less holy than they are. The Redeemer was celebrated for modesty as well as meekness; both of which traits were, perhaps, eminently suited to his time, and to his divine character. The English nobility, however, have effected changes, in this particular, no less striking than appropriate. He rode into Jerusalem, on a certain occasion, upon the back of an animal, whose venerable appearance cannot fail to win our respect, while the distinguished services rendered by his ancestors, of which mention is made in suitable and flattering terms, by history, sacred as well as profane, places him in the very front rank of four-footed animals. But now, Timothy, Lord Snizzle, and Sir Pertinax McFlummux, would ride their *own* legs from London to Newcastle, rather than be seen mounted upon a respectable donkey, in the centre of Hyde Park.

There is this striking reason for a modification of the crude morality of the Son of God. He was born in a manger, a place that would, of course, preclude him from establishing rules for the government of those who consider poverty highly reprehensible. His circumstances or his inclinations were such, that he neither rejoiced in purple and fine linen, or indulged in the pleasures of the table. There is a marked contrast between his humble career and the dashing life of the English nobility. There is a manifold propriety in the free indulgence by the latter in extravagance and folly, else how could they create a *sensation*, not having a sufficient amount of brains wherewithal to do so. Their only chance of winning celebrity, is by expending with liberal hands the money which is moistened by the tears of the poor—tears that are entitled to no sympathy, from the aristocracy, because *they* do not shed them!

But seriously—no thoughtful mind can fail to observe, the zeal with which the nobility and politicians of England seek to withdraw public condemnation from their own political and social organization, by concentrating it upon the peculiar institution of the southern states.

Leaving the tyranny unrebuked, which has debased the spirit, and broken the constitutions of their lower classes, they assail the Americans with a vindictiveness which is only equalled by its unblushing effrontery. Overlooking the absolute control of the Czar of Russia over life and death, through the terrible agency of the halter, the knout, and the snows of Siberia, they launch their curses against those who are allied to them by the bonds of a communism of language, of interest, and of blood.

What is the motive for this energetic and persevering crusade against a people who, so far from having wronged them, are furnishing cotton for their manufactories, employment for their laborers, food for their starving population, and homes for those who are driven by famine from their native land?

Recognizing with apparent sincerity the existence of those ties which trade and commerce would rivet more closely every succeeding year but for an *impertinent* interference in the domestic affairs of the great republic, why is it that they assail their transatlantic brethren with the combined power of money and abuse?

The motive is indubitable. They have everything to gain and nothing to lose from the example of Russia, and everything to lose and nothing to gain from the example of the United States. The principles upon which the constitution of the model republic is based, are not confined to the western continent. They are wielding a silent but irresistible influence upon the masses of the old world, who are awakening to the grand idea that absolute power is vested in the people alone. To save their rotten institutions from crumbling beneath the tread of the Goddess of *Liberty*, her great exemplar must be destroyed.

Therefore, they leave their own hemisphere to labor beneath a load of oppression which cries aloud for vengeance, while they cross the ocean in search of objects upon whom they can expend their sympathies, and shed the tears of commiseration. Abolition agents are sent forth, money is expended, the press of London groans under the weight of misrepresentation and calumny, and the pulpit and the forum swarm with Pharisees, who thank God because they are not like other men. To cap the climax of absurdity, the most illustrious of England's Aristocracy, and the favorite of her Queen, indulges herself in the agreeable pastime of chaperoning a negress!

The patience of a long-suffering people is exhausted. There is a point beyond which detraction cannot go unrebuked. There is a period of time when the assailed will turn upon their foes. That point of time is the present, and by the powerful aid of facts, the author has, in the following pages, exposed the monstrous iniquities which are hourly perpetrated by the slavery-hating government and aristocracy of Great Britain; and with the trenchant blade of truth has assailed cant and hypocrisy, where they seek to entrench themselves behind Pharisaical protestations, a false religion, and a disreputable philanthropy.

New York, January, 1854.

ENGLISH SERFDOM AND AMERICAN SLAVERY.

CHAPTER I.

"Behind the master walks, builds up the shocks."—THOMSON.

THE threatening cloud that had been gathering its forces in the west, urged the already wearied laborers to renewed exertions. Shocks of wheat thickly studded the field, but there yet remained upon the earth long rows of gavels ready to be bound into sheaves. The young farmer cast frequent and anxious glances to the dark mass that rose like a moving wall, and then, by his voice and example, stimulated his companion to increased activity. But the relentless storm heeded not his imploring countenance. It hurtled onward, and vivid flashes of lightning gleamed along the base of the cloud and darted into the blue ether above, followed by quick, sharp peals of thunder that increased in violence as they rolled away until the last report shook the earth. Turning his eyes upward to the summit of the cloud, his vision ranged along the broad belt of whirling vapor, until it rested at the point where the dark mass swept along the ground. There his gaze was riveted, and a look of awe overspread his features. Through the mist that partly shaded the body of the cloud, he saw that the storm was raging furiously. Here and there a tree was twisted off, and the roof of a cottage upon a neighboring hill was carried away. He looked toward his own humble dwelling—the chimney was thrown down. Folding his arms, while his teeth set in despair, he saw the advance guard of the storm sweep up the ascent, heralded by large drops of rain. As it reached the wheat-field, it made a swoop, and those shocks that had been reared with so much labor were scattered over the earth. The next moment the rain descended in torrents.

"Begorra! Misther Christie, thaive lift divil of a shock standin' at all at all."

Christie Kane turned gloomily away, and without seeking shelter from the storm, walked slowly out of the field.

"No wonder the lad takes it to heart, for we've tried hard enough to dry this batch of whate, and now, be me sowl, we must be afther spreadin' it all oot again. Never mind, we poor divils have only got to work *all the time*; that's some comfort ony how. So here goes for a dry skin, and a thatch that don't lake."

Saying which, Phelim Savor rapidly proceeded towards the house, dividing his thoughts between the rain that beat through his tattered hat, and the song that had pleased him so much at the last wake, short snatches of which burst from his lips between the peals of thunder.

"Be the holy St. Pathrick but the rain, bad luck to it, finds siveral crivices in this coat. Never mind, if it *lakes* now, it is *airy* in dry weather, that's some satisfaction, ony how.

'They walked,
And talked.
He tormented.
First she sighed,
Then consented
To be his bride.'

"Niver a dry rag will Phalim Savor have upon his back in the matter of ten minutes."

'He tormented.
First she sighed,
Then consented—

"Arrah! that's the way wid the darlints :—

To be his bride.'

"Whoop, wan't that a smasher! The faycher of the blacksmit' fraternity is forgin' some big thunder to-day, onyhow—

'Then consented.'

"Suzy Gowrie, what dul ye think of this," said Phelim, as he entered the house.

"It's a braw storm, ee'n for the heelands. But where is Mr. Christie?"

"He's offinded bekase the wind blowed over the whate."

"It did not show mickle care in its course, sure enough."

"Nivir mind complainin', Suzy. It's the duty of the lab'rer to work all the time. Don't the praists tell us that we must be satisfied wid our condition, and if the nobility hiv it all their own way in this world, that, perhaps, we shall be as happy as thim in the nixt?"

"I doan't think it roight for half of the human family to work for the other half; and you *know* I doan't."

"Be azy now, Miss Gowrie darlint, don't git on that subject untwil you have something for me to ate. That's a jewell of a gal; cold praties and bread. Now, let me rayson the matter wid you. Do you suppose the nobility and gintry would like to come out of their iligant houses, into the hot fields and bind up the shafes of whate?"

"Hoot! what a question!"

"Well, of coorse you will say no. An' why should they? Wouldn't the sun scorch their white skin? and wouldn't the rough grain, and the *thristles*, too, hurt their dilicate hands? Isn't it azier for us, who are accustomed to such hardships, to labor for thim, than for such gintlefolks to work for thimselves? Come now, Suzy, ba ginerous, an' admit it."

"And because we have been their slaves, shall we always be so? Oin't we all flesh and blood? If we receive a blow, do we not feel? If we are cut, do we not bleed? If we are hungry, do we not want food? If we cease to breathe, do we not die? Hoot mon, you *deserve* to be a slave!"

And Susan Gowrie proceeded about her work with great impetuosity.

"There you go now, Suzy, there's no rayson in a faymale, *onyhow*. Now see here, Suzy, suppose you was Ellen Knowles, would it ba the likes of yez that would be plazed to scrub the kitchen, and stan' all day fernenst the fire?"

Suzan Gowrie deigned no other reply save the indignation that flashed from her eyes.

"*Havn't* they been towld from their hinfancy that they hiv a dervine right to our services; that we are to work while they are not to do a haperth, and when they hiv such expectations, shall we ba afther baing so mane as to chate thim out of their blissed rights?"

The blue veins were swollen upon Susan's forehead, and she replied with great energy.

"An' we, every mother's chiel of us, must suffer hunger, disease, and death, to gratify the lazy aristocracy! We must toil and sweat from morning till night to minister to their whims. We must broil over the fire, or beneath the scorching sun, while they roll in their carriages, or recline upon their couches! Phelim Savor, you are a fool!"

A merry twinkle appeared in Phelim's eyes, during the nervous retort of the girl, but the reply that rose to his lips was checked by the entrance of Christie Kane, whose dripping garments bore evidence of the severity of the storm. Passing through the kitchen, he entered the humble sitting-room, and throwing himself into a chair, reclined his head upon his hand.

"In the dumps again, are ye?" exclaimed the harsh voice of a female.

The young man remained silent.

"Christie Kane! am I always to see you gloomy and discontented? Ever to look upon a frowning brow, and hear nothing but complaints?" continued the woman, querulously.

Still he deigned no reply.

"Come, come, Christie," she said more kindly; "do not look so disconsolate; your cousin Ellen is in the other room."

A momentary smile crossed the features of the young man, and then they assumed once more an expression of deep gloom.

"Mother, my patience is entirely exhausted."

"Pooh! child; compare your situation with that of your neighbors: is it not far better?"

"No! look at the condition of the upper classes, from the Duke of Sunderland to Sir William Belthoven: what occupation have they but to spend—often in wanton extravagance—the money which is earned by toil and suffering?"

"Yes, but see how many there are who are not so fortunate as ourselves. Look at the poor families in our parish. They can hardly obtain sufficient food to keep them from starvation."

"Aye, that is the result of the accursed political system which is grinding the lower classes—*the substratum*—into the dust."

"What would you do?"

"Do! I would equalize the condition of the people; educate and elevate the masses; abolish the hunting-grounds and parks of the nobility, and surrender them to the plough; reduce the salaries of corrupt public officers; curtail the benefices of avaricious clergy; and abolish the standing army by rendering its existence unnecessary, when the government is sustained by the affection of the nation. *Do?* I would apply the knife of reform to the social regulations and laws of England!"

The door was opened, and a girl glided into the room. She had numbered eighteen years, and her form was round and well-developed. Her eyes were blue, and of a strange expression. While the glance of Christie Kane was directed towards her they were demurely turned to the floor, but no sooner was his look withdrawn, than a cunning look gleamed from the sidelong glances of her eyes.

The features of the young man softened as she seated herself in the chair just vacated by Mrs. Kane.

"Ellen, it was kind of you to come over when the sky looked so threatening. I am glad to see you. Did you get here before the rain commenced falling?"

"A few minutes," replied the sweet voice of Ellen Knowles, as her hand rested upon that portion of the chair nearest to Christie Kane.

"What a beautiful hand, Ellen," he said, softly, as he placed the point of his fingers upon it.

As he raised his eyes to her own, the cunning side-long glance was withdrawn. He started to his feet, and turned towards the door.

"You will not encounter the storm again, will you, cousin Christie? The water is still dripping from your coat," said Ellen's gentle voice.

"The rain is over," he replied gruffly, as he stood in the doorway.

"Have I offended you, Christie?" inquired the maiden, as a tear gathered in her mild blue eyes.

"Oh, no, Ellen; you *could* not," said the young man, as he turned frankly toward her. "Come, will you not walk with me? See how the drops of rain glisten upon the trees. I will show you what sad havoc the storm has committed in my wheat field."

"Excuse me, Christie; I fear the damp earth."

"Good-bye, then, Ellen."

"Good-bye," replied the gentle voice.

"She is a strange girl, and I am half afraid of her," muttered Christie Kane, as he emerged from the house. "Why is mother so anxious for me to marry her?"

The storm was raging still far to the east, but the west presented an unclouded sky. Directing his steps down the lane, Christie entered the high road crossing the small stream, which was swollen by the rain. He was proceeding slowly through the forest that spanned the valley, when his steps were arrested by a carriage which lay in the middle of the road with one of the axle-trees broken, and a wheel lying upon the ground. Looking around to see what caused the accident, his eyes rested upon the form of a young lady, who was standing beneath the bending trunk of a large oak, which had sheltered her from the storm. The maiden gazed half terrified at the young man, but observing his look of open and respectful admiration, the warm blood returned to the cheek from whence alarm had banished it; so truly can the gentler sex interpret the impression which their loveliness has produced.

Christie advanced, and with innate courtesy raised his hat.

"Will you suffer me, madame, to inquire the cause of your misfortune?"

"A defective axletree;" and the young man thought the voice exceedingly musical.

"Will you allow me to tender my services?"

"They will hardly be required. My companion has been absent at least half an hour, for another carriage."

"But I shall consider it a great favor if you will permit me to bring a conveyance. I am *certain* you will take cold, if you remain long exposed to this damp atmosphere;" said Christie, pleadingly.

A smile wreathed the lips of the young lady at the earnestness of the stranger. After hesitating a moment, she replied,

"Very well, if you return first, perhaps—"

Christie did not wait to hear the conclusion of the sentence, but with a gratified look, proceeded rapidly towards the cottage.

By the exertions of Mr. Savor, the dapple grey was soon harnessed to the plain gig, and having changed his hat, coat, and boots, and donned a smart pair of gloves, Christie Kane, with a flushed countenance, drove rapidly away.

"Why didn't he ask me to *ride*, as well as walk?" exclaimed Ellen, sulkily.

"I can't tell what has come over the child. He has changed for the worse lately. Formerly he was so gentle and obedient, and now he is morose and abstracted;" replied Mrs. Kane.

"Would yez belave it," said Phelim; "he grumbles bekase the likes of us hiv to support the nobility. He niver wonst remimbers that whilst we do that same, we live ourselves; whin the poor divils who are starvin' hiv no support at all at all. But even they hiv the satisfaction of swelling the population of this mighty koontry, though by the holy St. Pathrick its little their amaciated figgers can swell it, onyhow. What's your opinion, Suzy?"

Susan's only reply was a look of mingled pity and contempt.

As young Kane arrived at the spot where he had left the lady, he observed an equipage approach from the opposite direction, from which a young gentleman descended, and offering his arm to the maiden, observed:

"I hope you have been put to no inconvenience by my long absence."

"And if I have not, it surely cannot be because sufficient time has not elapsed since your departure," she replied, tartly.

"I do not deserve *that* sarcasm," he said, reproachfully; "I made all possible haste. But come, do not delay any longer."

"I shall ride in this conveyance," and the maiden approached Christie's vehicle, disclosing as she did so, the most bewitching little foot and ankle, encased in the most bewitching little boot that ever caused a thrill in the hearts of the sterner sex. Christie sprang from the gig, and deferentially tendered his hand to aid her ascent, but mentally pronouncing a malediction at the folly which prompted him to wear a glove upon his right hand, thereby depriving himself—*voluntarily* depriving himself of the pleasure which a touch of the taper fingers of her ungloved hand would produce.

"Thank you," said the musical voice; and she adjusted her dress so as to make room for Christie Kane by her side.

"And now, Melville, let us see who will reach home first."

The person whom she addressed as Melville, stood with folded arms, and frowning brow.

"Ha! ha! ha!" rang forth the merriest laugh Christie had ever heard. "Come, take the reins," she exclaimed; "I dare you to the trial."

Scowling at young Kane, the stranger sprang into his gig, and wheeling his horse's head, dashed furiously onward.

"Thou art a craven," said the merry girl; "but you may have the advantage of the start. May I test the speed of your horse?" she asked, turning to Christie.

"To the death," replied the young man, to whom she had imparted her own enthusiasm.

"Then let me take the whip and reins. Stay, change sides—there, that will do. Now forward, my gallant steed," and the lash fell lightly upon him.

The horse had observed with impatience the departure of the other steed, and now, as he felt the touch of the whip, he darted eagerly onward.

"Soho! a spirited fellow," said the damsel, as with form thrown back, she guided the course of the flying animal. Several times she avoided a collision with the trees, as they rapidly crossed the valley, but now they began to mount the ascent that led from the river. Thus far, the leading horse had gained a little upon the other, and the distance between them perceptibly increased before they reached the summit of the hill. Christie watched the two as though life and death depended upon the result.

"Gently, my noble fellow; you have weight against you. Gently, ho! we shall soon be at the summit. *There*, now!"

The horse advanced at a tremendous rate of speed, as she gave him the reins, and it was soon apparent that he was the fastest horse of the two. The road now led down a gentle descent, and then stretched out across a broad level plain.

"Untie my hat strings," she said.

The hat had fallen back upon her shoulders. Christie's trembling hand approached her ivory neck, and he made several ineffectual attempts to untie the ribbon.

"What a blunderer!" she exclaimed, pettishly. "There, now, make haste;" and she turned her flushed countenance towards his own. With a desperate effort he succeeded, and as the hat was removed, a large mass of dark brown hair fell down her back.

"Did *ever* any one see such a bungler? You have made me lose at least ten feet by your awkwardness." The horse bounded forward under the application of the whip.

As they swept by each field, the laborers turned their wondering eyes to the road, and twice men were seen advancing rapidly, to arrest what they supposed were runaway horses. Christie's horse was not more than ten yards behind the other, and was fast gaining upon him, when the latter diverged from the road, and entered the private carriage-way leading through the grounds and up to the castle of the Earl of Rossmore. To his astonishment, the young lady also drove through the gate, narrowly missing one of the posts, as the horse swerved to one side.

"For heaven's sake, madam, are you not aware that these are private grounds?" he observed, anxiously. She deigned no reply. Her attention was entirely absorbed by the race; and her triumph was now at hand. The head of her horse lapped the wheel of Melville's gig. Twice she requested him to yield part of the narrow way, but he obdurately kept the centre of the road. They now emerged from the grove and swept along the open space in front of the castle. Its inmates collected upon the portico, as if surprised at the unwonted intrusion upon the grounds. The panting and struggling horses were approaching a small sheet of water that spread out directly in front of the castle. Along its border, and elevated three feet above it, ran the road. Each driver was aware that now was the moment for the final struggle.

"Will you yield part of the road?" exclaimed the maiden.

He did not diverge a hair's breadth from his course.

"Then take the consequence!" She wheeled her horse out upon the greensward. A loud cheer was heard. Casting his eyes toward the castle, Christie saw the waving of hats and handkerchiefs. He had no time for contemplation. They steadily drew forward—she turned the head of her steed and crowded the other toward the lake. He was forced nearer and nearer, until one wheel rolled over the bank, and Melville was precipitated headforemost into the water. The gig, relieved of its load, bounded upon the bank again, and the horse ran towards the lower end of the park.

Christie anxiously gazed after the form of Melville, but seeing him ascend the bank unharmed, once more addressed the maiden.

"You have triumphed; let us now leave these grounds: we may seriously offend the owner."

The laughing girl heeded him not, but with unabated speed drove in the direction of the goodly company who were cheering and waving their hats and handkerchiefs from the portico. Christie's glance turned from them to his companion, and then back again.

"Why, Kate, mad girl! what prank have you been playing now," said the cheerful voice of Lord Rossmore, as she sprang from the vehicle into his arms.

"Only teaching Melville that he is but an indifferent whip, notwithstanding all his boasting. See what a sorry figure he cuts. Come this way; *this* way, my Lord Melville."

But he took his dripping garments around an angle of the castle, without confronting the merry party.

"A right noble horse, papa;" said Katharine Montague, caressing the head of the panting steed.

"And swift of foot," replied the Earl. "Will you sell him?" he continued, addressing Christie Kane, who sat in blushing silence.

"I should be loath to part with Surrey, my lord."

"Where did you pick up your country beau, Kate?" inquired the Countess of Rossmore.

The blood rushed to Christie's face.

"You are wrong, Ma'ma; he picked *me* up:" replied the maiden, quickly; "and what is more, enabled me to achieve a triumph over the vain Lord Melville. Let this be a slight token of the gratification which that triumph has given me," and she took the rose that rested upon her bosom, and placed it in the hand of Christie Kane. He returned his thanks, and raising his hat, bowed to the company; then picking up the reins, proceeded slowly homeward. He started as if an adder had stung him, as a masculine voice observed,

"A well-behaved fellow, for a plebeian, and a clodpole."

"Such are the distinctions of society," he muttered gloomily, as the laughter died away that had recorded the unfeeling jest.

CHAPTER II.

"On man, as man, retaining yet,
However debased, and soiled, and dim,
The crown upon his forehead set—
The immortal gift of God to him."—*Whittier.*

It will be necessary, to give the reader a more formal introduction to our characters than was obtained in the last chapter. This we will now proceed briefly to do. Katharine Montague was the only child of Lord and the Countess of Rossmore. With a small circle of friends they were passing a few weeks at the castle of Montague. Lord Melville and his parents, the Duke and Duchess of Sunderland, with their guests, were also tarrying at their country-seat upon the adjoining estate. Christie Kane was a tenant of the Duke of Sunderland, and Ellen Knowles was the grand-daughter of a noble duke, her mother having eloped with, and married, a young ensign, who afterwards rose to the rank of a colonel. Mrs. Kane, the sister of Colonel Knowles, had married more humbly, and since the death of her husband, had barely escaped from the horror of want. Robert Kane, Christie's brother, had been in London several years, and only paid brief visits to the paternal roof as a temporary relief from severe toil. The character of each will be delineated during the progress of the story.

Upon the morning of the day succeeding the events recorded in the first chapter, Lady Rossmore was seated in the elegant drawing-room of the castle, entertaining the Duchess of Sunderland and her son. Lord Melville was lounging upon a sofa, casting occasional glances towards the door. If he expected Katharine Montague to enter, he was disappointed, for she was at that moment a mile from the castle, upon the back of a spirited horse.

"Are you troubled with complaints and excuses from your tenants?" inquired the Countess of Rossmore, as she adjusted herself more comfortably in the large arm-chair.

"Constantly. One would really suppose the lazy creatures had nothing else to do but to annoy their masters. And they are so *importunate*, too. You must listen to the entire catalogue of their grievances, from the failure of the crops to the death of the only horse. It was only this morning that a brazen-faced woman persisted in forcing her way into my presence, and nearly crazed me with her volubility. Her husband had deceased, the rot had destroyed their potatoes, the storm had blown down their chimney, and, to come to the point of the whole story, they could not pay the rent, and she begged me to direct the steward not to turn her out upon the 'wide, wide world,' to use her own expression."

"And what reply did you make, my lady mother?" asked Melville, as he languidly raised his head from his hand.

"I said the steward had informed me that I must expect such applications frequently," replied the Duchess; "but that I should pay no attention whatever to them. He further remarked, if I believed one half the tales of suffering that were poured into my ears by weeping mothers and distracted daughters, every moment of my time would be occupied."

"Well, what said the woman?"

"She assumed a threatening aspect, and half wildly exclaimed, 'have a care, madam, how you treat my request. I may have it in my power to humble your pride.' I called the waiter, and directed him to remove the disagreeable person. She erected her form to its full height, while her eyes flashed fire, as I pointed to the door. My nerves were very much shaken, very much shaken indeed, at the rudeness of the horrid creature."

"What was her name? she shall be taught to respect our position," said Lord Melville.

"I did not take the trouble to recollect it. Some common name, I believe; the steward can tell you; Keen or Kine, perhaps."

"Was it not *Kane?*" inquired Melville, eagerly, as he started to his feet.

"Yes, that was it. But what possible interest can you take in such vulgar affairs?"

"More than you suppose," muttered the young nobleman as he left the room.

In a few moments Katharine Montague entered the drawing-room, and addressing her salutations to the visitor, seated herself at an embroidery frame.

"What have we to do with their hardships?" said the Duchess. "They were born upon our soil, and are sheltered by our roofs; we have claims upon their services instead of being under obligations to them."

Katharine Montague divined at once the subject of conversation, and observed, while a demure expression sat upon her countenance:

"If they hesitate to pay the last farthing, even if it does reduce them to the verge of starvation, it is only exhibiting a proper degree of gratitude and respect for those who are the *accidental* owners of the soil."

"Very true; I am glad to see you have a just appreciation of our prerogatives. There is nothing more important, my dear Countess, than to apprise the young nobility of the exact scope of their prerogatives."

"And is it not quite as essential to teach the ***substratum*** that their duties consist of unceasing toil and suffering?" inquired Katharine Montague, whose eyes were bent upon her embroidery.

"You are right, my young friend," said the Duchess; "there is nothing like commencing a thorough training early."

"And it is quite as important to continue it. There should be no relaxation—no moment of ease—when the toiling millions can raise their heads and wipe the sweat from their aching brows," observed Katharine Montague.

"Precisely so. There is probably no class of serfs so admirably drilled as the English. They yield a princely revenue to the nobility and clergy. They enable us to indulge in costly excursions abroad, and to gratify our taste by the most lavish expenditures at home. We have no trouble in watching over them, except to enforce the payment of rents. It makes not the slightest difference to us whether they are sick or well. They pay their own doctors' bills, and if their crops are blighted, they must resort to the most pinching economy, for the rent must be paid. If long continued suffering or the whispering of demagogues make them restless, the authorities have only to swear in an additional number of constables, and they are reduced to submission. I really can conceive of no condition of society more charming," and the Duchess flourished her ivory fan with the greatest satisfaction.

"And the beauty of the whole system," said Katharine Montague, while a covert meaning played upon her lips, "consists in its justice and fair seeming. We receive the fruits of their labor, but do we not cause them to be respected by other nations? They pour the money earned by days of exhaustion and nights of anxiety into our laps, but do we not arouse the envy of a less fortunate aristocracy. If their own honor and that of England is assailed, do we not evince a disposition to redress it, even to the extent of employing a press-gang to drag them from their helpless families; and rather than permit the indignity to go unavenged, and the stain to remain upon our flag, do we not wash it out with their own blood?"

"Kate, my darling, where *did* you obtain so just an appreciation of the rights and duties of the English aristocracy?" said the Duchess enthusiastically.

"I think any person of ordinary discrimination cannot fail to observe them. The *substratum* display great ingenuity in adapting themselves to this condition. They bestow vast wealth upon the clergy, but how are they repaid? By being permitted to stare with open-mouthed gratification at splendid churches, gorgeous robes, and magnificent equipages. They shower untold sums upon the nobility, and how do we reward them? They are allowed to gaze at processions, crowd around the ball-room, opera-house, or private dwelling, wondering how much their own money can adorn manhood and beauty, and thank us for *generously* permitting them to take note of the magnificence with which we lavish their gifts."

"It never occurred to me that there could be a *system* in our exhibitions of splendor," said the Duchess of Sunderland.

"Really, my dear madam, you must allow me to think you are too modest. It occurs to me that nothing could be more palpable than the effect which pomp and splendor are designed to produce upon the vulgar. Do you suppose if the famed aristocracy of England should be clothed in the humble garb of the laborer, and suffer the sun's heat to brown their complexions and the rude contact of implements of husbandry to crack and soil their hands, that they could for forty-eight hours overawe and control the peasantry of the British Empire? No! it is the result of no ordinary forethought and sagacity, this wringing its fruits from the hand of labor with the design of ostentatiously displaying it for the purpose of dazzling the giver, thus creating a necessity for still further contributions to be expended in the same manner. And the poor creatures manage by some sort of a mental process to blend our extravagance with their own celebrity."

"Well, that is a fortunate circumstance," said Lady Rossmore, "for it makes them contented with a social position that—that—"

"That none but the *substratum* are desirous of occupying," interposed Katharine Montague. "They ought to be satisfied with the privileges, which, in our gracious condescension, we have deigned to confer upon them," continued the young lady, while the slightest possible approach to a sarcastic smile played about the corners of her mouth. "Are they not allowed to furnish us with food? Do they not construct our railroads, and pave our streets? Are they not suffered to bring to our shores the luxuries and necessaries of life? Have they not our full, I may say *unqualified* permission to perform the most menial offices? Are they not allowed to fight our battles, and to bear the cross of St. George in triumph upon the bosom of every sea? And as a climax to our generosity, do we not make their laws and relieve them from the trouble of governing themselves? Nay, suffer them to throw up their hats, and cheer, while we pass, without even permitting a look of displeasure to cross our features at such familiarity?"

Katharine Montague worked with increased diligence while she gave utterance to these opinions. It was evident that her lady mother listened with a feeling of intense pride to what she considered the wisdom of her daughter.

"But how do you account for the fact, that the aristocracy of England, although occupying different social positions, all unite in defending the system?"

"Easily. It is because there is no one so humble but that he can point to an inferior. The Duke can doff his hat to royalty because the Earl must yield him precedence. The Earl can give up the post of honor to the Duke, because the Baron must recede at his approach, even if by doing so he treads upon the knightly toes of the Baronet, and so on through all the gradations of society, until you come to the substratum upon whose shoulders rests the vast fabric of British despotism."

The last words were uttered by Katharine Montague with energy, and as she concluded, putting aside the embroidery frame, she withdrew.

The day succeeding the storm the weather was changeable. The sun emerged from the clouds at short intervals, and then the sky became again overcast, and the rain descended. Christie Kane watched the heavens with the greatest anxiety, for his wheat lay scattered upon the ground. It had already been exposed to one storm since the reaper had performed his task; and he was fearful that before it was ready for the stack it would become mouldy. He was more than usually alarmed, because he not only depended upon it for bread, but with it he expected to lessen somewhat his liabilities for rent. It was, then, with an anxious eye that he saw evening approach before the sun broke through the clouds. It was too late then to accomplish anything, and he was slowly proceeding towards the cottage, when he heard the sound of horses' feet rapidly approaching. Turning his head he saw a party of ladies and gentlemen riding up the road, and a momentary thrill of pleasure was produced as he saw Katharine Montague among them. He was in the act of raising his hat as she passed, but her eyes rested upon him mechanically for a moment, as upon a person she had never seen before, and were then withdrawn.

"Of course she will not deign to recognize me, fool that I was to think so," exclaimed the youth bitterly.

"Yonder is Lady Katharine's gallant," exclaimed Lord Melville, tauntingly, as the rear of the party were riding past. Half-a-dozen persons looked in the direction that he pointed, and then a peal of laughter rang upon the air.

A momentary pang shot to the heart of the poor fellow, and then he bore himself bravely up in the strength of innate nobleness and conscious rectitude.

He met his mother at the gate.

"Well, Christie, I went to see the Duchess for the purpose of getting the time extended for the payment of the rent."

A flash of displeasure shot across the features of her son.

"Mother, how could you so degrade us?"

"Hoot, boy! Degrade us, indeed! What have the poor to say against degradation. Where is the money to pay the rent? What is to keep us from the highway even now? Potatoes destroyed, and with a fair prospect of the entire loss of the wheat, methinks you have little to do with *pride*, unless you expect to carry your aspirations to a ready market. Degradation, forsooth!"

Christie turned gloomily away.

"Well, she heeded your prayers, did she not?"

"By the foul fiends, no! With a haughty languor she replied that her steward had informed her she might expect frequent applications of the kind. She could not, she *really* could not think of troubling herself about such vulgar matters! May heaven desert me if she shall not repent, aye bitterly repent, her insolence."

"Ha! ha! ha! Well repaid, my gracious mother, for your condescension."

"Have a care, sir, how you are wanting in respect," said Mrs. Kane, fiercely.

"It is useless for you to attempt to treat me as a child, mother. And while I am upon that subject, let me say once for all, that your tyrannical conduct towards me since I was an infant—the marked contrast in your bearing towards me and Robert—has given you small claim upon my gratitude and affection. I am a man now, and will no longer be treated as a child!"

The air of calm determination with which this was announced, overawed Mrs. Kane for a moment, but her form trembled with rage as her son entered the house.

The pensive eyes of Ellen Knowles met his, as Christie Kane seated himself upon the old fashioned sofa. The subdued bearing of the maiden contrasted so strongly with the harsh demeanor of his mother, that the irritated feelings of the young man were soothed.

"Cousin Christie, I sympathize with you sincerely in your misfortunes."

"You are a good girl, Ellen, and I am grateful for your kindness."

"Why do you not compare your condition with that of others?"

"I do."

"But you compare it with the fate of those who are more bountifully supplied with this world's goods than yourself."

"It is natural to do so."

"Nay, but Christie is it *wise?*" said Ellen hesitatingly.

"Perhaps not."

"I was glancing at the paper while waiting for you to return; that is, I was reading it, having nothing else to do," stammered Ellen, confusedly.

"I understand; well?"

And it gives the most terrible description of the suffering of the peasantry upon the western portion of the Duke's estate."

"And the next column describes the brilliant ball given by the Duchess at his country seat, where the strains of music blended, as they floated away, with the wailings of despair?"

"It does," said the maiden sadly.

"I thought so."

Ellen looked at him with tearful eyes. Their glances met.

"Come, Nell, I will gratify your pitying impulses by listening to those tales of suffering. Read, Nell."

With a grateful look the damsel read extracts from the report made by commissioners appointed by the English Parliament to inquire into the condition of the hand-loom weavers.*

"One witness called before the commission, said—

'Children of seven years old can begin to turn the wheel to spin

*The quotations are taken from a report which was actually made to the British Parliament in 1840, and can be found copied into a speech made by Hon. Charles Hudson (a member of Congress from Massachusetts), in 1842.—*The Author.*

flax, which is very hard work, and they are kept at work from five in the morning till nine at night. I might enumerate the number of weak and crooked-legged children in towns—an evil that is attributable to this sort of work.'

"A manufacturer testifies that—

'Their dwellings, their clothing and that of their children, evince great misery. There is often great distress among them. They are generally sober, industrious, steady men; but, with the best intentions, at the present wages, they cannot get a living. Many of the weavers are obliged to apply to the parish for assistance.'

"Mr. Otway, the commissioner who examined into the condition of the weavers in Ireland, says:—

'The cabins that the weavers live and work in are fearful specimens of what habit will enable human beings to endure. The weavers are obliged to pay as high rent for these dens as they ought to get comfortable cabins for. Nothing can equal the distress of the poor cotton weavers. I never witnessed greater misery than in their cabins and mode of living. The houses of some of the lower classes of weavers are in the most wretched state, with only a little straw and a coverlet for a bed; plenty of children, but scarcely a chair to sit down upon.'

"Erasmus Charlton, a police sergeant, testifies:—

'Sometimes he has had occasion to search the houses of some of the weavers on suspicion of stealing yarn, and had witnessed very distressing cases—children crying for food, and the parent having neither food nor money in the house, nor work to obtain any.'

"Another witness says:—

'A poor weaver came last Sunday to my house, and stated he had had a poor Sunday, not having a potatoe, or even a bit of bread in his house. The weaver had a wife near confinement and three children.'

"Another witness testifies that:—

'He has no doubt many of the weavers and their children, especially *young* children, die from disease brought on by want of proper nourishment.'"

Christie Kane moved uneasily in his chair. At that moment the merry laughter of the party of equestrians was heard, and, as they cantered by the house, the young man's brow was contracted into a heavy frown. "Others starve while they laugh," he muttered between his teeth.

A suppressed sob escaped from the overcharged bosom of Ellen Knowles. She raised her kerchief to her eyes, and then asked Christie if she should continue. "Oh yes, let us scan the picture in all its details."

Ellen continued—"One of the weavers testified before the commission as follows:—

'Question.—Have you any children?'

'Answer.—No: I had two, but they are both dead, thanks be to God!'

'Question.—Do you express satisfaction at the death of your children?'

'Answer.—I do. I thank God for it. I am released from the burden of maintaining them; and they, poor dear creatures, are released from the troubles of this mortal life.' "

"Hold! for God's sake! this is too frightful! Accursed despotism, that can perpetrate such horrors; and abominable hypocrisy, that affects great sanctity while it points at and condemns the faults of other systems," exclaimed Christie Kane, as he abruptly left the cottage.

The eyes of Ellen Knowles followed him; but the whole expression of her countenance had changed. Instead of sympathy, a look of triumph sat upon her features as she soliloquized:

"I have pricked your confidence in the nobility, my aspiring cousin, while I have convinced you that persons in your humble position ought to be grateful. If this fails to elicit a declaration of love, I must e'en try some other plan. Shall this inexperienced boy baulk one who boasts of her power to baffle and deceive? Never!" and her pearly teeth pressed her nether lip as she vowed he should yet kneel humbly at her feet.

CHAPTER III.

> "Ah! that deceit should steal such gentle shapes,
> And with virtuous visor hide deep vice!"—*Shakespeare.*

Christie Kane rose from his bed at an early hour the following morning, and eagerly scanned the appearance of the heavens. His spirits sank as he observed the scarlet-tinted clouds gathering in the east. Slowly the sun mounted from the horizon and cast his rays with a red, angry glare upon the earth, while occasionally a hot breath of air came up from the south. Kane looked anxiously over the field where his wheat lay, fast mouldering upon the saturated ground. The clouds heeded not his imploring glance, but rallied their force until the whole firmament was overcast. Then the rain descended in torrents, and with an imprecation, forced from him in the excess of anguish, he turned moodily away.

"Niver mind, maister Christie, the world owes us a living, for Sir Wm. Belthoven told the fraymen so, and said they mustn't make thimselves onasy or discontented, no matter what might be their sufferings, for they'd niver die ontail their time come; an' if they did, for the matter o' that, become a little pinched wid hunger, they must consider it a bountiful affliction of providence as a punishment for their transgressions."

"And what response did the people make?"

"Why, yez say, the farmers who hiv provisions to sell cheered vahamently bakase they *did* hiv provisions to sell."

"But what said the day-laborers?"

"Why, the ungrateful spalpeens towld him that was mighty poor consolation to a man wid an empty stomach; and then the farmers began to hustle them out; but Sir William, wid one of his banivolent smiles, towld them not to molest the people, bekaze they had nothing to do wid the matter, as the parliament ralieved thim from the trouble of voting; and said they were compensated fur any little inconvanience they might suffer be manes of hiving nothing to ate, in the magnificent and splendid government that was provided fur them wid their own money. Which rasoning satisfied all parties, and they said Sir William would make a jewel of a mimber."

"Fools! fools! thus to hug your chains," said Kane, passionately.

The storm now raged, and Christie Kane saw the utter loss of his crop, which he foresaw would be succeeded by civil proceedings, ejectment, and ruin.

The brow of Mrs. Kane wore a deeper frown as they were seated at the dinner-table.

"What think you now of my application to the Duchess of Sunderland? Does your pride still revolt at it? Or does the apprehension of adversity, or rather absolute want, smooth down your self-esteem?"

"Whatever misfortunes destiny may have in store for me, I will never stoop to ask favors of the oppressor. Fate may do her worst."

"We shall see—we shall see. Hunger is a conqueror of stubborn wills. But, Christie," she continued, in a milder voice, "Why do you not seek the hand of your cousin Ellen; I am certain she loves you?"

"Do you think so, mother?" he replied, while a gleam of pleasure lit up his features.

"There is not the slightest doubt of it. Besides, you will always be able to secure a competence through the influence of Colonel Knowles."

"And become a pensioner upon his will," replied Christie, sternly.

"Did ever any one see such a suspicious and unmanageable boy."

"I am no longer a boy, and I *will* take my natural position among the thinking, resolute men of my time."

"And bravely, no doubt, will a *peasant* succeed. Ha! ha! Without money, without friends, without a name. Go on, my self-willed child, and let us see how far you will ascend the ladder of fame!"

"But, mother, renown has been acquired by the humbly-born." said Christie, in a low, half-imploring voice.

"Yes, by a few pampered menials of the crown."

"No! no! by some of the ablest and purest of philosophers, orators, and statesmen. Newton, whose mind could not be controlled by the shackles of nature—Boyle, who dissected with the knife of a master the organization of matter—Thurlow, the dispenser of equity, and the custodian of the king's conscience (which I assume to have been a very difficult task)—Locke, who laid bare the process of reasoning, and the foundation and development of human judgment—Erskine, whose magic eloquence swayed the senate and controlled the bench—Cromwell, glorious Cromwell, who convinced a despotic king and a corrupt nobility that popular vengeance is sometimes terribly appeased when justice is outraged—and

Washington, immortal Washington, who taught a rapacious monarch that an empire was the price of unmerited rashness: all—*all* of those illustrious men carved their renown *with their own hands*, and in characters that time can neither mutilate nor efface."

Christie Kane spoke with the fire of enthusiasm, and for a few moments his mother was startled by his language; and then she remarked, with cutting irony.

"And, pray, is it in the field of philosophy, eloquence, or war, that you intend to commence your career? Will you become a competitor of Newton in philosophy, of Locke in ratiocination, of Erskine in oratory, of Cromwell in treason; or does your patriotism prompt you to emulate the conduct of Washington by instigating the Canadians to revolt, or, mayhap, to place yourself at the head of some tribe in Hindoostan, or of a few straggling cannibals in South Africa? If these enterprises are not sufficiently lofty for your ambition, you can mount Surry, and, placing Phelim astride the cow, for the want of a more showy animal, start forth, Don Quixote like, in search of adventures."

"Mother," said Christie, with a forced laugh, "I am sure, if you had been an acquaintance of Job's wife, you would have caused her to break one of the commandments."

"Why?"

"Because she would have coveted your tongue for the purpose of putting the patience of her long-suffering husband to a final test."

The conversation, which was in danger of becoming personal, was interrupted by the entrance of Ellen Knowles, who extended her hand to Christie Kane. Her voice was subdued, and the melting eyes were cast to the floor, as if her bashfulness could not remain unmoved in the presence of Christie.

"Ellen, you are always welcome; I am glad to see you."

"Thank you, Christie; the assurance gives me much pleasure. I came to offer my sincere condolence upon the distressing condition of your agricultural affairs. I fear your wheat crop will be destroyed; is it so?" and the maiden's voice trembled with anxiety.

"Hopelessly."

"And what will you do, Christie?"

"Do? that is difficult to tell; only I shall preserve my independence."

'Faugh!" exclaimed Mrs. Kane, with extreme disgust.

"No, no, Aunty, you are wrong," said the mild voice of Ellen.

"You are always defending his absurdities. In your estimation Mr. Christie Kane cannot err."

"Oh, Aunty, why did you divulge—"

"Never mind, cousin Ellen, she has only increased the high opinion I have always entertained for you."

The blushing cheek of the girl was shaded by a mass of curls as she turned her glance to the window, but her features wore an expression of triumph which the young man did not observe.

"Come, Ellen, your presence has brought sunshine once more. Will you walk with me?"

This time she did not refuse, and together they passed through the garden and entered the little thatched roofed arbor that was separated from the highway by a hedge.

"Ellen, you have manifested an interest in my affairs. I will confide to you my hopes, for I am certain of your sympathy."

She smiled gratefully.

"I cannot pay the rent, and unless I greatly misunderstand the disposition of the Duke's steward, if not the Duke's son, I shall be ejected from the house in which I was born."

Ellen Knowles eagerly caught at his words.

"What reason have you for supposing that Lord Melville will prove your enemy?"

"It is needless to explain them; suffice it to say, I cannot be mistaken."

Again a gleam of triumph shot across the features of the girl, but was as quickly succeeded by a look of solicitude, which Christie attributed to an intense interest in his affairs.

"In the event of such disasters befalling you, what will you do?" and the large, expressive blue eyes were fixed tearfully upon his face.

"I will leave England for ever."

Ellen was visibly affected by this annunciation, and her cheeks rested upon her hands. But her mind was eagerly revolving the results which must ensue from such a course. With the quickness of thought she foresaw it would aid her own views, but she had too much tact not to appear unhappy at the prospect of a separation. The tears trickled through her fingers and a deep sigh escaped her.

"Dear Ellen, does this intelligence give you pain?"

Another, and a louder sob succeeded, but she did not speak, for she knew that silence was more eloquent than words. Christie contemplated her well-formed head and blooming form, and taking her soft white hand in his own he bent his head down until her glossy curls touched his cheek. His attention was attracted by the approach of his mother who stalked into the garden. Perceiving that the intrusion was untimely, she retraced her steps, but the spell was broken, and Christie rose abruptly to his feet. Ellen Knowles bit her lips, and a scowl of rage disfigured her brow, as they proceeded towards the house.

The conversation between the aunt and niece was brief after they separated from Christie.

"You are always thrusting yourself where you are not wanted," said Ellen, with calm insolence.

"Indeed, Miss Malapert! and I should like to know what prospect you would have for winning Christie's hand without my assistance, eh!"

"On the contrary, your offensive and turbulent interference is the most formidable obstacle I have to contend with. It is strange what a savage beast you make of yourself."

Mrs. Kane seized Ellen by the arm, and bending a fierce glance upon her, exclaimed:

"You are a deceitful, lying, hypocritical hussy, and can cloak the most intense meanness under an appearance of candor and gentleness. Have a care, miss, or I will thwart your designs upon Christie."

"No you won't, because in doing so you will thwart your own, my precious Aunty. So good bye. No, you will think better of it, because you can't *afford* to thwart my designs upon Christie Kane, and you told a *lie* when you said so, *dear* Aunty. Just peep into the glass now, and see how beautifully you look when you froth so at the mouth. See how much better my placid face appears, especially when I smile. Good bye, Aunty; you won't thwart my designs upon Christie, will you?. Ha! ha! ha!"

With a graceful courtesy she departed, leaving Mrs. Kane overcome with rage.

Slowly the maiden proceeded homewards, revolving in her mind the most effectual plan to accomplish her designs upon her cousin.

"It is strange how difficult it is to force a declaration from the obstinate fellow," she soliloquised, "and yet I am considered handsome, and, thanks to my powers of deceit, as Mrs. Kane calls it, I am thought very agreeable. Others call me beautiful, for their eyes tell me so. And Lord Melville, too, could not disguise his admiration. It is strange what an influence his lordship exercises over me since I was magnetised by him at Bath. I am certain there is a peculiar charm in being magnetised by a lord that a common person cannot elicit. The sensation that stole through my limbs and crept along my arteries, was, I am sure, more extatic than if any one but a lord had produced the excitement. And then the dreamy delight which succeeded was more soothing and profound. Most decidedly should I prefer being excited into the delicious state of magnetism by one of the nobility; the pressure of whose fingers could produce such delight as those of a lord? Who could, with such assurance, instil the mysterious and rapturous bliss into my frame! But the reaction that succeeded! I attended a concert the same evening, and when *he* entered the room, a cold shudder passed through my frame, which, without my seeing him, warned me of his approach. I was obliged to leave the room, and during the long night they were anxiously watching over my couch. The restoratives produced a temporary relief, but it was only by several days of repose that I was freed from the excess of animal magnetism with which my body was surcharged by the graceful Lord Melville. Mrs. Skewton was affected by his lordship in the same way. It is strange that her form is so easily excited, for she is quite thirty-four; a period of life when it is supposed the nerves of the human form are not so easily influenced by contact, as at a more youthful age, especially if, as in the case of Mrs. Skewton, the female has given birth to three or four children, besides having been troubled for any number of years with those complaints incident to our sex. Be that as it may, Mrs. Skewton declared that she should never, she was certain she should not, be relieved from the overdose of magnetism which Lord Melville condescended to give her. And her eyes did have a languishing appearance, and her form did tremble as if it desired the sustaining arm of his Lordship, notwithstanding she is upon the shady side of life, and her frame has been tested in the manner—but here I am talking to myself. Enough of Mrs. Skewton. I shall suffer Lord Melville to cultivate me, and perchance he can assist my 'designs,' as Aunty calls them, upon Chester Kane."

The unscrupulous girl, with a sneering response to her mother's salutation, entered her room and banged to the door. Standing in front of the glass, she gazed with savage delight upon the gentle face that was now transformed into the lineaments of a fiend.

"Ha! ha! won't I astonish master Christie when he is mine? I'll teach the prudent and courteous boy that hell is preferable to my company. *Won't* I adopt every expedient to torture the gentleman? Hatefulness shall, for the future, be what deception has been for the past—my study—my thought by day—my dream by night; and when he turns to upbraid me and meets a look like this, won't he shudder? Ha! ha! ha!"

And the face of the girl was contorted into an expression that a maniac would have envied.

Throwing herself upon the sofa, her face once more assumed its natural beauty and repose. It was one of those clear, open, frank, countenances, which, as well as the fair complexion and the light auburn hair, may sometimes be called emblematical of gentleness, but whose possessors often become notorious for their diabolical cruelty. It was that complexion and color of hair which we find so difficult to associate with Lucrezia Borgia, while we mistakingly attribute to her the darkest hair and lineaments of her country.

She matured her plans by resolving to call upon Lord Melville for assistance. It was necessary for Christie Kane to be persecuted. The most rigorous enactments of the law were to be put in force for the collection of rent, even to the extremity of turning her aunt and cousin from home. She saw no other way of humiliating Christie so that he would apply to her father for that assistance which would alone save him from absolute want, if not from the rigors of a prison. With a triumphant expression upon her face, she approached the window and clapped her hands with joy as she saw Lord Melville riding up the avenue leading to the house.

She welcomed the young nobleman with downcast eyes and faltering words, as though she was agitated by his presence. Melville made his salutation with that easy assurance which the English aristocracy exhibit while in the presence of their inferiors, and which, by the way, is in marked contrast to their bearing when confronted by their superiors.

"Existence has been unendurable, Miss Knowles, since I saw you last, and it gives me the most *intense* delight to behold you again."

And he gave the hand of the placid maiden a prolonged squeeze.

"Your lordship is altogether too condescending, to keep my poor self so long in your memory."

"You do me shocking injustice, 'pon me honor you do, me charming damsel. Now, really, I have been dying to see you again."

"I cannot believe your language is candid."

"And why not, pray?"

"Because you act cruelly towards my relations."

"Don't say so. To whom have I been guilty of wrong? I was not aware that you had any lovely cousins."

Ellen could not repress a feeling of disgust at the egotism of the nobleman, yet she replied calmly:

"I do not refer to any one who may have found the graces of your person, and the fascination of your manners too powerful for their susceptible hearts."

"To whom, then, can you possibly allude, loveliest of your sex."

"To my cousin, Christie Kane."

Melville started.

"Is it possible, Miss Knowles, that the boor, Kane, can be your cousin?"

"It is true; but I hope your lordship will have the kindness to overlook a fault which cannot strictly be laid to me, as we may not always have it in our power to locate our relatives in precisely the grade of society most suited to our tastes. This fact your lordship will not be disposed to controvert, as your great aunt formed a tender connection with her footman."

"Hell and damnation!" muttered the nobleman.

"Now I have a great favor to ask of your lordship," continued Ellen innocently, as if unconscious of the affect produced by her sarcasm.

"Oh, very well, you have put me in the proper mood for granting it," said Melville savagely.

"That was what I was desirous of doing. My cousin is a tenant of your gracious father. It is hopelessly out of his power to pay his rent."

A gleam of joy, which did not escape the notice of Ellen, flashed across the countenance of Melville.

"He cannot pay the rent, hey?"

"Your lordship understood me correctly."

"And you wish me to interfere in his behalf?" he continued, rubbing his hands gleefully.

"If your lordship can forget how immeasurably he is beneath your family in position, if we may except the great aunt whom I mentioned as having formed an attachment for her foot——"

"Your cousin shall hear from me," exclaimed Melville in a loud voice, as he rose abruptly.

"Pray be seated, my lord. I hope you will not mention to Christie Kane, or to any one likely to communicate the information to him, that I have been instrumental in averting misfortune from him."

"He shall remain profoundly ignorant of all the benefits which your information will confer upon him," said the other sarcastically.

"I thank your lordship," said Ellen, with a grateful look, "for the pleasure which this assurance gives me. You know we cannot feel otherwise than solicitous for our kindred, notwithstanding their plebeian origin, as in the case of my cousin Christie, or any departure from the strict rules of propriety, as in the case of your great——"

"Good morning!" shouted Melville, as he closed the door violently.

Ellen Knowles watched the receding form of her visitor as, plunging the rowels into his horse, he rode furiously away.

"He is in a delightful mood now for attending to the case of Christie Kane. Thanks to the *faux pas* of his great aunt, I was enabled to stimulate his ferocity and arouse his revenge by lancing his family pride. Every conceivable crime of which England's monarchs and England's nobility have been guilty, gives the humbler born a glorious opportunity of calling a little of the 'best blood' to the cheeks of their descendants." Thus soliloquized this flint-hearted girl, whose native talents were desecrated to the purposes of malignity and revenge.

She had not miscalculated the effect produced upon Lord Melville by her information and the taunts by which it was accompanied. That person had not forgotten the part taken by his father's tenant in the race which resulted in his immersion in the sheet of water that ornamented Montague park. It was, then, with the most determined malice that he sought his father's steward and gave him specific directions to enforce every remedy which the law gave him upon Christie Kane. Leaving wickedness to its work, we must call the reader's attention to Robert Kane, another character whose career we have undertaken to delineate.

CHAPTER IV.

"Go, then—'tis vain to hover
Thus round a hope that's dead;
At length my dream is over;
'Twas sweet—'twas false—'tis fled!"—MOORE.

In a narrow street in the city of London was a small tenement inhabited by several families. They belonged, with one exception, to that poor but honest class who manage, by the aid of pinching economy, to live from "hand to mouth," as the independent sometimes call it. Although to the uninitiated it may be a very amusing expression, yet to those accustomed to test its bitter experience, it often presents the dread reality of anguish and despair. The tenants of this dilapidated building, however, were, in the main, exempted from those vicissitudes which the day-laborer so much apprehends. They managed to return, at a late hour, with sufficient money to supply their moderate wants for the next twenty-four hours. One family, however, that helped to make up the little world, possessed no ostensible means of support, and yet they were rather more bountifully supplied with the necessaries of life than the rest. In what manner they were acquired, no one knew, although all had their suspicions. The members of this family consisted of the father, two boys, and one little girl. They remained at home during the day, but sallied out at night, and returned long after their wearied neighbors were asleep. The father was a diminutive fellow, with a dark, sinister-looking countenance. It was impossible to encounter his furtive glance without a feeling of apprehension. He conversed with no one; and if by chance he was met in the little hall, or upon the narrow stair-case, the only recognition he vouchsafed was a stealthy look from his half averted eye. His children, too, were morose; and if they met those of their own age, it was with grim little countenances. Even the girl, a toddling thing, three years old, had an elfin look. The whole family were regarded with a feeling of apprehension by all who knew them; and, to add still more to their unpopularity, the father was suspected of being an agent of the press-gang, whose recent operations had carried terror into the houses of the poor. This man was known as Matthew Riley. It was in this humble dwelling that Robert Kane, the brother of Christie, resided. He occupied but one room, and within its narrow limits were his wife and children. The former had won the affections of Robert Kane by her sweet face and gentle deportment, and despite his humble prospects they were married. Three children were the fruits of this union, a boy eight years, a girl four years, and an infant eight months old. Into this lowly habitation we will now introduce the reader. Mary Kane was busily engaged in preparing the morning meal. Her countenance wore a contented expression; and she alternately talked with Robert, and addressed a few words, in the language of a mother, to the baby. Kane was dressing the little girl in his awkward way, while Henry, the oldest child, was playing upon the floor with "Frank Tot," as he called the infant.

"Why, what an awkward fellow you are," she exclaimed, as she held the tea-kettle in both hands; "you have put Dolly's shoe on the wrong foot, and, as I live, one stocking is wrong side out. Men never can do any thing right."

"Only rig ships well, Mary."

"Yes, you can do that, for I heard the foreman say there was not a more skillful rigger in his employ."

"And I can do something else."

"What's that?"

"Love you."

She put down the tea-kettle, and coming over to where he sat, pinched his ear, while his stalwart arm encircled her waist.

"I believe you are a humbug, Robert. But come, breakfast is ready, and I want you out of the room so that I can put it to rights, for I have *ever* so much to do to-day."

"What?"

"Why, wash, and iron, and mend Henry's coat, and cut out Dolly's frock, and get your supper ready, for you always come home so hungry, you know."

"Yes, that is one consolation the poor have."

"What is that?"

"Plenty to do, and a good appetite."

"Ha! ha! Come, now, every thing is ready; place Henry's and Dolly's chairs to the table, and give me the baby."

"Sha'nt I hold him?"

"Catch me trusting him with you; Frank is too precious to be scalded." Squeezing him to her bosom, she inflicted half a dozen kisses upon his rosy cheeks.

"And now," she said, when the frugal meal was over, "you may go. Mr. MacDougal likes punctuality. Here is your dinner; all ready."

"Thank you, Mary."

"What a careless man you are. Don't you see it looks like rain, and you going without your thick coat. There, now, good-by."

"Good-by, baby; give me a kiss."

He raised the child cautiously, as though he was fearful that his rough hands would mar the delicate limbs. The boy waited until his father's face was within reach of his dimpled hand, and then he inflicted a little blow upon his cheek. Straightening himself up for a moment, as if he had performed a wonderful feat, he broke out into an infantile laugh, which was re-echoed by Dolly and Henry. Robert bent his head until his stout beard came rather roughly in contact with the baby's face. The laughter was hushed, the lip curled, and a sob—a premonitory symptom of a tear—was heard, when he was suddenly raised to the full height of Kane's elevated arm. Clapping his hands, every sign of grief disappeared from his chubby countenance.

"There, there now, will you never have done with such folly. It was only last week that Daniel Doughty let his child fall, and broke one of his legs."

"I'm going. Take good care of the children."

And the happy fellow went whistling down stairs. In the lower hall he met Riley, who was just returning from his night wandering. He threw a stealthy glance at Kane, and was sneaking past him, when the latter arrested his footsteps by placing his stalwart form in the centre of the passage.

"Don't you touch me, Robert Kane, if you do, I will call in the police," exclaimed Riley in a sharp voice.

"Look you," said Robert, sternly, "it would require a strong provocation to induce me to soil my hands by touching your carcass. But if, as I suspect, you are in any way connected with the press gang, you had best get your neck insured, that's all."

"Threaten me, do you? I'll see whether her Majesty's liege subjects are to have their lives put in danger." He made a motion as if to approach the door, but his progress was arrested by the strong arm of the other.

"Mathew Riley, I am a hard working, honest man, and support my family by daily labor. You never work, and it is thought you obtain money by means that only a villain would resort to. Now then, if you take food from the mouths of my wife and children, by causing me to be arrested, I will slay you as if you were a mad dog. Go!"

The malignity of a fiend gleamed upon the cadaverous features of Riley as he glided away.

Mary Kane, with a light heart attended to her household duties. She first washed up the breakfast things, and then commenced cutting out the frock for Dolly.

"Ma, shan't Dolly and I go out and play while you put Frank Tot to sleep?"

"Do you want to leave me?"

"No, but ma, I can't keep Doll from laughing, and she will be sure to wake Tot. She is always a-giggling."

"And for the matter of that I think you are fond of laughing as well as Doll."

"That's because she says such funny things. She told me yesterday she should be very happy if I could be quiet, for she was sick and tired to death with my nonsense. What a speech for little Doll to make, wasn't it, ma?"

"It was rather funny," replied the fond mother.

"Ma, let Henry and me go into the great park in the next street and play with all the fine little boys and girls."

"You can't go there, my dear."

"Why not, ma?"

"Because no one but rich people's children go there."

"And why are no poor little boys and girls let go in?"

"Because—because—"

"Because what, ma?"

"Because the parents of poor children do not own the land?"

"What does own the land mean?" inquired Henry, for Dolly was pondering over the hard fate of poor little children.

"To do with it as they please, I suppose."

"Then I will tell my father to buy some land, for it would make Dolly so happy to run through such shady walks as those in that park. And brother, too, wouldn't he clap his hands? Father must buy some land when he goes out to-morrow. And then I would let all the poor children—all the *good* poor children, run through the park, and all the rich children, too; for they must all be good or they would not be dressed so fine."

"Oh, yes! do let pa buy a park, won't you, ma? He will do anything for you," exclaimed Dolly, joyfully.

Mary Kane was silent, and tears gathered in her eyes as she contemplated the hard fate which her offspring were doomed to encounter in their brief journey through life. Thinking it better to apprise them at once, as far as she was able, of the distinctions made by the political and social laws of England, she laid the baby in the cradle, and quietly rocking it with one foot, took Dolly upon her knee, and proceeded to reveal her stock of information.

"Well, ma, tell us; me and sissy."

"You have, my children, seen ladies and gentlemen riding on horseback and in carriages?"

"Yes, ma."

"Dressed in rich clothing?"

"Oh, yes, such beautiful dresses!" exclaimed Henry.

"Well, those are called *favored* people."

"Why so?"

"Because they perform no labor, and go where they please."

"Don't they eat?" asked Dolly.

"Of course they eat."

"And don't they work so as to get bread like father does?"

"No."

Both the children paused in mute wonder, for they could not comprehend how people could live without work.

"But, ma, aint they human beings, like we are?" said Henry, returning to the attack.

"Yes."

"Well, the bible says that the descendants of Adam shall earn their bread by the sweat of their brows. But perhaps they are *not* the descendants of Adam, for they look so much handsomer than ragged persons."

"They are all descendants of Adam and Eve, and the reason why they are so much more beautiful is because they have never been accustomed to toil."

"If they are human beings they ought to obey the bible, and work," said Henry positively.

"Ma, if they don't work, who gives them bread, and meat, and tea?" asked Dolly anxiously.

"A certain portion of the inhabitants of England, by the operation of laws which they have themselves made, live in idleness, while all the rest labor to support them."

Dolly pondered over this information as though she was sadly puzzled, but Henry, after a few moments' reflection, inquired,

"Did God make these laws?"

"No."

"Then why do the poor people obey them?"

"Our masters are so powerful that we have to submit."

"But father, I am sure, is stronger than either of those richly clothed gentlemen; why don't he make them work?" said the boy eagerly.

"They make some of the lower class, as they call them, force the rest to perform labor."

"And do they?"

"Yes."

"*I* would not," he exclaimed stoutly.

"Then they would make the others kill you."

Dolly opened her eyes at this intelligence, and throwing her arms round her brother's neck, clung convulsively there.

"I will explain the matter to you as I have heard your father tell it. The nobility, and gentry, have divided the kingdom among themselves, each renting the portion allotted to him to landlords, who in turn underlet to the farmers. The landlords pay rent to the nobility, and gentry, and the farmers pay rent to them, so that the land is cultivated, the crops are raised and sent to market, so that the privileged classes receive their rent and live without work. But as the laboring part of the people think this is wrong ——"

"So do I!" cried Henry.

"The government have taken measures to see that it is done."

"How, ma!"

"You have seen the soldiers marching through the streets with flags and drums?"

"Oh yes; and I have often wished that I might be a soldier too."

"These soldiers are dressed up and armed with guns and swords to make the poor people perform their tasks."

"Father, too?"

"Yes."

"Then I will never want to become a soldier again."

"But they will make you, perhaps."

"And force me to fire upon poor creatures?"

"Whose strength cannot endure the heavy burden they are compelled to perform, and upon whose cheeks the sweat mingles with their tears."

"I tell you I *won't* do it," exclaimed the child passionately, as his lips curled, and the large tears gathered in his eye.

"I will tell you how they will force you. They will reduce your wages as a laborer so low that you cannot buy bread enough to keep you from starving; and when you are very, *very* hungry, you will be willing to do anything to obtain food, even if it is to enlist as a soldier."

Henry rested his head upon his hand as he felt the truth of her words.

"If they should fail in this, they will seize upon your person if necessary."

"What, ma, in free and happy England, as Mr. Kossuth said it was."

"My child, there is *no* freedom in England for the poor; it only exists for the favored class. We are crushed to the earth by laws that force us to toil from daylight until dark for the paltry pittance which is scarcely sufficient to keep starvation from our doors, while the rest is exacted to fatten a pampered aristocracy. No, Henry, there is no freedom for you, for when the government requires your services as a soldier or a sailor, the press-gang will seize you as they have seized thousands before."

"But, ma, why do they become soldiers?"

"Because a disobedience of orders is punished with death."

"I would die, then."

"No, you would not; you would follow the examples of those foolish men who, for the shadow of military glory, will turn their arms against friends as well as foes."

"What is the shadow of military glory, ma?" asked Henry.

"It is losing one's health, and limbs, and life, for nothing but to confer honor and glory upon one's masters. The common soldier gains nothing by the battles in which he perils his life; on the contrary, he rivets more closely the chains which bind his class, because he increases the power and renown of his tyrants."

"But I heard father say that money and honors had been given the *iron Duke*. Why do they call him the iron Duke?"

"Because he won those honors and that money by sacrificing, without remorse, the lives of his men. Yes, they have showered honors and wealth upon the Duke of Wellington, but what has become of those poor fellows by whose aid he acquired his renown?"

"Do you mean his soldiers, ma? Ain't they the officers I see so handsomely dressed and who ride such splendid horses?"

"Alas! no, my child. Most of them have crumbled into dust, and now enrich the soil of Portugal, Spain, and Belgium, or are lying far down in the deep, dark sea."

"But if they cover up soldiers in the ground, and, as father said, without coffins, and put the sailors into the sea, for the fishes to eat, why are they so careful to put the dead bodies of the Iron Duke and Lord Nelson where not even the worms can get at them? Didn't the soldiers and sailors fight for their country too?"

"Yes, they suffered more than the officers."

"Then why should they be treated like dogs?" said Henry impatiently.

"Because, having won victories for England, and lost their lives, the government could gain nothing by decently burying their remains. But they can strengthen their own power by fawning upon the chieftain."

"Are Wellington's and Nelson's men all dead, ma," he inquired sorrowfully.

"Not all; there are some survivors."

"*They* must be well fed and clothed," he said, confidently.

"Henry, did you ever pass by the Workhouse in ——street?"

"Yes, ma," he replied with a shudder.

"And you have seen half a dozen old men with trembling limbs, snow white hair, and shriveled faces?"

"Oh, yes, and I have pitied them so often. The boys call them crazy."

"Want of food and hard labor caused a loss of mind, and now those helpless old men are left to drag out the remainder of their miserable lives, with no home, no relations, no friends."

A loud sob burst from Dolly, whose cheek rested upon her mother's bosom, as she listened with all her little might to the conversation.

"Mother!" exclaimed the boy, springing from his chair, "you don't mean to say them old men were at the battle of Waterloo?"

"All."

"Then if I wasn't afraid to swear, I would curse the government for its meanness."

"Hush! you must not talk so."

"I would, ma, *so* I would, and I will too when I am old enough not to be afraid of swearing."

With doubled fists he paraded across the narrow floor for several minutes, until his excited feelings were calmed down, and then he seated himself again, while Dolly continued to weep over the sufferings of the poor old men.

"But why don't they give them something more to eat?"

"It takes all the money to pay for the fine clothes, splendid carriages, and magnificent buildings of the nobility."

"And the old soldiers and sailors must be hungry?"

"Yes."

Henry was silent for several minutes, and then he exclaimed, joyfully,

"Ma, ma, I'll tell you what can be done for them. Food can be raised from the ground, and then they will not be hungry."

"The earth will only yield a certain quantity."

"Yes, but the earth is not all cultivated. Don't you remember when we were at grandma's I saw a large park belonging to the Duke of Sunderland, in which nothing grew? Now, enough wheat and potatoes would grow in that park to feed all the soldiers and sailors, I am sure there would; and then they would look cheerful and be happy, wouldn't they, ma?"

Dolly's face brightened at this new idea, which she managed, with some difficulty, to comprehend.

"You forget, Henry, that those parks belong to the nobility. There are deer, and pheasants, and other game in them, which the rich people hunt during certain portions of the year."

"And be the parks only used by game?"

"That is all. They are devoted to the pleasure of the nobility."

"And does it give the nobility pleasure to do anything that will make the poor hungry?"

"What odd questions you do ask, Henry! Come, you had better get your hat and go out to play. I don't like to think, much less to talk, upon this subject, for it always puts me in an ill humor, and then I'm not cheerful when your father comes home."

"Dear ma, answer my question. Does it give the nobility pleasure to make the poor hungry?"

"Oh! I suppose they don't think anything about it."

"But don't they see the ragged clothes and pale faces of the poor?"

"Doubtless."

"Then why don't they tell them to go into the park and raise food, instead of letting wild beasts occupy them."

Mrs. Kane did not reply.

"Perhaps they think the old soldier is not as good as wild beasts?"

"Heaven forbid that I should say that!"

"Well, they don't think an old man is as good as a hound."

"Why?"

"Because I saw Lord Melville strike an old man with his whip, when he slily picked up a piece of meat that Lord Melville threw to his dog."

"The English nobility inherit their power by descent, my child, and they are accustomed to think of nothing but their own pleasure. They regard the lower classes only as soulless, feelingless instruments to minister to their happiness."

"What is inheriting power by descent?"

"The wealth and power of the father belongs to his oldest son after the parents' death."

"What becomes of the other children?"

"They have to take care of themselves."

"What funny people the nobility are. Don't you love brother and sis as well as you do me?"

"That I do," and she pressed Dolly fondly in her arms.

"Why do they love the oldest child the best then."

"I suppose they do not, but the law, I believe, settles the property upon the oldest child."

"Don't they make the laws?"

"Yes, but they wish to keep the wealth and power of the kingdom in the hands of a few individuals."

"The nobility," said Henry, musingly, "give their property to the oldest son, and they would let poor little brother, Frank Tot, take care of himself, and they feed beasts and let poor old people starve. I think the nobility are bad, mean, persons; *that* I do."

"Come, now, take Dolly and go play in the street. I will call you when dinner is ready."

With compressed lips and a stern brow the boy took his sister's hand, and together they descended the staircase, muttering as he went—

"Poor old soldiers treated worse than dogs."

"What's dat you say, Henry?" asked Dolly.

"Let us go and sit down upon that bench, and I will tell you all about it."

Together they seated themselves upon the old bench, and Henry recapitulated all that he remembered of the grievances of the lower classes, and the oppressions of the rich. Her tears flowed afresh, and she sobbed herself to sleep. Resting her head upon his lap, he took off his coat to prevent her from catching cold. And there he sat, watching over the sleeper until the sun had mounted to the meridian. She was sleeping sweetly when three boys smartly dressed came down the street, loudly talking and laughing.

A flush of anger overspread the face of Henry Kane, when he discovered they belonged to a class who were guilty of such heartless cruelty as his mother had portrayed. The youngsters, who were about his own age, stopped near where Henry sat.

"Oh, here is fun for us!" exclaimed one of them, as he directed the attention of his companions to the sleeping child.

Henry raised his hand with an imploring gesture as they approached; but their laughter awakened her. Rubbing her eyes, she looked up, and, gazing upon the derisive countenances of the rude boys for a moment, she clung to her brother for protection.

"See how his sweetheart clings to him. Ha! ha!"

"She is my little sister; go away, you frighten her."

"His little sister. Come, little sis, look this way, and let us see if you are handsome."

"You are bad, *bad* boys, to scare a little child so. Go away, I tell you. Pray, Mr. Riley, make these wicked lads leave us alone."

The mischievous fellows turned in momentary alarm; but seeing the malicious grin upon the face of Riley, and the smile of the one-eyed man who stood by his side, they followed the retreating forms of Henry and his sister.

"Go it, my young gallants!" exclaimed Hurdy, the one-eyed fellow, who was known as a savage member of the press-gang that infested the neighborhood.

One of the boys seized Dolly's frock, and held her fast.

"Leave her alone!" exclaimed Henry, fiercely.

The only reply was a violent jerk, which threw her upon the pavement, from whence she arose with the blood flowing from a cut in her cheek.

A sudden blow from Henry's clenched fist knocked the offender down. Springing to his feet, he returned the assault.

"At him, my little gentleman; show the beggar how you can beat him," cried Hurdy.

Again the aggressor tumbled upon the pavement; and this time he ran bawling away, with the blood spouting from his nose.

"Let them both at him," whispered Riley.

"I'm d——d if you aint right. At him both of you," exclaimed the brute.

"No, no! be Jasus! fair play is a jewel; one at a time," said a stout voice from across the street.

During this scene Dolly stood by a post, watching them in silent terror.

Another of the boys now rushed upon Henry, and they fought until their strength was nearly exhausted. He seized Henry by the hair, and bending his head down, kicked him several times in the abdomen. Dolly screaméd. "Foul play!" exclaimed the man who had already interposed in behalf of the persecuted lad.

Rallying his strength, Henry released himself; and grasping the other by the throat, bore him back, until, no longer able to maintain his feet, he fell, and his head came violently in contact with the curb stone. He lay upon the ground still and motionless.

Henry stood in the street; and with panting form, but flashing eye, awaited the attack of the remaining boy. But, rendered cautious by the fate of his companions, he recoiled a step from before the glance of the little hero.

"Now's your time for an easy victory," said Hurdy, patting him on the shoulder.

"But he fights so."

"He's weak and exhausted, and you can beat him easily," whispered Riley.

"Oh don't, pray don't let them hurt brother any more. See, his face is all bloody," cried Dolly.

"At him, my little gentleman," said Hurdy. "This way;" and taking the boy's hand in his own, he thrust it with such violence against Henry, that, already weakened by the prolonged conflict, he fell heavily to the ground.

"You have killed my poor brother Henry—I know you have killed him," sobbed Dolly, as she tried to raise his bruised head upon her lap.

"That was a mane act of yourn, Master Hurdy, an', be the holy St. Patrick! I'll tell Robert Kane."

"Will yez?" replied Hurdy, imitating the Irish brogue. "Thin, by the inemy of all the toads in that same koontry of yourn, I don't care if yez do tell him."

"Away wid yez, for a bragging kidnapper, as ye are."

"Take care, Mr. Pat, that I don't kidnap you."

"Ye'll get a broken pate first."

"May be so."

Mary Kane, coming in search of her children, saw her boy lying upon the pavement, with his face bruised, from which Dolly was trying to wipe the blood away. A crowd, who had enjoyed the spectacle, were standing around making their comments upon the scene; the more humble portions of it congratulating themselves upon the bravery of Henry Kane, while those whose affinities were with the aristocracy were saying that the spirit of the lower classes must be subdued. Through this assemblage Mrs. Kane forced her way, and raising the helpless body of her child, bore it towards the house. The motion roused him, and opening his eyes he looked around as if rallying his thoughts. When at last the recollection of the conflict burst upon him, he exclaimed, "My sister—where is my sister!"

"Here I is," said the troubled voice.

The assurance satisfied him, and his head fell upon his mother's bosom.

"Oh! that I should ever witness such a spectacle as this. And what will his poor father say when he sees this mangled face," said the agonized mother.

"Don't cry, ma, I am not much hurt. I shall soon be over it. I would rather been hurt a great deal more than have them bad boys frighten Dolly."

Sadly she ascended the stair-case, and laid Henry upon the bed. Dolly pushed a chair to the side of the bed, and ascending it laid herself by him, and placed her cheek, down which the tears trickled, close to his own.

Slowly the day wore along. Mrs. Kane bathed his face, and prepared some soup for the sufferer, and although he tried once to sit up, so as to be well when his father returned, a sudden dizziness forced him to lie down again. It was evident that when he fell last his head was very much injured. Darkness now began to steal over the earth, and the anxious mother expected every moment to hear the welcome sound of Kane's footsteps upon the stair-case. But time wore on. She had never known him to remain out so late before. The suppper was already upon the table, except the tea, which was never drawn until he entered the room. His chair was at the right spot; the boot-jack was placed beside it, and his slippers lay upon the hearth-stone.

"What can have happened," said the anxious wife.

Henry raised his throbbing head.

"Has father come?"

"Not yet," replied Mrs. Kane, in a cheerful voice.

"I want to see him."

"He will come soon, I hope."

"He will be hungry," she murmured to herself, "*very* hungry; and he cannot be much longer away. I will draw the tea. Oh, no, he must return immediately, for it is nine o'clock."

And humming an old song, as if that would hasten his return, she placed the steaming teapot upon the table.

"There, now, all is ready."

The minutes flew by. The clock struck ten; eleven; and the hands indicated a near approach to midnight. Still her husband did not return.

"Oh, I was certain misfortunes would not come singly; what can have happened to poor, *dear* Robert? If he should be taken from me. And Henry too; how his head throbs; and his pulse beats so fast, and his mind wanders, I am sure it does, for he talks so wildly. Hark! *that* is Robert."

Opening the door, she rapidly descended the stairs, and throwing her arms around his neck burst into tears. Silently he pressed her in his arms.

"Oh, Robert! what could have kept you away so late?"

"Is—it—late—dar—ling?" he stammered.

A terrible thought flashed like fire upon her brain. Her steady and industrious husband had for the first time returned intoxicated.

"And at such a moment, too," she said, as she sank upon the steps.

"What's the—the matter—Ma—ree—"

"Matter? why our boy, Henry, is going to die, but, alas! you are too drunk to comprehend me. Come, go up to your bed."

"Hush! not—drunk—no, not *drunk*—Ma—Mary," he muttered, as he staggered into the room.

Mary anxiously scrutinized his countenance as the light fell upon it. His features were hueless, a white foam was upon his lips, and a crimson stream trickled down his face from a cut in his forehead.

"Too true. Poor dear Robert, how could you so have forgotten yourself?"

Reeling forwards, he gazed for a moment upon the flushed cheeks of his boy, and then muttering—

"Doctor—send—" he fell upon the bed.

Mary started.

"Why did I not think of that before; yes, the Doctor, I must bring the Doctor."

She hesitated as she was closing the door. Could she leave them alone? A drunken father and a sick child. But there was no other recourse, and emerging into the open air she proceeded rapidly along the street in the direction of Dr. Aldway's office. Fortunately he was at home. Explaining her wishes, she started upon her return, and had nearly reached the house when she encountered Matthew Riley. His sinister face was more than ordinarily forbidding, and a low chuckling laugh issued from his grinning mouth, as her progress was involuntarily arrested.

"Your husband is out late to-night, Mrs. Kane?"

"How do you know that?"

"Wives have to sit up late when Dwyville Hurdy nabs their mates."

"What! the leader of the press gang?"

"Ye'll find it out, soon enough, pretty dame."

"Tell me, monster, have the press gang been after Robert Kane?"

"Monster, indeed! yes, they have, and it's a sore head Mr. Kane will have the morrow on board the king's ship. Dwyville Hurdy don't let his stick fall upon the heads of his victims for nothing."

"Dear Robert, how have I wronged you!" exclaimed Mary, as she sped onwards.

Throwing open the door, she knelt by his side.

"Robert, Robert, look up; forgive me, say that you forgive me, only say that, and I will be happy."

The sufferer breathed heavily, but made no response.

"He will die, I am sure he will die," sobbed Mary, "and I wronged him so. Dear Robert, wake up, only say that you forgive me."

He opened his eyes, and a thrill of anguish darted through her frame as she saw they were lead-like.

Footsteps were heard mounting the staircase, and the Doctor entered the room.

He looked upon the form of Kane.

"What, honest Robert intoxicated ?" he said in a low voice.

"No, no, not that, I was guilty of harboring the thought. He has been in the hands of the press-gang."

"So, so, and they inflicted a blow here, is it not so ?"

He parted the hair upon the forehead.

"Yes, here it is, and an ugly cut too. Don't cry. I trust it is nothing serious."

"Then why don't he awaken from that stupor ?"

"The functions of the brain are suspended by the blow. Bring me a bowl, I must bleed him."

With that perfect reliance upon the doctor, which is so often witnessed, she obeyed his directions, and with blanched cheeks saw him tighten the cord upon the arm ; but averted her face as the polished steel entered the vein. The dark blood flowed slowly at first, and then, as the body began to reassume its powers, the crimson tide spouted forth from the stalwart arm.

The sleeper opened his eyes and asked for water.

"I am much better now," he said.

Mary pressed his hand in silence.

"Has the Doctor seen Henry ?"

"What, another sick person ? why, this has been a day of wrongs !"

"Has Henry been abused too ?" asked the father, quickly.

"Come, Mr. Kane, you must remain quiet. He is not dangerously hurt, and you will both be better to-morrow. You must keep them quiet during the night, and I will call early in the morning."

The next day Mary told her husband all that had occurred during his absence, and learned from him, that returning home at the usual hour, he was attacked by the press-gang, under the leadership of Hurdy. After a desperate resistance, during which he was knocked down, he was bound and carried to the Thames. He managed, however, to make his escape, and eluding his pursuers, reached his home—that *castle* in which the most humble of England's subjects are sovereigns.

"But there is no safety for us here, Mary," he continued.

"Where shall we go ?" she anxiously inquired.

"Any where, rather than be torn from you and our little ones. To leave you to starvation, perhaps to insult, if not dishonor ? The thought is too horrible."

"But have you no plan for the future ? Have you no idea in what direction to escape ?"

"I have thought," he said in a low voice, "we had better seek the friendly shores of America."

"And leave England forever?"

"What have we received from England but ill treatment?"

"But here we were born; here repose the ashes of my father and mother; here lies buried the dead body of our first child; and here, too, are my brothers and sisters." She wept at the thought of a separation from every tie that bound her to the land of her nativity.

"Yes, but Mary, look upon the other side of the picture; nothing but wrongs here; a happy home with no one to make us afraid in the United States. One of my cousins has been there several years. He has now a farm of his own, and he writes to me that they are happy and contented."

"Well, Robert, I am willing to do anything that you think best," replied Mary, as she wiped the tears from her eyes and smoothed down her white apron.

"Thank you, dear Mary, and now you have said that, I will frankly tell you that during the long hours of the past night I have pondered upon the subject, and have come to the conclusion to leave England at once."

"Indeed, Robert?"

"Yes, there is no time for delay. We cannot tell how soon I may be again seized by the press-gang."

"Oh, let us go at once, then," she exclaimed eagerly.

"I have enough money to pay for a steerage passage, and if the voyage is not too long, the supply of provisions which I shall be able to buy will be sufficient to prevent us from suffering much for want of food. When once we get to the United States I can earn enough to keep you all comfortable, and to educate the children."

Mary's face brightened at his cheering words.

"I am willing, Robert. We will go as soon as you please. Shall you visit your brother and mother?"

"I would gladly do so, but the necessity of leaving England at once is too pressing to admit of delay——what was that?" he whispered, proceeding towards the door. His cheek turned a shade paler as he saw Riley moving stealthily from the door. "In less than a week we must bid adieu to *merry* England," he said bitterly.

CHAPTER V.

"Do I merit pangs like these,
That have cleft my heart in twain?
Must I, to the very lees,
Drain thy bitter chalice, pain?"—MORRIS.

THERE was no prospect of a harvesting day. The sky still looked threatening, and at short intervals the rain fell copiously. Christie Kane filled a portmanteau with provisions, and, accompanied by Phelim Savor, started in his gig for the western part of the Duke of Sunderland's estate, situated six miles distant.

"Phelim, what makes you always so cheerful?" inquired Christie Kane, abruptly.

"Is it me, maister Christie?"

"Yes."

"Och! plinty to ate, an' no care, I belave."

Christie was struck with the reply. He thought there was philosophy in it.

"Plenty to eat and no care," he said, musingly.

"But suppose you did not have plenty to eat, Phelim?"

"By me sowl, but I belave in that case there would be a fierce struggle betwane natril good humor and rebillion."

"We are going where, I fear, we shall witness absolute want."

"Thin there is one matter of consolation to the parties interested. They will be the better plazed whin the temporary restriction is removed, and the supply is equal to the demand, as Sir William Belthoven said tother day to the independent fraymen."

"How is that?"

"You see, the Baronet was a candidate for mimber of Parliament, and so he made the fraymen—yez see they call them *fraymen* bekaze they fall upon others to bate knowledge into other's heads wid shellalaghs—an' he towld thim that it gav him uncommon satisfaction to address voters so remarkable for their intilligence as that same body of men tul whom he was at that moment spaking. Yez say, they are called wery intilligent becaze they don't begrudge the use of thim same shillalaghs. Whin they heard sich gintlemanly language from Sir William, all about their own wisdom, and sich like, they giv their hats a tirl and cheered untwil they got red in the face. When he had done justice to their mirits, he tould thim a heavy duty must be laid on foreign importations, so as to exclude them from our markets. Bad luck to his strange words, I didn't know what *heavy duty* meant, and so I axed a stout bit of a lad, who was a very intilligent frayman, for his scalp was cut in siveral places. He said I must ha' coomed from the koonty Clare, which he towld me was the greenest koonty of the Green Isle. 'Not know what *heavy duty* manes,' he cried in a voice so loud that Sir William paused, and all eyes were directed to me.

'Why, *heavy duty* means to attach something so weighty to the importations that they sink into the depths of the ocean, and don't land at all at all.'

"The crowd chared, and Sir William smiled, and bowed graciously, and said:—

'A very good explanation, my intilligint frind.'

"An' the person who was thus publicly complimented looked as wise as St. Pathrick, afther the small toad investment, and the fraymen tirled their hats again, for they were plazed that Sir William appraciated their intilligence. Yez say people like to hear nice spaches all aboot their own good qualities, and especially their intilligence; it puts them in good humor directly, and makes thim feel decidedly comfortable."

"Well, what more did Sir William say?"

"Afther he had done justice to the frayman wid the cut head, he towld us—for having obtained the valuable bit of information about the heavy duty, I considered meself a frayman in embree—he towld us that a heavy duty would exclude—sink thim, mind ye—

foreign provisions, and thin the supply would be less thin the demand, which would make the price of food very high. An' thin the fraymen twirled their hats agin, for yez say they had provisions to sell. At that moment some unlucky divil said, 'that if it was to increase the price of food, thin he for one, was fernenst heavy duties.' Ye ought to hiv been there thin. Och! but didn't they hustle out the '*Paddy whack*,' as they called him. 'Is it the likes of yez that'll ba afther expressing an opinion? Sure an' you hiv no vote, onyhow, an' what business is it of yez whether provisions is high or low.' Two or three brawny divils flourished their shillalaghs over me own head, and axed me did I endorse the treasonable sentiments of me ignorant coonthryman. I towld thim I had inflixible confidence in hivy duties. An' thin they said I might hiv the binefit of Sir William's spach. But Sir William was determined to be universally popular, an' so he towld thim to listen to his explanation, which was to the effect that if provisions did become higher, thim's as had praties and whate to sell would be plazed, and thim as had to buy, would hiv sich excellent appetites, be razon of the *scarcity*, that they would relish amazingly what they did git to ate. An' thin the fraymen, an' the 'Paddy whack,' an' mesell, tirled our hats. Some gintleman, who was sated fernenst Sir William, on the stand, laughed an' towld him he explained that matter beautifully. An' his benevolent countenance was covered wid smiles too: an' then I exclaimed, begorra, nis honor's an illigant spaker. The gintleman smiled agin, but the frayman wid the cut head thumped me in the ribs, and towld me not to spake agin untwil I was axed, an' so I—"

"This is the house, Phelim," interrupted Christie Kane, and they alighted from the gig.

Passing through a narrow wicket gate, the lower hinge of which was broken, they approached the door of a hut. It was scarcely twelve feet square, and a bank of dirt encircled the outside to the height of four or five feet. The dilapidated thatch roof was elevated about two feet above the bank, and, between the two, was an aperture—it could not be called a window, because there was no glass—for the admission of light and air. The entrance to the hovel was reached by mounting three steps, and as Christie Kane ascended, he saw the miserable apology for a cellar was tenanted by a very weakly pig. In the corner of the hut was a filthy straw bed lying on the floor, upon which the water was dripping from the thatch. The room—for there was but one—was entirely destitute of furniture, save one chair with three legs.

With folded arms Christie Kane contemplated the objects of destitution around him. Upon the straw bed was the skeleton form of a little girl, some eight years of age, whose wan cheeks and sunken eyes, betrayed the effects of hunger and disease. Her lips were dry and cracked, the eyes were bright and restless, and the body emaciated to such a degree, that the bones protruded from the skin.

"Be me *sowl*, but this is too bad, intirely," said Phelim, in a low voice, while big tears rolled down his cheeks.

The wistful glance of the tortured child rested upon the portmanteau, while her fleshless fingers played convulsively with the ragged bed-clothes.

"Ye needn't be coming after the rent, for it's nothing you can get but the pig below, and ye'll have to carry him away, for he can't walk," said the mother, in a cracked voice. It was evident her sensibilities were deadened by suffering.

"You mistake the object of our visit, good woman," said Christie. "Although poor ourselves, we come to commiserate, if we cannot relieve."

"Well, it's all the same to us now. Little Mary can't live long," replied the woman, with a look of hopeless despondency.

"Do not say that," exclaimed the young man. "She cannot, she *must* not starve to death, in a country which boasts of its wealth, power, and philanthropy. It would be too horrible."

"I tell you it is too late," said the female, sternly. "Not all the wealth of the avaricious Duke of Sunderland could now preserve the life of that victim."

"Hush, you will alarm her."

"Not at all, she is as willing to die as I am to part with her. Her form is too weak to suffer any more."

"My God! I cannot endure this!" burst from the lips of Kane.

"Then you are more tender hearted than our landlord."

"Does the Duke know of your condition?" eagerly inquired Christie.

"Of course. Lord Melville, his son, came here with the steward yesterday, accompanied by a distress officer, but it's very little they found to seize, except the pig, and he couldn't stand."

"But surely Lord Melville relieved your wants."

"Hoot! you must have lost your senses. He told the officer to turn us out of the hut. But the steward, as unfeeling as he is was shocked at the proposition, and so they left Mary to die in peace."

"May the divil get the unfaling spalpeen," cried Phelim, whose good nature was not proof against such atrocities.

"Mother," said the child, faintly; and she pointed to the portmanteau.

"The darlint little crater shall hiv something to ate amadately," said Phelim, as he hastily opened the leather-bag.

She turned her eyes away with an expression of utter hopelessness, as she felt that the nourishment, which a few days before would have been so eagerly seized, the stomach now loathed. Her glance fell again, but mechanically, upon the portmanteau, and then she whispered, "Mother," with more earnestness, for she saw a bowl of fresh and delicious blackberries.

"Ah! that may prove a welcome present," said the woman, more gently.

The little, wan face seemed to brighten as her look followed the movements of her mother while she pressed the juice from the berries, mixed it with water, and sweetened it. An expression, almost of happiness, overspread her pale and attenuated features, as the female raised her head and applied the grateful beverage to her parched lips. But as she swallowed one draught, she coughed violently, the lower jaw dropped, the eyes closed, the pallor of the countenance deepened, the rattle was heard in her throat—she was dead.

Loud laughter was heard in the highway. Christie turned to the door with a frowning brow, as if he would rebuke unseemly merriment. It was a party of equestrians convoyed byLord Melville.

Their laughter mingled with the sob of the mother, and the last moan of the dying child.

"Proud and boastful government, unequal and tyrannical laws, exacting and unfeeling aristocracy, may the trenchant blade of truth lance thy canting hypocrisy, and expose thy unblushing wrongs!" said Christie Kane, as his eyes followed the receding horsemen.

Heart-broken sobs burst from the bosom of the mother. It was evident, notwithstanding the willingness she had manifested to have her child relieved from suffering, that now the link was severed which bound her to her offspring, the uneffaceable strength of a mother's love would reassume its dominion over her feelings. She laid her down upon the homely bed, and adjusted her body and limbs with a tenderness which the living form could have felt without pain; and then, falling upon her knees, with the hand of the dead clasped within her own, she wept long and violently.

Christie waited until the first outburst of grief had subsided, and then he uttered the words of consolation.

"Oh! if you only knew," said the wretched mother, wiping the scalding tears from her cheeks, "how her poor father and I almost worshipped her when she was an infant—what happy hours we passed watching over her cradle, for we were then well off. How often he came during the day to look at her, for he said he was afraid to touch her with his big hands. And then when she grew to be a little toddling girl, and could run about the room, with what gentleness he raised her to his knees, and how patiently he taught her to lisp her first words. I am sure when he comes home—if he ever does come—and finds she is *dead*, it will break his heart; I am *sure* it will," and the poor creature cried as though her own heart was breaking.

"Where is your husband? Why is he not here to aid you in the hour of affliction?"

"Alas! sir, he cannot return. Three years ago we were happy. We had a small house in London, and my husband, by his industry, obtained a comfortable living. One evening he did not return at the hour when I always expected him. The minutes flew by. Mary cried, for her father always petted her before she was placed in her little bed. Midnight, morning came, still he was absent; I had not closed my eyes during the long hours of darkness. I started forth in search of him, but when I reached the next street, I met an acquaintance. He was terribly cut about the head. The truth at once flashed like fire through my brain. My husband had been seized by a press-gang! The wounded man informed me that as my husband and himself were returning home, having been unavoidably detained until after dark, they were beset by a press again. They resisted stoutly; but my husband's right arm was broken, and then he was knocked down. In piteous accents he implored them to release him. He told them he had an unprotected wife and a helpless child at home, who would be reduced to beggary, perhaps to starvation, if he was forced away. They replied with derisive laughter, and told him that his wife would console herself with another lover, and his child would find another protector. On his knees he supplicated; but they answered him with scoffs. At last he implored them only to suffer him to bid his wife and child a last farewell. Enraged at his pertinacity, one of them dealt him a heavy blow upon the head, and he was borne insensible on board ship. The other sought an opportunity, when the attention of the gang was directed elsewhere, and by a powerful effort made his escape. But my poor husband was less fortunate, for I have never seen him since."

"Have you never heard from him?" inquired Christie, deeply affected by the tale of woe.

"Only once. He was then attached to one of her Majesty's regiments in the East."

"An unwilling victim, pouring out his blood as an offering to the Moloch of insatiate ambition!"

"We remained in London until we were reduced to beggary, in the hope he would return; for I looked forward to that event, oh *so* anxiously. Then I saw the cheeks of my darling—*his* darling, Mary, becoming pale and thin, and we left London; and hearing there was employment here, we came down to the Duke of Sunderland's estate. Bitterly have I repented the step. For eighteen months we have existed in this hut. My exertions alone could not keep us from want; and Mary, at the tender age of seven years, began to turn the wheel. I tried to have her task lightened; but they required her to work from five in the morning until nine at night, *sixteen hours*, or else to give up the situation. I told them it would kill her. They answered it was not their fault; they could not change their regulations; the precedent would be a bad one. The dear child saw that labor and anxiety had enfeebled my frame, and with the most touching devotion she insisted upon performing her daily work, until over-exertion in the performance of labor too great for her strength, brought on an attack of sickness. I could not leave her side; and then commenced that pinching want, which gradually increased to starvation. Aye, to starvation! Do you know what that means?" she inquired, with a look of wildness. "Starvation! that yearning for food until you feel that your frame is in the grasp of dissolution—that horrible torture of the nerves and fibres, the bones and sinews of the body, as though about to be severed by mortal agony! It is too, *too* frightful for contemplation."

The poor creature started to her feet, and staggered wildly around the room.

At length she became more calm, and seating herself by the wretched pallet, gazed upon the wan features of the dead.

"It is better that she is relieved from suffering. Her whole life would have been one of toil and hardship. Yes, yes, I am glad she is dead!—glad she is dead! But what will her father say? Oh, the thought is horrible!"

And again the foundations of her grief were broken up, and the tears streamed down her cheeks, while her body moved backward and forward in the intensity of woe.

Christie Kane saw that consolation could avail nothing, and promising to make arrangements for the burial of the child, left some food, and emerged from the hut.

As he entered the gig he saw Lady Katharine Montague seated upon a horse, some twenty rods down the road. She appeared to be looking for some person, and beckoned to Christie, as soon as her eyes rested upon him. Without regarding the signal, he wheeled his horse in the opposite direction.

" See, yon lady wants yez," observed Phelim.

" I care not if she does. If I am poor, I am not a lacquey."

" Ah! but maister Christie, she may be in danger."

On the instant the horse was turned, and they rapidly approached the lady. Phelim sprang to the ground, and touching his hat, placed his hand upon the rein of her horse, while young Kane sat erect in the gig. She tossed a small portmanteau, which hung upon the frame of her saddle, to Phelim, and then sprang lightly to the earth.

" Thank you, my good man. Take charge of these horses until my return. Here," she continued, turning to Christie, " take the portmanteau, if you please, and come with me."

The hot blood mantled the cheek of Christie as he replied quickly,

" I am neither your father's tenant nor the footman of your ladyship."

She gazed at him a moment with a look of surprise, and then a glance of approval flashed across her features.

" Tie the bridle of my horse to the fence," she said, addressing Phelim. " If your master, if such he be, is too proud to aid me in a mission of charity, he will not be so ungenerous as to refuse me your aid."

" I beg your pardon for misjudging your intentions. Here, Phelim, take charge of both horses. Your ladyship may command *my* services."

" Then take up the portmanteau."

Passing over the stile she entered the narrow path. Raising the folds of her apparel, so as to prevent the rich and spotless material from coming in contact with the grass and weeds which surrounded the way, she disclosed the exquisitely shaped limbs where they tapered into the well booted, small Norman feet. Sinner as he was, Christie Kane could not withdraw his gaze from those little feet, as they quickly but noiselessly touched the ground, as she rapidly proceeded, only pausing to gather up her clothes as the obstructions of the pathway loosened them in her grasp. The lady was extremely modest, only her companion was far below her in rank, and her thoughts dwelt upon her mission.

Passing through a portion of the Duke of Sunderland's park, they emerged into a small country thoroughfare, upon the wayside of which several small huts were situated. Grateful voices welcomed Katharine Montague; children ran out from each of the houses to kiss her hand, while some of them pressed their lips to her dress. Several aged persons clasped their hands, while tears of joy coursed down their furrowed cheeks. Even some emaciated dogs staggered forward, wagging their tails, and whining, to express their pleasure at the approach of the maiden.

"Will you open the portmanteau?"

"Certainly," responded Christie.

From its ample store each person was supplied, and even the curs were not forgotten. She now beckoned Christie to follow her. They entered the most wretched of the hovels. There were two rooms upon the ground floor, if, indeed, that could be called a floor which was only misshapen boards with wide crevices between them, made by the touch of time. The rude door was opened, and Katharine Montague entered the first room.

"Many, many thanks to your ladyship," said the weak voice of a female. "I am grateful to you for your kindness; indeed I am."

"You are better?"

"I feel like a different person since I eat the food you brought me."

"Very well; here is something still more nourishing. How is the occupant of the next room?"

"He was able to go out in search of work, though I fear it's little he'll get for it. But there is a still more distressed object down yonder."

"What! in the cellar?"

"Yes, ma'am. He rented the apartment yesterday, and to-day he has a raging fever."

"The apartment!" muttered Kane, bitterly.

"We will descend; give me a light."

The woman obeyed, and delivered the candlestick into the hand of the maiden.

They descended the damp and mouldy stairway, which possessed scarcely sufficient strength to support their weight. The cellar was dimly lighted by an open space beneath the sill of the house, but it was too indistinct to enable the visitors to discover the dweller of the miserable abode of wretchedness, without the aid of the candle. Their attention was attracted to the corner of the cellar by the quick, short breathing, and restless motions of the sick man. He had rolled from his rotten bed of straw, and lay upon the cold, damp earth. His feet were in a pool of stagnant water, upon whose slimy surface there was a dark green coating. His head rested by another festering and loathsome pool, from the border of which several toads leaped sluggishly away as Katharine Montague and Christie Kane approached. In his delirium, the sufferer quenched his raging thirst in this fetid and putrid mass.

The cheek of the lady grew pale, her head swam round, and she would have fallen had not Christie sprang forward to her assistance. In a moment she rallied, and passing her hand across her brow as if to dispel an unpleasant dream, when her sight again rested upon the stern and terrible reality.

"Such are the fruits of an accursed system," said Christie Kane, as he raised the form of the unconscious man and placed aim upon the miserable pallet. His eyes met the glance of the maiden. Perhaps, as one of the class who exist upon corporal and mental agony, she felt herself justly accused, for her eyes fell.

Kane turned moodily away.

The mind of the sick man wandered. He spoke at first mutteringly, and then his fevered thoughts became more connected.

"Ah! that's it," he said. "The vast mass; the physical power of this empire are no longer to be crushed into the earth. They are going to do us justice! yes, sir, they have found out that we can suffer. Thank God, for teaching them that *we* are human beings, as well as themselves. And now they are enlightened upon this important subject, they voluntarily right our wrongs. Ain't they generous?"

He muttered incoherently for a few moments, and then he exclaimed, vehemently—

"I tell you, I am *not* mistaken. I have reflected too long, *suffered* too long, to be mistaken. Can you not see for yourself? Look yonder! The magnificent hunting grounds attached to the domain of Sunderland are now fields of waving grain. No not *all*, for he has been suffered to retain—let me see—ten acres for a park. But the remainder, instead of feeding worthless deer, and affording cruel sport to hunter, horse, and hound, will now feed those who are starving. So courage, friends—courage, brave friends; our sufferings will soon be over. They are, indeed, terrible; oh, almost too terrible for human endurance."

The sick man pressed his hand upon his side, and then in the delirium of his fever inflicted a heavy blow upon his forehead.

"They cannot last. See, the grain assuming a golden hue, waves in the breeze as I loved to see it in infancy. How deliciously it smells. Let me see: That field of grain will be ready for the sickle in one week. In one day more it can be cut down; then it will take one day—will one day be enough?—yes, if it is a fair day, it will be dry enough to thresh. But suppose it should rain? Ha! ha! that would be delightful; *delightful* to persons starving. Ha! ha! ha! how merry it would make them. Ho! ho! ho! By the gods, it's too funny." The dreary abode rang with maniacal laughter, but suddenly assuming a serious look, he continued—

"There would even then be one cause for congratulation, we should have water, yes water. The earth would no longer be parched with thirst, I could then wet my fevered lips. Thank Heaven! There is a cloud even now. See, it grows darker and darker; but Father of Mercy! can it withstand, much more overspread, that painfully lurid and scorching sky? It pales before the intense heat, it will be consumed. No! no! by heaven, no. It struggles bravely. Noble, gallant cloud, move on! Now it spreads out its dark wings like an army with banners. Hark! listen to the roar of cannon; the rattle of muskets; the neighing of steeds. Let me buckle on my sword and once more join my regiment. Alas! I am too weak. But I can witness the conflict. Now they are moving hitherward. Take care; the enemy is crowding his legions upon your left wing. Fool, fool! reinforce it, or he will cut you off in detail. Ah, that was well done. Glorious! Now follow it up with another charge. How the cannons roar! It is music—sweet music. Blood is poured out like rain; see, the earth is saturated with its crimson tide. It forms a rivulet. If it would *only* flow this way I could quench my raging thirst. It does! it does! Nearer, nearer, here it is. Thank God!"

He crawled eagerly in the direction of the putrid water. As Christie Kane arrested his movements, he struggled fiercely, but soon, overcome with exhaustion, sunk upon the ground. A sob burst from the aching bosom of Katharine Montague.

She pointed to the portmanteau. Kane eagerly searched its ample folds, and drew forth a bottle of cordial. Raising the head of the sick man he applied the grateful beverage to his lips. With a convulsive start he pressed it for a long time to his mouth, and then sunk back, while a calm smile played upon his fevered countenance.

"The man has seen better days, but poverty is a remorseless leveller," said Christie Kane in a low voice.

The feelings of the spirited girl were subdued in the presence of such horrors.

"What shall we do for this poor fellow?" she inquired.

Young Kane's heart thrilled as her melting eyes rested upon him.

"He must be removed from this loathsome spot, and receive medical assistance."

"Yes, and at once," she responded energetically.

Giving directions to the occupant of the room above to watch over the sufferer, she retraced her steps to the place where she had left her horse in the charge of Phelim. Suddenly halting in her progress, she confronted Christie Kane with the bearing of an accuser.

"You scan with a sharpened vision, each fault of the aristocracy; what excuse can you offer for the brutal conduct of those people who permitted a human being to toss upon the damp earth without an attempt to alleviate his sufferings?"

"Their exculpation is found in the fact that their sensibilities have been brutalized by the aristocracy. Brutalized, because it was necessary to gratify their inordinate vanity," replied Kane, with an unflinching gaze.

Katharine Montague pondered upon the reply a few moments, and then she resumed her walk. Arriving at the stile, she mounted her horse, and bestowing some pieces of silver upon Phelim, galloped rapidly away, without recognizing the existence, even, of her late companion.

Christie Kane gazed after her, until her form was concealed by the foliage of the wood.

"Be me sowl, she is a beautiful and ginerous lady, thot same, and long life tul her," exclaimed Phelim, as his eyes wandered from her receding form, to the silver, before he consigned the latter to his pocket. "It's well there is two, to keep each other company, for its few of the likes of yez that iver pay a visit to the pockets of Phalim Savor, onyhow. An' ye needn't ba afeerd of mating wid an inimy of another color. Begorra, the Pace Society might rist from their labors if foes were as scarce outer dooers as these bits of siller in the breeches pockets of Mr. Savor. Fur the matter o' that, I might as well have no pockets at all at all, ony its better to ba afther kaping up apparances, like the rest of the world; though if there was as little rayson fur thim same apparances, in gineral, as there is fur mesell hiving *pockets*, the world is beautifully humbugged, onyhow, don't yez think so, Maister Christie?"

But Kane suffered the observations of Mr. Savor to pass unheeded, and bidding him enter the gig, proceeded homewards, muttering, *sotto voce*, "She is a haughty maiden, but she may find me as proud as herself."

CHAPTER VI.

"Will no man throttle him, once for all?"—SCHILLER.

"WHAT kind of a country is America, ma?" inquired Henry Kane, when he had sufficiently recovered to be apprised of the contemplated emigration to the United States.

"The people are the sovereigns there."

"Is there no king?"

"None."

"Nor nobility?"

"No."

"Well, who abuses poor people there?"

"No one, Henry."

"Then I shall like America," he said, quietly. "But ma, who governs the people, for they must have rulers?"

"They chose their own public servants, as they call them."

"What does that mean?"

"Persons to make laws for them."

"Just as they wish them?"

"Yes."

"And will the press-gang ever seize father?"

"They have no press-gangs in the United States."

"I am sure I shall be happy there. Why don't *all* the poor people go to America? If they did, the nobility would have to wait upon themselves, and I think they wouldn't like that."

"They are emigrating by thousands, and more would doubtless go if they were not so poor, or if they were not so lamentably uneducated as to be ignorant of the advantages which a more favored country possesses."

"Does the English Government try to keep them in ignorance?"

"The government plays what is called a *shrewd game*. It manages to let out as many of our *criminals* as possible, and also the *very* poor from the impoverished districts, while it practises the most ingenious methods to retain the hardy and serviceable."

"That is cunning of John Bull, ain't it ma? But when shall we start; I am so anxious to go."

"We shall know when your father returns; and here he is; come in, Robert, what success had you?"

His cheerful countenance bore evidence of flattering hopes.

"Phil Hogan says I shall have my money to-morrow."

"But can you rely upon his word?"

"He has never failed me yet."

"If he pays you, father, when can we leave this hateful place?" asked Henry.

"The day after."

"Oh, I shall be *so* happy," and he clapped his hands with joy.

With smiling faces, they commenced packing their little store in a substantial wooden box purchased by Kane; even little Dolly contributing her feeble aid, with troublesome zeal.

The next day Robert started for the money that was absolutely necessary to ensure the success of his plans. As he reached the hut, he saw Hurdy and Riley in conversation. They hoth regarded him with malicious eyes, and for a moment the strong man faltered beneath their glance. His agitation elicited a coarse laugh from the kidnapper.

Kane approached them.

"Have I injured you in any way, Mr. Hurdy?" he asked in a steady voice.

"I won't tell you."

"Why do you persecute me? Have you no compassion for the humble? You ought, for you belong to that class yourself."

"Aye, but I am not so humble as to work, Mr. Kane. I can live without that. He! he!"

"Because you live by means that none but a scoundrel would resort to," exclaimed Kane passionately.

"Very well; *very* well. You only strengthen a determination I had already formed, Mr. Kane; so be on your guard, Mr. Kane."

"Miscreant, you will find me prepared. It will be more than your carcass is worth to attack me again."

"We shall see; he! he! he! We shall see."

With frowning brows Robert strode onwards, inwardly resolving to inflict a terrible chastisement upon Hurdy if he molested him again. Arriving at the house of Hogan, he was excessively disappointed to learn that the money he expected to receive could not be paid for several days. This was the more vexatious because every hour's delay periled his liberty. It was, therefore, with a sad heart that he returned to his wife.

With that hope which is so firmly implanted in the female mind she attempted to reassure him.

"God will not desert us, Robert; I know he will not. We have injured no one, and we are only trying to escape from oppression; be assured, then, all will be right, yet. You incur no danger in the house, and they will not attempt to seize you in the day time. So we must wait patiently."

"But our limited means, Mary. We shall require them all to take us across the Atlantic. I would continue my employment, but it is so late when we are dismissed that it is dark before I can reach home."

"Then do not attempt it. It is better to suffer a little for the want of food than to lose a home where you will indeed enjoy freedom."

Slowly the days rolled away to this anxious family, but at last Robert returned with the much coveted money—that pitiful amount of dross, upon which was staked the happiness of five human beings. Rarely do those who are accustomed to the immunities of wealth think how much of joy or woe is periled for the want of what, to them, is the merest trifle. The importance of money is measured by necessity, and when that necessity is pressing in its demands, at what point will honesty wage an unequal conflict with crime? Let him who has been put to the test answer; none other can.

The final preparations had been made, and Robert Kane and his family were seated at their last supper in the city of London. Now the time for departure had arrived, all the recollections of the past crowded upon them. Memory, with a gentle hand, softened the hardships through which they had struggled, and gilded with a bright radiance the joys that had checkered their career. A subtle negotiator is memory, when it seeks to elevate the realities of the past above the dread uncertainties of the future; for it presents the beautiful outlines of an existence that is seldom entirely destitute of green spots, while the unseen terrors of that which is to come are impressed upon the imagination with ineffaceable power. Life had been, however, to this humble family, chary of its favors, and with pleasant recollections, there was sprinkled too freely the remembrance of suffering and wrong. It is true that a final separation from the presence of the living, and the ashes of dead, relatives, caused more than a temporary pang. But to them alone was paid the tribute of a tear. The municipal and social laws of England merited and received the bitterest execration. That which the privileged classes so often favor with their laudations, and with such offensive bigotry require others to endorse, was viewed by the Kanes, as it is by all who are not bribed to defend it by money or position, with the most intense disgust. If there is any one thing which becomes a subject of amusement to foreigners, more than another, when the transparent egotism of John Bull—we mean the well fed John Bull, if, indeed, it would not be considered a "bull" to intimate that a person pinched with hunger *could* represent that burly character—is displayed, with his hereditary vanity, it is the complacency with which, overlooking the misery that is plainly visible to the whole world beside, he congratulates himself upon the evidences of wealth and power which his country exhibits. With such ludicrous intentness are his eyes riveted upon these objects of his idolatry, that it is utterly impossible for him to see, much more to relieve, the world of human agony upon which rests the vast and hideous superstructure of British despotism. But while he invariably overlooks the suffering that is visible upon every square yard of the British Empire, he engages with characteristic zeal in the small business of pointing out the short-comings of his neighbors. He manifests at this game more than his accustomed malignity and tact. In short, John Bull, by his prying habits, has acquired the reputation of being among nations what the musquito is to the insect tribe, always busy, never satisfied; and like that loquacious insect, no crevice is too small for him to enter while attempting to instil his poison. Such, at least, is the general reputation of John Bull among those who know him sufficiently well not to be deceived by his pretensions, or who do not suffer their judgment to be controlled by his own opinion of what constitutes a powerful, wealthy, and charitable people.

So far as his experience guided him, Robert Kane entertained these opinions. And it was, therefore, with a satisfaction greatly overbalancing regret that he severed the tie which, to him and his, had been fruitful of misfortune.

"And now, Mary, since we have concluded to start to-morrow, how do you feel?"

"Very happy, Robert."

"And you, Henry?"

"I shall never have to fight any more to keep sis from being hurt."

"That seems to run in your head."

"Because the pain hazent left my head yet, I suppose."

The fond parents exchanged approving glances.

"And what says little Dolly?"

The little girl brushed away the drowsiness that began to settle upon her eyelids.

"I'se will go any where wid you, and ma, and Henry, and—and Frank Tot."

A knock was heard upon the door. Mary's cheek blanched, while the lines on Robert's brow deepened into an angry frown. Walking to the desk, he took from it a long dirk-knife, and inserted it in his bosom; and then, elevating his form to its full height, he said, in a stern voice,

"Come in."

The door creaked upon its hinges, and the round, jolly face of Hogan was seen. Robert's features relaxed.

"Welcome, Phil, I am delighted to see you."

A glad smile was Mary's only salutation; the reaction was too powerful for words.

"You leave to-morrow, Robert?"

"If no unforeseen difficulty prevents me."

"Will you have the kindness to walk over to Martin Lennon's; he wishes to send a message to his son."

"Oh no! no! he must not go into the street to-night," almost shrieked Mrs. Kane.

"Why not? Surely no harm can happen to him going the matter of half a dozen streets."

"To tell you the truth, Phil, I am fearful of being attacked by the press-gang."

"Oh, if that is the case, I will not insist. I would not have asked you to go over at all, only the old man seemed so very anxious to see you."

"Did he seem so?" asked Robert, musingly.

"Yes."

"Why did he not send a letter?"

"I axed him that, an' he said he was too old to write."

Mary, with parted lips, watched the thoughtful countenance of her husband.

"It is shameful that an Englishman should be afraid to carry a message from an old soldier to his son. I will go."

Robert raised his head from his bosom, and, taking his hat, stood in the door-way.

"But dear, *dear* Robert, if any thing *should* happen to you, what will become of us?" and her eyes wandered to her children.

"Mary, that old man assisted me once, when I thought all mankind were my foes. He has but one son, who is now in the United States. If I can lighten the grief of the scarred veteran, and make his few remaining days happy, shall I hesitate to do so, because we apprehend, perhaps, imaginary dangers?"

The lip of his wife trembled, while she regarded him with tearful eyes.

"Father, I would do so much for the old soldier."

"You are right, my boy."

"But if they should—oh, if they should——"

She could say no more, for she burst into tears.

"Mary, don't cry; Phil will go with me, and I will return in half an hour. There, now, cheer up."

He encircled her waist with his arm, and pressed his lips to her own.

"Good-night, Mrs. Kane, I will see you off to-morrow."

"Good-night," she replied, sorrowfully, as she followed the receding form of Robert to the door; and as he left the house, she sank upon the floor overcome with apprehension.

Robert, accompanied by Hogan, proceeded rapidly towards the house of Martin Lennon. The streets were quiet and deserted, and there was no appearance of danger.

But Robert's departure had been observed by Matthew Riley; and with stealthy steps he descended into the street a few moments after the other left the house, and swiftly proceeded towards the head-quarters of Dwyville Hurdy and his band.

"I have him now," he muttered, with fiendish joy. "Fool that he was to venture out to-night. And I have him, too, just at the moment when he thinks he will escape me."

"What—are you *talk*ing about ship-*mate!*" exclaimed a gruff voice, whose language was accented by drunkenness.

"About nothing that interests you," replied Riley, as he attempted to pass the other upon the narrow side-walk.

"Heave to and show your colors, or I'll stave in your bulwarks," retorted the seaman, as, steadying himself with great difficulty, he prepared to exercise a little of that "wholesome discipline," to which, having been freely subjected himself, he felt at liberty to practice upon all the queen's subjects who happened to be under sail at that late hour.

"I tell you to let me pass or I will call the police."

"Avast there, comrade, don't you know that martial law is supsu-supe-su-*pe-re-er* to civil law. Heave to, and run up yer colors or I'll sink yer."

"Let me pass, you drunken beast," cried Riley fiercely.

"Boarders, to the assault," shouted the sailor.

Poising his huge frame for an attack, totally unexpected by Riley, he hurled himself forward, rather than aimed a blow, and his fists coming in contact with the stomach of that individual, he was doubled up, and before he could regain his natural attitude, he came violently in contact with a lamp-post. The sailor would have been seriously injured in his fall upon the sidewalk, but for the relaxed condition of his frame; a circumstance to which all inebriates, as well as opossums, are indebted for an exemption from broken bones.

With endeavors that appeared for some time of doubtful success, the sailor attempted to regain his feet, but seeing the difficulty of accomplishing that desirable object without the aid of extraneous assistance, he scratched his head, and setting his hat firmly upon his brows, proceeded to "take possession of the disabled craft," as he called the insensible form of Riley. To that end he crawled along upon his hands and knees, and pulling out a flaming handkerchief turned Riley over, and commenced binding his arms to his side.

"You see the victor always runs up his own colors, messmate, so you will be after excusing me for displaying this little bit of bunting."

Riley slowly returned to consciousness, and at length fixed his eyes upon the sailor with a perfect recollection of what had taken place. Retaining a firm grasp upon the handkerchief, the sailor addressed his captive with the confidence of a man who had performed a brilliant exploit.

"Steady, ho! Don't remain any longer upon your beam ends. Right yourself, man. There now, hoist my sheet anchor; the wind is fair, heave away! You see, I'm not the first heavy craft that's run aground in following a light one into shoal water."

"Now I hope you are satisfied. Let me go."

"Not so fast, I must take you into port. You'll make a handy little craft for the cabin."

"What, you don't mean to say you are going to impress me," shrieked Riley, appalled at the fate he was endeavoring to inflict upon Kane.

"Call it what you like, landlubber, though in seaman's phrase it is known as making use of a prize, so come along."

"But I have a helpless family at home who are dependent upon me for bread," said Riley, as the cold sweat gathered upon his forehead.

"Shall we try it yard-arm and yard-arm again," said the sailor, squaring himself.

"Oh, no, not that," replied the other, shivering with terror.

"Then let me bring you into port."

The old salt reeled along the sidewalk, and at every lurch hauled Riley after him. The latter individual, now almost palsied with fright, cast eager glances around in hope of a rescue, but no footsteps fell upon the pavement except their own.

At length a thought flashed upon his mind. He had often heard of the liberality of sailors.

"Come," he said, coaxingly, "you will not take me on board ship without treating me?"

The sailor arrested his footsteps, and in gaining an equilibrium the form of Mr. Riley was made to swing back and forth like the vibrations of a pendulum.

"For a small craft what a lurch you have, shipmate. Treat you? To be sure I will, if I have any money left. Let me overhaul the old chest. I gave that soldier one crown; his pretty daughter another. By the shade of Columbus, her build is beautiful. I spent another at the Ball and Anchor, and I had four, so there ought to be another amidships."

Releasing his hold upon Riley, he was attempting to find the crown that, perhaps, existed only in his imagination, when his prisoner suddenly darted away and ran swiftly down the street.

Only for a moment astounded by the audacity of the escape, the sailor gave chase.

"Heave to! how dare you set sail from beneath my very guns. I'll pour a broadside into you. Heave to! heave to!"

But the sailor ran awkwardly, and with legs wide apart so as to meet any sudden lurch of the earth. In the meantime Riley turned down first one street and then another with such rapidity that at last he disappeared altogether.

The sailor, completely baffled, drew up against a post.

"I'll rest here for a fresh breeze. Did any one ever see a prize '*cut out*' more beautifully; and if the piratical villain has not cleaned me of my last crown well, he deserves it, for, by the shade of Columbus, it was handily done."

Matthew Riley, notwithstanding his narrow escape from imminent peril, felt no commiseration for Robert Kane; on the contrary, he was prompted by a fiendish impulse to lead him on to that doom, the mere contemplation of which had palsied his own heart with terror.

With heaving chest and trembling limbs Riley entered the room where Hurdy could usually be found.

"Where is Hurdy?" he inquired, eagerly.

"Gone to Fletcher's."

"Hell and furies! was ever any thing so unfortunate. Here, release my arms. There may yet be time;" and he rushed into the street.

Courage! noble, generous Kane, there is still hope for you!

He had received the message of the aged soldier with a promise to deliver it, and was retracing his steps homeward, having assured Hogan that his presence would not be required. His heart bounded with that strange delight which is rarely felt, and then only when some great success is the reward of an enterprise, upon which doubt serves to rivet our hopes with greater intentness.

So absorbingly did his thoughts dwell upon the picture, that he failed to observe the crowd tnat was gathering around him. One by one they dropped into the street from before and behind, from each dark alley, or more public thoroughfare, until, as he stood motionless, he was surrounded by a dark, and evidently a hostile group. Conspicuous among them he recognized the face of Dwyville Hurdy, from whose solitary eye gleamed an expression of ferocious joy, while across the way stood the scoundrel who had betrayed him. For a few moments they glared upon their victim. Kane paused like a stag at bay, and then aware that his only chance of escape was to act on the offensive, he drew his dirk and bounded forward. Knowing that to shed blood where none but perjured villains could witness the provocation was almost as much to be dreaded as to be overpowered in the conflict, he endeavored to force a passage without using his weapon. Three of the gang were hurled to the ground by his muscular arm, and but one foe opposed his flight, when the powerful grasp of Hurdy was laid upon his shoulder; the dirk was wrested from his grasp, and he stood powerless in the midst of his enemies.

"Men! men! *why* do you hunt me like a beast? I am flesh and blood like yourselves; for God's sake let me return to my wife and children. They will starve without me."

The only response to this appeal was a roar of laughter.

"I implore you, in the name of your mothers, of your sisters, of your wives, to release me. If you only knew the agony that my poor, dear, helpless wife will feel when she hears of my fate, I am sure, oh, I am *very sure*, you would release me."

"Tush, man, don't bellow so. I'll take your wife under my protection."

Again a coarse laugh, accompanied by rude jests, rang upon the night air.

"Merciful heaven! is our fate indeed so terrible?" groaned Robert, in the anguish of his heart.

The sound of wheels was heard approaching, and by the light of the moon Robert saw a liveried driver seated upon the box. A faint hope that one of the aristocracy might have a greater respect for what that class are so fond of calling the *rights of Englishmen*, than the fiends in whose clutches he found himself, prompted Kane stoutly to resist the attempt to force him into a dark alley leading from the street.

The resistance aroused to desperation the angry passions of the gang.

"Kill him if he will not yield," shouted Hurdy, as he leveled a blow with a heavy cane which fell upon the side of Robert's head with such force that the blood gushed from a long cut in the temple. He staggered under the effects of the blow, and came down upon one knee.

"Will *that* make you go quietly?" exclaimed Hurdy, savagely.

"My wife, one more struggle for my wife!" and with a mighty effort he shook off his assailants and reached the carriage.

"Oh, Lord Melville! thank God it is you! I know your lordship will save me."

"I don't know you, fellow; you are impertinent," replied his lordship, mincingly.

"But let me wipe the blood from my face; there, you recollect me now; I am the brother of Christie Kane, your father's tenant."

"Then to hell with you, as well as your brother," said Melville, fiercely.

"But mercy, have mercy, my lord; my wife—"

"Drive on, Hartman."

"She will die—"

"On! on!" screamed his lordship.

"What an obstinate brute!" yelled Hurdy. "But may perdition seize me if I do not subdue you." Again the staff descended upon Robert's devoted head, and this time it fell upon the scarcely healed wound he had received a few days before. Human nature could endure no more, and the poor fellow sunk powerless to the earth. Raising him in their arms they bore him to the Thames, where he was taken on board a small government craft and heavily ironed. Thus were crushed the bright hopes of liberty and protection which that humble family had so fondly cherished. And yet such aggravated cases of human woe are never alluded to by those who are always boasting of the bliss enjoyed by the inhabitants of *merry* England!

There was a solitary person near the scene of the late conflict. Matthew Riley was still gloating over the recollection of human suffering. So intense was his delight that he could not tear himself from the spot, and he rubbed his hands and chuckled gleefully. Suddenly he was aroused by a heavy hand that grasped his shoulder. The marrow in his rattling bones seemed to crawl as he cowered beneath the glance of the sailor.

"I've overhauled you, shipmate, after a long starn chase, and this time I will take care that you don't escape under convoy of my good nature. And first of all, I will release your hold of the crown you piratically took from me. Yes, here it is. You not only escaped with arms, but captured prize money."

Riley saw from the determined manner of the sailor, who was now sober, that remonstrance would be useless, and with bloodshot eyes and hueless features, submitted to his fate.

"You have only to serve his majesty faithfully for three years, and then if there is no necessity for your services, and you fight gallantly, or are killed, or so maimed as to be unserviceable, perhaps you won't be wanted any longer. So cheer up, messmate. Lord love you, I have been pressed into the service three times. First it went hard, as it will with you, mayhaps. But avast there, you will get accustomed to it, and like it, too. And they have such wholesome discipline: the beating which seemed to give you so much pleasure a few minutes ago, is nothing to it."

Riley groaned.

"To be sure the officers break heads sometimes in moments of passion; but the genteel way, and one which they enjoy the most, because it requires no exercise—nothing but calm, placid delight—is to see the skin of the sailor cut and mangled by the cat. It often happens during a voyage, and sometimes when it is deserved. My back has been cut into every kind of shape, and I have the satisfaction of knowing that, although the operation has been performed seven times, it was *merited* twice. That's some gratification. They didn't lacerate my skin them times for nothing, anyhow;" and the old salt chuckled gleefully. "But here we are on the bank of the Thames."

"Will you, oh! will you release me?"

"Avast! shipmate, I might have let your wretched craft escape before the wind if you had not stole my money under the false flag of good fellowship. Even that I might have forgiven, if you had not proved yourself so destitute of feeling when that gallant fellow begged so hard for his wife and children. In then with you, and thank yourself at the prospect of the world being rid of such a monster through the agency of a cannon-ball or boarding-pike. Into the boat with you."

The terror that had appalled the craven heart of the coward faded before the feelings of shame and rage that took possession of his soul as he found himself in the presence of Robert Kane, like him heavily ironed and strictly guarded.

CHAPTER VII.

> "A troop of tall horsemen! how fearless they ride!
> 'Tis a perilous path o'er that steep mountain side."—NEAL.

A SUCCESSION of stormy days utterly ruined the wheat crops of Christie Kane. This misfortune destroyed all prospects of paying the rent, and there was no other recourse but ejectment from the premises. This was a hard fate, because Christie Kane had exerted his energies to the utmost for the purpose of keeping a home for his mother. Now, hope had abandoned him, for he expected in a few days to be turned houseless and homeless upon the world. Not a result to be much dreaded by a young man with a strong frame and a stout heart, but to be feared as a calamity when a female relies upon him for shelter and support. Christie Kane became more gloomy and morose, notwithstanding the taunts of his mother and the cheerful sallies of Phelim Savor, whose good humor was unconquerable. A settled conviction had fastened itself upon his mind that the political and moral structure of the English government and society was all wrong. He felt that he walked the earth as noble and as worthy of freedom as the proudest lordling in the kingdom; and yet the strong arm of the government, which ought to protect him, only sought to crush him. It first tried to debase the spirit that God had implanted in his bosom, and then seized upon the earnings that had been won through storms and heat. He was conscious of possessing a cultivated mind, generous impulses, and honorable principles; nevertheless, fashionable society had placed its ban upon him, and he was socially outlawed. His position was expressed by one word—he was a *plebeian*. It is not strange that his proud spirit fretted at its destiny. It perhaps would not have forced itself upon his mind with quite so much power, if he had not daily witnessed the exercise of authority by persons in every way inferior to himself. Power was conferred upon titled spendthrifts, to control the happiness and health of tenants and operatives, and in some instances he had seen it wielded with a remorseless cruelty that brought its victims to their graves at an early age. And yet the infamous laws of England legalized these atrocious murders.

While he was contemplating the destruction of his crops, the festivities in the castles of Momlow and Montague were at their height. Large accessions had been made to the guests of the Countess of Rossmore and Duchess of Sunderland; and as both of those ladies moved in the same circle in London society, there was a constant interchange of civilities between them, so that their guests were often thrown together. They had exhausted all the ordinary sources of amusement, when it was determined to have a grand steeple-chase, to be followed by a magnificent ball at the Castle of Montague. Great preparations were made for both events. Not only the nobility and gentry, who resided in that part of the kingdom, prepared to attend, but large additions were made from the list of those who could only be induced to leave "charming London for the stupid country" by some extraordinary attraction. The day at length arrived. The sun, tired of having his rays obscured by the clouds which rolled up from the west as if they would never cease, now burst through the wall of vapor, and cast his beams over the earth. It was a "glorious day," was the universal exclamation.

Phelim Savor had taken more than ordinary pains with the dapple gray. He was favored with a bran new pair of shoes. His hair had been rubbed until it exhibited a beautiful gloss; and, in the estimation of Mr. Savor, Surry was as fine an animal as could be seen in the United Kingdom.

"Yez needdent ba ashamed of yersel' to-day, Maister Christie, ony how, for the likes of that horse will ba hard to find at the steeple-chase. I wish *he* could have a trial wid the rest of them; for, be the holy St. Patrick! there's niver a horse of bitter pidigree in all England. And why should'ent ye? if yersel', Maister Christie, aint quite as noble-blooded as the lords beyant, Surry can make it up, for he can boast a longer line of distinguished ancestors, on both sides of the house, too, than any nobleman who will ride to-day; and sure, honey, that ought to make the thing aquil."

"Do you wish to see the race, Phelim?" asked Christie Kane, as he threw himself into the saddle.

"Very much, indade, if yez plaze."

"You will have to walk there."

"I would walk the matter of ten miles ony day to see a steeple-chase."

"You can witness it from here, as the course crosses a portion of our farm."

Phelim resorted to that method of his class to show his embarrassment. He scratched his head.

"Well?" suggested Christie.

"I should like to see Surry among blooded horses, Maister Christie, it is so sildom he gets into the company of thim as can call thimselves aristocratic horses. Though, be my sowl! there's divil a horse will ba seen on the estate of Lord Rossmore this blissed day that can boast sich a noble birth as the dapple gray."

"Go, then," replied Christie, as he turned Surry's head towards the castle of Montague.

"Whoop!" ejaculated Phelim, as he sprang into the air, and cracked his heels twice together before he came down: a flourish that, we regret to say, was performed without the usual appendages of shoes and stockings. They were not considered by Phelim as absolutely necessary appendages to that portion of the human frame which is brought in contact with the ground. An opinion which he had been known to defend, upon the assumption that the feet were no better than the earth, because Adam's whole body, feet included, were manufactured from that material, and he did not consider himself any better than Adam. If made out of the earth, he was wont to say, it could be no disgrace for them to come freely in contact with it, if it was only to show a proper regard for kith and kin. Mr. Savor admitted that, with gentle folk, it might be altogether a different affair, because their feet having been so long separated from the ground, there was no obligation to recognize the relationship, only so far as they condescended to *cozen* it out of nearly all the generous bounties it bestowed upon the human race.

From an early hour throngs of people crowded to the spot selected for the competitors to start for the prize. They came in carriages, on horseback, and on foot. From far and near, the wealthy, the aristocratic, and the poor gathered to witness an event which is always regarded with interest by the patrician and plebeian. No obstacle was interposed by Lord Rossmore and the Duke of Sunderland, upon whose estates the steeple-chase was to occur, to the ingress of the lower classes. It was one of the *cheap* ways of purchasing their acquiescence in the present order of things, for they had a happy faculty of identifying the princely exhibitions of the landed proprietors with their own humble fortunes. The sight of a steeple-chase made hundreds unmindful of hunger when they went supperless to bed.

The carriages of the Duke of Sunderland and the Earl of Montague had arrived upon the ground, each followed by a long train of distinguished persons. The judges' stand was erected upon the brow of an elevated plateau, commanding an extensive and beautiful view of the surrounding country, including hill, dale, woodland, lakes, and streams.

Along the slope of the hill were ranged the carriages of the most illustrious of the spectators; and in the centre of the group, Katharine Montague, who was to bestow the reward upon the succesful competitor, sat upon a milk-white steed, that scattered the foam upon his glistening hair as he impatiently shook the reins. She was attired in a black riding-dress of rich material, and wore a black hat without feathers.

"My lord, I hope you may be more successful in your trial today than you were on the occasion of your unwilling visit to the lake in front of Montague Castle," said Katherine Montague, as Lord Melville rode up and made his salutations.

"Lady Katherine, I hope you will forget that affair some day," he replied, with evident annoyance.

"Not until memory fails me," said the merry girl.

"What adventure do you refer to?" inquired Sir William Belthoven.

"Lord Melville will relate it."

"Lord Melville will do nothing of the kind, with your ladyship's permission," responded the irritated noble, as he spurred his horse to the judges' stand.

He was mounted upon a black horse that had made some attempts at the Derby stakes, and not without fair prospects, if he had been ridden with judgment.

He was a thorough-bred and powerfully-built animal. He had many admirers too among the fairer portion of the company, but whether the brilliant prospects, and really fine person of his rider, added to the beauty of the animal, none of them took occasion to explain.

"Lord Melville seems annoyed at your remarks," observed Sir William Belthoven, who being an M. P., did not think it just to his constituents and the government, to peril his invaluable life in the uncertain chances of a steeple-chase.

"It will make him contend with more fearlessness for the prize, though to do him justice, he is a bold rider."

"Well, Kate," said the Earl of Rossmore, a fine specimen of the English nobility, "a goodly number of gallants will contend for the prize you will have the pleasure of bestowing."

"How many have entered the lists?"

"Fifteen, already, and half an hour more must elapse before they will be closed. What, my lord of Delmore; it is an unexpected pleasure to see you once more on the turf."

This salutation was addressed to a gentleman somewhat advanced beyond the morning of life. His whiskers and bearing betrayed the old bachelor.

"How could it be otherwise, when your charming daughter bestows the guerdon of beauty?"

Lord Delmore gracefully raised his hat, and bowed.

"Always yourself, my lord," replied Katherine Montague, extending her gloved hand, which the veteran and accomplished beau reverently pressed to his lips, as an acknowledgment to what he considered a graceful compliment.

"Your lordship is well mounted," observed the lady, casting an admiring glance at the superb bay Lord Delmore strode. "I am glad to see his points indicate great powers of endurance, for your form appears more portly to me than when I first saw you, now some fifteen years ago."

Lord Delmore was very sensitive upon the subject of his size, and nothing annoyed him more than an allusion to his increasing weight, for not many years had elapsed since he considered himself little less faultless than the Apollo-Belvidere. His lordship, however, had been too long in society to suffer his annoyance to be observed, and he replied with a grateful smile,

"I am glad your ladyship is kind enough to notice the relative extent of my proportions, for to be observed by the fair sex is evidence that we *are* still of some consideration."

"Doubtless, my lord, you *are* yet of very decided importance, for I heard old Lady Margaret Summerville observe the other day, with a simper, that she knew of no one who would be more likely to tempt her so far to forget the dear defunct Sir Charles Summerville, as to enter the holy estate of matrimony, as Edward Lord Delmore."

"Why, she is old enough to be my mother!"

"She says you attended the same school; that you were her beau; and even as a child possessed something of that fascination as a lover, which has rendered you so dangerous to our sex, as a man for the last twenty-five years."

Lord Delmore did not know whether to be pleased or angry, the biting sarcasm of her words being so modified by what he regarded as a delicate compliment.

Before he could reply, the venerable Marquis of Hungerford rode to the side of Katharine Montague. Her look, half merry, half defiant, at once changed, and her countenance assumed an expression of the most deferential regard.

"My lord, this is an unexpected honor," she frankly said, removing her glove, and pressing his shrivelled hand with her soft, taper fingers.

"I could not suffer the occasion to pass, my young friend, without witnessing the scene over which I understood you were to preside. I thought I should realize again something of the poetry of youth, and I am grateful to you because such is the fact."

"Oh, thank you, I can assure your lordship that the pleasure is mutual, for to be honored by the presence of one so celebrated for every quality that proclaims a man, gives me no ordinary pleasure."

The marquis bowed profoundly. The attention of Katharine Montague was drawn to "a horseman who might have been seen" riding rapidly towards the judges' stand. She immediately recognized the dapple gray, and, in the rider, her quondam acquaintance Christie Kane.

The young man rode into the centre of the group of competitors with a bearing quite as lofty as the most imperious. All eyes were turned upon him, for he was unknown, except to Lord Melville, whose eyes flashed scornfully as he recognized the "country beau of Katharine Montague."

"What seek you here, fellow?" he exclaimed, fiercely.

Kane cast a glance of contempt at the interrogator, but deigned no other reply. Turning to the judges, he said,

"I come to enter the list of competitors for the award of beauty." And he cast a furtive look at Lady Katharine, whose countenance was impassive.

"Why, gentlemen, he is my father's tenant; a clodpole by the name of Christie Kane," replied Lord Melville.

"And does that deprive me of the pleasure this day's amusement must afford?" said Christie, still addressing the judges.

"That depends upon circumstances," replied one of them; "in your case it probably will."

Katharine Montague looked with admiring eyes upon the splendid animal which Kane bestrode. He had enabled her to achieve a triumph over Lord Melville, and she felt a strong desire to see the dapple gray enter the lists.

"Why in my case?" replied Kane, calmly.

"Because by the rules we have established, no person under the rank of a baronet can become a competitor unless he is allied to the nobility, by affinity or consanguinity, within the sixth degree."

"That I am."

"How, fellow?" cried Melville, haughtily.

"Who can prove your statement?" asked the umpire.

"The word of a man of honor ought to be sufficient."

"A man of honor!—the *plebeian* a man of honor!" retorted Melville. "I will have you punished for this insolence."

"If no one will vouch for you, it will be our duty to exclude you," replied the judge.

Lady Katharine Montague was in the act of addressing the judges, and had turned her horse for that purpose, when the clear, authoritative voice of a gentleman in the undress of a colonel of infantry, said,

"I know him; he is the nephew of my wife, a daughter of the Duke of Rollston."

"Ah! Colonel Knowles, your word is sufficient," replied the urbane voice of the oldest judge; "the young man may enter the lists."

"Then I will withdraw from them," said Melville. "A prize for which *he* contends cannot be worth the wearing."

A flash of indignation overspread the face of Katharine Montague, which was succeeded by an ashy paleness.

"Come, Melville, you are wrong," replied Lord Delmore. "We will have the satisfaction of showing him that a relationship to the well-born by affinity merely, will not enable him to contend successfully with the best blood of England."

"He shall bitterly, *bitterly* regret thrusting himself where he is known only to be despised."

"And, Lord Melville, you, too, shall pay dearly for your unmanly taunts," retorted Christie Kane, haughtily.

"Gentlemen, you will assume your positions," said the judges.

The course marked out for the horsemen to take led along the level plane to the right of the judges' stand for one fourth of a mile, and then passed through an open wood, the "underbrush" from which had been removed. The ground sloped gradually through this wood; and just before it opened into the valley, the horsemen could not be seen from the judges' stand. At the termination of the forest, a brook wound its course, the banks of which were very abrupt. Here was the first serious obstruction to the riders. After passing the valley, a hedge, five feet in height, crossed the course. This presented a formidable barrier, because the ground was uneven on both sides. But now commenced a succession of rocky and dangerous hills, and hollows, terminating in a low piece of ground that was marshy in certain places. This brought them to a stream whose banks were separated a distance of nearly twenty feet. The summit of each shore was of solid earth, yet the leap was fearful. The river at that point flowed in the direction of the judges' stand, so that it was in plain view of the spectators assembled upon the plateau. A succession of gentle slopes succeeded, until the course led to the foot of the plateau, when a formidable hedge and ditch crossed the way. This barrier safely passed, and the acclivity of the hill which teminated upon the plateau was the only obstacle to be surmounted by the horsemen. The herald proclaimed the conditions of the steeple-chase, which were, that the horseman who passed around the course between the flags, and arrived first at the stand, should receive the prize from Lady Katherine Montague, and be honored with her hand in opening the ball that night at Montague Castle.

Seventeen horsemen sat upon impatient steeds that were grinding their bits between their teeth and stamping the earth, while they shook their reins and occasionally reared in the air. They were a splendid collection of horses, nearly all being thorough-bred. Not one among them was more beautifully formed than the dapple grey. Both Surrey and his rider attracted much attention in their humble position upon the left, and slightly in the rear of the line of aristocratic horsemen.

Christie Kane saw in that vast crowd the face of but one anxious friend, and that was Phelim Savor's. The solicitude which was stamped upon the features of the honest fellow, strange as it may appear, reanimated the courage and the hopes of the young man, as he sat among that group, the only untitled competitor for the prize. And he mentally exclaimed—

"Do not doubt me, for I will vindicate the claim of the *plebeian* to the honors of the day, or perish."

The bugle gave the signal; the ground trembled beneath the charge, and the excited spectators breathed more freely. Lord Melville took the lead as they descended the slope through the woods, having, in the impetuosity of his feelings, plunged his spurs into the flanks of his horse. Lord Delmore followed next, and Christie Kane, with his form thrown back in the effort to check the speed of his horse, brought up the rear. As they emerged from the bank of the brook which we have described as flowing past the foot of the declivity, four riderless horses dashed across the plain, but neither of them was the dapple grey. As the horsemen reached the open country, and approached the hedge, their relative positions were the same.

"Neither of the dismounted horsemen is Melville, for there he is, nobly leading the way," said Lord Rossmore. "I am afraid, Kate, the horse with whose assistance you accomplished a triumph over Melville will prove less successful in a struggle with practiced thorough breds. See, he is still far behind."

"But four miles is a long way, and they have not accomplished a fourth of the distance. My noble grey may yet triumph."

The earl shook his head incredulously. They approached the hedge and Melville gathered the legs of his horse well under him and then darted at the barrier. The horse passed it with a splendid bound.

"Well done, Melville," said the Duke of Sunderland.

"Yes, that *was* a magnificent leap," replied Katharine Montague, approvingly.

Lord Delmore came next; his horse stumbled upon one of the hillocks, and his rider was thrown heavily to the ground. The ladies shuddered.

"A few more such falls as that, and Delmore's bachelor days will be over," said the Duke of Sunderland, coolly.

Only eight horses passed the hedge when the dapple grey approached. With a tremendous bound he cleared the barrier, landing several feet beyond it.

"By the memory of Queen Bess, but that was splendidly taken," said the Marquis of Hungerford, enthusiastically. The dapple grey swept by one after another of the horsemen until only two led him. They crossed the uneven part of the course, and approached the marsh. Christie Kane, instead of attempting to pass them, suffered his horse to follow in the footsteps of Lord Melville's, being convinced that his lordship had often examined the ground, while he had never crossed it before. But as his horse reached the plain which bordered the river, for the first time he gave him the reins. His powers had not been overtasked, and he rapidly approached Lord Melville; the head of the dapple grey lapped the the quarter of the leading horse; he drew ahead until, as they struck the bank of the stream, they were neck and neck. It was evident the riders were utterly reckless, for they made no attempt to arrest the headlong speed of their horses. As they sprang from the bank with fearful bounds a thrill of awe ran through the frames of the stoutest hearted. A moment of intense anxiety succeeded, while the noble animals swept through the air. It was succeeded by prolonged cheers as both horses alighted upon the opposite bank at the same moment.

"Well done! *well done!*" exclaimed the Marquis of Hungerford, as he waved his hat in the excitement of the moment. "He is a splendid rider, if he is a plebeian."

Katharine Montague did not reply, but she eagerly watched the progress of the headmost horsemen. Sir Edward Donnelly, who next approached the stream, did so more cautiously. His horse made a gallant attempt to pass it, but his strength failed him, his fore feet struck the bank, and he rolled backward into the water. The next horse shared the same fate, and warned by their fate the other competitors drew up their steeds upon the bank and watched the progress of the two horsemen who alone now contended for victory. And it was a matter of doubt which must triumph, for a blanket would have covered them as they crossed the plain between the river and the inequalities that grooved the land at the base of the acclivity. The excitement became intense as they ascended and descended hills, and bounded across chasms. Quick, almost, as thought, the panting steeds reached the formidable hedge and ditch that now presented the only obstacle that intervened between them and the termination of the course. Christie Kane checked the speed of Surrey so as to approach the hedge cautiously. Lord Melville followed his example. Both riders reached the barrier with frowning brows and set teeth. For the first time Christie applied the spur to the flank of Surrey. With an angry snort he cleared the hedge and landed upon the solid earth beyond the ditch, and then gallantly dashed up the hill. Lord Melville also passed the barrier at the same moment. Cheer after cheer rewarded these splendid efforts, and upon the brow of the plateau could be seen a long line of waving hats and handkerchiefs. Katharine Montague alone sat apparently unmoved, upon her white steed, but excitement was perceptible in her dark blue eyes.

"Magnificently done," said the Marquis of Hungerford, as he re-covered his silvery hair with his hat.

With the last great effort of passing the hedge and ditch, the powers of Melville's horse were exhausted; from that moment the dapple-grey slowly left him, and Christie Kane arrived at the judge's stand a dozen yards ahead.

The nobility received the victor with faint praises, with the exception of the Marquis of Hungerford and Lord Rossmore, whose magnanimity rose above the pride of caste, but the humbler portion of the spectators were vociferous in their demonstrations of joy.

A solitary figure emerged from their midst, and regardless of the distinguished presence in which he found himself, threw his arms around the neck of the panting Surrey.

"Och! but this is the blissedest day of me whole life. Surrey, *Surrey!* its mesel know'd you would bate every mother's son of thim, an' now yez hiv jist done it, an' so beautifully." And the happy fellow stroked the arched neck of the dapple-grey, while the tears ran down his cheeks.

Christie dismounted, and delivered his horse into the charge of Phelim Savor, to be led away—surrounded by the admiring but humble portion of the spectators.

The young man was conducted by one of the Heralds to the side of Katherine Montague's horse, and bowing, while his face was covered with a deep crimson, awaited his award.

Her voice was steady and musical as she said:

"Mr Kane, you have contended successfully for the prize which I have been selected to award to the victor in the hazardous, but manly amusement of the steeple-chase. By your boldness and skill as a horseman, aided by the splendid qualities of your magnificent steed, you deserve the reward which I now bestow."

Bending forward, she placed the ribbon, elegantly embroidered by her own hands, and to which a gold medal was attached, upon his neck. For a moment his eyes met her own, as he raised his head. He spoke not, but their eloquent glance betrayed the emotions of his heart.

Having performed her duty, she lightly touched her horse, without further noticing the humble victor, and led the way to Montague Castle.

CHAPTER VIII.

"And thus I clothe my naked villainy
With old odd ends, stol'n forth of holy writ;
And seem a saint when most I play the devil."—SHAKESPEARE.

It is impossible to describe the agony of mind experienced by Mrs. Kane, when her husband did not return at the time she expected him. She did not close her eyes during the long hours of the night. She started early in the morning for Martin Lennon's, with the faint hope that he might still be there. She was doomed to disappointment. A visit to Hogan's was alike unsuccessful. The most rigid search was instituted by her humble friends, and even the police, as is unusually the case, with that self-sufficient and independent fraternity, *promised* to rectify an evil they ought to have prevented. But they meant nothing by their promises, for like all idle words, they cost them nothing. Mrs. Kane could not promise a *reward* to stimulate their sense of duty, or what is of far greater importance, their vigilance was not aroused by having a bribe placed in their hands. It is amusing to see with what complacency these gentry pocket rewards for the recovery of articles, when they are employed to prevent the thief from stealing them. When an amount sufficiently valuable is stolen to justify the offer of a liberal reward, the property is often recovered, a consummation that seldom gratifies the sufferer who cannot arouse the cupidity of our "guardians" by the tender of money. Nothing has such a magical effect in impressing upon the minds of these worthies the absolute necessity of maintaining justice in all its purity, as a liberal bribe, slily thrust into their hands, when no one can observe the delicate operation.

The machinery of justice runs much better on gold, and if the reader doubts it, let him make the experiment, not only in England but in any other corner of the earth, where he may require the services of the police. But there is one condition which must not be forgotten, the tender must be made in private, as their sense of duty and propriety would be outraged provided a third person should witness an open assault upon their virtue. This makes all the difference in the world, as any one will discover by the angry rebuff he will receive provided he thoughtlessly tenders money *before folks* to an individual who would take it without the slightest qualms of conscience; under the very different circumstance, however, of there being no witnesses present. The efficacy of the bribe depends upon secresy; and there is a manifest propriety in the fact, because the goddess of justice is represented as being blind; and what is unnecessary for her to see, the agents of her will should not of course be required to divulge to the gossiping multitude.

Hogan thinking himself not altogether blameless, although his intentions were honest, with what money he could command sought the presence of one of those Bow-street officers who are so often employed by persons who *can* "*bleed*" *well*. It was with many misgivings that he ventured into the presence of the renowned officer, painfully conscious that his rough garb was not in keeping with the place. The officer looked at him from behind his spectacles with a suspicious glance, and Hogan involuntarily trembled for fear some rascality, unknown to himself, would be ferreted out by the most celebrated of the detective police. He could not rally his thoughts, so thoroughly had the officer confused him. There was something about him strangely inconsistent. His form was stout, even corpulent, and when Hogan looked at that he thought the mind which controlled it must be frank, if not jolly. He verily believed that it would not be too much to attribute downright jollity to such a rotund figure. But when he encountered the piercing gaze of those coal-black eyes, he doubted if the figure had ever felt the luxury of one good, hearty laugh.

"Well," grunted, rather than spoke, the officer.

Hogan was certain he had unconsciously been guilty of some monstrous rascality, and that, from behind those spectacles, there was being taken a detailed account of the whole transaction.

"Well!" more loudly grunted the voice.

Aroused to a pitch of desperation, Hogan muttered—

"I never—done any thing of the kind—"

"Are you certain?" thundered the other.

"At least not that I know of. It must have been some other, or I did it in my sleep."

"What do you want then?" responded the officer, with a rumbling kind of a laugh at the effect produced by his glance.

"I come to see if you would undertake a little matter for me, and I brung some money to pay any expenses that might—if there be any—"

He took from his pocket a handful of coin, among which there could be discovered only one piece of gold.

"How dare you think of bribing one of her Majesty's executive officers?"

"With such a paltry sum," distinctly whispered a voice.

The policeman frowned, and Hogan looked furtively about without being able to ascertain from whence the voice proceeded.

"If I could have—brought—more I would have done so—" he faltered.

"Silence! Here, Fizgig, see what you can do for this fellow. Are you positive, sirrah, that you were not, at least, an accessory before the fact in the murder case?"

"Never! sir, never!"

"Then begone; but if I ever set eyes upon you again I shall be sure to think you were an accessory either before or after the fact."

Hogan found himself in the presence of Fizgig. That individual received him blandly, and Hogan came to the conclusion that he had found the right person, and his supposition was true, for Mr.

Fizgig had only acquired sufficient reputation to justify any one in bribing him, unless he belonged to Hogan's class in society.

Mr. Fizgig received him blandly, but it was a *cool* blandness, that could be either softened or hardened as pecuniary considerations might justify.

Hogan began his negotiations by drawing forth his small store. The sharp eyes of the policeman saw nothing but copper coin, here and there set off by a piece of silver, that varied in amount from a sixpence to a crown. The face of the officer said as plainly as words could have expressed it,

"Your case, my dear fellow, is utterly hopeless."

But Hogan, not being skilful at translating the shades and lines of the human countenance into words, proceeded to unfold his wishes, backing up his solicitation for aid by turning over the coins in his hand so as to make as great a display as possible of the silver pieces aforesaid.

The blandness of the policeman stiffened very perceptibly as he replied,

"I fear there is no hope for your friend. He has doubtless been arrested by the press-gang, and it is with great difficulty that we can rescue him, even if they have not taken him from their haunts on board a government vessel. Besides, an attempt would put me to very great trouble and expense."

The blandness of the officer became as stiff as buckram while he cast a contemptuous glance at the copper and silver which Hogan, instead of continuing ostentatiously to display, now sought to conceal with both hands, as though he had been guilty of stealing it.

But a sudden light broke upon his mind; he had not offered enough to stimulate the confidence of the officer in the success of the undertaking or the justice of his cause. He thrust his hand again into his pocket, and ushered into the light a bright yellow piece.

The starch disappeared from the blandness of the policeman like snow before the warm sun. In fact, it wilted right down into the most affable complaisance. He was happy in his mental conformation, was Mr. Fizgig, for his good nature possessed a sliding scale that was capable of expressing either the most insinuating regard or the most frigid politeness.

"I expected, of course, to remunerate you for all your trouble, but as you think there is no hope—"

"I trust you will excuse me for saying you slightly, *very* slightly misunderstood me; a misapprehension that was doubtless owing more to the want of copiousness and flexibility in the English language, than to any fault of mine or your own."

Hogan stared at Fizgig as though he did not exactly comprehend him. The officer paused with a smiling countenance, to give him an opportunity of making a further demonstration; but Hogan suffered the money, gold and all, to slide into his right-hand pocket, for that was his treasury; the other being devoted to his knife and tobacco.

"I am sorry the prospects of my friend are so gloomy, but if it can't be helped, it can't, that's all. Good morning."

The affability of Mr. Fizgig took another slide, as the prospect of obtaining the money, especially the sovereign, diminished.

"My language must have been unfortunate, indeed, if it led you to suppose that your friend's—your *insulted* friend's—case is hopeless. Nothing was farther from my intention. The exertions of so generous a person as you are willlng to prove yourself, ought not, I may say, *must* not, be unavailing."

Hogan began shrewdly to doubt the good faith of the officer, and he therefore buttoned up his pocket as he said,

"I tell you what, Mr. Fizgig, I'm a poor man, but I would spend all my money to rescue Robert Kane, because, you see, he has done me a good turn afore now, and he is an honest, hard-working fellow, with a family dependant upon him; and there's no saying how soon I may want him to keep a fatherly eye upon my own little children. Now, Mr. Fizgig, if you will produce Robert Kane to me, face to face, I will give you all the money I have here, and as much again, besides."

Fizgig suffered a starchy laugh to escape from his thin lips. "You are too kind, Mr. Hogan, but we like to have these trifles arranged beforehand, you know, to prevent it from escaping our recollection; a mere matter of form, you will bear that in mind, Mr. Hogan."

"My memory is likely to be quite as good as yours. Not a penny will I pay till I see Robert Kane." And with something of the sturdiness of the old English character, Hogan set his hat firmly upon his head.

Mr. Fizgig's blandness underwent another change; for the atmosphere of London is not susceptible of more frequent variations than was the humor of Theophilus Fizgig.

"Do you agree to my terms?"

"You are pleased to be facetious."

"You refuse?"

"Can you doubt it?"

For the first time the smile of Mr. Fizgig looked spiteful, yet it was so blended with a not unpleasant grin, that Hogan was for a moment doubtful whether he had interpreted it correctly; but he was then satisfied, and involuntarily his fists doubled.

"I *thought* any one who would suffer himself bribed, must, in the end, turn out to be an infernal scoundrel, and now I'm certain of it. An' yer all alike too, the fat devil in there, whose eyes makes one think he's a villain when he is not; an' yer own smooth, deceitful manner, that leads one to believe he's an honest man, when he may be just as far from the truth. The only difference is that you are a *cheaper* rascal than him. Out upon ye all for a set of thieves."

"Mr. Hogan, you will please to recollect that you have been aspersing the honest and faithful officers of the realm," said Mr. Fizgig in a soft voice.

"Honest and faithful!" retorted the other scornfully.

"And that severe and condign punishment awaits all such disrespectful and contumacious individuals."

"Is that person here yet?" exclaimed the officer with the spectacles, throwing open the door of the adjoining room.

"Yes," responded Fizgig.

"Well, if he is to be found here in one minute from this time I will have him arrested, not as an accessory, but as a principal in the—"

Hogan waited neither for the minute to expire, nor for the policeman to finish his sentence, but moved with great vivacity towards the door, muttering, with dissatisfied earnestness, as he put that barrier between himself and the eyes that made him so nervous, "I'm *damned* if I aint afraid of that cuss."

Every attempt made to find Robert Kane proved unavailing; and at the end of a week the painful truth was ineffaceably impressed upon Mary's mind that she should never see him again. The money he had obtained from Hogan he thoughtlessly took with him on that fatal night, and she was now penniless. It is true, Hogan insisted she should accept the small amount he intended to expend in searching for her husband; but that sum would soon be gone, and even if he was inclined to aid her further, he would not have the power, for his own family entirely depended upon him for support. Great as were her trials, the spirit of the noble woman was not crushed. Happiness, it is true, had taken its departure; but that unfaltering and holy love which a mother feels for her offspring, especially when they are threatened with danger, now exhibited its power. They would soon cry for bread, and she could not—oh! she could not let them starve!

Dolly hourly asked for her father, unconscious of the tears that her mother often turned her head to wipe away. Almost from the moment of their misfortune, Henry had become apprised of their loss, and with a sad face wandered about trying his best, but unsuccessfully, to let his mother see that he would be a little man.

A week after the disappearance of Robert Kane, they were in the room together, about the time when he used to return. Mrs. Kane was rocking the cradle, in which the baby, at an earlier hour than usual, had nestled herself to sleep. Her features were much paler and thinner than when the reader last saw her. It was apparent that she had quaffed the cup of misery deeply; and yet her eyes beamed with devotion as they rested upon her children—*his* children. Dolly was humming a tune her father had taught her a few weeks before as she put her doll to sleep. Henry stood by the window leaning his head against a pane of glass, as he was wont to do, while watching for the welcome wave of his father's hand as he turned the corner of the street. The big tears were rolling down his cheeks, while a suppressed sob, in spite of himself, occasionally reached his mother's ear. It became darker and darker, but still no father appeared. Every body else passed by that he had ever seen before; but the one whose approach would have sent an indescribable gush of joy through the hearts of that family, was still absent. It was too much for the little fellow; and throwing himself upon the bed, he wept long and bitterly.

"Poor child," said Mary, as she parted the hair upon his forehead and kissed it.

With a heroic effort he closed the fountains of his grief, and, taking his mother's hand, looked anxiously into her face.

"Ma, we have no one to give us money, now father is gone."

She shook her head despondingly.

"And we cannot get bread without money."

"No, dear."

"And without something to eat, you, and sis, and I would starve; and Frank Tot, too, for I heard father tell you to eat a good deal, or you would not have enough milk for Tot."

Mrs. Kane was visibly affected, in spite of herself.

"I diddent mean to make you cry, ma; only I thought I should like to know what we are to do to keep from starving."

"God only knows, Henry."

"But if God knows, what good is that going to do us; he don't give people manna now, does he?"

"No."

"Well, if neither God nor any body else is going to help us, mussen't we help *ourselves?*"

"God sometimes extends aid to the unfortunate, with an unseen hand."

Henry pondered upon these words.

"Mother, I am hungry now; and do you think, if we get no assistance from heaven by to-morrow morning, it would be any harm to help ourselves?"

"What do you mean by helping ourselves?"

"Take bread from the baker, and meat from the butcher."

"Why, that would be stealing."

"If it is only to keep us from dying?"

"That makes no difference."

"But are we not God's creatures?"

"Yes."

"Does it make him happy to see Frank Tot hungry?"

"No, he is a kind and merciful being, and the happiness he destined for his children has been destroyed by the nobility and aristocracy of England, who appropriate that which would otherwise keep us from suffering, for the purpose of gratifying their own caprices."

"Why does he let them act so wickedly?"

"Because the human family are free agents."

"What is that?"

"They have the right—no, the *power* of doing as they please."

"Then it will please me to steal some bread and meat," he answered, promptly; "to keep us all from being so very hungry."

Mrs. Kane was puzzled, for she saw her explanation was somehow or other, incorrect.

"Perhaps my answer was not right, Henry; I believe the multitude—the nation, possesses the power of doing as it pleases, but that individuals are restrained by laws."

"If the nation, which must mean the English people, have the power of doing as they please, why don't they make the rich a little less happy, and the poor a little less miserable?"

"How?"

"Why, by giving the rich money enough to buy chickens, and game, and turkeys, and geese, and cakes, and wine, and ever so many *good* things, and let the poor people keep enough to buy coarse bread, and the cheapest and toughest kinds of beef, *most* as good as the nobility give their dogs; would that be unreasonable, ma?"

"No."

"Well then, why don't they do it?" he exclaimed, impatiently.

"Because those most interested in keeping things as they are, have induced the majority to believe that it is all right."

"What, them with empty stomachs?"

"Yes, even some of them, I believe."

"Then they have no brother, or sister, or mother, to pity when they hear them cry for bread."

"There are not many, probably, who can make themselves happy while they endure pinching want, but others, who gain a precarious subsistence, prefer the evils that are not quite intolerable, to the certainty of death or transportation if they attempt to uproot the despotism which is so strongly protected by those whose interest it is, in a greater or less degree, to defend it."

Henry reflected upon this answer, while his mother placed half of the pittance left in the house upon the table. At length his face brightened.

"Ma! ma! oh! I've got it, I've got it!"

"What, my child?"

"The plan to relieve us. I'm *so* happy. Tot won't look so pale to-morrow night; none of us will be hungry then. Ha! ha! why *didn't* I think of it before?"

"Hush! Henry, you are crazy!"

"No I ain't, ma, I'm only very happy, that's all. You see this is it," he continued, with a look of immense importance; "I went t'other day up into Dexeter Hall, with another boy, Bill Wilson, and we sat down, way far back and listened. There were ever so many kind, good natured people in that great big Hall. They seemed all pious persons too, for they wore white cravats, and they had such sweet amiable faces; and they were such charitable men and women too, for there were a great many women in the Hall—Dexeter Hall. Well, one of the most pious looking among the men, with long white hair, and such a *good* face, stood up and commenced speaking. He told them how degraded were the negroes in America, and his voice was so tender, and he told so many stories of how the slaves were whipped and beat, that nearly all the men and women cried, and Bill Wilson and I cried too. And then another man got up and said they had collected, I don't know how much, but whole oceans of money, for the purpose of sending it to America, and the people clapped their hands, as I do when I want to amuse Frank Tot, and Bill Wilson and I clapped our hands too, for it seemed to make the speaker happy, and we thought such a good man ought to be made happy. And then they agreed to send all this money to liberate the poor slaves. They were not decked out in silks and ruffles, them good people wasn't. Their clothing seemed to be rich enough, but they was cut plain, and

Bill Wilson said he knew some of them were economical, and wanted to save as much as they could, to send to the slaves, for they wore broad brimmed hats, to keep off the rain, so they would not have to buy any umbrellas."

"Well, what has all this to do with our situation?"

"Why, don't you see, ma? You must go up to Dexeter Hall to-morrow, for I heard them say they would meet there again to-morrow, and you must tell them you have three children, who would work their fingers off to get bread for you, if they were old enough, but that they ain't. Tell them father has been stolen and carried off to fight; that he may be killed," and the tears gathered in his eyes, and his lip quivered—" and—and—that we shall starve to death unless they give us a little bit, only a little bit of that money they are going to send to America."

"And do you suppose they would give me a penny?"

"Yes, wouldn't they?"

"Not if it was to save us all from starvation."

The boy was appalled; his bright hopes were instantly dashed to the ground.

"But ma, they said they were going to send away all that money for charitable purposes. Do they know there is any need for charity here?"

"As well as you and I do."

"Then their bible is not like ours, for that says charity beginneth at home."

"It is precisely the same."

Henry seated himself, and crossing his legs, tried to divine the cause of this inconsistency. But apparently his efforts were unsuccessful, for he again leaned his arms upon his mother's lap.

"If they know there is need of charity here, *why* don't—they—they—"

"I'll tell you why they seek distant objects upon which to bestow their alms. It is because they obtain more notoriety by doing so."

"What is notoriety?"

"It is getting their names frequently in the papers, so that the world may talk about their generosity and goodness."

"But you must tell them that the bible says the left hand must not know what the right hand giveth."

"I am afraid that would be the most unpleasant thing I could say to them. You must think of some other method of obtaining money, Henry, for an application at Dexeter Hall would be unavailing. But it is time for you to go to sleep now."

Henry lay awake a long time, and the result of his reflections was a determination to go to Dexeter Hall himself the next day, in the hope that his mother had been misinformed as to the character of those pious and charitable looking men, who had made such a powerful impression upon his mind.

After breakfast he told his mother he would go out a short time, and having found Bill Wilson, they proceeded towards Dexeter Hall—that renowned building, within whose walls cant and hypocrisy hold their court—where the meek and truly charitable spirit

of the Redeemer seldom finds an entrance, and then only to be grieved by the unblushing effrontery with which miscreants seek to cloak their impure and unholy ambition with its spotless and divine character.

Turning into a thronged street, their progress was slower than suited the excited feelings of Henry Kane.

"Let us get into the next street, Bill."

"Oh no, this is so bustling and gay, I like it best."

"But it will be so long before we get there," pursued Henry, as he turned his head first on one side and then another, in the hope of finding some opening in the crowd.

"Them long-winded chaps take a good deal of time to pray up in old Dexeter, which is very kind of them, considerin' how much better they all are than anybody else; and besides, we shall be sure to see somebody punch somebody else's head this morning, the street is so crowded;" and William Wilson looked up and down the street to see if the hackmen, carmen, and omnibus drivers would not emphasize the gesticulations they were favoring the air with by a few blows administered with an earnestness indicative of a superabundance of bile and a hearty good will. His expectations were gratified, for there were unmistakable signs of a difficulty at the knot of drays, carriages, and stages that seemed to be inextricably wedged together at the corner of the street. The belligerents were favored with an impromptu and more attentive audience than generally rewards a dull lawyer or a stupid preacher.

"Here's a good place, Henry," said Bill, as he scrambled up a tree; "a capital—place—can see—it—all." He made a parenthesis at each hitch, and a rent, likewise, in his pantaloons, that could already boast of as many colors as the garment which excited the virtuous indignation of Joseph's brethren. But William at last reached a knot upon the tree whose unaccommodating outlines forced him to change the local part that was submitted to its sharp point, oftener than was consistent with his comfort or an attentive observation of the hostile parties below.

A dray and hackney-coach had locked wheels. The respective drivers tested the strength of their horses, and all the draymen cheered because the two hackney-coach horses could not move the enormous dray horse.

"Take 'em out; lean 'em up agin a post to rest."

"Put them in bed; *thems* weakly hanimals!"

Aroused to fury by these taunts the coachman lashed the beasts unmercifully. They sprang forward, and under the impetus which the start gave them, they rolled back the dray. The drayman turned the head of his horse until he cramped the wheels of the coach, and it was again brought to a dead stand.

The coachee, whose red head and squinting eyes by no means gave indications that he possessed the placid temper that has been attributed to Job the myth, changed his whip into his left hand, and knocking the hat up from his forehead with the right, squared himself for an indignant speech.

"You scum of the earth, how dare you treat the driver of ha hackney-coach *so?*"

The other belligerent was a short, stout, thick-set little man, whose bullet head was set jauntily on his bull neck. As the preliminary flourish to a reply, he doffed his round skull-cap, and retaining it in the same hand that he scratched his head with, exclaimed—

"I *per*-sume a honest drayman is as good—as—the superfluous driver of *ary* hackney-coach in Lon'on!"

The low obeisance with which this annunciation was accompanied was followed by a sudden erection of the drayman's figure into rather more than its natural attitude, which position it retained with the scornful eyes elevated above the head of the coachman at an angle of at least forty-five degrees, where they remained immovably fixed, as if the pompous little man expected to see a foe worthy of his fists emerge from the sky. But if such were his ambitious aspirations they were doomed to disappointment, for a blinding cut fell from the whip of no more exalted a person than Timothy Spriggins, the coachman, upon the uplifted eyes of Daniel Buzzle, the drayman.

"Take tnat, ye vagabond."

"An take *that*, you damned old Hessian, and that, and *that*, too!" exclaimed the drayman, who had leaped upon the box of the coach, and having encircled the neck of his antagonist with one arm, was poking sundry blows with the doubled-up end of the other, into the abdominals of Mr. Spriggins, an unwarrantable proceeding which the coachman acknowledged with divers grunts, that corresponded exactly to the number and vigor of the aforesaid applications.

The combatants were cheered on by their respective friends until the police gathered in sufficient force to separate them and disperse the crowd.

"Come, we have been here too long already," said Henry.

"Yes, the fun is all over. I told you we should see them punch each other. Didn't they do it well?" And he trudged along much better satisfied than before.

Collisions that end in blows are not common among the drivers in London, owing to the efficiency of the police in preventing obstructions in the great thoroughfares. In that particular the reader will recollect the great metropolis is much better regulated than many smaller cities.

The two lads now pursued their walk diligently, and soon arrived at the Hall. Bill Wilson, after obtaining a glimpse at the stand where all the most sanctimonious and celebrated of that charitable congregation were assembled, whispered to Henry—

"I'm blowed if they ain't prayin' yet; I told you they were long-winded, them good people, for nobody but the most piousest have religion enough to put up sich long prayers."

"Oh, no, they ain't praying yet."

"I tell you they is." replied William Wilson positively.

"Don't you hear his voice; *do* they ever say '*yah*,' as if they would never stop; and so through their noses, like, when they are *not* praying? you—"

Here the dissertation of Master William Wilson on nasal intonation, becoming rather too audible, was cut short, by an ominous frown from a police officer; an arbitrary interference with the freedom of opinion, and the right of speech, which that youngster, not having the privilege of denouncing in set phrases, contented himself with showing his horror and detestation of, by divers contortions of the mouth from right to left, and from left to right, accompanied by sundry flourishes of the tongue, all of which are known to the initiated as giving expression to illimitable contempt and aversion.

The hammer of the president was now heard upon the desk, the sound of which echoed through the spacious hall with a gloomy distinctness, calculated to impress the lounging spectators with a solemn respect for the cause that had elicited the prayerful attention of the *salt* of the English Church.

"The subject for to-day's consideration is now open for remark," said the venerable president; "it is the *awful* condition of American slaveholders. Brother Rumfelt will address you."

Brother Rumfelt did not discredit his name; and, therefore, an audible titter ran along the benches upon the frontiers of the hall, when his florid countenance and rotund figure became visible upon the speaker's stand.

"I'god, he don't belie his cognomen, Harry; his face is as red as a beet."

The man who made this most unfeeling and irreverent observation was sitting near Henry and his friend. William Wilson had not observed it before, but now he thought the Reverend Ebenezer Rumfelt's face *did* look like a beet—decidedly like a beet. The likeness became so strong, and the idea was so ludicrous, that when the general titter had subsided which greeted the advent of Mr. Rumfelt, and he had begun to charm the vast auditory with his eloquence, a young, shrill, uncontrollable, though brief laugh, ran through the hall, at once and forever upsetting the most brilliant period in the exordium of that celebrated orator. Every body's eyes were turned in all directions to discover the culprit whose profanity merited condign punishment. But no sooner had Master William Wilson's throat given vent to his feelings than his countenance resumed an expression of the severest gravity. The policeman happened to be in another part of the building, and the person whose comparison caused the involuntary explosion was the only person who was certain that the lad was the offender, and as he felt an interest in one who laughed at his joke, it was not probable he would expose Master Wilson.

Mr. Rumfelt pursued very much the same line of argument that the abolitionists have adopted since the days of Wilberforce; indulging, perhaps, rather more in anecdote and pathos than is customary with even that sympathetic class, which aroused the deepest indignation of the audience at the cruelties practiced upon human beings—*all the way off in America.*

"I have, Mr. President, ladies, and gentlemen, reflected much and deeply upon the crimes of our transatlantic brethren, and I have wondered, Mr. President, that divine wrath has not, in some special manner, like the destruction of Sodom and Gomorrah, been poured out upon them for their iniquities. To buy human beings! —to sell parents and children, body and soul, into endless captivity, is too horrible for contemplation! What a contrast does the soil of England present, for the foot that once rests upon it is instantly free." (Loud and prolonged applause.) "Yes, sir, free, noble, happy England; rich enough in Christian faith, moral culture, aye, and in pecuniary wealth, too, not only for her own population, but with abundance to spare for benighted Africa and slavery-accursed America." (Loud and prolonged applause.)

Henry, who managed to catch that part of the speaker's words, which intimated that there was money enough for suffering mortals in England and America, and Africa, too, thought that was the time to proclaim the distressing condition of his mother, and, with the courage prompted by affection and despair, he mounted the bench, and, with a preparatory hem, was in the act of interrupting Mr. Rumfelt in his sublime peroration, when the police-officer, in a stern tone, bade him descend from the bench. He would have demurred to the proceeding if the policeman had not taken him by the arms and seated him, but with a pressure upon his delicate limbs that made him writhe with pain. The vast assemblage, unconscious of the pain, as they were of the agony he was trying to avert when the authority of England first laid its hands upon him, with vociferous applause rewarded the last eloquent flight of the Reverend Ebenezer Rumfelt in denunciation of every thing like oppression —*without* the limits of the British empire.

"Please, sir, I want to tell them mother's starving," said Henry, imploringly, as the tears fell fast upon his hands as they were clasped before him.

"Hush! you beggar's brat," exclaimed the policeman, in a savage voice.

"I ain't a beggar's brat, sir, only my mother has three children, and I am the oldest; and I'm only a weak, little boy, and she hazent got a bit of food in the house; and it's almost dinner-time, and they will be so very *very* hungry; *do*, pray do let me tell them to give me only a few shillings of all the money they are going to send away, far away from England—oh, pray do, sir, *do!*"

"Why, the brat is up to all the beggar's tricks. Now, you little whelp, if you do not keep quiet, I'll pitch you out at the door, d'ye hear?"

If any one had thought he was a practiced beggar after observing the earnest manner of Henry Kane, and had seen the tears that fell as he pleaded so hard for his dear mother, the indignation that flashed from his eyes when the officer, calling him a second time a "beggar's brat," assured him that he thought so, would have removed an impression so degrading to the feelings of even that poor child. A gentleman who sat near him observed the agony that was visible upon the face of Henry as he urged his request, and it deepened his enunciation as, rising, he said, in a voice that filled to its entire compass the spacious hall—

"Mr. President."

There was something ominous and startling in the harsh voice, as it grated upon the nerves of the self-lauding audience like the application of a rusty saw. It was therefore with a slight trepidation that the president inquired—

"Is the gentleman a member of the charitable association for the abolition of slavery in the United States, and for the reformation and amelioration of our black brethren in Africa?"

"I have not the honor of being numbered with that *sanctimonious* class of Englishmen. Yet, I suppose, a person who has contributed to benevolent institutions elsewhere may be heard here." There was a prolonged and biting emphasis upon the word sanctimonious, which caused the president to move uneasily in his soft chair; yet the saving remark that he had contributed to benevolent institutions, produced a marked effect upon the less discriminating members of the society, and therefore cries of "hear him! hear him!" came from all parts of the hall, and no where more vociferously than from the "outsiders," who were crowding together in the vicinity of the stranger; drawn thither, not more by his clarion voice than by the scorn and contempt that flashed from his light grey eyes.

"As it is the wish of the society to hear the gentleman, he will please ascend the stand and gives his name," said the president.

With a form slightly stooping, the stranger walked up the aisle, and mounted the stand. "John C. Jones," he said in a low voice, replying to the secretary.

The stranger was rather more than six feet high. His thin, wiry frame seemed indurated by exercise. His face, too, was long and thin; his mouth large and capable of wonderful expression; his voice, sometimes sonorous, had also tremendous depth of compass, that ran down like the harsh and grating lower notes of an organ, sending the blood thrilling along the arteries.

"Mr. president, ladies and gentlemen," he began, with the self-possession of a practiced orator—"this society is world-renowned." As this announcement flattered their vanity, it was of course loudly applauded. "No other has acquired such extensive notoriety for its *far* reaching charity." This annunciation was also loudly cheered, and the cheers were, of course, disinterested, because they were uttered by men who were blowing their own trumpet; and they were vigorous, for who else would expend their breath with such hearty good will. Having thus exhibited their entire concurrence in all the complimentary things he could possibly say about them, they prepared to listen with sympathies expanded to any imaginable degree, to the soothing words that might fall from the lips of the orator.

"The human family can never sufficiently express their gratitude to this society for taking under its especial control the fallen members of our race. No other society is favored by almighty power with such a superabundance of piety, which enables you to lift up your eyes in public places, and thank God, like the Pharisees of old, that you are not as wicked as other men. Few, *very* few associations called into being by a desire to ameliorate—I believe, Mr. President, that was your expression—ameliorate the condition of mankind, and to obtain for the members thereof a gratifying *notoriety*, have been favored with such marked success as the one I have now the honor of addressing."

The speaker dwelt upon "notoriety," as if he would never enunciate the word, and the president did not breathe half so hard when each prolonged syllable had visited every nook and corner of the hall. That sagacious individual listened as if they had been "sold" from the start, and he now intimated that he trusted some of his more illustrious associates were of the like opinion, by exchanging ominous glances with them. Profound silence reigned in the hall as that harsh, emphatic voice continued to pour forth a resistless torrent, the effect of which was, to bring the irreligious portion of the audience to their feet, and to cause the members to cower involuntarily in their seats.

"You have been fortunate, wonderfully fortunate, for renown such as you have acquired is enough to gratify the ambition of the most aspiring. When you, Mr. President, are seen in public, the welcome shout reaches your ears, 'There goes the benevolent President of the Dexeter Hall Society.' What could be more soothing to your feelings? You exhibit a commendable improvement upon the example of our Saviour, whose modest demeanor, and secret charities, though, perhaps, very proper eighteen centuries ago, and no doubt in strict consonance with the divine character, is quite inconsistent with this enlightened age, and totally at variance with the ostentatious and pharisaical religion of the present day. And herein lies the grand secret of your success, Mr. President. It is idle to suppose that money will be freely given for charitable objects, if the *ex—cel—lent* donor is not to reap a quick return upon his investment. He cannot, with reason, be asked to give liberally of his abundant store, to relieve those who are less fortunate, if the sound of his contribution, as it falls into the box, is never to be echoed by public approbation. It is not enough that bread scattered upon the waters shall return after *many* days. Quick returns and large interest are more suited to these commercial times, than to that primitive period when one of the most illustrious of the apostles engaged in the humble avocation of a fisherman. And if the Saviour should make a second appearance upon the earth, for the purpose of regenerating the human family, he would doubtless call to his assistance the members of this society, who have made such decided and *highly respectable* improvements in the method of extending alms over that practiced by the Redeemer and his lowly followers when they were satisfied with the simple plan of giving in secret."

The President honored with a reproving glance one of the leaders of the Society, who joined in the call made upon Mr. Jones to address them, which said, unmistakably,

"*Now* I hope you are satisfied."

And the humble way the chastened brother met the glance plainly indicated he was.

"But what adds still more to your fame, and merits the attention of the civilized world, is the fact that you have religiously obeyed the glorious mandate, that '*Charity beginneth at home*' before seeking to reform abuses in another hemisphere."

The eyes of the President were fixed still more remorselessly upon the offending brother.

"You have relieved the suffering and oppressed throughout England. The streets are destitute of beggars, the wail of anguish is no longer heard in the factories, the howl of despair is hushed in wretched hovels, crime walks no more in London, vice has left the great metropolis. Shivering, clotheless forms are no longer exposed to the blasts of winter; and starvation, withall its untold horrors, stalks no more, Mr. President, among your tenants. You no longer take bread from infants, no longer wring parental hearts with agony, that you may make an ostentatious display of your *charities!*"

The terrible irony with which these words were uttered caused the President to start to his feet, and exclaim with great agitation,

"Order! order!"

Turning upon him a glance of fire, while his mouth was contorted into an expression of overwhelming contempt, the orator said,

"I am *not* out of order, unless to recapitulate what you ought to have done, before *im—per—ti—nent—ly* meddling with the affairs of others, is considered out of order." and he shook his bony finger threateningly at the President.

"In order! in order!" came like a tempest from the outskirts of the building.

"Resume the chair, Mr. President!" he continued in a stern, commanding voice.

The President sunk into his seat.

"My mission here is to expose cant, to uncloak hypocrisy, and to tear the thin, but impervious covering from that which you have dignified with the appellation of charity, but which is no more than the *painted sepulchre* condemned by that blessed Redeemer, in whose name you have perpetrated the most infamous rascalities, practised hypocrisy that would have disgraced the most abject felon, and consummated iniquities that a just God will punish with eternal damnation. You shall now hear what an AMERICAN thinks of you."

This annunciation produced a marked effect, but the silence with which it was at first received, was broken by the thunder of applause that shook the building. Cheer upon cheer welcomed the speaker from the vast throng of spectators who, having filled the rear of the hall, now crowded along the aisles, so that the members of the society could not escape the malediction of the indignant orator, if they would.

The President now sat in stupid silence until the storm, which the American had raised, should pass away.

"The gentleman who preceded me indulged in remarks that displayed a lamentable ignorance of the peculiar institution of my country, from the moment it was founded, against our wishes, by British obstinacy and cupidity, to the present hour. Admitting, for the sake of argument, that slavery is an evil, it is one that English avarice established, and one that English jealousy, and not English philanthropy, now seeks to destroy."

This assertion was loudly applauded by the outsiders.

"It cannot be forcibly eradicated without the total destruction of our government. And does it not come with a bad grace from those who planted slavery in America, to ask us to abolish it at the imminent risk of subverting the most glorious system evoked by the wisdom of the human race! And for what? To uproot the principles upon which the great Republic is based, *solely* for the purpose of strengthening the crumbling foundation of despotism.

"The gentleman referred to the dreadful sale and separation of families in the southern states. Who does not know that necessity, stern, implacable, *resistless* necessity is daily sundering the bonds which rivet the affections of your serfs? Nay, within this hour I heard a poor child say that his father had been seized by a press-gang, and that his mother has been left to wage an unequal contest with hunger, if not with dishonor; and he begged *so* piteously to have the privilege of asking you, *you*, Mr. President, for a few shillings of that vast sum you are about to expend in the cause of abolitionism to keep his mother from starvation. And here—within the walls of Dexeter Hall—where rotten-hearted philanthropy revels in its foetid corruption, yonder minion of power, whose livery conceals the heart of a hyena, savagely repulsed him."

A storm of hisses were levelled at the officer, and fierce cries of, "He's a brute—he's a brute," met his startled ears.

"Now, Mr. President, how much will this society appropriate of the money collected to forward the unholy crusade of abolitionism, for the purpose of ameliorating the condition of that noble little boy, and others, in the same situation?" The speaker paused.

"Come, sir, I will yield the floor that the motion may be made."

"The proposition is out of order," muttered the president.

"Out of *or—der!* Yes, it is out of OR—DER to relieve the agony that is visible upon this floor, and that pleads with a child's voice for succor; but it is not out of *or—der—English* order, to let him starve. Well, sir, what will you give out of your own funds for the relief of this family?"

"Your conduct is unusual, sir; your remarks are personal, sir," responded the presiding officer.

"My application *was* personal; it was made to you, Solomon Greasebeans, in your individual capacity, and the response is accompanied with quite as little aid as when I appealed to Solomon Greasebeans, the president of a celebrated society. What is the conclusion that must be forced upon every unprejudiced individual in this assemblage? That a contemptible ambition is the groundwork of your benevolence. In the United States we sell the father, but the wife and children are fed, clothed, and nursed in sickness. The law in its mercy requires it; the interest of the owner is a double guarantee for its fulfillment. Here you *steal* the father, through the agency of a press-gang, and leave the wife and children to misery, dishonor, sickness, and death! There families are separated by executive sale; here by a necessity quite as irresistible. There our slaves are well fed and clothed; here the traveller is at a loss to know whether to laugh at the scanty raiment, which is sometimes an apology for clothing, or to weep over the emaciation that nakedness reveals. There the young negroes are rarely taken from the play-grounds; here little white serfs drop into the grave, with broken constitutions, at seven years of age. Such are the contrasts drawn by stern reality. I will leave you to contemplate them, remarking, in conclusion, that we are annually giving homes to thousands and tens of thousands of what you complacently call the 'surplus population' of England. We feed, clothe, and educate those whom you would mercifully starve. We enable them to send five millions of dollars annually to relieve the wants of those who are so unfortunate as to be unable to escape from servitude—who are still subjected to the oppressive laws of the British empire. While we remember these facts, we can afford to *despise* the canting hypocrisy which emanates from the renowned society of Dexeter Hall."

The orator descended from the stand, after having given utterance to the most caustic speech ever heard in that temple of the philanthropic. The president sat motionless, while the speaker was greeted by prolonged cheers, that had more of earnestness in them, and less of sanctity than was usually vouchsafed to that venerable pile.

Henry was as much excited as the most enthusiastic, and he exclaimed, as he clapped his hands,

"Oh! he'll do something for ma, I know he will do something for ma."

"Now you little rascal, out with you," said the officer, as, seizing him by the collar, he led him towards the door.

"Oh don't, don't, till I've seen him; pray don't."

"Will you hush?" screamed the policeman, as he shook him violently.

"Shame! shame!" cried several of the crowd.

The officer paused for a moment and scowled upon them. "Perhaps you will try to effect a rescue, gentlemen?"

They were appalled by his words, and moving on, he pitched the child into the street.

When Mr. Jones reached that part of the hall where his attention had been attracted to Henry, he paused. "Have you seen the little child to whom I alluded," he asked of a bystander.

"Yes, but a moment ago the officer thrust him out."

The gentleman pushed his way rapidly through the crowd, but when he arrived at the portico, the boy was no longer to be seen; his slight figure had been borne irresistibly along by the vast multitude.

CHAPTER IX.

"Cheerful glows the festive chamber;
In the circle pleasure smiles:
Mounts the flame, like wreath of amber,
Bright as love its warmth beguiles."—Percival.

Scarcely had the full moon risen and faintly brought the angles and turrets of Montague Castle into view, gently mellowing and subduing the evidences of decay, as we love to see them represented upon canvas, when the flower of the English aristocracy began to assemble, for the purpose of joining in the festivities of the occasion. Carriage after carriage rolled up beneath the portals of the castle, with their liveried coachmen, and their precious freight of wit, beauty, and intelligence. A long line of magnificent robes and sparkling diamonds swept into the hall and mounted the staircase to the dressing-room. The castle was brilliantly illuminated. Each window, tower, and balcony sent its rays into the night. Lamps were placed among the trees that ornamented the ground, and their light mingling with the smile of the moon, presented an appearance of more than oriental beauty. Among the guests who arrived at an early hour were Lord Delmore and Sir William Belthoven. The former carried his arm in a sling, which, from pure accident, no doubt, was made of the finest material the market afforded. Sir William Belthoven was radiant with satisfaction at being still preserved for the benefit of his constituency and the service of his queen; which, in his estimation, consisted (of what, in England, is not a peculiarity), of a willingness to tax his constituents to any amount the wants of her majesty or the public service might require. This, he imagined, entitled him not only to the lasting gratitude of those whom he enabled thus to manifest their loyalty to the throne, but to a seat in parliament so long as he could succeed in humbugging electors not hitherto remarkable for their sagacity in detecting the grossest impositions. As John Bull is fond of being humbugged, Sir William considered himself as occupying, to some extent, the position of a public benefactor, which added in no inconsiderable degree to his complacency.

Lord Delmore having paid his salutations to Lord and Lady Rossmore gracefully bowed his way through the crush of laces and silks, to that part of the room where Lady Katharine was surrounded by hosts of admirers.

"I regretted to see, Lord Delmore, that my forebodings were too well founded."

"How so?" inquired his lordship.

"That you have become so corpulent it is no longer safe for you to encounter the hazards of a steeple-chase."

"The fall was occasioned by anxiety lest I should fail to win the prize your fair hand was to bestow."

"Over weight, my lord."

"The dread of failure."

"Too much rotundity."

"Have it as you will, I am still spared, and remain the most devoted of your admirers," replied the veteran and unconquerable beau.

"Oh! *thank* you," replied the lady, as she made a low and graceful courtesy, in mock humility.

"My mother says you have often made the same observation to her," remarked the young and transparently simple Lady Emily Snizzle, sister of the reader's acquaintance of the same name.

"An observation I am fearful your ladyship will never elicit," remarked the peer, with a stately air, which had the effect of rendering that young lady extremely taciturn for the rest of the evening. He put a quietus upon her in his own peculiar manner, which, by the way, he always adopted in silencing "sap heads." And it is a remarkable fact, that in the estimation of his lordship, it made not the slightest difference whether the "sap head" was attached to the shoulders of a person whose great-grandfather was a peer of the realm or a tinker; and therein consisted the solitary proclivity of his lordship for republicanism. A proclivity which had its origin in a contempt for dullness, whether it was palliated by social position and costly raiment, or displayed itself in the garb of poverty, rather than from a constitutional love for the lower orders.

Timothy, Lord Snizzle, now advanced to pay his respects to Lady Katharine. It was observable that "Tim Snizzle," as Lord Delmore irreverently called him, (with a reprehensible disregard for the said Timothy's position, as the heir apparent to a dukedom,) could see much better in genteel society without requiring the assistance of his eye-glass, than among the wealthy parvenus, who assumed that every thing done by a lord *must* be worthy of admiration. His grimaces were not, therefore, half so painful to contemplate, as when he was conscious of awakening mingled emotions of envy and delight which his contortions elicited from that portion of his acquaintance. Habit, however, sometimes made him unconsciously thrust the glass into the socket of his eye. Upon such occasions the left orb instead of the right performed the unpleasant task of making him short-sighted, and the grimaces thereby awakened were not half so fearful to contemplate as those with which the right eye was accustomed to favor the substratum of London society.

"Look here, Snizzle," said Lord Delmore, "they have an eye infirmary in the city; why do you not have an operation performed? for you cannot, of course, expect any prudent young lady to ally herself to such a face as you now present. Judge for yourself; look in the mirror."

Lord Snizzle turned to the mirror, and for a moment regarded the contortions that had drawn up the lower part of his left cheek to meet the upper part which had a corresponding depression. The exertion had the effect of disclosing several sharply pointed teeth, thereby giving to his mouth a voracious expression.

The muscles of his face collapsed as he finished a rather cursory examination, and the eye-glass fell to the length of a pretentious chain.

" Snizzle," continued Delmore, " it is a great mistake to suppose that any defect of vision can add to the attractions of an individual. The eyes are remarkably true evidences of mental conformation. Thus, if a person is cross-eyed, you will find a corresponding obliquity in his moral perceptions. If he is near-sighted, his conduct will seldom square with the recognized standards of propriety or common sense. There may be exceptions to the rule, but I have not been so fortunate as to meet with them. In either case, you will find their possessors have crafty or turbulent dispositions, wayward and uncontrollable passions, or are governed by a thorough contempt for the sacred and necessary regulations which morality has established for the control of society."

Lord Snizzle had a great respect for the opinions of the veteran beau, because he was always cordially welcomed in the most select circles, and he inwardly resolved never to use his eye-glass except among plebeians, where he knew it couldn't fail of producing a sensation.

The guests continued to arrive, and the spacious rooms were thronged. The hour had come when the ball was to " be opened."

" Kate, has the hero of the steeple-chase yet presented himself?" asked Lord Rossmore.

" No, pa'pa," she replied.

" Has he sent no message ?"

" Not that I have received."

" It is remarkable. I should not judge from his bearing that he could be guilty of discourtesy."

" We could expect nothing else from a person occupying his position," said the maiden, as her nostrils dilated and a flush suffused her cheeks.

" Perhaps he may be ill, or more probably, his bashfulness could not brave this array of illustrious names."

" He certainly ought not to expose me to the taunts which the impertinent will indulge in, notwithstanding my hand in the dance would be an honor the most illustrious noble in the castle might be proud of. But it is idle to look for well-bred manners in a boor," replied Katharine Montague, as her eyes flashed, and her little foot impatiently tapped the velvet carpet.

At this inopportune moment Lord Melville made his way through the press of silks to the side of Lady Katharine.

" I congratulate your ladyship," he said spitefully, " on the happiness which is vouchsafed you in being honored with the hand of my father's tenant in the dance."

" An honor for which I am indebted to your lordship's want of skill and courage as an equestrian, whereby your father's tenant convinced your father's son, that so far at least as *one* accomplishment is concerned, which denotes a man, the high-born noble is not the equal of the humble retainer ," replied the maiden sarcastically.

" Baulked, hey, Melville ?" exclaimed Delmore gayly. " Why, man, have you not measured lances often enough with Lady Katharine Montague to discover your inferiority in the tournament of wit!"

"And if I have, I believe I am not the only one who has been favored with the same experience," replied Melville sarcastically.

"Perhaps not; but at all events you are the only *case* that has come to my knowledge where experience has not produced caution. But there is an old adage, scriptural or classical, I have forgotten which, that says, whom the gods would destroy they first make mad. If there is any truth in it, your prospect for a long enjoyment of sanity is very slender."

Melville controlled his indignation with a powerful effort, as he walked away.

"Bilious, *decidedly* bilious," remarked Sir William Belthoven; "he ought to offer for a seat in Parliament; that would teach him patience, I'll be bound."

With an anxiety that caused Katharine Montague to smile through her blushes, she glanced around the room. But the humble tenant whose presence, under the circumstances, would have caused a thrill of pleasure, did not make his appearance.

It was with a face flushed with a scarlet hue that she addressed even Lord Delmore, the oldest and most esteemed of her acquaintances.

"My lord, I hope you will excuse the liberty I take in asking you to favor me with your hand in opening the dance to-night. The individual who was to have had that honor, has, it seems, proved a recreant knight," and a faint smile wreathed the lips of the haughty beauty.

"Certainly, my dear Lady Katherine; nothing could give me greater pleasure than this unexpected honor," replied Lord Delmore with the greatest deference.

The dancers took their places, and the gorgeous music floated through the spacious saloon. The figure was the stately quadrille which so well shows off the beauty of form and grace of motion. The polka and waltz were excluded: the polka and waltz, for whose voluptuous embrace less refined maidens pant, as though with it their fortunes—thereby meaning rich husbands and fine establishments—were made, and without it they were doomed to perpetual celibacy: the polka and waltz, borrowed from the outdoor, sky-ceilinged, leaf-walled ball-rooms of the Rhine, and the less romantic and respectable quartiers of the Parisian grisettes. The polka and waltz, intended to display the accomplishments of those whose heels can be cultivated, but whose heads cannot: the *polka* and *waltz*, whose days are numbered, and whose votaries will soon go to the wall, when *heels* will occupy the position where *brains* have long been stationed. Then the class known as the species snip, instead of thrusting their capering stupidity, where wisdom modestly appears, will resume their rightful position among the outsiders. No more will be seen the forms of men who, gifted with imposing presence, yet stoop to the attitude of monkeys for the purpose of enabling gaudy-dressed sapheads to show off their figures advantageously. The beardless stripling may no longer attempt to strain himself up to manhood, by the waist of some spinster who could boast of maturity at least half a dozen years ago. That enchanting combination of hops, shuffles, and skips, that is simply a prelude to the more violent features of the main performance, though surpassing them in the spasmodic motions which strongly resemble a double representation of St. Vitus's dance, will never more cause the hearts of adoring mammas to overflow with happiness; never more cause the feminine member of the jigging partnership to cast devotional glances into the eyes of the male member as a reward for encircling her waist with a more vigorous arm, under an implied understanding that it is not squeezing—though very like it—only necessary support. Never again suffer demure yet observant glances to flash around, as she whirls past, to see if some other beau is not dying of envy because his arm is not around her zone; to estimate the probabilities of that fine-looking stranger desiring an introduction, to encourage which she suffers several additional pounds of her invaluable weight to rest in the arms of her partner. Never again will she whirl around the room until her strength is completely exhausted, in the hope that all the spectators will have an opportunity of admiring the grace with which she can balance herself upon one foot, while the other cuts two or three fantastic flourishes unseen, if it is fashioned after a shovelish mould; a performance that is duly rewarded by suffering that foot to obtain a few moments' rest in gratitude for its vigorous demonstrations, while the other is made to cut the same fascinating shake.

The figure was the graceful and stately quadrille, and the most observed among the dancers was Katherine Montague. Her spirit was not in the amusement, for she dreaded the biting sarcasm of Lord Melville. To avoid meeting him she withdrew from the saloon when the figure was over. Passing along the balcony, she turned an angle of the castle. The night was exceedingly lovely. The moon had mounted above the trees, and was casting a flood of light upon the rich foliage that surrounded the castle. The stars were good-naturedly winking at the festivities of the hour. The soft breezes of departing summer gently agitated the trees, and upon the fragrant air, mellowed by distance, floated the music of the band.

The maiden contemplated the scene with emotions of tranquil delight. Hers was a mind that could elevate itself above a dance, the newest fashions, and the opinion which one-half the world had formed and expressed of the other half. With all her pride of ancestry, and of caste, there was at the foundation of her character a lively regard for the rights of the masses; less philosophical, perhaps, than impulsive. It was this that prompted her to indulge in those ironical allusions to the government and social regulations of England which were listened to by the Duchess of Sunderland and the Countess of Rossmore with such lively satisfaction. The abolition opinions of the former she assailed with a power of sarcasm that nothing but the wretched condition of the tenantry upon the Sunderland estate could have enabled her to indulge in.

She gladly turned from the gay crowd for a few moments to gaze upon the beauties of nature. The private grounds of the castle, with their flowers and shrubbery, lay invitingly open. The beckoning trees waved her onwards, and descending the staircase she entered the garden, slowly proceeding along the gravel walk leading to the stream that bounded the garden in that direction.

She seated herself in a bower that overlooked the water and commanded a view of the undulating park which stretched away to the south. She was aroused from her recumbent posture by the wailing of a child. Ever alive to the voice of distress she listened. The cry became fainter, not as she thought by distance, but by weakness. It seemed to proceed from the carriage-way that led through that part of the grounds. Her sympathies were excited, and apprehending no danger where she was known to the humble only to be idolized, she descended the pathway leading to the stream and crossed the rustic bridge to the other side. Ascending to the summit of the acclivity, she paused to listen. The voice of a man uttered words of encouragement and consolation. There could be no risk in meeting one who was evidently engaged in the cause of mercy, and she advanced in the direction from whence faint moans were now heard.

As she emerged from the cluster of trees that bordered the carriage-way, she saw the form of a man bending over a child, whose head he was sustaining upon his arm. He turned his head at her approach, and she met the glance of Christie Kane. The young man raised the boy to his feet, still sustaining his weight with his arm.

"And this is the reason why you did not keep your engagement at the castle?" she observed, in a tone that was in the slightest degree tremulous.

"No, madam," responded Christie Kane, decidedly.

"And, pray, to what other cause may your rudeness be attributed?" she curtly inquired.

"Not to thrust myself where I should only be welcomed by scoffs, can hardly be termed an act of rudeness."

"You misunderstand, sir, the courtesy of our house. Whom we admit within its precincts, we know how to treat with civility."

"Probably, after they *are* admitted; but there is a way to exclude an individual who may know what is due to himself, if he *is* a peasant," replied Kane, sarcastically.

"How?—what do you mean?"

"I mean, lady, that nature has endowed me with too much pride, if I *am* humbly born, to pledge the grateful offering of the spirit's fealty at the summons of a mortal like myself," said Christie, sternly.

The smiling eyes of the lady apologized for the curling lip.

"Enough, sir. Whom have we here?"

"One of the unfortunate tenants of the Duke of Sunderland, who has been so long without food that he cannot stand alone."

"Poor child," she said, in a tone of deep commiseration.

"Withhold your sympathy, madam; the most illustrious of the guests, who are now enjoying the festivities of yonder castle, can boast of at least a score of human beings who are dying, literally *dying* of starvation; and they will soon thank God at the near approach of death, unless her grace, the Duchess, with the assistance of the charitable ladies who meet at Strafford House for the purpose of ostentatiously displaying their benevolence, should, at a sufficiently early day, succeed in ameliorating the condition of the whole world beside, when she may, possibly, find time to direct her benevolent eyes to the appalling situation of her own peasantry. While there is a foreign subject, however, upon which her charities can be expended in a way to arrest attention and command applause, she will not be able to discover the miserable condition of her own tenants. Her grace's moral eyesight possesses the rare faculty of only coming to a focus beyond the limits of Europe. So nearly parallel are its rays, that domestic suffering never meets with domestic alms."

The boy moaned.

"I can carry you to the gig; it is only a few steps now. I hope your ladyship will pardon me for trespassing upon the grounds of Earl Rossmore."

"Yes."

"Good-night, madam."

"Good-night."

Raising the child in his arms Christie Kane proceeded down the road, and his form was soon lost amidst the shrubbery that overhung the way.

"An implacable enemy of our class," said Katharine Montague, as she retraced her steps to the castle.

The grounds in front of the castle were thronged by the retainers of the houses of Sunderland and Montague, and the peasantry of the surrounding estates. The most healthy portion of the population were out; and as Lord Rossmore had ordered tables to be loaded with food beneath the trees, gayety prevailed without as well as within the castle. He was known as one of the most liberal and kind of the English aristocracy, and he was, consequently, very popular with the *substratum*, the country round. He had sufficient tact to comprehend that such gorgeous displays as were now witnessed in the castle of Montague, if not participated in by the substratum, might occasion heart-burnings, if not disaffection. He knew how easily they were satisfied, and wisely conceded something to natural prejudice by giving an humble entertainment upon the greensward, which proved quite as satisfactory to them as the display within the castle did to his courtly guests. With two violins and abundance to eat, the few might for them rule the world. And Lord Rossmore knew it.

Among the happiest and most grateful of the out-door guests was Mr. Phelim Savor. Phelim was ordinarily blessed with unquenchable good nature: but a well-lined jacket added surprisingly to his facetiousness. It created a well of thankfulness that he considered inexhaustible, and he, therefore, drew largely from it.

Phelim was the centre of an admiring circle, and he proceeded to expatiate largely upon popular themes, for Mr. Savor possessed enough sagacity to know, that to become a favorite, one must never broach unpleasant subjects. He therefore *enlarged* upon the generosity of Lord Rossmore for his bounty, which he was then availing himself of to an extent that a strict regard for truth will not justify us in pronouncing *moderate*. Having, after the manner of more literary and refined gentlemen, expressed his gratitude to his entertainer, (which elsewhere is manifested by personal laudation of the host, or in extravagant praises of what he may have invented, or may have to sell, or, as by no means is unfrequently the case, may have prepared for the benefit of the travelling public) for his liberal hospitality, he launched off into praises of Christie Kane, the hero of the steeple-chase. As Christie belonged not exactly to their set, but to a few shades, only, above it, he was deemed worthy of almost as much applause as Earl Rossmore, and if the occasion had been any other than one which displayed the Earl's generosity, and therefore awakened their gratitude to an unusual degree, the name of Christie Kane would have been welcomed more enthusiastically than any other.

"Fill yez glasses," said the cheerful voice of Mr. Savor; "wid the permission of the gintleman beyant, whose iligant spach have been so properly and purposely praised, I will prayface me last toast wid a sintiment which will, as Sir William Belthoven says, meet wid univirsal approbation; bekase, as Sir William says, it will be unmeasurably liked. Christie Kane, the gintleman—the *humble* gintleman"—(added Mr. Savor, upon perceiving the word gintleman was not well received by his audience, and he had learned from Sir William that offensive remarks were to be avoided) "who so significantly triumphed over the nobility beyant at the steeple chase, is me imployer." Phelim paused when he announced the relative position of the idol of the hour and himself; a position that in fact consisted of service upon the one side for the consideration of very plain fare, and no wages on the other. Phelim did not attempt to be accurate as to terms; he only wanted to apprise his hearers that he was something more than an ordinary acquaintance of the victorious horseman. In this respect Phelim Savor followed the example of thousands who are satisfied with reflecting the honors that are showered upon favorites by merely knowing them and being seen in their presence; a common failing, by the way, of sapheads in general, who are conscious that the observation of the curious can be won by no other process.

"Be rayson of me faymiliarity wid Mr. Christie Kane," continued Mr. Savor, after an impressive and significant pause, "I can spake understandingly, as Sir William Belthoven says, maning thereby, *under* the comprehinsion of the fraymen; a bootiful fagure of spache. Mr. Kane is proud of his success to-day, bekase he balongs to the poor divils (three vociferous cheers) who give the nobility money to display their extravagance, as they are doing this blissid night in yon castle, (scowling visages were directed to the illuminated building) an' enable Lord Rossmore to give us a magnificint intertainmint like a noble gintleman as he is. (Earl Rossmore was loudly cheered.) Yez say its kind in the aristocracy to ba afther lettin' us enjoy a sight of steeple chases and balls, for empty stomachs don't feel half so bad for siveral days, bekase whin the mind runs fernenst a jolly time, its amazin' how it takes one's thoughts from temporal affairs. Some discontinted divils thry to make us belave we are human beings, and hiv rights, *nathural* rights, aquil tul the proudest nobleman in England. But don't we all know they are unrasonable spalpeens? Jist look at Arthur Wellington William Pitt Smithers, yonder, wid his knees through his pantaloons, thrying tul scrape acquaintance wid his elbows, which are in the same predicament, as yez will obsarve. Now will ony man say that Mr. Smithers is a human baing to the same extint as Earl Rossmore?"

"No! no!" and derisive laughter.

"Of koorse not. Thin Arthur Wellington William Pitt Smithers must be thrated accordin. He can't expict onything but savare labor for thim as has more naturaller rights thin himsilf. If he was a human baing tul the same extint as thim blissid aristocracy up yonder, we would all work and toil and sweat for Smithers as charefully as we would for ony other superior baing."

"How do you make it out that they are superior beings, Mr. Savor?" asked a voice in the crowd.

"How do I make it out? There's an ignoramus for yez! Don't we labor and suffer, and don't they laugh and enjoy thimselves Ain't we ragged? ain't they well clad? Ain't we hungry? ain't they well fed? Ain't they bootiful? ain't we ugly as sin, especially yezsilf? How do I make it out?" quoted Phelim indignantly; "don't the blissid prastes, whin they cancel ony little rascalities we hev committed, tell us obadience to the laws is the nixt thing in importance to paying the tithes? Begorra, the gintilman who axed that question must be a heretic who has niver been blissid wid the pardonin' power of the prastes—long life tul thim and may they ba long spared to open the hivenly gates for poor divils to enter—or been fayvored with the illegant diskoorse of Sir William Belthoven. Didn't that distinguished parliamentary man tell the fraymen the day *afther* he was elected whin they coome to congratulate him, that obadience to the government was the best koorse for them tul pursue, and that they must not expict much from the government, bekase the government had all it could do tul take care of itself, and that if they obayed the laws, paid the rint and the tithes, and all other taxes, and conducted thimselves as orderly citizens, the government would be satisfied, and would not molest thim, unless it wer nicessary to hiv their sirvices in foreign parts, whin they would be fayvoored by a visit from the press-gang, whose praysadings would be very quiet and orderly. One ongrateful spalpeen said it wer his opinion that foreign parts claimed too much attintion, bekase the philanthropists were neglicting the poor white people here to send money tul the niggers, and the government wer stealin' white people to send off to Africa to prevent niggers baing stolen, and it seemed to him the niggers wer considered more of gintilmen than himsilf. By the holy St. Pathrick, but yez ought to hiv sane how they hustled him out, an ongrateful boogger as he manifisted himsilf. But—"

"Mr. Savor, don't you think you had better let us drink your toast and conclude your speech afterwards. Eloquence has made us very dry, down here," said a voice from the lower end of the table.

"I returns me thanks to the gintleman for the compliment," observed Mr. Savor, bowing. "Allow me to propose the health and happiness of me employer, Mr. Christie Kane, who niver carries two faces under one hat."

The sentiment was drank with all the honors, and by none with a *deeper* expression of regard, than by Mr. Phelim Savor himself, who imbibed the grateful beverage so freely that his ideas became rather confused, and he did not feel altogether equal to the work of continuing his brilliant discourse.

The company began to leave the castle, and soon with that unaccountable apprehension of being last—which is almost as much dreaded as being first—the gay throng bid adieu to their hospitable entertainers, and the castle was deserted, save by those guests who were to remain all night beneath its roof.

Following the example of the aristocracy, that portion of the Earl's company who had been enjoying themselves where there was plenty of air, also withdrew; prompted, however, by the annunciation that the gates were to be closed, rather than by an apprehension of being last, which we are bound to admit would, in a considerable number of cases, have been deemed a consummation devoutly to be wished, in view of sundry bottles of liquor yet uncorked.

The moon was hiding her roguish smile behind the trees; the stars were slily winking, and the gentle breeze was rustling the green foliage. Katharine Montague leaned from the casement. Her cheeks were still flushed with excitement, and her disheveled hair fell to her feet. How much happier was the accomplished, beautiful, and idolized daughter of that illustrious house than those who made themselves miserable by envying her lot!"

"*We all have our troubles*," she sighed, as she closed the casement.

How many of the sorrowful and harassed pilgrims to the other world can repeat her language, as they toil along the dreary pathway of life, across which despondency would cast its dark shadow, if it was not dispelled by rays from the lighthouse of hope?

CHAPTER X.

"Who dare confide in right or a just claim?"—GOETHE.

IT was with a heart bursting with grief that Henry Kane returned from the meeting at Dexeter Hall. His hopes had been raised to such a height before he entered the edifice dedicated to the cause of *foreign* charities with loudly proclaimed asseverations of *domestic* piety and abstinence from all sinful desires or gratifications, that now, when he was convinced they would not stoop from their exalted situation to his lowly condition, the reaction in his feelings made him very miserable. He could not eat the pittance his mother had kept for him, and he was glad of it, too, for both his mother and Dolly looked as though they were very hungry.

"But you must eat, Henry, indeed you must, or you will be sick."

"I cannot, ma, I am so full here," and he clasped his throat with his hands.

"Do, oo feel sick, Henry?" said Dolly, taking his hand.

"Not very, Dolly, only I can't eat. Here, take the bread; eat it yourself, Dolly."

"No, ise wont." But she eyed it wistfully.

"Yes, you must."

"No."

"But I *don't* want it, Dolly."

"Don't, oo?"

"No."

"Pon zoo honor?"

"No," he said, smiling.

"Take half of it, then."

And she broke the hard piece of bread, with great difficulty, and gave him the largest part.

"Ma, why don't you write to grandma, and tell her all about our condition?"

"I have."

"And what did she say?" he inquired, eagerly.

"That they had been turned from home by their landlord."

"And could not help us."

"No."

He reflected a few moments.

"Ma, I'll tell you what I must do," he said, resolutely.

"What?"

"Go and get employment in a weaving establishment."

"At your tender age—it is impossible."

"Oh no, it ain't; there's ever so many little boys, and little girls, too, no bigger than I am, who work there."

"But what good would it do?"

"I heard 'em say a smart, little boy could earn six or seven pence a day, and that, you know, would buy us a loaf of bread; and I will be *so* smart, I am sure I shall please them."

"And ruin your health at the same time," responded Mrs. Kane, sadly.

"Better that than starve, ain't it? I shall stand it bravely, for I shall think all day long how happy it will make Dolly to eat the bread I bring home to her at night."

She pressed him silently in her arms.

"And if I do that nobody can call me a beggar, as that bad officer did. You will let me try, won't you, ma?"

"Yes, you may try," she said.

"Thank you, dear ma—to-morrow?"

There was a brief struggle in her mind at the idea of having his tender form so soon tested by hard labor. He observed her working countenance.

"I shall be very miserable and unhappy if you refuse."

"Well, well, you may go to-morrow—yes, to-morrow."

His countenance lighted up with as much pleasure, as if her consent had exempted him from every care little people are in the habit of thinking their parents concoct, with a great deal of ingenuity and no small amount of labor, for their particular and individual annoyance.

At an early hour the next day, Henry Kane sallied forth with a clean face, and in the clothes that had but one patch upon them, and that one neither upon the seat, nor paid for by the public as a judicial and, therefore, necessary expenditure. He sought no adventure, like the worthy knight, Don Quixote; but his stomach, poor boy, was as destitute of food as that redoubtable champion's head was of brains. No; the lad set forth with hopeful feelings in search of the practical, unromantic employment of a wheel-spinner, that he might contribute, in a small way, to the support of his destitute family. What an example did he set to the youth who live only for pleasure, without bestowing a thought upon those who are less fortunate, or pausing to raise their eyes for a moment to Heaven in thankfulness for every earthly blessing! Faint with hunger, he threaded the streets, only kept from sinking in despair upon the ground by a sense of duty. He passed confectionery shops, where cakes and fruits were temptingly displayed; refectories from which issued the smell of beef and the aroma of coffee; into these he cast wistful, but momentary glances, and sped onwards. Passers by noticed his pale cheeks; yet the sight was so common in London that they did not proclaim it a novelty by turning their heads. One boy, trimly dressed, and who had evidently been favored by some liberal person with an extravagant amount of pennies, judging from the artillery of rolls, the magazine of cakes, and the embankment of candies with which his person was fortified, spied Henry from afar off. As they approached each other, the stranger sidled away, not that he supposed the pale child was about to forage upon his possessions, but only to obtain a more accurate survey of his person. His jaws moved less and less rapidly as they neared one another, until, as Henry was passing him, they altogether ceased masticating the compound of cake, bread, and candies, with which his mouth was distended to its greatest, not to say its most alarming capacity. Whether there was something in the emaciated appearance of the wan face that excited his compassion, or whether the superabundance of good things with which he had supplied himself, had enlarged his sympathies as they had his stomach, and made him desirous of imparting something of the superabundance, as a new convert does that blessed religion which is more than enough for his own bliss, will to the latest time remain unexplained. Either the emaciated appearance of Henry, or the world of good things which the stranger possessed, one or the other, or both, prompted him to advance a step and make earnest gesticulations. Henry stood still, while his eyes followed the bread which the other was flourishing diligently in default of speech, for his mouth seemed to be hermetically sealed by the compound there imprisoned. Finding that the gesticulations did not have the effect of expressing his charitable desires, he thrust the bread into Henry's hand, articulating at the same time with manifest difficulty.

"Take it."

The face of Henry was crimsoned in a moment, as he drew back. He had never taken alms.

"Do take it," said the other in a kind voice. "You look so pale and thin. Come, I've got ever so much beside, and see all the pennies too."

Henry took the bread.

"I am sure I am very much obliged to you," he said, gratefully.

"You're welcome. Here, take this roll too."

Henry looked surprised at his generosity.

"Oh, I've eaten enough myself, I couldn't swallow as much as would choke a mouse."

The child thought of the hungry ones at home, and he put the roll in his pocket, and then he thanked the good boy again, and then he walked along more briskly than ever. The sun seemed t shine more brightly, and the faces of all the people he met looked more cheerful, and he turned his head to catch one more glimpse of the kind stranger, who was still watching him, with a pleasant consciousness that he had made him happier than he was before.

Henry soon reached the large weaving establishment, and timidly entering the office, stood by the door, with his hat in his hand. One of the partners was there, and seemed to be in consultation with a foreman of the establishment. Henry modestly waited until their attention might be directed to him. A large black Newfoundland dog, whose fat proportions spoke of good living and gentle treatment, regarded the child with sleepy eyes, and seemed to be in doubt whether he was, in fact, a veritable boy, or the huge form of the mastiff, that had been troubling his dreams. After a long examination, during which, judging from a growl, he had a reasonable—or rather an *instinctive*, conviction that the identical mastiff was then and there present, and that too, in a most offensive position. When this impression had ripened into certainty, the shaggy monster was not long in defining his position. Without attempting to disguise his purposes with gracious and complimentary notes, intended only to deceive, such as our renowned diplomatists are accustomed to write to each other, the gallant Newfoundlander sprang to his feet, and without any more formal declaration of hostilities than a bark, prepared to repulse the enemy from his territory. No sooner, however, had he thus proclaimed his ultimatum, and that too with a dog-matical resolution to enforce it—an example which might be appropriately followed by certain crowned heads—than he was apprised of the futility of even canine opinions. If his warlike preparations were unhesitatingly made, no one, not even the Emperor of France, could express more undisguised satisfaction, that peace could be preserved upon honorable terms. If one could not brook a continental war that would light the fires of a revolution, which must turn up the rotten foundations of despotic governments, because his sympathies were aroused for those who might fall in a conflict that must give freedom to Europe, the other could not visit that indignation upon a poor little boy, which might rightfully be poured out upon the head of an offending mastiff. So he walked up to Henry with a separate and distinct proclamation of neutrality in each wag of his tail, and the offer of an alliance offensive and defensive in every glance from his good-natured eyes.

"What do you want?" said the partner, as he surveyed Henry over his spectacles—those lighthouses standing out upon the nose, as a disregarded warning that he was rapidly approaching the great port to which his sea-beaten craft had directed her course for more than half the brief period allotted for a passage from time to eternity.

"Please, sir, I want employment."

"Employment! It seems to me all the brats in London come to me for employment."

"Perhaps they can't find it anywhere else?"

"Hity, tity! and if they could, I suppose they would not come here; eh?"

Henry was grieved to think he had made a disagreeable remark, and he was silent, not knowing what to say.

"Hey! is that it?"

"I don't know, sir, only I didn't mean to offend you."

"Didn't you? Well, I should not think it would be worth your while *to* do it, if you think of working for me! Hey, Dykeman?"

"No."

"Hear that, you little spawn?"

"Yes, sir."

"Well, what can you do?"

"I don't know, but I am *willing* to do anything."

"And how much will you give me to learn you to do something for yourself?"

Henry was appalled, for a moment.

"Give you, sir? I've not got one single penny in the world. I am very poor."

"I do not see how you could well be more so; do you, Dykeman?"

"No."

"You don't expect me to pay *you* anything, do you?" he asked in a voice calculated to make Henry believe that such expectations were little less criminal than theft.

But despair was not to be put down by looks, or words either.

"I must have money, sir."

"You must; why?"

"Because if I don't, my little sister and little brother, and mother too, will starve!"

"The old story, Dykeman."

"Yes."

"The same."

"Yes. Poor people will persist in the foolish idea that if they don't eat they must die!"

"Preposterous notion!"

"Monstrous!"

"Especially when bread is scarce."

"And potatoes have the rot."

"How much do you expect a day?" said the commiserate Mr. Greasebeans, for he was no less a personage than the President of the Dexeter Hall Association, for the Amelioration, &c., &c., of the African Negroes, &c., &c., and the American Slave, &c., &c.

"I hope seven pence a day will not be too much?" said Henry, alarmed at the magnitude of the amount, as he mentioned it.

"Think of *that*, Dykeman!"

"Yes."

"Sevenpence a day!"

"A day!"

"Ain't they coming to it?"

"Fast!"

"They have no consciences."

"Nor bowels, except for food."

"You may think yourself fortunate if I give you three," said the charitable Mr. Greasebeans, who had subscribed five hundred pounds at the recent meeting at Dexeter Hall, to aid the cause of Emancipation in the United States.

"Then I can't work for you," said Henry sadly, as he put on his hat and moved towards the door.

"Well, how little will you take?" inquired Mr. Greasebeans; "come, now, if we make your work light;" and he winked at Dykeman, a freedom totally at variance with the orderly and well-regulated features, such as the president of a renowned society might be supposed to possess.

Henry recollected that his mother had expressed her anxiety about his health, and he was grateful, therefore, to Mr. Greasebeans for the intimation that he would make his work light. He hesitated for a few moments, and then he thought he would come down a penny, and that was a great deal to him.

And he told him so.

"Sixpence! Do you hear that, Dykeman?"

"Yes."

"Did you ever hear such exorbitant demands?"

"Never."

"The world is surely coming to an end!"

"On fire now!"

"Where?" exclaimed Greasebeans, in evident alarm.

"Deep down in the earth, so the geologers say."

"Pshaw!"

"Nonsense!"

"I'll give you fivepence, boy."

Henry again moved towards the door, and the rich man, thinking that he had chaffered long enough with human misery, not only to satisfy his partners of his business sagacity, but also to maintain his own reputation in tact, finally agreed to give Henry the *liberal* sum of sixpence a day, adding sternly—

"But recollect, I have bought your time, youngster, from five o'clock in the morning until seven at night."

"So many hours as that?" asked the child falteringly.

"Yes, every moment of it. For that time you are sold to me. If you come one minute too late it will be theft; do you understand *theft?*"

For a moment he thought of giving up the place at once, but

then the images of his mother and Dolly and Frank Tot rose up before him.

"Yes, I will do it."

"Very well, now you may go."

Henry left the office, and then he thought the time for receiving his wages had not been fixed, and he returned, honestly wishing that there might be no mistake.

"Please, sir, you will pay me the sixpence every night, won't you?"

"Do you hear that, Dykeman?"

"Yes."

"Is it not too outrageous?"

"I told you they would persist in not letting their stomachs grow up," replied Dykeman cynically.

"Must I humor him?"

"I suppose so, unless you can make him believe it is just as agreeable and quite as well in the long run, to fast for a month or through one quarter, as it is to eat. And I do not know why you should not, for you accomplish things in a money-making way almost as difficult."

"He! he! he!" shrieked the delighted Mr. Greasebeans. The compliment of Dykeman had evidently expanded the heart of his patron, for that individual said with an expression of benevolence upon his features—

"Yes, my little man, you shall receive the *total* amount of sixpence each day."

"Thank you, sir," replied Henry, and he went home very happy to think he had obtained a situation where he could get sixpence a day to support his family and pay the house rent, and for which he only had to task his strength *fourteen* hours a day, and that, too, in the service of a person who had written his name upon the record of humanity in unmistakable characters by his liberality in the crusade of Abolition. A crusade which sought to improve the condition of young negroes who, at the age when Henry had sold himself to work fourteen hours a day for sixpence, were scampering unchecked in their playgrounds, or earning double that sum by holding "Massa's horse."

CHAPTER XI.

> "To whom with dark displeasure Jove replied:
> Base and side-shifting traitor! vex not me
> Here sitting querulous; of all who dwell
> On the Olympian heights, thee most I hate
> Contentious, whose delight is war alone."—HOMER.

IT was a severe trial for Henry Kane to get up every morning at four o'clock, for it took an hour to eat his breakfast, and get to the factory at five. An hour was allowed at dinner, so that in making up his complement of fourteen hours, he could not start upon his return until eight. A great many children were employed in the same room with him, all of them engaged in the laborious task of turning wheels. That it required too much exertion for their strength was proved by the deformed limbs, that had become misshapen under the ordeal. Crooked legs, uneven hips, arms out of all proportion, round shoulders, and bent heads, that presented upon their little bodies the most quaint, old fashioned, grotesque appearance. To see them at work, with their sad faces and bent forms, would make a person think he had been favored with one of those sights which were vouchsafed to Gulliver, and which he recounts (after the manner of the present day) with such apparent truth, in his "personal recollections." He would come to the conclusion that he was in the rightful territory of a nation of Lilliputians, and with all due speed would beat a retreat before "each individual hair" on his cranium was made to "stand" out by a peg.

Mr. Dykeman had the overseeing of this part of the establishment, and to do that functionary justice, he was by nature and a thorough training sufficiently unfeeling to do credit to the discipline of "Messrs Greasebeans, Snodgrass & Co," the successors to the celebrated house of the "Snodgrass Brothers," who had themselves succeeded the "Brothers Snodgrass," business descendants of "Snodgrass and Son," the original founders of the establishment, and supposed, also, to have been the originator of the partnership term of "Brothers Snodgrass," and also that of "Snodgrass Brothers," a phrase whose mellifluousness of tone and easy gracefulness of expression, finds much favor at the present day. Be that as it may, Hugh Dykeman had no more feeling for human suffering than might be supposed to emanate from a piece of leather that had undergone the process of tanning for seven years. Hugh prided himself upon his stolidity; so did Messrs. Greasebeans, Snodgrass & Co. It suited him to annoy the poor creatures over whom he was set as guard, for he seemed to revel in human suffering. If he could not, by taunts, wring tears from them, he sought an opportunity, when overpowered nature took a few moments for rest, to steal softly up to the offender and dash his raw hide into his flesh, and then he would laugh gleefully, and rub his hands as the victim danced about the room. No galley slave ever dreaded the approach of his task-master more than that band of helpless children did the presence of Dykeman. It was useless to complain to the proprietors, for he at once exculpated himself to their entire satisfaction by informing them that their *interests* would be advanced if he was allowed to use the raw-hide freely. And so their lacerated forms continued to bear evidence that Dykeman still enjoyed his favorite amusement.

Henry had hitherto escaped the vengeance of this monster. This was probably owing to the fact that he was strong and resolute compared with those who had been longer subjected to arduous labor. But after he had performed his task a few days, his strength began to fail him. He required more nourishing food than bread, which was all that now passed his lips. Exhausted with fatigue, he had fallen asleep during the hour of rest, and failed to hear the bell which called them again to their work. Dykeman saw it, and stole on tiptoe with the rawhide stretched forth. His companions would have aroused him, but for the ugly frown of the overseer. A smile was upon the face of the boy; he was happy, for he was dreaming that his father had returned, and that he once more sat upon his knee, and his mother clasped his hand, and Dolly sat upon the other knee, and Frank Tot was cooing, and unraveling whole bales of happiness with his busy little hands. In the excess of his joy he gently whispered,

"Father, *dear* father."

The only answer was the rawhide, as it fell upon his quivering flesh. Henry sprang to his feet, and rubbed his eyes.

"You struck me, sir," he said indignantly.

"Yes."

"I'll tell Mr. Greasebeans."

"Do, and then I'll strike you often."

He went straight to the office. Mr. Greasebeans and his partners were indulging in the luxury of the best regalias.

"Please, sir, Mr. Dykeman struck me."

"I dare say you deserved it," replied Mr. Greasebeans, as he daintily removed the ashes from the cigar, so that it might not soil his elegant shirt bosom.

"Nobody ever struck me afore."

"Probably that is the very reason why the correction was proper now. Hey, Snodgrass?"

"It would have been thought so in the days of Snodgrass Brothers"

"And Brothers Snodgrass, too?"

"Yes."

"Hear that, you young scapegrace?"

"I'm not a scapegrace, sir, and I don't think the meeting in Dexeter Hall, when you sat in that big chair, (for I know it was you, although you don't look half so good, and pious-like, as you did then,) thought it was right to beat little boys; that is, *black* little boys, and I don't know why white boys ain't as good as black ones."

"Did you ever hear such impertinence, Snodgrass?" said Mr. Greasebeans, with as much horror imprinted upon his countenance as if a live negro was in the act of being roasted; or, what would have been deemed still more revolting, his master had just put his initials, in clear and legible characters, on his shoulder, with a red hot iron, as slaveholders are convicted of being constantly in the habit of doing, upon the unimpeachable testimony of Mr. Roorback, a gentleman whose veracity is undoubted in the United States! Where any one can vouch for the truthfulness of his statements, who is disposed to do so.

"Impertinent!" cried Mr. Snodgrass, ferociously. "I do not know what you, in the well-known tenderness of your disposition may think of it, but I can tell you that the Brothers Snodgrass would have pronounced it monstrous; yes, MON-strous!"

"There, sir, you hear what my partner, Mr. Snodgrass, a lineal and business descendant of the founder of this establishment, thinks of my humanity."

"Ain't I as good as a negro?"

"Ahem! That—that—depends upon—circumstances—yes, upon circumstances, youngster. If the negro is a slave, you are not as good as he is, because, by virtue of his sufferings, he obtains an exaltation like the martyrs of old; yea, verily, like unto the apostles. *Yah!*"

"If he is not a slave?" asked Henry, anxious to obtain information from his excellent master.

"That depends upon circumstances also. If you are both industrious, and bear chastisement without murmuring, I don't know why your skin should prevent you from being considered as good as a negro. Hey, Snodgrass?"

But Snodgrass was silent; he was reflecting upon the point, and it was clear his mind was not prepared to endorse the proposition of his partner, to its full extent.

"Well, *I* won't be beat," said Henry positively.

"I am sorry to hear you express yourself in that way, for it not only interferes with our admirable discipline, which by breaking your spirit, prepares you for the position of servitude so well fitted to the mental conformation of your class, and so necessary to uphold the government and aristocracy of England, but it sets an example of insubordination destructive of all authority in the wheel-room."

"I don't understand half what you say, for you don't talk with father's straight-forward, plain words; but I won't be beat."

"I'll speak to Dykeman about it."

"And tell him not to strike me again?"

"Yes."

"Thank you, Mr. Greasebeans, I will work ever so much harder for you; *that* I will," said the child gratefully as he left the office.

"That lad's spirit must be broken, Snodgrass," said the pious Mr. Greasebeans, savagely.

"Crushed," said Dykeman, laconically.

"Say you so?" replied Mr. Greasebeans.

"Yes."

"Then I take it master Kane will have an ugly time. But hark ye! you mus'n't strike him, that is, not yet; his rebellious spirit will not brook the rod; that is, *not yet!*"

"It will shortly," replied Dykeman cynically.

"You understand, I see: Dykeman, your wages must be increased. What do you suppose is the net profit per day on the labor of the sixty boys under your control?"

"Don't know."

"Six pounds."

"No!"

"Eighteen hundred pounds a year."

"Incredible!"

"My share six hundred pounds; why, I can easily give one hundred pounds for the purpose of lighting abolition fires in the United States; and if (as I think it quite probable, owing to the general scarcity of food and the consequent suffering among the poor folks) we can reduce the wages of the boys to five pence a day next year,

I shall be able to add another fifty pounds to the general fund, by way of a flourish, and as a climax to my generosity. Even now, there is but one person in the kingdom who gives so liberally in the good cause as myself, and that is old Ned Thoroughwort."

"Him with the starving tenantry?"

"The same."

"But what do you *gain* by all these gifts; for I presume a shrewd calculator like yourself does not make so large an investment in charities without a corresponding return?"

Mr. Greasebeans winked at Dykeman—a proceeding which that individual, in the early days of their intercourse, supposed to be caused by a nervous affection of Mr. Greasebeans's eyesight, for he could never bring himself to believe so faithful an observer of the ten commandments as his patron had the credit of being, would be guilty of the levity which a *voluntary* contraction of the eyelid would indicate. But when their mutual qualities begat confidence, Dykeman discovered that both eyes indiscriminately were made to express the sly humor which abounded in the conformation of Solomon Greasebeans. It was, therefore, with a consciousness of something good coming from the senior member of the establishment that Dykeman seated himself in a comfortable arm-chair.

"I don't mind telling you, Dykeman, because your good qualities have almost made you one of us, and will, when we increase the number of successors to the celebrated house of Snodgrass Brothers ——"

"Successors to *Brothers Snodgrass*," interposed Mr. Snodgrass, majestically.

"Successors to Snodgrass and Son. If it ever does happen, and it probably will, since it has been promised every month for the last six years, I shall feel duly honored," observed Dykeman, with an imperturbable countenance.

"You must know there are *two* reasons for this liberal expenditure. I have told you how important it is to advertise our goods. It is not enough that we have them to sell, the world must know it. Now half the manufacturers in the kingdom do not know the importance of advertising. They have goods to sell, many of them better than ours, between *ourselves*, and yet they cannot imagine, stupid creatures, why the house of Greasebeans, Snodgrass & Co. ——"

"Successors to Bro——," interrupted Snodgrass.

"Don't interrupt me, Mr. Snodgrass; the whole world knows who our predecessors were. Why, as I was saying, the house of Greasebeans, Snodgrass & Company is amassing an immense fortune, while they are doing nothing. Now the secret of the whole matter lies in a nut-shell; buyers have found out that we have goods to sell. And how do you suppose they found it out? I'll tell you. Whenever my name was announced as president of the Dexeter Hall Society, or as a patron of the abolition cause, I managed to have added thereto, 'senior member of the great house of Greasebeans, Snodgrass & Co——'"

"Successors to Brothers Snod——," interrupted Mr. Snodgrass.

"Mr. Snodgrass, if *I* am to relate the modus operandi of our system (and which, with all due respect for *Brothers* Snodgrass, *Snodgrass* Brothers, or *Snodgrass* and *Son*, would never have been conceived if I had not become a member of the firm), you will please remain silent. I was going to say, Mr. Dykeman," continued Mr. Greasebeans, with his stateliest manner, "when I was interrupted—I must be allowed to say, and will say, *disrespectfully* interrupted, that I always managed to have the name, style, and place of business—*place of bnsiness*, you understand, Mr. Dykeman—the street, *the number of the street* where our establishment is situated, inserted after my own name, so that it read something in this way, 'The meeting was called to order by,' or 'This munificent donation was made by Solomon Greasebeans, senior member of the celebrated house of Greasebeans, Snodgrass & Co——'"

"Formerly Brothers Snod——"

"'Who have amassed an immense fortune in the manufacturing business at their enormous establishment at Nos. 20, 22, and 24, ——— Street, London,'" concluded Mr. Greasebeans, only acknowledging the interruption of Mr. Snodgrass with an ominous frown.

"These notices are easily procured by slipping a few crowns into the hands of reporters, or by making them good-natured with soft chairs and good opportunities for reporting. I have obtained the insertion of some capital advertisements, which have gone the round of the London press, without the London press knowing they were *uscd*, simply by talking kindly to the reporters, and giving them easy chairs. Lord, I knew the value of the position of president of that society, when I flattered all the pious old women, and treated all the religious old sots, who were supposed to have any influence in the society. And I paid off no small amount of debts, too, for some who were the most clamorous in Dexeter Hall. But I have been doubly, trebly paid. I could afford to be liberal. Why, I would not lose the position for five thousand pounds a year; that is to say, not at present. I don't know how long it will be considered reputable to advertise in that way, for it is becoming rather a *common* business. All the hatters, tailors, and small fry, have resorted to it. It won't do much longer, because they will make it decidedly vulgar, and then it will be beneath the notice of Greasebeans, Snodgrass & Co., and——"

"Successors to Brothers Snodgrass!" shouted Mr. Snodgrass, in a voice which indicated a determination to be heard.

"Yes," replied Greasebeans, savagely.

"Well," said Dykeman, "that is one good and sufficient reason for bleeding so freely; what is the other?"

"The one I have mentioned is of a private nature and inures to the benefit of our house, the other is of a public character, mainly, though it also will not be without its effect upon our pecuniary affairs. It will not do to have the truth proclaimed to the world, for there are thousands and millions in this country who fancy that a republican government is preferable to our own, and if they thought we hopefully contemplated the downfall of the only republic on earth worth the name, we should have a *domestic* opposition to the great work."

"Do you seriously intend to dissolve the American confederacy?" asked Dykeman.

Mr. Greasebeans winked expressively. It was a protracted wink, calculated to make a profound impression upon Dykeman. When he had thus with a single ray of light opened a path to the convictions of the overseer, he proceeded in his own peculiar way.

"We are satisfied with things as they are in England. We want no change. There is danger of a change while the government of the United States remains intact. Their example is silently, but steadily undermining every representative monarchy in Europe. It cannot be otherwise, for to the masses there is nothing so attractive as self-government. The Constitution of the United States must be destroyed. But how? Not by a forcible pressure from without; the combined despotisms of the whole earth could not effect their purposes in that way. They must be made to destroy it themselves."

"Surely they are hardly so green as that?"

"No doubt of it. Fanaticism has accomplished far greater triumphs. Did it not exhibit the folly of man in the crusades? Did it not proclaim its power in the expulsion of the Moors from Spain? Did it not water the streets of Paris with blood on the eve of St. Bartholomew? Has it not over and over again deluged Europe with human gore? Did it not, too, exhibit its relentless power at the time of the Salem witchcraft? Tush, man! *anything* can be accomplished under the leadership of fanaticism. We intend to destroy republican institutions under the specious banner of liberty."

"Ha! ha!"

"You may laugh, but I tell you that is the programme."

"You intend to attack liberty under the banner of liberty. Well, it is difficult to tell what you may not successfully accomplish."

"It required very little sagacity to make out the programme. We shall strengthen the abolition party through the agency of lectures, newspapers, and tracts. Already they hold the balance of power in the free States, and we advise them to demoralize and corrupt the two great parties by requiring them to make concessions, in order to get their votes. Becoming familiar with a sale of principles, by frequently setting them up at auction, they will at length view anything like public faith with supreme contempt, when it stands in the path leading to political promotion. When thus thoroughly corrupted, they will yield an easy victory to the abolitionists. The whole north will be abolitionized, and then they will force the southern states to emancipate their slaves, or fight. A fight is the consequence; and such a fight as civil wars only can exhibit. A dissolution of the Union takes place; a dozen confederacies spring up, and anarchy and bloodshed is hourly witnessed, where the beautiful constellation of states now revolves in exquisite harmony. All this will take years; the work may not be consummated during my life. It will be resisted by patriots, north and south. The Union will several times be saved, but at last their patience will be thoroughly exhausted, and the crash will come."

"And you expect to accomplish all this, by the aid of those who ought to defend the constitution, if necessary, with their lives?"

"Yes," replied Mr. Greasebeans, serenely.

"With what arguments? you would hardly inform them that such was your neighborly designs."

"Of course not. We shall constantly proclaim our abhorrence of slavery; we shall tell them how disgraceful it is to uphold involuntary bondage in a country where they profess to believe that all men are born free and equal. We shall covertly arouse their jealousy and envy against their southern brethren, because they live without work. We shall say that to live in idleness is bringing down to too late a period the aristocratic habits of the cavaliers who settled the southern states. We shall contrast their own industrious habits with those of the gassy, starchy, aristocracy of the south, and we shall make them believe that it will be in strict accordance with the genius of their institutions to require southerners to labor, by stealing their slaves, or by forcing them to choose between the dread realities of emancipation or insurrection. All this we shall accomplish under the banner of liberty."

"Why, from this candid statement it would seem the American abolitionists are your tools, with which you work out their own destruction."

"Yes, and the most stupid, ignorant, demented tools that ever man attempted to work with. It does not require an amazing amount of cunning to lead them on to their destruction."

"Are all of them *blind* instruments of your will?"

"No; it is shrewdly suspected that some of the ringleaders in the plot are working understandingly for the destruction of their government. These traitors hope to gain something in the general crash. But to do the great mass of the abolitionists justice, they are thought to be honest in their belief."

"Are you not fearful they may question the purity of your motives by making an examination into the horrible condition of the poorer class in this country?"

"The southern press have launched this argument against us, but it does not possess as much weight as you would suppose. The abolitionists have not witnesssed the suffering among our population, and to hear about it, is one thing; to see it, another."

"Well, how is the house of Greasebeans, Snodgrass & Co.—" "Suc—suc—suc—cess—" snored Mr. Snodgrass, almost arousing himself from a deep sleep at the mention of the firm's name,—"to be benefited by all this?" persisted Mr. Dykeman.

"We want no change; we are satisfied with things as they are. If a republic should be established, and there should be a more equal division of the real and personal estate of the kingdom, do you suppose I could get boys to work fourteen hours a day for sixpence?"

Mr. Greasebeans closed his right eye in a prolonged wink, calculated to impress Mr. Dykeman, not only with a proper respect for the world of far-reaching sagacity that was enclosed within the compressed lids, but also to cause a reasonable doubt in his mind as to whether the lids aforesaid were not under the influence of an obstinate paralysis, a conclusion that was formed by the ghastly smile that was drawn up into a knot at the corner of his mouth.

"And I am to put the youngster through a wholesome discipline?"

"Yes, break his obstinacy."

"If it breaks his constitution?"

"It matters very little, in this vast system of ours, Mr. Dykeman, where a solitary individual is, no more than a grain of sand on the sea shore; whether he dies under the operation of a healthy discipline, or lives to exemplify the excellence of our regulations. It will be all the same one hundred years hence," said Mr. Greasebeans thoughtfully, for he was always sad when he reflected upon that terrible leveller—Death.

"That's some consolation to the poor folks, Mr. Greasebeans; there will be very few of the distinctions of society in the grave. It is true that the rich may build tombs that will for a greater or less period shut out the worms that are not to the body born, yet the inherent corruption of the human frame will ultimately destroy the limbs we are so tender of. One by one they will rot away; the disgusting gangrene will visit the loveliest cheek; festering decay will prey upon the fairest bosoms; loathsome worms will crawl through sockets which were radiant with beauty, and teeth that coral lips were wont to reveal will grin a perpetual and ghastly smile at the triumphant revelry of corruption. This, *no* tomb can prevent. I believe you are now building one with more than ordinary care, Mr. Greasebeans?"

That gentleman's usually placid countenance had gradually paled. "I'll thank you to indulge in such remarks as rarely as possible, Mr. Dykeman. Can't a person put off the hour of his death until it comes, without dying every day in the week," he said petulantly.

"The preachers say that it is not a safe operation to do so. But probably you know best, whether they are right or not; only the costliest tomb won't keep the worms from eating you up, any more than the body of Jem Shoelocks. I don't really know if they won't prefer a rich man, because his flesh must be tenderer than one whose sinews have been indurated by hard labor."

"That will do," chimed in Mr. Greasebeans nervously.

"At all events, it will be the same in the end, for I presume, unless the millennium makes its appearance within a century, very nearly all that remains of rich and poor will be—dust."

"The boys must require your attention, Mr. Dykeman."

"There is one consolation, however," said Mr. Dykeman, rising; "that the rich man possesses. He has the consciousness of knowing that his dust is kept safe from the contaminating touch of the poor man's ashes; and that, I take it, will be no small satisfaction during the years upon years it will remain imprisoned in the dark, silent receptacle for the dead. That is to say, unless the necessities of after ages may require the use of the soil for more urgent purposes than to keep a few handfuls of mother earth. Even in that case you will have one consolation; it is far more cheerful without than within a tomb, for your ashes may receive the heat of the sun and the showers of heaven, and watch the ever-changing seasons as they record the mutations of time, and the fiats of destiny."

CHAPTER XII.

"Existence may be borne, and the deep root
Of life and sufferance make its firm abode
In bare and desolate bosoms."—BYRON.

LORD MELVILLE, in the depth of his wrath, sought counsel of Ellen Knowles. It was his opinion that the female mind was gifted with a subtle ingenuity for the purposes of tormenting, that might in vain be looked for in the mental organization of his own sex. He was doubtless wrong, though he was wont to say he had satisfactory proof that such was the case. He occasionally remarked, also, that the consanguineous tie of cousin possessed the miraculous quality of exercising and bringing out the most bitter and vindictive hatred of which the human mind is gifted; and as he thought there must be a great deal of satisfaction in hating *scientifically*, it was a subject of deep regret to his lordship that he had not been favored with collateral relations in the fourth degree. To the interest which he took in this matter was Melville indebted for the knowledge that cousins *were* related in the fourth degree; and he often essayed to enlighten the informed, uninformed, and misinformed—the relative proportions of which, in the human family, he often said, were about equal—by remarking that the degree of *relationship* was computed by counting up one degree to the father, one more to the grandfather, down one degree to the cousin's father, and one more to the cousin—four degrees in all. This was all the information to be found in Blackstone which his lordship thought worth possessing in order to qualify him for a seat in the House of Peers; that body of respectable gentlemen whose most illustrious members are elevated from the commons; often creating thereby a sparseness of talent in that branch of the government, which makes the appellation appropriate, when applied to them, of "*Short* Commons." Melville found Ellen Knowles an eager assistant. The triumph of Christie Kane in the steeple-chase added strength to the determination she had already formed of compassing heaven and earth to win his hand. She perceived that her designs could only be accomplished by humbling his native pride. The opportunity now presented itself, and she entered into the schemes of Lord Melville with an ingenuity and an ardor that he claimed to be an illustration of his opinion of the craft of the sex, as well as an exemplification of consanguineous hatred. She welcomed him graciously as he entered the parlor at the lodge.

"This cousin of yours, Miss Knowles; he is a constant source of annoyance to me," observed Melville, as he seated himself with that easy carelessness which the cockney aristocracy know so well how to assume.

"Get rid of him, then."

"How?"

"How? He your father's tenant, and in arrears, and you ask me *how!* Your lordship would be an adept at revenge, and yet you are as ignorant of the means as your great aunt was of some of the proprieties of life."

"Another allusion to that affair, madam, and you may work out your own revenge upon this boorish cousin," replied Melville, haughtily.

The maiden bit her lip. It would not do to quarrel with him yet; and she forced a laugh.

"Come, my lord, we cannot get along without each other. Let us be serious. You would humble the arrogant pretensions of Christie Kane; so would I. For the means, then. You have them in your power, and I am only astonished that you did not avail yourself of them before you were beaten in the steeple-chase in the presence of the assembled nobility of England."

An angry flush spread over his features.

"But why did he not avail himself of his rights, and claim the hand of Lady Katharine at the ball?"

"Because he fancied the conduct of the lady was contemptuous when she gave him the reward of his triumph. You do not know Christie Kane."

"I will though."

"I hope so."

"But how shall I take the most summary and terrible vengeance?"

"Sell his property; eject him from his farm; throw him into prison," she coolly replied.

"Cousins can hate, can't they?"

"When they have cause."

"And Master Kane was imprudent enough not to perceive your beauty and accomplishments. Hey?"

The glance which the maiden cast at him made his lordship start.

"I beg your pardon."

"It is well that you do. Ellen Knowles, the grand-daughter of a Duke, will not ally herself to the tenant of a nobleman whose patent is not so old as that of her ancestor," she replied, scornfully.

"I did not mean to offend you," he said, deprecatingly.

"I hope not. The daughter of a colonel in her majesty's service need be under no apprehension of insult."

"Calm yourself—calm yourself; our interests run too much together for us to quarrel about trifles."

"It is not a trifle to insinuate that a lady has been jilted," she replied, while her eyes still flashed.

"Have it as you will. If I pursue the plan you suggest, will the spirit of the fellow be crushed, *aye, crushed*," he said, fiercely.

"Doubtful; but you may tame him."

"I'll try; *won't* I try?"

"Hark you, my Lord Melville; in all that you do, have a care

6*

that you mention not my name, either to Christie Kane or to his mother. D'ye hear?"

A gleam of triumph shot across the features of Lord Melville. It as much as said—"And so, Miss, I have *you* in my power, as well as your cousin."

"Not a word, upon the honor of a gentleman," was the audible response.

"The programme is, to sell him out, turn him out, and lock him up?"

"Precisely so; you have expressed it laconically, and well."

"Immediately?"

"At once."

"Very well."

"That satisfies you?"

"It does; so you do not falter."

"Falter!" and he laughed sardonically.

"He will be locked up in a week?"

"In four days."

"You will not relent?"

"Never! why?"

"Because weakness is a family failing. You know your great aunt in the matter of the footman—"

"Hell and damnation! am I to be insulted thus. You shall pay for the taunt," and he dashed from the house.

Ellen Knowles watched him from the window, with something like grim satisfaction, as he threw himself upon his horse and rode furiously away.

An officer, accompanied by the steward of the Momlow estate, levied upon the property of Christie Kane. He regretted the loss of all less than the sale of Surrey; though his grief was not so apparent as Phelim Savor's, who felt a simple, but earnest attachment for the horse.

"Sure yez will not be afther layding away bootiful Surrey, will yez?"

"Surrey must be sold, unless you have the money to pay the arrearages with," replied the steward.

Phelim thrust his hands where his pockets ought to be, but they were long since worn out by similar attempts, *unavailing* attempts, to find there some of the likenesses of her majesty stamped upon the coin of the realm.

"Divil a ha'porth hiv I at all, at all; bad luck to me extravagant habits, that could not save up anough to kape this noble baste n the family."

The extravagance of Mr. Savor consisted in spending the matter of eleven pence half-penny, for tobacco; the total amount of his earning for the last eight months.

"Have you the funds at hand?" asked the officer with a professional leer.

"No, nor at mouth, nayther, where yer honor kapes sich gintlemanly and witty remarks."

"Better let Phelim alone," said the steward.

"Ugh," grunted the officer.

Phelim seated himself upon a hen-coop, and eyed the officer as he took a list of the personal property belonging to Christie Kane.

"I hope your honor won't forget anything," said Phelim.

"If there is any probability, you will oblige us by mentioning it," responded the steward.

"Yez honor may rayly upon me fedelity," said Mr. Savor, as, filled with the importance of the trust, he rose from the hen-coop, and assumed a position more in accordance with his new responsibilities, upon the fence, where he scraped together his sandy hair in front, and set his crownless hat perpendicularly thereon. For it was the practice of Mr. Savor to place his dilapidated beaver uphis head in a slanting direction, so as to protect his cranium from the sun or rain, only when he felt like repining at the ills of fortune. But when, as at the present moment, he felt called upon to exhibit all his importance as a responsible human being, he bid defiance to the scorching rays of the sun, which found an unobstructed passage to the red covering of his skull. The hat to which allusion has been made with a respect commensurate with its venerable age, was the sole article of the kind belonging to Phelim Savor. In justice, however, to that gentleman, it is proper to add, that this fact was owing to the sparseness of her majesty's handsome likeness in the custody of Mr. Savor. Though, had he been more favored by fortune in that regard, it is doubtful whether he would have deemed it consistent with his principles to become the owner of two hats; for, in his estimation, nothing could be more dishonorable than to carry two faces under one hat, a condition of things that he found it difficult to distinguish from one face under two hats.

"Yer honor wont forget the speckled pig?"

"No."

"And the big rooster?"

"No." The officer continued with his memorandum.

"Perhaps yer honor can make something out of yon oold hen, for nayther I nor the rooster—"

"You are becoming trouble—" interrupted the steward.

"Not in the laist," interrupted Phelim. "I'm a gintleman now, and am intirely at yer disposal, fur yez hiv livied on ivery tool upon the farm. Divil a thing hiv yez left, excipt mesel, and yez had better take me, for the holy St. Pathrick only knows how I am to live now."

"Why, if you are a gentleman, as you say, you can live without work."

"Without money?"

"Yes; by your wits," said the officer.

"Its meself is afeared the capital would not ba profitable, as yez have found the invistment yaldes small profits."

"Ugh!" grunted her majesty's representative.

"Yon is the billy-goat; his riverence, maister Scrimpton, the Apiscopalian minister, would giv yez the matter of one pound ten for that billy-goat."

"What for?"

"Tul make his riverence a wig, or a goaty one, for he niver

passes this way that he don't stop and cast invious eyes at that same billy-goat."

"What would you sell your wit for?" asked the constable.

"If it was markitable yer honor ought to buy it."

"Why?"

"Bekase blissid Ireland is not frayer of snakes thin yer honor is of that same."

"Ugh!"

"There's the skeleton of the old cow, as died last summer, in the lot beyant. It's in a good state of preservation; prehaps yer honor can make something out of that; though she niver was much of a milker in her life-time. Some people can raise the dead, they say. Perhaps yer honor is one of thim."

"No; but I'll tell yez (irreverently imitating Phelim's 'rich Irish brogue') what I can do. It's mesell that can take every bit of skin from the back of yez," said the enraged officer.

Mr. Savor placed the fence between the constable and himself.

"Be vartue of yez office, money is raised, and I hope yez will not consider it offensive whin I supposed the skeleton of the old cow beyant might be raised likewise. As nothing is too low for yer honor to do, yez might try an expiriment on the skeleton of the old cow; it might help you to make up arrareages, ba rayson of which the Duke of Sunderland might not lose a hayperth of his rent. Shall I show yer honor where the skeleton——"

Phelim was not permitted to conclude the sentence, for the officer, dropping his memorandum, sprang over the fence. Mr. Savor, conscious that his body would suffer in the hands of the officer in his present mood, departed with great vivacity. They were both fleet of foot, and, consequently, made foot-prints rapidly across the potato patch, in the direction of the wheat field. Phelim's hat-crown gathered so much wind in his flight that it blew off. He had a partiality for that hat, imperfect as it was, and he turned to pick it up; but the constable applied his foot to it with so much vigor that it sailed through the air with the addition of another hole in its already imperfect proportions.

"Hiv yez no riverence for a man's bayver?" he cried, indignantly, as he confronted the officer.

"Take that, and see," replied the constable, as he disrespectfully punched Mr. Savor's ribs with his fist.

Phelim acknowledged the blow with a grunt. Offended by such unwarrantable familiarities, and having an indistinct idea that the present proceeding of the constable was not fully authorized under the power to make a levy, and conscious of having aided justice instead of obstructing her mission, in so far as making suggestions as to additional articles to be levied upon, including the skeleton, the pig, and the billy-goat were concerned, he assumed the reserved right of an English subject to defend himself.

"It's a bootiful officer yez are not to know that a man is protected in his castle. And, bad luck tull yez, don't yer say me hat is all the castle I hiv? Begorro, I'll tache yez yer duty ony how."

Saying which, Phelim seized the hat of the constable, and, muttering that "thim haythinish officers always have other castles except their bayvers," proceeded to jam the hat down over the eyes and ears of the constable, where he held it with determined vigor.

"Yez may tramp about as much as yer plaze, fur it's yer own prates yer spileing."

"Let go—let go!" gasped the constable, from within the hat.

"Acting in silf-defince."

"Let go, or I'll have you transported."

"It's transported I am already wid amusement at the capers yer honor is cutting."

The steward now advanced to the assistance of the officer. Phelim waited until he was within a few yards, and then giving the hat one more vigorous thrust downwards, made with renewed vivacity for the wheat field, much strengthened and gratified in the inner man by the infliction of justice, after his own peculiar fashion, upon the executor of the law.

Every thing belonging to Christie Kane was sold, and he expected every moment would witness his own arrest and the ejection of his mother into the highway. Overwhelmed with anxiety, less on his own than her account, he welcomed the gentle and confiding Ellen Knowles as she entered the little parlor, where he was reclining upon the sofa.

She looked at him with tearful eyes.

"You see, Ellen, fate is busy."

"I do, I do. But cannot its more fatal decrees be revoked?"

"How?" inquired Christie.

"By soliciting the Duke of Sunderland to arrest these proceedings. I do not believe he is aware of what his son is doing."

"I would not follow your advice if by doing so I could save my life," said Christie, sternly.

"I hope I have not offended you, Christie," she replied, sadly. "I was only prompted to make the suggestion by the interest I feel in your welfare."

"I am sure you were not, dear Ellen. Do not remember my rudeness; I am not conscious of what I say."

He took her hand and pressed it in his own.

A triumphant expression flashed across her features; but in a moment they resumed a pensive cast.

"What *will* you do, cousin Christie," she asked, imploringly.

"Meet the reverses of fortune with a manly bearing."

"But how far can you be affected by the malevolence of Lord Melville?"

"To the extent of being thrown into prison."

He thought the beautiful girl shuddered as she turned away her head.

"What! in free, enlightened England, a man, actuated by the vilest motives, to control the liberty of a freeman; to make him tremble at his approach; to thrust him into prison; to keep him there so long as his vindictive passions remain unappeased; and all because a small matter of pounds, shillings, and pence—the dross of earth, the root of all evil—remains unadjusted between them?"

"Even so, dear Ellen," replied Christie, grateful for the words, and the warm blood that mantled her cheek as she spoke.

"And you think he will thrust you, *you*, my dear cousin, into jail."

"There is not a doubt of it."

"Why do you not foil his malice by fleeing?" she inquired, while a peculiar expression crossed her features.

"Because I am an Englishman, and scorn flight."

The maiden seemed to breathe more easily.

"Can I do nothing for you, Christie?"

He thought for a moment it was strange she did not ask if her father could do nothing, but he dismissed the thought as unworthy of himself and his gentle sympathizing cousin. She rose to take her leave.

"I fear we may not meet again, soon," she said, while tears filled her eyes. His heart was touched by her solicitude for his welfare, and he walked by her side, with her soft hand resting upon his arm, as she proceeded homewand.

The hour was propitious for love. The light of day was gracefully yielding its scepter to the sway of night, through the melting agency of twilight. Upon the mellow air floated the song of the nightingale, that companion of lovers, and upon the scene stole the soothing influence of melody and affection.

The following night Christie Kane slept within the damp walls of a prison.

The sceptre of England was still swayed by a firm, though a female hand; the world continued to roll through space under the guidance of omnipotent power, and these two facts, the most important in the estimation of the English aristocracy, that divine goodness could bestow, still rendered them deaf alike to social wrongs and political rights; so far, at least, as the humbler portion of the population of the British empire was concerned. The earth will still roll on, and England will still be governed by the strong arms and feeble minds of hereditary sovereigns, until the people, roused to a sense of their inherent rights, assume the prerogatives which the God of nature placed under their control. Till then labor in the cause of *foreign* philanthropy, ye benevolent aristocracy of the British Empire; until then, ye stolid, slumbering subjects of despotism, present your willing limbs to the lash of your task-masters, until the *scourge* awakens you to a sense of your wrongs, for nothing else will!

CHAPTER XIII.

"O, gentle sound,—how sweetly did they fall
In broken murmurs, like a melody
From lips, that waiting long on loving hearts,
Had learned to murmur like them."—SIMMS.

KATHARINE MONTAGUE proceeded at an early hour upon her accustomed visit to her father's tenantry. The sky was cloudless, the air was balmy and fragrant, the sun was only brightening the tree-tops with his golden rays, for he had not yet kissed away the dew, those tear-drops shed by night for the loss of day.

Her spirits were light, for she felt a consciousness of doing good. It was one of the chief attractions of this beautiful girl that her heart thrilled with tenderness in the presence of suffering. She daily visited the old, infirm, and unfortunate, and her presence was always greeted with exclamations of gratitude.

She observed a person approaching, whom she recognized as the serving-man of Christie Kane. Phelim removed his crownless hat and observed with mechanical and characteristic fluency,

"Long life tul yer ladyship, and may yez bless us for many a day wid yez booty and charities."

"Thank you, Mr.——Mr.——"

"Phelim Savor, if yez plaze," he replied, pulling his red top-knot, and favoring the gravelled road with a semicircular scrape with his right foot.

"Phelim Savor; a pleasant name. And where are you going, Mr. Savor?"

"Its mesel' don't know that same."

"Do not know where you are going?"

"Indade it's the truth. I'm like a dismantled ship on her beam eends, widout compass, rudder, or pilot, as boatswain McScudder used to say."

"Have you left the service of Christie Kane, for methinks you were his retainer?"

"Maister Christie, God bliss him, has no sarvice now, and he is under a retainer himsilf."

"What do you mean?"

"He's in jail."

"In jail? What crime has he committed?"

"He has been tried and found guilty of the hainus offince of baing poor."

"You are merry, Mr. Savor."

"Troth I fear I shall niver be that again," he replied sadly.

"Who caused him to be imprisoned?"

"Lord Melville, of koorse."

"Why of course?"

"Bekase it was wid his horse, yer ladyship bate his lordship in the race, at the time he made a small expiriment in the lake fernenst the castle."

"Did Christie Kane boast of that?" she asked quickly.

"Divil a word, begging yer ladyship's pardon for mentioning the name of that unpopular gintleman. I was tould it by the people at the castle."

"Was that the only cause for ill will that Christie Kane has given his lordship?"

"Sure yez hiv'ent forgot the steeple chase. Didn't me masther win the prize from yiz bootiful hand, whin Lord Melville would hiv died fur it, as, indade, would onybody else," said Phelim enthusiastically.

A blush mantled Katharine Montague's cheek at the warm language of her humble admirer.

"And his mother; I believe his mother is living?"

"Since her son's arrest, she's gone to her sister's, Mrs. Knowles."

"And is Ellen Knowles a cousin of Christie Kane's?"

"She bes that same."

"'And I suppose they are friends of each other?"

"I don't know, but I should think they would be, for she is very bootiful as well as yersel."

"Yes, she is very handsome," replied Katharine, thoughtfully.

"Yez say she is constantly at my master's house; at laist was a condolin wid him upon his thrials and misfortins."

"Undoubtedly," she replied tapping the mane of her horse with her riding whip. "And the dapple gray is to be sold?"

"To-morrow."

"What is to become of you, now?"

"I don't know. I've niver thought much how to get along in the world, for yez say Master Christie has always done me thinking."

"You have no home?"

"Niver a bit. But I spose the world owes me a living onyhow; or at least it ought to; fur I had no choice whether I would come into it or no; and the blessed praists say I have no choice whether I will go out of it or no."

Katherine Montague took some gold pieces from her purse.

"Take this money; purchase a suit of the Montague livery, and inquire for me, at the castle."

"May the Almighty Powers forever bless your ladyship," said Phelim Savor, fervently, as he fell upon his knees, and pressed the border of her riding-dress to his lips. "Och! that iver I should be so blissid! Sure, yer ladyship will injure the Bank of England, by giving me sich enormous sums!" And Phelim gazed upon his wealth as if its possession materially interfered with the financial arrangements of the government.

"If it plaze yer ladyship, may I davote the rist of this, afther purchasing the suit, to the payment of Master Christie's debts, and to buying him something to ate? for it's nothing but very poor bread and water he'll be afther getting, in that same prison, where he is confined. If you knew what a kind, good, gentlemanly master he always wer tul me, I'm *sure* yez would not refuse."

"Do with it as you please," she replied, as she gave her horse the rein.

Phelim watched her receding form with emotions of gratitude.

"It's the blissed praistes would think me devotion for that bootiful creature belonged to thim, but may the holy St. Pathrick help me, for I niver expect to fale sich gratitude for mortal man, be he ten times a praiste, as I feel for that young lady. But the divil a word will I mention about it, the next time I confess, to Father McQuodling. All this goold, too, besides taking me into her service. I'll be damned if Father McQuodling mai'nt expict a long time afore he'll make me riverence him tul the same extent as I do yon lady. Divil a bet the wiser will his riverence ba, though I dare say his riverence—heaven pardon me—do'nt ravale all his villanous thoughts to the Almighty; and why should he expect poor divils to make a clean breast of it if the clergy do not. It's mesel wouldent carry two faces under one hat, if I had the right, tul the same extint, as the praistes, to confess directly to the Supprame Being, and ask blessings amadently from him, widdout the intervention of Father McQuodling."

Reflecting upon the superior advantages of Father McQuodling, in the matter of a direct spiritual intercourse with Omnipotence, which, in his opinion, was denied to laymen, counting over and over again the gold pieces, and regretting the dilapidated condition of his pockets, now that, for the first time, during their existence, he was possessed of something to make them "fale comfortable;" and expressing the liveliest satisfaction, in broken soliloquies, at the generosity of Lady Katharine Montague, Phelim Savor sought for one of those useful and highly respectable individuals, known as drapers and tailors.

Christie Kane occupied a narrow cell in the county jail. It was scarcely three steps in length, and only wide enough for a foul berth, and room to stand. It was one of the tier of cells under ground—far under ground—being the third tier from the surface of the earth. The merciful law-makers thinking all persons who cannot pay their debts, no better than fossil remains, whom to put out of sight were as much a duty as to bury the dead.

It was not enough, in this charitable and wise estimation, to restrain the debtor of his liberty; to withdraw him, as something that might contaminate society, from its presence; to put him aside as a man would old furniture; to conceal him from public observation, as the hypocritical do their vices. All this would not suffice. He must be *punished* for his misfortunes; for, what right had he to be poor? If tightness in the money market resulted in failure, the victim should have known what was to happen. If the wheat crop failed, he should have sown rye; if oats were blighted, he ought to have planted more potatoes. Not being as wise as omnipotence, he must be well punished. As thoroughly, at least, as the most depraved villain in the land, because thieves and blacklegs occupied adjoining cells. But there is one excuse for the creditor; he will obtain his money so much sooner by keeping the debtor in prison! He can raise such quantities of grain from the productive soil of the stone floor; his commercial pursuits will prove so profitable, beneath the earth, because his ships can tack or run before the wind upon the moisture of the walls; and, laden with the wealth of the Indies, can sail through the channel of darkness which fills the aperture of the door. If the prisoner is a poet, the vanities of the world will not become a rival to the spirit of song with which his soul must be inspired. He will unravel whole acres of harrowing poetry of the Byronic description, (or what is the same, in its effect, whole acres of poetry, the language of which has been harrowed with a painful disregard for the rules of Lindlay Murray and Noah Webster) which those persons who love to have their feelings wrought up to the most intense pitch of agony and despair, may sigh and weep over to their heart's content.

The jailor turned the key and the ponderous door swung upon its hinges—not *rusty* hinges, as the architect of that renowned "solitary horseman" delights in having it, but plain, unpretending, unromantic hinges, that frequent use had kept free from rust, and a piece of mouldy bread and a mug of unsavory water, which the owner of one of Ham's descendants would think food too mean for a slave, were placed upon the floor.

The jailor scowled at his prisoner as if he thought it a special exhibition of divine mercy that he was allowed to live.

"Can't pay your debts, hey?" he said, in accents strongly emphasized by disgust.

Christie Kane made no reply.

"Proud, too. I should jist like to know what a *poor* man has to do with pride?"

"You estimate the worth of a human being by the amount of money he possesses?"

"Certainly; by what other rule can he be weighed?" said the jailor, with a look of surprise.

"I am ignorant enough to suppose that moral and intellectual qualities may be entitled to some consideration."

"You *are* ignorant if you can believe such folly. Why, sir, mind will soon kick the beam in the scale with money," replied the man of keys, looking complacently at those instruments of power.

Christie Kane felt the force of his remark, and it lessened the value of human nature several degrees in his estimation.

"Do you hear me?" demanded the keeper savagely.

"I do."

"Well, you will see the truth on't, afore you leave these walls. For the mind you boast of will rust, and your limbs will rot, here, *here*, unless you are liberated by money."

"At all events, as a slight compensation for the loss of liberty, you ought to bring me food more inviting than these crusts," said Christie, good humoredly.

"The crusts to-morrow shall be like rocks, and the water green, *dark* green, if I can find it," replied the earthly St. Peter, shaking his keys.

"You do not approve a free expression of opinion, my worthy friend?"

"Look ye, my precious cove, Herrick Hellkirk calls no man friend who can't pay his debts, and for your impertinence in calling me such, I shall shorten your allowance of food, and I'll begin by taking this away."

"You will only incur the risk of removal, Mr. Hellkirk, for I shall proclaim your villainy."

"Ha! ha! ha! Ho! ho! ho! That's too good, by God! it is. Who will believe you when I pronounce it a lie, a damned wilful and malicious lie! Look-a-heah!" he added fiercely; "Who will be the wiser if I do not visit the cell for a week, after I have knocked you down with this bunch of keys and gagged you?"

"Monster!"

"It would not be the first time I've done it, and if you dare to look at me thus, may I be eternally damned if it shall be the last," he said, in a low savage tone.

Christie Kane folded his arms and gazed at the other with an overwhelming expression of contempt upon his features. The jailor sprang upon him with the fury of a demon. The attack was unexpected, and Kane was hurled to the ground by the herculean strength of the jailor. His head came violently in contact with the stone floor, and he lay there motionless. The faint moans that escaped him did not penetrate to the outer air, and he was gagged and bound. The face of the jailor gleamed with the fierceness of a tiger as he twisted the rope which he had brought with him between the teeth of his victim.

"Now, vagabond, let us see how long you will preserve your haughty bearing. The poor to threaten! Bah! Lord Mellville will pay well for this." And kicking the unconscious body with his heavy boot, he withdrew from the cell and locked the door.

Christie Kane remained a long time upon the damp floor, and when at last awakened to a consciousness of his situation, the cold sweat stood upon his forehead, for the terrible conviction flashed upon his mind that he was buried alive.

With great difficulty he rose from the floor. His head swam round, and he staggered against the wall. At last he managed to roll into his berth, where he lay overcome by the most painful reflections. The rope was drawn so tightly across his mouth that it gave him excessive pain, and the cord which confined his arms behind him cut into the flesh and stopped the circulation of his blood. The designs of the jailor were apparent. He was to be thus confined until so exhausted, by hunger and suffering, that his cries could not be heard, when the cords would be removed, and his death attributed to general debility, brought on by unwholesome air, want of exercise, and the fretting of a proud spirit at confinement. There would, in the careless inquisition held upon his body, be no clue to murder most foul.

He looked upon the four walls as a living tomb—the portals of that unheralded burial, which would soon follow. It is terrible for the young to die; to yield the realities of earth for the untraveled future. But to die the most lingering and painful death that human ingenuity could invent; to linger in the grasp of the fell destroyer as he gradually tightened his grasp upon the suffering flesh, without the cheering presence of affection, was too horrible! He was unsustained by hope, and he prepared to meet death with what resignation a manly spirit could summon to his aid.

His mother had, for the last few weeks, assumed a stern and unforgiving manner towards him, which he attributed to a failure upon his part to comply with the request, which she had often made, to solicit the hand of Ellen Knowles in marriage. When he offered his hand at parting, Mrs. Kane obstinately declined to take it, scornfully asserting that he deserved his fate for refusing to return the love of one who adored him, and by whose assistance alone he could effect his release from prison. He had no expectation that his mother would interest herself so far in his fate as even to desire an interview, until he was sufficiently humbled in her estimation. Of Col. Knowles he could expect nothing, for he had always disliked him. And Ellen, gentle, loving Ellen, what could she accomplish? He had, with the exception of Phelim and his brother Robert, (neither of whom could assist him,) no other friend among all the members of the human family, who would turn upon his heel to do him a favor. From the philanthropists, who direct their exertions exclusively to foreign sufferings, he had no hope. As an Englishman, he had claims upon them. He was a neighbor, and charity ought to begin at home. But they could not withdraw their gaze from the United States.

It was strange, too, for their conduct strikingly contrasted with that of many distinguished individuals, whose pretensions are properly very high, and especially that of the senior partner of the greatest American publishing house, whose native Americanism is so intensely patriotic, that it can tolerate nothing foreign, except the unpurchased works of English authors, for which he is supposed to have a partiality so strong that his honesty has found it too powerful for successful resistance; a slight, yet *profitable*, deviation from the path of rectitude, which it is presumed he palliates upon the ground that a moderate amount of thieving, in that regard, is allowable, in consideration of the fidelity with which he maintains the balance of his native American principles (?) the sale of which don't pay.

The weary hours rolled on, uncounted by Christie Kane, for no ray of the sun ever penetrated his dark and silent abode. And there he lay, without the power of motion; the image of the Almighty, suffering the penalty of the law authorizing imprisonment for debt—a law that would have disgraced the statute-book of Draco, and which should be consigned to irretrievable oblivion by every legislative body on earth, whose members aspire to a greater elevation in the scale of civilization than the Hottentots can boast.

His sufferings became intolerable. The blood could not be thrown from his heart to the extremities of his arms, and his hands became cold as ice.

He fancied so much of his body was dead, and he tried to estimate the time which must elapse before the grim monster would move his freezing hand along his limbs, until his grasp was fastened upon his vitals.

Misery proceeds at a slow pace, and days might have elapsed since he was aroused from insensibility, and he was fast sinking into a state of unconsciousness, when he thought a ray of light flashed upon the wall. He rallied his drooping spirits. Was there still hope? With eager gaze he watched the door.

The key turned in the lock, the door rolled back, and the trembling form of the jailor entered the cell, followed by the stately figure of the Earl of Rossmore.

The nobleman folded his arms, and looked first at Christie Kane and then at the jailor; the one met his gaze with a look of gratitude, and the other with the aspect of a craven-hearted coward.

"And this is the reason why you interposed so many objections to showing me hither?" said the Earl sternly.

The jailor did not reply, but his hands shook, as though they were in the grasp of dissolution.

"Release him," said Lord Rossmore.

Christie could not stand.

"Rub his limbs."

"Yes, your Lordship," and he servilely bent to the task.

"Your lordship has saved me from death," said Christie, gratefully.

"And this miscreant for transportation. Yield those keys; such a monster may not retain them an hour."

"Can you walk now?" he asked of Christie.

"I will try," and together they emerged from the bowels of the earth into the air. One victim of the disgraceful law authorizing imprisonment for debt, escaped the clutches of his persecutor, and walked the earth a freeman once more.

CHAPTER XIV.

> "How hard we strove to save her, love
> Like ours alone can tell,
> And only those know what we lost
> Who've loved the lost as well."—EASTMAN.

MRS. KANE sought employment with her needle, but the small compensation she received would not, with the pittance earned by Henry, buy food for them and pay the rent. Her landlord had already called twice, and the last time he threatened to turn her into the street, if the rent was not paid in one week. Some other plan must be adopted. She reflected long and painfully upon her prospects, and at last she could see no other way of keeping want from her fireside, but to wean her baby, and wet-nurse some other child. It was after many struggles that she brought her mind to sanction this painful alternative, but there was no other recourse. She made inquiries, and found a man whose wife had died, leaving him four children, the youngest of which was six months old. He consented to let Mrs. Kano take the child to her own house. And now commenced the disagreeable task—disagreeable to every mother who is *fond* of her offspring—of weaning the poor little fellow whom necessity had forced to yield his natural sustenance to a stranger. In no way are the distinctions of society more vividly illustrated than by the career of two infants. One, a hale rosy-cheeked girl, plainly but neatly clad, is the joy of a lowly dwelling. The father thinks of her often during the long day of toil. Her bright face interposes itself between him and the fierce rays of the sun; it wards off the rain; her breath cools him in summer, and her eyes warm him in winter. She is the angel that stands between him and the bottle. She arrests his hand when it is raised in anger, and she soothes, and guides, and controls his passions. Well, necessity forces him to send her away; it is hard, *very* hard; but they can get her wet nursed for half the money that his wife can earn by nursing some other child. The little girl is sent among strangers, to encounter neglect, sickness, and death. Its mother, always under the eye of her foster child's parents, cannot, if she would, neglect her duties; and the boy thrives, and coos, and doubles up his chubby hands, as if he could successfully battle with life. And as she bends over her new charge, the tears fall upon his cheek; he looks up wonderingly, for he don't know that the price of his health and happiness, is the cold, silent form that was locked up a few days before in the ground; never more to gladden the hearts of its parents by its winning smile, never more to lay its cheek but upon the bosom of its mother earth.

Mary Kane proceeded to execute her plans, when they were once matured, with as much resolution as she could command. When the child tasted the bitter substance upon her bosom, he drew, at first, angrily away. It was his first taste of life's bitter experience. For hours he lay in the cradle with his large round black eyes riveted upon her countenance, as though his wee bit of a brain was trying to find some reason why his mother, always so kind before, now treated him so cruelly. Wearied out at last, he fell into an uneasy slumber, from which he often awoke, crying as if his heart would break. And his mother wept, too, burning tears, yet necessity still urged her on. At length he turned his eyes with a look of disgust towards the sweetened drink prepared for him, and with a little groan, swallowed it. Frank Tot was weaned, and now she took the motherless stranger to her bosom. She was kind to him, for she thought of her own baby placed, as this helpless thing was, among strangers. No female but one who has known maternity, can feel that love for children which their helpless condition demands.

All her sacrifices proved unavailing; she could not pay the rent. An officer was sent to remove her into the street. It was a dark, cold, raw day in December when he came to perform his duty. The wind, clothed in fog, thrust its cold grasp into the hands and faces of all who were exposed to its rude touch. Not content with such familiarities, it pulled aside the ragged garments of the poor as if it scoffed at their sufferings; it seized hold of their nerves, and went shrieking with laughter among the houses and along the streets, because they trembled in its grasp. Even the rich and well clad shuddered at its approach, and hastening home, seated themselves by the blazing fires. The sun was going down, and he, too, expressed his dissatisfaction at the rude assaults of the wind upon the city, for he cast an indignant glance upon the clouds from his flushed countenance.

On such a night as this did the officer, accompanied by Hurdy, enter the room where Mrs. Kane and two of her children were, for Henry had not yet returned. The unhappy woman sank, overcome with terror, into her seat.

"Prepared to liquidate, madam?" he inquired, glibly, as he cocked his hat on one side, and drew a lease from among a package of papers.

"You have not come to demand the rent now?" she asked, faintly.

"I *have*, Mrs. Kane," he replied, in a voice intended to close all discussion.

"Then we are undone."

"Doubtless; I've frequently known it—bureau—to be the case —bedstead—"

"But the landlord told me I should not be molested for ten days when he was here last, and that was only three days ago."

"Very likely—straw mattrass—he ain't your landlord any longer—cradle—"

"Not my landlord?"

"No—table—"

"Who is, then?"

"Tongs—Mr. Greasebeans—"

"The manufacturer?"

"Solomon—pot—Greasebeans—"

"Oh, then, I implore you to wait. Mr. Greasebeans is rich; he is charitable; and I know he will not turn me into the street, and sell this small stock of furniture."

"Don't know—shovel—him told me an hour ago not to let you —trunk—stay here—that's all—another night."

"What *shall* I do? what *shall* I do?" exclaimed Mrs. Kane, wildly.

"Can't say," coolly replied the officer.

"Mrs. Kane, I can furnish you with an apartment until you can find another," said Hurdy, with a sinister expression upon his features.

"Monster! do you think Mary Kane is sunk so low as to receive a favor from the brute who kidnapped her husband?" said Mrs. Kane, indignantly.

"Oh, very well; we shall see how long you will carry yourself so bravely, my pretty dame," said the Ogre, scornfully.

At this moment Henry Kane entered the room. His features were attenuated; his lips were blue, and his thin form trembled with the cold. But his strength seemed to return as he saw the officer and Hurdy.

"Ma, that bad man has made you cry."

Mrs. Kane only wept the more bitterly.

"Well, youngster, what have you to say why your mother should not be ejected by Solomon Greasebeans, your landlord."

"Mr. Greasebeans?"

"Yes."

"A great deal to say. Mr. Greasebeans won't let you act so cruelly, for he is president of a charitable society."

"Which will benefit you about as much as it will me. But, come, I can't dally here, so march out."

"Mr. Officer, we shall freeze to death in the streets to-night. If it was summer, we could all sleep under the tree near the park, for the leaves would keep off the dew. But now there are no leaves on the tree; the limbs are all covered with icicles, and the cold wind makes the branches creak and groan. Poor Frank Tot woulddent live there till morning, Mr. Officer. Now pray think, if your boys and girls should be turned into the street to-night, what would you say?"

"I would say it was a d——d rascally, unfeeling business," exclaimed the officer, whose eyes had moistened during the appeal of Henry Kane.

"Better think of what Mr. Greasebeans will say," whispered Hurdy.

"What can I do?" said the officer.

"Let us remain here until morning, and I will then go and see Mr. Greasebeans," said Henry.

"Perform your duty, or I willl tell Mr. Greasebeans to-night," remarked Hurdy, with rage imprinted upon his countenance.

"You see I cannot let you remain, however much I may desire it," replied the officer, sheltering himself, as is customary with his class, under the mantle of delegated authority.

"Will you let my mother stay here one hour?" asked Henry, eagerly.

"I don't see how the law will admit of delay," said the officer.

"Certainly not," replied Hurdy, positively.

"For one hour; only for one hour," said the child, imploringly. The officer hesitated.

"Yes, I will do that much for you, my lad."

"Thank you."

Henry put on his straw hat, and moved towards the door.

"Henry, Henry, where are you going?" said his mother, anxiously.

"To see Mr. Greasebeans."

"But, my child, you will perish this cold night."

"Better for me to die, than all of us. But I shall not die. It is not more than ten blocks; I'll soon be home."

"Stay, then, let me tie this handkerchief about your ears."

She put another around his neck, and buttoning his coat up to his chin, kissed his cheek, and calling him her noble boy, bade him return soon.

"Stop, Henry," she said, as he was unclosing the door. "You have had no supper; let me give you some warm tea."

"No, ma, we must not expect the law to wait for boys to eat. I'll be back soon, though;" and he went out into the cold, stormy night. His teeth chattered, his blood receded to his heart, and his fingers became numb, as the wind pierced his thin clothing, and shook the rim of his straw hat, as if in derision at its unseasonable appearance; still he pressed onward. His mind dwelt not upon the cutting storm, as it rudely seized him, and made his form stagger beneath its grasp. He only thought of his mother, Dolly, and Frank Tot, and the little stranger, too, who was intrusted to their charge. In imagination, he saw her clasp the two babies to her bosom, and weep, because there was not sufficient warmth to keep their limbs from stiffening. There was a swelling in his throat, and he hurried onwards.

"I shall be too late—I *know* I shall be too late," he exclaimed, redoubling his speed.

While he was hurrying in the direction of Mr. Greasebeans' mansion-house, we will introduce the reader within the walls of that building.

Mr. and Mrs. Solomon Greasebeans had yielded to the solicitations of their son and daughter, and had consented to give them a party. Indeed, as they sat by their cheerful fire on the evening before their consent was announced, Mrs. G. suggested to her husband, that it was time, in her opinion, to make an exhibition of their furniture, and to give Seraphina an opportunity of displaying her diamonds. And Marcian, too, required some relaxation, for he had become paler, she thought, than usual, the last week, Which paleness was in fact attributable to the quantity of sweetmeats that remarkable individual was in the daily habit of consuming, combined with the attractions of Miss Dancy Dodds, a lank, sallow-skinned maiden, who favored him with loving glances from her bilious eyes, twice a day, as they passed each other upon the street. No young man's susceptible stomach could withstand such appeals, and Marcian Greasebeans grew pale with love. Mr. Greasebeans did not know that the request of the dear children *was* unreasonable. As for exhibiting the furniture, he could see no particular necessity for doing anything of the kind; for, like all men, he thought every responsibility was discharged when he gave his check for it. It was the women, alone, who knew that then was the moment when the responsibility of making a proper exhibition of the furniture commenced. So it was agreed that Seraphina and Marcian should have a party. And now the difficult task commenced of deciding who should be invited, and who should be cut. For if the uninitiated think it is a pleasure to make out a list of our friends for the purpose of making them happy, they are most woefully mistaken. Does it not require the most intense discrimination to know whom to invite? If an invitation is extended to Miss Jones, what will Miss Smith say? If Miss Brown is cut, what will her cousin Miss White say? And if she sends a regret because Miss Brown is not invited, will not the party be a failure? *Could* a party be "a go" without the presence of Miss White? Had the tallow-chandler in the next street amassed sufficient money to make his daughter respectable? They would try and come at it as nearly as possible, by getting papa to ascertain what his balance in bank was. Had Lawyer Dibblee acquired sufficient notoriety at the bar, to prevent people asking who Miss Laura Dibblee was? Had Dinctum Dowdy withdrawn from the commercial house of Feejack and Dowdy (a house engaged extensively in the manure line) long enough to make his daughter a proper associate for Miss Greasebeans? There could be no doubt of it, if his fortune was correctly stated at one hundred thousand pounds, and not twenty-five thousand, as it was sometimes put down. Seventy-five thousand pounds would make an enormous difference in the claim of Miss Dowdy for admission into genteel society. Would it do to have the Dunlaps, who were at the head of society—that branch of society—one year ago, but who were now very considerably reduced in circumstances, owing to several heavy losses? Did the Longs dress well enough?—Of their respectability there could be no doubt. Would the splendid diamonds of Mrs. Baxter obliterate the recollection of the slight *faux-pas* that was associated with the name of Maj. Duke, in the life-time of the excellent but now defunct William Henry Baxter? Could saddlers, under *any* circumstances, be requested to come? Were merchant tailors admissible? If not, were *tailleurs?* Should retail merchants be considered presentable, and if so, would it do to invite wholesale grocers? Would it be possible to induce Lord Snizzle to "drop in" for a few minutes, just to give an air of fashion to the entertainment, and make the Durgins burst with envy? He had ogled Miss Greasebeans with impertinent condescension at Bath, for one whole evening, when her dress was worn so low in the neck as to make a liberal display of her really very fine bust. And twice he had sweetly addressed her in the street, by raising his hat. But this was not all. He had, at Brighton, so far stooped from his lofty position, as to magnetize her—his lordship *did* sometimes condescend to magnetize plebeians, provided they were good-looking, and young; for he had been heard to say, that, although he did occasionally favor ladies who had arrived at the matronly age of thirty, with a few sparks of magnetic fire, yet it was only in obedience to their imploring glances, and the benevolence of his heart, as he not only found, after they had arrived at the age of thirty, that their nerves were not so sensitive to the touch, but that in several instances he had found them decidedly tough; some few of them having, in addition thereto, favored him with very bad breath. A most unfeeling remark, which, having gained credence, prevented any further annoyance from females who had numbered thirty years of age, especially whose breath was not fragrant. It was supposed Lord Snizzle had a preference for young and blooming maidens, because it was a more pleasant operation to magnetize them; and therefore, among the plans that were suggested for the purpose of inducing him to "drop in" for a few moments, on the night of the party, was to let him take a few "innocent liberties" with Seraphina, as that was known, in certain cases, to have a magical effect. Of course such a proceeding would alone be admissible in the case of a lord; the social position of the party, thus to be favored, making all the difference imaginable. It was considered indispensable, also, to secure the attendance of Lady Madaline Flouncy, the natural daughter of the late Earl of Dumpy. It is true she was not born in wedlock, but what of that? Did not the blood of an earl flow in her veins? And what offspring of matrimony, among the middle classes, could claim equality with her? The fame of her mother was dishonored, but then her father was a belted earl, and besides she was ENORMOUSLY rich, and that, of itself, was enough to elevate her to any conceivable height, above the less favored, though decidedly more respectable, plebeians of the town.

These and a hundred other considerations were perpetually suggesting themselves, not only to Marcian and Seraphina, but to Mr. and Mrs. Solomon Greasebeans. At last every obstacle was surmounted, and their plans were matured; a consummation which was announced in the following letter from Seraphina to her bosom friend Henrietta Maria Flukins.

"No. 10 Dumpy Court.

Darlingest Henrietta Maria Flukins. Dear Friend.

I intimated to you somewhat perspicuously in my last, that papa and mama had yielded to my and Marcian's entreaties to give us a blow-out, in honor of my twentieth birth-day. *Seventeenth* birth-day as we tell the world, but in confidence, it is the twentieth. I told ma it was the most unreasonablest thing in the world not to give me a party until four years after I had completed my heducation, and she said she thought so too. So we *are* to hev a blow-out. It is to be a particular affair, very. We hev maid up our minds to cut all but the rich, and consequentially, respectable, of our friends, because ma says the house of Greasebeans, Snodgrass & Co. is looking up. What do you think, Henrietta Maria Flukins? I'll tell you. I'm all but *positive* Lord Snizzle will honor us with his presence!! Them hateful Smithers said last week, after I had boasted that his lordship would drop in at our party, that Lord Snizzle was not much thought of among the best society of London, he was so—I forget the word, it was something like them things that the farmer folks use when they gether hay—oh, I hev it—so *rakish*. I didn't know what that meant until I looked at the dicshonary. But ma said that is not considered an objection to a lord. So I said last night, loud enough for the Smithers to hear me, *I* can tell you, that Lord Snizzle didn't bestow his attentions upon some people. They said it "was a fact, for he was not permitted by some persons to look at them when their veils were up." I replied we—Lord Snizzle and myself—*despises* common vulgar folks like some I could mention, and they said their "contempt was supremest for both me *and* Snizzle." Snizzle! Think of calling him Snizzle! without the alliteration of *Lord!* Contempt for Snizzle! *Lord* Snizzle! Eldest son of the Duke of Minkey. Won't he feel unhappy when he learns in what estimation he is held by the Smithers? For I shall tell him every word they said about him, it will make him so grateful, and I know they are dying to get him into their house.

We shall have a grand affair. Pa says it will require several things to make people believe we are the cream of fashion, and the leaders of quality. *Fust*, we must have at least twenty musicioners. *Second*, it is indispensably necessary to have Mr. Brown to open the carriag-odoors and whistle so that the servant may open the hall-door; for he says it absolutely requires Brown's presence to give the affair a distingee—as the French say—appearance, and without him everybody will think us nobodys. I told pa I didn't see how sich a fat, greasy-looking fellow could make us fishionable, but he said Brown opened the carriage-doors of the Spradlins, and Spriggins, the Jones, and Rimes, which you see was conclusive. *Third*, the world judges of your claims by the quantity of bokays you can muster, and so he has sent to all the florists in London and Liverpool for all the bokays they can make. Ma told him the guests would think a great deal more of the party, and praise it ever so warmly if they had plenty of good things to eat, and that, too, without being crowded, for when they were crowded and jostled they got their brussels up, like hogs. So we are to have a table loaded down with every thing nice. Pa said he should be forced to give a little less to the abolition cause at the next meeting; which he can safely do, for he has got his name up for being liberal. He thinks what he can save in that way, and by reducing the wages of his operatives, and being very severe upon his tenants here and in the country, he can afford to give what will be called a *magnificent* entertainment.

But you can judge for yourself, as you will not fail to be present. And you must—excuse me for the liberty—dear Henrietta Maria Flukins—get a splendid dress and wear *all* your diamonds. We have given out that it will be a grand affair, so that the ladies will dress superficially, and in good taste, for costly dresses go half way to make up a splendid party.

As ever thine, till death, and afterwards through my mortal existence

Dear Henrietta Maria Flukins

Thy friend

Seraphina Greasebeans.

P. S. Dearest Henrietta Maria, I shall ask Lord Snizzle if he will consent to be introduced to you, as my *per*ticular friend; which I am sure he will, if you wear your dress modestly, invitingly low in the neck.

Thine

Seraph. G.

N. B. P. S. Don't hint anything about the *low neck dresses* to the Membertons; if you do, his lordship will be too permiskus in his devotions.

Till death

S. G. beans."

After a world of anxiety and preparation, the evening of the party arrived. Mrs. and Miss Greasebeans stood in the front parlor, near the door, looking quite fatigued, but receiving their guests as they poured in, with the sweetest smiles imaginable, as if the particular period of time when each individual was presented, constituted, by many thrills of pleasure, the happiest moments of their whole lives. Not that all were received with the same bend of the neck, or welcomed with the same expressions. Still the condescension which was exhibited to one, and the fawning sycophancy observed to another, seemed to give them equal joy. It was really

affecting to remark how winningly Seraphina displayed a charming regard for maternal example; for if Mrs. Greasebeans seized the right hand of a new comer in both her own, as if one could not express the overflowing effusions of her too ardent impulses, Seraphina availed herself of the aforesaid right hand as soon as it was suffered to escape, when it passed through another pressure, significant of unbounded and irrepressible affection. If, on the contrary, a stately, yet patronizing reception only, was awarded by the mother, it was reiterated with as much precision by the daughter as if she was merely that lady's shadow.

And thus they continued bowing, and squeezing, and smirking, and smiling through two mortal hours, when the rooms were filled to an acceptable degree of suffocation; that is to say, acceptable to the Greasebeans, who, like all hosts, care very little how uncomfortable their guests may be, provided they are well jammed. It is essentially necessary that they pass through that ordeal, if the party is to be stamped as "a go." There was one drawback, however, to all this splendid exhibition of beauty, diamonds, and lace, and it caused Mrs. and Miss Greasebeans several unpleasant sensations. The most distinguished of their friends, and those who they particularly desired should be present, absented themselves, as is invariably the case; while the common people, whose absence nobody would remark, were there in full force. This fact did not escape the notice of the anxious mother and daughter.

"Ma, why don't the Tadpoles come?" whispered Seraphina, as she cast her eyes at the clock. "See, it is half-past ten, and not a Tadpole here."

"And the Rumpdings, too?"

"As I live, yes. If the Beldens *only* had stayed at home instead of the Kimpdings; but such good fortune never could be expected."

"And Lord Snizzle has not made his appearance yet."

"*Don't* I feel it, ma? but I hope my face does not proclaim my chagrin. There, that hypocritical minx, Henrietta Maria Flukins, has asked me twice to-night if I was not going to introduce her to his lordship, and with such a demure countenance, too. I am confident she knows he is not here. There, see her now, she is whispering to that ojeous Miss Twisdale, and smiling so maliciously, and she the friend of my bosom. Thank Heaven! Lord Snizzle *has* come."

And the happy maiden gave the *noble* man an exceedingly low courtesy, as he stood in the hall a few moments before ascending to the drawing-room, superciliously examining the company with the single glass that he thrust into the socket of his right eye, retaining it there by a contraction of the muscles that are located in the neighborhood of the brow and the upper region of the cheek, that was fearful to contemplate, and giving to a usually placid countenance a most malignant and sanguinary expression.

Miss Greasebeans was impaled upon any conceivable number of thorns, until he was seen descending the stair-case with that mincing gait, presumed to be so appropriate in the son of a duke. She had never imagined it possible that half an hour of precious time could be frittered away in the dressing-room by even Lord Snizzle. She was not aware that his lordship, by a frequent reference to his repeater, was making a nice calculation as to the probable time which must elapse before the splendid supper—that was, to him, the most important item in the entertainment—would be announced. It was then, with patience whittled down to the merest point, that the young lady saw him reach the hall floor. Again the eye-glass was thrust into the socket, with a painful disregard of consequences, a decent respect for the feelings of spectators, and a reckless contempt for the sympathies which the extraordinary procedure could not fail of eliciting. It was alarming to think what a horrible corpse he would make if his face should freeze in that condition; a dilemma, the mere apprehension of which will, no doubt, induce all who are in the habit of indulging in such fiendish grimaces to abandon the practice forever.

Miss Greasebeans lost sight of all her other guests, and seizing Lord Snizzle by the arm, walked back and forth between the admiring line of spectators, with as much certainty of monopolizing universal admiration, as Mr. and Mrs. Gimcrack did, while they were dancing the mazurka on the night of their wedding, in pursuance of the heraldic announcement that the company would yield a sufficient space, while Mr. and Mrs. Gimcrack, the bride and bridegroom, performed the dance aforesaid: a performance which the reader is assured did actually take place.

The attention of Miss Greasebeans was absorbed by his lordship; and all the intimation she gave of there being any other person in the room was in side-long, spiteful glances at Henrietta Maria Flu kins. Not that his lordship indulged much in conversation, for the Cockney nobility are sometimes extremely taciturn, which those gifted with rare colloquial powers have maliciously attributed to a want of ideas: an opinion that no doubt had its origin in the envy inspired by a consciousness of occupying a lower stratum in the social organization.

Several times Henrietta Maria Flukins threw herself in the way of an introduction so significantly, that Seraphina was forced to give a negative shake of the head, intimating thereby that Lord Snizzle might not wish to extend his list of acquaintances. But his lordship did not twist his face into diabolical contortions for nothing. The remarkably fine bust of Miss Flukins was "modestly, invitingly" displayed, in pursuance of Miss Greasebeans' suggestion; and every time the *noble* man passed her, the stare with which he honored her was materially prolonged. That young lady was at a loss to divine his intentions. At one moment she judged, from the shadows upon his convulsed physiognomy, that he was in the act of addressing her, like Niobe, with tears, for she had noticed similar grimaces upon the face of her little brother, Sydenham, previous to an explosion; but while she was in the act of getting her handkerchief and her sympathies ready for the catastrophe, the muscles seemed to contract, the face assumed a fierce expression, as if he contemplated a violent assault upon her person: a revulsion partly attributable to the gas-light, and somewhat to a spasmodic effort necessary to retain the eye-glass in its position. As she was timidly watching the transition, the muscles of the brow and cheek suddenly collapsed, and the eye-glass fell to his waistband.

"Demmed foine queter that; who 's she?"

"Your lordship is kind to ask about any of my company," replied Seraphina, simperingly, as she permitted more of her precious weight to rest upon his arm—thus revealing, as a counterpoise to the physical attraction of Henrietta Maria Flukins, what Sir Walter Scott thought right to call "faint glimpses of a breast of snow." The exhibition seemed, however, to fail of its intended and indeed its *legitimate* effect, for his lordship's gaze was riveted upon the voluptuous form of the Flukins.

"I think she'll do. Yeas—you may—I *think* you may present her."

There was now no other alternative, for the request was made with a distinctness of tone which reached the ears of Miss Flukins.

"Lord Snizzle, my most perticlerest friend, Miss Henrietta Maria Flukins."

The *noble* man vouchsafed one of his fiercest glances, as he set his eye-glass with an inclination more decidedly towards the nose than usual. Seraphina now found an opportunity of showing ordinary politeness to the rest of her guests, as the signs were favorable to a monopoly by Miss Flukins of Timothy, Lord Snizzle. It was readily seen that Miss Flukins was elated to a degree which foreboded no permanent benefit to her nervous system. There was no evidence of that languor which is sometimes begotten of indifference; on the contrary, her motions indicated the vivifying elasticity of every nerve, muscle, and tendon of the body. She seemed to be set on any number of springs, every one of which had a violent proclivity for teetering, which strongly resembled St. Vitus's dance in its most aggravated form. Her gesticulations were absolutely spasmodic, when earnestly impressing some trifling matter upon his lordship's attention. If he deigned to interrupt her, the spasms ceased, except so far as they were made available in assisting her to keep step with his somewhat erratic strides. This difficult feat was accomplished—for it *was* a difficult feat, because Timothy, Lord Snizzle, considered it one of the prerogatives, that rightly appertained to his superior rank, to take short or long steps, without regard either to the convenience of his companion, or the length of her legs—by paying undivided attention to his motions, and taking enormous strides, or halting abruptly, as the exigency of the case required. From what has been said, it will not be inferred that any of Miss Flukins' *everyday* admirers were brought within the circle of her smiles. For aught that could be discovered in her demeanor, she might never have listened with blushing cheeks and beating heart to more humble swains than her present aristocratic companion; and yet, there were not less than a dozen gentlemen present, made up of a promiscuous assortment of clerks, sub-lieutenants, bank-tellers, merchants in a small way, &c. &c., who had, each in his turn, been made happy, in believing that the dearest, sweetest smile, of the Flukins was lavished upon them. One of the number, a highly respectable *merchant* tailor, on the strength of sundry of those dearest, sweetest smiles, that, not being more than forty-eight hours old, still played about his heart, and emboldened, also, by the well-known dogma that the "tailor makes the man," which he assumed more particularly referred to Timothy, Lord Snizzle, and gentlemen of his calibre, walked *deliberately* up to Miss Flukins, and hoped, as she was looking extremely well, she was enjoying herself correspondingly.

No stately swan ever bent its neck more haughtily, at the approach of a vulgar goose, than did the queenly Flukins, at the salutation of its prototype. Mr. Presswell, not entertaining the slightest doubt that he had spoken in too low a key, reiterated his hopes.

"Do you not see, sir, that I am engaged, *particularly* engaged," replied the beauty, decidedly.

The features of Lord Snizzle became unusually convulsed, as he thrust the glass into the socket of his eye, and coming to a dead halt, critically examined Mr. Presswell from crown to toe.

"Who is the queter, Miss Fukins?"

"Your lordship *ought* to know me, for there is a charge on my books for that suit, and a dozen others," replied Presswell, with sturdy independence.

"I'm blistered if 'tain't my demmed tail-or!"

Miss Greasebeans thought she should make a hole in the floor about the size of her body.

"I told you, ma, not to invite that ojeous mechanic."

"Is he, aw, one of your *acquaintance*, Miss Fukins?"

"Never saw the fellow before, my lord."

"If the supper ain't announced soon, I'll quit this howid place," said Snizzle.

The supper *was* announced at that moment, and his lordship, however much he might despise tailors, and particularly those at whose establishments his credit had arrived at a "mature" age, was nevertheless fond of good suppers, and he therefore waived an expression of his indignation, at being thus inveigled, by the Greasebeans, into such a mixed assemblage, until he had partaken of their hospitality, and thereby gained sufficient strength to denounce their meanness in fitting terms.

As the large company were ascending to the supper-room to the music of "Brittania rules the waves," Henry Kane rang the bell at the front door. It was opened by a servant in white kids, who was in the act of closing it again, but there was something so abjectly miserable in the appearance of the boy, that he hesitated, and at last suffered him to enter. A purple hue had overspread his emaciated features, his teeth chattered as if they were loose in their sockets, and his body shook as though it was in the grasp of dissolution. He essayed to speak, but his tongue clove to the roof of his mouth: yet his countenance expressed the most intense anxiety and alarm. It was altogether a picture of human woe that melted the heart of the menial. The child pointed toward the receding party.

"Poor little fellow, he is hungry," said the servant, as he ran for some cake that was lying upon the silver waiter.

Henry shook his head impatiently.

"What can the boy want? Drink perhaps. Some wine, at all events, will not harm him, this bitter night."

He could scarcely hold the glass in his trembling hand while he swallowed a few drops. The wine and the warmth of the room enabled him to speak.

"Mr. Grease—be—beans. Let me see Mr. Greasebeans," he gasped.

"To-night? it is impossible."

"No, no, no; don't say that. I *must* see him; indeed I must."

"It is impossible. Can't you see there is a party here to-night?"

Henry came up to the man and whispered in a low solemn voice, "If you don't let me see him they will turn my mother and my little sister and brother into the street this cold, *cold* night."

The servant hesitated.

"You won't let them freeze to death in the street, will you?"

"By my soul, no; not if I can help it."

"Then you must call him quick, for I promised to be back in an hour, but I lost my way coming here, and I am sure it is more than an hour; much more than an hour, so you will call him quickly, won't you?"

The waiter ascended the staircase, and the wan child remained in the hall, with his straw hat in his hand, from which he had shaken off the snow and sleet that had fallen upon it. Small particles of ice still glistened upon his rough garments, but they were fast thawing, like the congealed blood in his veins, under the influence of the warm atmosphere. The strains of "Brittania rules the waves," still rolled through the mansion, but his heart sickened at the sound, for he had heard that Brittania ruled the waves by means of the agony and despair which the press-gang entailed upon every family within whose circle a victim was seized.

Mr. Greasebeans descended with strong marks of impatience upon his countenance, but these words faintly express the mingled emotions of surprise and rage that were visible there when he discovered in the person of the intruder, one of his operatives. His brow contracted into a frown as he turned his glance from Henry to the waiter.

"James, is this guest here upon your invitation, or that of the cook?"

The serving-man hung his head.

"Neither of them invited me here, Mr. Greasebeans," said Henry, earnestly.

"Then why *are* you here?" he replied savagely.

"Because, sir, they were going to turn my mother into the street to-night—yes sir, to-night; and don't you hear how the storm rages? listen!"

"And why were they going to do that?"

"She could not pay the rent."

"You expect, then, to live without paying rent, perhaps?" said the benevolent man, with a hard expression upon his features.

"Oh no, sir, we do not; if you won't let us stay until we can earn it, only say we may sleep there to-night. *Just this one night!*"

"Not one minute; do you hear. Not one minute. I intend to make an example of you for the benefit of all dilatory and refractory tenants. James, shut that door; I would not have my guests shocked by a sight of this vagabond."

"What shall I do? what *shall* I do?" exclaimed the wretched child, in tones that pierced the heart of the waiter.

"Do? march out of my house. *I* can tell you what to do soon enough."

"But, Mr. Greasebeans," he sobbed, falling on his knees; "*dear* Mr. Greasebeans, if you turn us into the street to-night, we shall freeze to death before morning. My dear, *dear*, kind, *good* mother will freeze to death. Dolly, *gentle* little Dolly will freeze to death. Frank, too, who is a little baby, and can't tell how cold he is, will freeze to death too; and I shall freeze to death too; but I don't care for myself—".

"Out with you."

"Think how they will suffer; what a *hard* death it will be—"

"Won't you go out?"

"Do, Mr. Greasebeans, pray do, for mer—"

"Then I'll throw you out."

Opening the door, the benevolent and charitable man seized the child by the neck and hurled him down the steps. He struggled to retain his feet, but the frozen rain had made the marble slippery, and falling, his head came violently in contact with the curb-stone. A slight groan mingled with the strain of "Brittania rules the waves," as the philanthropic Solomon Greasebeans closed the door.

"Now, sir, if you admit another rag-a-muffin, you'll lose your place."

"You may attend the door yourself, hereafter," replied the man, taking off his gloves and dashing them upon the floor.

"How is that, sirrah?"

"I mean, sir, that I will not wear the livery of a brute."

"Oh! think better of it, James; at all events, for to-night," said Mr. Greasebeans, graciously, for he could not well dispense with his services until the party broke up.

"Not one solitary moment."

Mr. Greasebeans considered it undignified to bandy words with a servant, and he therefore ordered another waiter to take his position by the door, and he then entered the supper-room with as much happiness impressed upon his benevolent features, as if he had emancipated the whole negro race, or what he would regard quite as satisfactory, involved the United States of America in the horrors of civil war. Upon his calm features was plainly written, "I am the liberal president of the Dexeter Hall Society for ameliorating the condition of the blacks in Africa, and liberating the manacled slave in the United States."

CHAPTER XV.

"Broad are these streams—my steed obeys,
Plunges, and bears me through the tide."—BRYANT.

LORD ROSSMORE conducted Christie Kane from the jail to his carriage. As he tottered into it, with feeble steps, he saw Katharine Montague seated upon the back of Surrey. A faint smile expressed the pleasure which the possession of the dapple-gray by the maiden gave him. She gazed upon his emaciated form and pale, attenuated face with painful interest. Her looks assured him there was one human being whose heart was touched by his sufferings.

The earl motioned to the coachman, and they proceeded rapidly towards the castle of Montague. Lord Rossmore suffered his glance to rest occasionally upon the countenance of the young man.

"It is an infamous law which thus surrenders the body of the debtor to the creditor," he said, in a low, stern tone.

"I thank you for your generous sympathy, my lord," said Christie Kane.

The earl did not reply.

When they arrived at the point where the road turned in the direction of the castle, Katharine Montague rode past them, bowing to her father with a smiling face, and suffering her eyes to rest upon his companion longer than a momentary glance. Instead of following her to the castle, the horses proceeded in the direction of Kane's former residence.

"Young man, nature destined you for a more elevated position in life than you have hitherto occupied," said the earl.

"I am satisfied with it," replied Christie.

Lord Rossmore proceeded without seeming to heed his remarks.

"Your rent has been paid; the lease is renewed, and for the present you can resume your farming operations. The future will unfold what is in reservation for you."

Christie Kane was silent, but his looks expressed the depth of his gratitude.

The earl spoke no more during the ride.

As the carriage drew up at the door of his house, Mrs. Kane walked out upon the portico. She expressed neither joy at his return, nor sorrow at his emaciated appearance.

"Good morning," said Lord Rossmore, as the carriage departed.

"Good-bye, my lord; your kindness shall never be forgotten."

The sound of the wheels swallowed up the last words.

"I hope you have had a comfortable time of it," said Mrs. Kane, sarcastically.

"This is my welcome home, and the reception a mother gives her son! Very well, it's in keeping with the ways of the world."

"In the blues still?"

"Tell Susan to come here, if you please. Ah! here she is."

"Mony's the day sin' I was so shocked," exclaimed the girl, with unaffected astonishment.

"Never mind it, my good lass; it is all over now, I hope. Assist me to my room, and then get me some light food."

"That I will—that I will. It is in the bonny hielands they would be ashamed to treat a human being so cruelly," replied Susan, as she assisted him to his room.

Several days elapsed before he had recovered sufficient strength to leave the house, and when at length he did breathe the pure air of heaven, beneath the clear sky of autumn, it was with a profound sense of enjoyment. As soon as he could leave his room, Ellen Knowles called to see him. Her mild countenance expressed the utmost commiseration, as she took his hand, upon which a tear fell.

"Do not weep, dear Ellen; I have suffered, but all is over now."

"How can I help it when I reflect how unjustly you have been treated. How often I implored my father to intercede in your behalf; but, but—"

"I am no favorite of his."

"I would have done something myself if I had possessed the ability," she added, with a heart-broken sob.

"Dearest Ellen," he said, tenderly, "do not distress yourself. I know very well you were powerless; but the will to aid me shall ever be taken as the deed, so think no more about it. You have endeared yourself to me by the anxiety you have suffered on my account."

"Yes, you can never repay her for the solicitude she has felt for you," said Mrs. Kane, ironically.

"I know it, mother; and Ellen shall discover how sincere is my thankfulness."

"Maister Christie, Maister Christie, it's mesel is delighted to say yez wonst more. I should hiv come amadintly, but I hiv been to town—to Lunnon," he added, setting his smart hat upon his left ear.

"I am glad to see you, Phelim. And so, you are in service?"

"Yez. Lady Kathreen Montague honored me wid her fayvur whilst yez were eximplyfyin the booties of imprisonment for debt, bekaze the crops would fale."

"And how are you pleased with the service?"

"No one can say the lovely smile and hear the sweet voice of her ladyship, widdout a loven her,"

"You think not, Mr. Savor," said Ellen Knowles, tartly.

"Yez may well say that. But me remark is applicable to me own sex, though, for the invious of yez own, cannot admire booty in ony but themsels."

"You will remain at the castle, of course," said Kane.

"Of koorse I will not! Desert yez, who have always been so kind to me? Never! It shall not be said of Phelim Savor, poor though he ba, that he is guilty of the fashonble vice of carryin' two faces under one hat."

Christie Kane pressed his hand.

"I shall not consent to have you sacrifice your fine prospects for me. I can manage the farm with other assistance; you must return to the castle."

"Niver!"

"Yes, I insist upon it."

"It can't be done, Maister Christie. Yez say, whin Lady Kathreen towld ma this mornin to ride Surrey here, and return him to you"—

"Did she say that?" asked Christie, quickly.

"Yez; that she did. I tell yaz, Maister Christie," said Mr. Savor, in a confidential tone, "that lady niver has two faces under one hat, and it izzent bekase she haint got booty enough, or aint married or koorted, ayther."

"And she told you to deliver Surrey to me?"

"Yez; and there he is; and looking, too, like there wazzent a horse his aquel in all the united kingdom of Great Britain, Ireland, Scotland, Wales, and the Koonty Clare."

"Surrey has been treated well, then?"

"Thrated well? Ba the powers yez may well say that same. He was after being roobed down three times a day, as if he was Lord Snizzle's boots, and no one but her ladyship iver ixercised him."

"Well, now, Phelim, you will ride Surrey to the castle, and present my thanks to Lady Katharine Montague, and say to her that I cannot accept the present she has so delicately offered me."

"Spoken like a man of honor, as you are," said Ellen Knowles, enthusiastically.

"Like a simpleton, as he is," responded Mrs. Kane, sarcastically.

"Yez know best what is right," said Phelim. "I will do your bidding, and then ax her bootiful and gracious ladyship to let me raysume me crownless hat, and quit her service for yez oon."

"No, no, Phelim. I will *not* consent. You cannot shake my resolution upon this point. The advantages are altogether too much in your favor to justify me in withdrawing you from her service. You will therefore say to her ladyship, when you make known my refusal to accept Surrey, that I shall consider myself under additional obligations to her if she will retain you in her service."

"If yez command me to do that same, I will," said Phelim, sadly.

"I do."

Without saying more, Phelim withdrew from the house, and mounting Surrey, rode slowly in the direction of the castle.

Christie Kane accompanied his cousin home. Her manner was tender and subdued. The winning softness of Ellen Knowles had the effect of soothing his spirits.

When he withdrew, her eyes flashed, and her nostrils dilated.

"He is mine, he is mine! The victory for which I have struggled, oh, so long! that has caused me to pass so many sleepless nights, and days of agony, is now within my grasp, and I will clutch it, clutch it, with the remorseless determination of a fiend."

Before she could compose her features, Lord Melville was announced. Her temper was still up, and she haughtily waved him to a seat.

His lordship did not seem to be in the mood to submit to her humor, for he threw himself at full length upon the sofa, and drawing forward a chair to rest his opera boot upon, smoothed his whiskers with the coolest air imaginable.

She endeavored to annihilate him with several fierce glances, but he seemed to be proof against their assault, as he continued to survey her person with a steadfast, supercilious gaze.

"Your lordship is rude."

"Your ladyship is shrewish."

"I could expect no better manners from one who has not tact enough to control the liberty of a debtor once in his power."

"Manners depend upon the ability of a man to play the tyrant and villain, eh! Miss Ellen Knowles, your code of morals ought to be generally established in fashionable society; for since the days of Cain, the first robber, it has guided the conduct of that respectable portion of the human family who live by rascality. Did it ever occur to you what an admirable female Captain Kidd you would make, Miss Ellen Knowles?"

"Insolence!"

"Truth, madam—naked, unvarnished truth. By the way, how far have your designs upon Christie Kane been forwarded by his imprisonment, and to what extent will they be embarrassed by his liberation, through the influence of Katharine Montague?"

"Did she liberate him?" gasped Ellen.

"Sets the wind so strongly in that quarter? I shall cause Mr. Kane to be informed of the interest that fair lady takes in his welfare."

"No! no! you will not. Say you will not do that?"

"I shall, though. You may remember having made frequent and taunting allusions to my great aunt."

"It made you feel sore, did it?" replied Ellen, triumphantly.

"Not half so sore as I will make you feel, my merry damsel, before I let you up," said Melville, with a sneer.

"Do your worst, fool and coxcomb, as you are. Nothing can prevent Christie Kane from making a declaration of his love, and me from accepting him."

"Indeed!" he said—showing his teeth like an enraged wolf.

"No, sir."

"Not if I tell him you instigated me to throw him into prison?"

She turned pale, and her form trembled.

"Ah ha! you are in my power, are you? Simpleton! did you suppose you could safely trifle with me—*me*, Lord Melville, who never forgave an insult?"

"Nay, my lord," she replied in supplicating tones; "you will not, let me implore you, inform Christie Kane that I urged you to cast him into prison. If you only knew how much I have at stake, I am sure you would not."

In the intensity of their passion, neither heard footsteps approaching the parlor: they were arrested at the conclusion of her appeal, and then receded to the outer door, which closed upon them. It was Christie Kane, upon whose ears fell the unwelcome intelligence of her heartless conduct.

"You cannot shake my resolution,"coolly replied Melville.

She raised her form to its full height, and casting upon him a look of intense hate, she said—

"You shall not tell him."

"Shall not?"

"No; if I am in your power, you are not less so in mine."

"Do your worst."

"Have a care, my lord. My *worst* will greatly exceed anything you can possibly imagine."

"I doubt it."

"You do?"

"I do."

"And you persist in your determination to injure me in the good opinion of my cousin?"

"As surely as I live long enough," he replied defiantly.

"Then I am your stern and irreconcilable foe; a foe whom you cannot thwart or elude; who will follow in your footsteps with the untiring ferocity of a tigress, until you are bereft of rank, fortune, every thing which you now enjoy but to disgrace. Begone, sir."

"Au revoir," he said, kissing his hand to the maiden, as he walked to the door followed by her flashing eyes.

"Beware," she exclaimed, shaking her trembling finger at him.

"Vive la Bagatelle."

Christie Kane had never felt a more tender sentiment for his cousin than gratitude. In their childhood she had often annoyed him by unkind allusions to the difference in their social conditions. It was only within the last twelve months that her bearing had changed; so suddenly, indeed, as to create distrust at first; but that had gradually yielded to time and the tenderness of her manners. It is true he had sometimes doubted her sincerity, and now that he had accidentally become possessed of a knowledge of her agency in his imprisonment, she was thoroughly unmasked.

In spite of the haughty mien of Katharine Montague, he could not think of her unmoved. At times, her eyes had dwelt upon him with an expression that caused his heart to thrill with delight. But oftener, his feelings had indignantly resented her contemptuous bearing. He could not divest himself of the belief, presumptuous as he often thought it, that despite the difference in their positions, she regarded him with greater interest than she would disclose. A union between them he knew was impossible, and he resolved to conceal within his own heart the emotions with which she had inspired him.

Katharine Montague, mounted upon Surrey, for she rode no other steed now, and followed by Phelim Savor, availed herself of the fair days in October to visit the poor and prepare them for the severe weather of winter. The strongest contrast in the character of the maiden was the tenderness of her manner to the humble, and the haughty bearing she presented to the worldly and assuming. It gave her more pleasure to relieve the suffering than to receive the adulation of the high-born. How different from the fine lady, whose mind cannot elevate itself above dress and the concomitants which make up the "fishionable" woman!

She was returning from one of these excursions, followed by Phelim Savor. She had been detained longer than she was aware by the bed-side of sickness, and she gave Surrey the rein. They swept rapidly across the open country that spread out some eight miles from the castle of Montague. She had observed a dark cloud passing over the head waters of a rapid stream, as they crossed it a few hours before. It was already swollen by heavy rains, and she thought at the time, the bridge was too frail to resist the mountain torrent. As they approached the stream she heard the roaring of the waters as they tumbled down the hill-side and rushed through the chasm across which the bridge was thrown. The road was one not much frequented, and due precautions had not been taken to reconstruct the bridge which was now weakened by age. A portion of the framework erected in the middle of the stream had been carried away by a previous flood, and now presented a feeble barrier to the fury of the waters.

As they reached the summit of the hill overlooking the river, she arrested the speed of her horse, and gazed with rapt delight, not unmingled with awe, upon the scene. The flood, from the point where it curved over the distant elevation, was one continuous sheet of foam. Fretted and angry, it tumbled onward, now rushing against this bank and then against that, as if it would force a passage through the rocky barrier. Checked in its career, it turned with renewed vigor upon the next obstruction, against which it furiously hurled itself. Logs and small trees were borne down the stream, and passing under the bridge were swept away.

"Look, look!" exclaimed Phelim eagerly. "Don't yez say yon big tree? If that same strikes the pier, it's little of the bridge will be left standing at all, at all."

"True; we must cross the stream before that tree reaches the bridge. Now to your utmost speed, Surrey."

The generous horse sprang away; but if his progress was rapid, that of the descending tree was still more so. Surrey was within a few yards of the bridge when, by a strong effort of his fair rider, he was thrown back upon his haunches. The promptness with which she acted saved the lives of both. The next moment the descending tree struck the framework in the centre of the stream. A loud crash was heard, the bridge trembled violently, and then sunk into the river.

"That was a narrow escape, Phelim."

"Yez may well say that, yer ladyship."

"What is to be done? I think that chasm is too wide even for Surrey to take."

"Begorra—barring your presence..Nayther Surrey, nor me own horse could lape this stream widdout an especial dispensashin from Holy St. Patrick, long life tul his blissed mimory."

"Is there no other way of crossing the stream?"

"There is a ford the matter of a kouple of miles up the river, that can ba forded almost any wither."

"In the autumn flood?"

"Yis, I have waded across it even thin."

"Lead the way thither."

"If I might assume the laiberty of suggisting what koorse should be pursued, it would ba to return to the wayside inn two miles back, or tul proceed down the stream to the castle of Monlow?"

"The ford *has* been crossed in high water?"

"Yis, ma-am."

"Then we will cross it now. Once upon the other side, it will be a short ride home. I must not cause the alarm my absence at the castle would produce unless it is absolutely necessary."

The road which it was necessary for them now to pursue was little better than a path, and their progress was necessarily less rapid than before. To add to the difficulties that seemed to gather in her way, the clouds began to collect again, as if threatening a storm. Daylight, too, would soon disappear. The prospect was anything but agreeable, still she continued her way as fast as the nature of the ground would permit.

"It's a cooming; what will your ladyship do?" said Phelim, anxiously. "Hadn't we better go back to the inn?"

"It is too late now. How far is it to the ford?"

"Betterer an a mile."

"So far?"

The path was now open, and she again proceeded rapidly.

The storm now burst upon them. The wind hurled the rain into her face, and her clothes were soon saturated. For a few minutes she paused, unsheltered from the storm, until the first blast had spent its fury, and then she again proceeded.

"Ba the merciful powers ba thanked, here is the ford."

"Can we cross here, Phelim?"

"It looks scary like, but I summit believe it can be done. I'll try onyhow."

"Do you think you incur no risk?"

"I think not. The main channel is narrow, yez say, although the stream is wide, an' if the horses do happen to swim, it will ba only for the matter of a few yards, which wiil be nothing, especially to Surrey, that is a bootiful swimmer. Yez will plaise take notice which koorse I go. There's no danger until yer git fornenst, the rock beyant. Wonst by that same, and yez are safe."

"Lead the way then, if you think there is no danger. Twilight is already setting in, and this rain is anything but comfortable."

Phelim rode his horse into the stream. Near the middle he was carried off his feet, but he was not borne down far when his feet again touched the bed of the river.

Encouraged by the success of Phelim Savor, Katharine gave Surrey the reins. As she reached the channel a dark mass loomed through the deepening gloom. The sagacity of the horse discovered the danger, and nobly did he try to avoid it. He saw he could not pass in front of it, and turning his head up the stream he endeavored to regain the shore which he had left. The bridle became entangled in a branch of the tree. The horse shook his head but could not extricate himself. They were borne down the stream. Katharine Montague did not shriek; she did not even utter a cry, but she leaned forward to free the rein. Her efforts, also, were unsuccessful. A thought flashed upon her mind in that moment of extreme peril. She detached the bridle and threw the reins over his head. With a glad neigh the animal rewarded the feat. They were now in the strongest part of the current, and were carried rapidly down the stream. The horse, instead of turning his head towards the bank, endeavored to stem the torrent. His efforts were unavailing, and Katharine shuddered as she heard the roar of the falls at the head of the rapids. She pressed her hands upon her eyes to shut out the fearful spectacle, when a firm grasp was laid upon her arm.

"Trust to me," said a calm, manly voice.

She slid from the back of the horse into the water in a state of insensibility.

The stranger spoke no more, but struck boldly for that part of the shore which fringed the summit of the falls. In this he acted wisely, for he did not exhaust his strength in a vain struggle against the current. Surrey with instinctive sagacity followed the lead of the stranger, but his powers were too much exhausted to reach the shore. As Christie Kane bore the unconscious maiden up the bank, the gallant steed was swept into the rapids, from which escape was impossible. Christie still held Katharine Montague in his arms, and a feeling of bliss pervaded his frame, as they were tightened upon her soft form in the effort to retain it there.

A few rods from the shore was a deserted cabin, whose thatched roof kept out the storm, and into this hut he carried the maiden. He had taken shelter here from the storm an hour before, and a cheerful fire blazed upon the hearth. Gently laying her down upon a bed of moss, in front of the fire, he rested her cold, pale cheek upon his bosom, while he rubbed her hands and arms for the purpose of aiding her restoration from insensibility. The blood returned to her lips, but as he bent over her he did not profane them with a kiss. She sighed, and turning towards him, placed one arm around his neck. His form trembled at the involuntary caress. She opened her eyes, but at first she could not rally her ideas. Her look was expressionless. Christie did not move, but he could not withdraw his fascinated gaze from her face. At length consciousness resumed her throne; she recollected every thing; the perils with which she was surrounded; the few, but cheering words of Christie Kane, whose features she now recognized. For a few moments she did not attempt to withdraw herself from his arms, and a thrill of pleasure indescribable ran along his nerves as her full, lustrous eyes turned to his own with an expression which revealed the depth of her gratitude and affection. For a moment only, was nature allowed to exhibit its powers, for she raised herself from his bosom, not hastily, like the timid dove, but proudly and collectedly, like the stately swan.

"Where is Surrey?" she asked.

"Alas! I fear the noble animal is dead."

"What! was he carried down the rapids?"

"Yes, the current was too strong for him; we barely escaped with our own lives."

The maiden shuddered.

"Poor Surrey! where is Phelim?"

"Here I am, and may St. Pathrick be praised for yez riscue, and by maister Christie, too," said the gratified fellow, as he proceeded to cut several dozen pigeons'-wings to the music of his own whistle and the rain that poured upon his head.

"Come into the hut," said the lady.

"A saycond adation of Noah's deluge could not wet me a hay-porth more than I am at this present moment."

"You can come and dry yourself," said Christie Kane.

"Not ontwil I hiv picked up some more turf. Yon fire wants replenishing."

"What is to be done now, Mr. Kane?" asked Katharine Montague.

"I hardly know what to advise, unless you remain here until Phelim can ride to the castle, and return with a carriage and dry apparel for you."

"How far is it to the castle?"

"Three miles."

"And the road?"

"Is passable for a carriage."

"Such a night as this?"

"I fear not until the moon rises, some two hours later. In the meantime I am apprehensive you will take cold."

"I do not fear that. But can Phelim find his way to the castle until the moon rises? to me it seems the darkness is impenetrable."

Christie went into the gloom that walled up the light of the fire. "It *is* impenetrable; he could not go a dozen rods without losing his way."

"It is an awful night," she replied, as she listened to the roaring of the wind, the falling torrents, and the rushing stream. "What will father and mother think?"

"They will undoubtedly be alarmed at your absence, but many hours shall not elapse before they are apprised of your safety."

"This turf will make an illegant fire," said Phelim, as he piled up the logs of wood in the chimney.

Christie adjusted a seat near the blazing fire for the maiden.

"By what accident am I indebted for your aid at such a perilous moment?" inquired Lady Katharine; for she could not withdraw her mind from the danger she had encountered.

"I have been upon the heath to-day, in pursuit of game, as you may discover by glancing at the corner of the room. Returning, I saw the storm approaching, and took shelter in the cabin, which has often been my resting-place for the night, under similar circumstances."

"If I am indebted to the storm for wet garments and the loss of Surrey, poor fellow, I am also under obligations to it for your aid."

"As several hours must elapse before you can leave this place, will you honor my culinary skill, unless terror has occasioned the loss of appetite?"

"And do you number cooking among your accomplishments?" she inquired laughingly.

"Of course; even the knights-errant did not think their education complete until they could prepare a meal; a result, indeed, which could not well be avoided, for in their warfare against real and imaginary enemies of fair ladies, they were often carried beyond the reach of that aid which is so generously afforded by females who understand making up substantial fare as well as grateful delicacies."

"Well, let us see what proficiency my knight-errant has made in such an important vocation," replied Katharine Montague, who began to enjoy the scene, as the warmth of the fire diffused itself throughout the cabin.

"Thank you. Occupying this hut so often during this season of the year, I am not altogether destitute of some of the necessaries of life, and especially to-night, for the sky looked threatening when I left home this morning. Here Phelim, dress this pheasant; or is your ladyship more fond of grouse?"

"Oh, grouse, by all means."

"Dress both, but the grouse first."

"Yez. I always did say," soliloquized Phelim, as he withdrew, "that me mistress is much more tasteful than the nobility in gineral, for yez say, they think nothing is so delightful as to live on the peasantry, and especially does his riverence, Fayther McQuodling, whilst her blissed ladyship prayfars grouse, me own delight."

Katharine Montague observed the motions of Christie Kane, as he prepareed the supper. The bright light that fell upon his manly form, and the heat of the fire, suffused his cheeks with a ruddy hue. Occasionally his eyes met her own, when they were suddenly withdrawn; but the glance deepened the color in his cheeks. He took a tea-pot and tin pail, which shone like silver, from a shelf in the corner of the hut, and went to the river, where they were thoroughly rinsed. He then placed the pail upon the coals so that the water could not be smoked. Some potatoes were covered in the ashes, and from the portmanteau that he always carried on his shoulders, upon his hunting excursions, he took bread, salt, cheese, and butter. These he placed upon a table with two legs, which he leaned against the wall. The maiden was very much amused at the scene, and could not repress her laughter as she witnessed his operations.

"I am glad you are in such fine spirits," he said, with a smile of open pleasure.

"I was never more delighted. This is a scene to be long remembered."

"I hope so," he replied with an expressive glance.

The lady blushed, and was silent.

Phelim now brought in the grouse and pheasant, and Christie, adjusting the former upon a crooked stick, requested Mr. Savor to hold it suspended over the coals. The pheasant was arranged in the same manner; and Phelim, taking that also, sat in front of the fire—his face red and cheerful: the very impersonation of comfort and good humor.

"You would make an excellent quarter-master, Mr. Kane," said the maiden.

"Do you think so? I have some thoughts of joining the army, and would do so, if I could, like some of the younger sons of our nobility, *purchase* promotion, when they have not been fortunate enough to *merit* it. But will you suffer me to turn your seat to our humble board?"

"Gladly; for I must confess to a most craving appetite. I ought, perhaps, to blush for it, because it mars the romance of my adventure."

"Which I will pardon, for the joy which your cheerfulness gives me."

Exercise and exposure gave a relish to the food, of which she partook with a sharpened appetite.

After Phelim had eaten, he was despatched to the castle, with directions to return with a carriage, and he was enjoined by Katharine Montague to assure her mother that she was safe and happy.

The last word gave Christie Kane indescribable pleasure, and in that seductive hour he forgot the distance which separated him from the being who had so completely fascinated him. He was vain enough to suppose that he possessed all the manly qualities which, stamped upon the image of God, rendered him one of nature's favorites. He forgot, for the hour, that, with all his mental and personal gifts, he was still one of the *substratum* upon whose shoulders rested the feet of the *patented* noble.

"You have not a high opinion of the class of society to which I belong?" said the maiden, interrogatively.

"The feeling with which your father, and, may I add, yourself have inspired me, will not justify me in saying that."

Katharine shaded her face with a lace handkerchief. She did not reply, and he continued—

"There is a portion of the English nobility whose conduct awakens the respect of the most ardent republican."

"And do you belong to that small section of our population?"

"Can you doubt it? Believe me, Lady Katharine, there is an imposing minority in numbers, if not in influence, who would gladly exchange a state of social and political bondage, quite as degrading as that of the African slave, for a state of freedom and independence."

He spoke earnestly, and she did not fail to observe that his fine eyes lighted with enthusiasm.

"Of what do you complain?"

"Can you ask me? Of everything to which human nature can be subjected. Oppression, contempt, contumely. Our services required, our health ruined, and our misfortunes punished as crimes. One law, which disgraces the statute-book, is enough to justify a revolution."

"And that?"

"Is the law authorizing imprisonment for debt. It not only inflicts punishment upon the unfortunate, as revolting as that with which you seek to arrest crime, but it increases the number of offences upon the criminal calendar."

"In what way?"

"By teaching the vicious and depraved that it is no worse to be wicked than to be unfortunate—for both are punished with equal severity."

The maiden was impressed with the remark, but said—

"It is an evil which the noble may suffer as well as the peasant."

The words, falling from her lips, grated harshly upon his ears. But he controlled his feelings.

"Pardon me. In *our* case"—and he dwelt bitterly upon the word—"it is involuntary; and we are made to suffer for results over which we cannot exercise the slightest control. With the aristocracy it is generally courted by voluntary indulgence in extravagance and folly."

She was still silent.

"And what makes the law ridiculous as well as unjust, is the fact that the government, which so mercilessly crushes the spirit of the debtor, is itself hopelessly and irremediably insolvent. An insolvency from which there is no expectation or desire to escape."

"No wish to pay off the national debt?"

"Not the slightest."

"And why not?" she asked with a look of surprise.

"Because the national debt is the strongest pillar that sustains the fabric of British despotism; more powerful even than a hereditary nobility, or the Church of England."

"I cannot conceive how that is possible."

"I will explain. The government is indebted to its subjects. The interest, which is annually paid upon this indebtedness, is the income of the subject. Do you not perceive that every creditor of the government would rally to its defence, were it in danger of being overthrown? for the reason, that their capital would be involved in the general crash, were the debtor ruined."

"Ah! I understand. There is much force in your reasoning," replied the maiden, as she rested her elbow upon the mossy bed he had prepared for her before the fire, and placed her cheek upon her hand.

The storm had passed, and not a cloud could be seen along the vast expanse of the sky. The moon was rising above the adjacent hill, and casting her mild beams across the turbulent river. Christie Kane re-entered the cabin, from which he had emerged a short time before.

"I can hear the sound of wheels; the carriage must be approaching."

"That is welcome intelligence."

The reply was natural, yet Christie did not like it. He seemed hard to please.

"Kate, my darling, I am glad to see you—and looking so fresh and blooming too, as though nothing had happened,"—said the Earl of Rossmore.

"But there has, though."

"Anything more than a worse ducking than the one you gave Lord Melville?"

"Yes, I have lost Surrey."

"How?"

"He went over the rapids."

"Never mind, you shall have another."

"There is no other Surrey."

"There are as good fish in the sea as were ever taken out of it."

"An adage that may possibly apply to the finny tribe, but not to horses."

"Have it as you will. But where is your preserver? Ah, here he is," and the earl grasped Christie Kane by the hand. "You have saved the life of my child, and you have made me your friend," he said, frankly.

"My lord, you saved my life. I could do no less than save that of your daughter, if I wanted a motive stronger than a sense of duty."

"But to Kate, not to me, are you indebted for a release from jail," said the earl.

"Hush! father," she said, placing her hand upon his mouth.

"I am certain the obligation I am under will never be considered less," he replied.

"To her all the credit is due."

She shook her head at him imperiously.

"Then I shall more than ever thank fortune for leading me to this spot to-night."

"And so will I. But come, Kate. Drive the carriage this way, Donald," said the earl, from without the door.

Katharine paused before following her father.

"You will come with us, won't you?" she said to Christie.

The invitation was strongly seconded by her eyes. Christie hesitated for a moment, and then said,

"I thank you, no. I shall remain here to-night."

"Does it possess so many attractions?" she inquired, archly, as she cast a glance around the rough walls of the hut.

"Never so many before; but now I will often make pilgrimages hither, and with as much devotion as ever Mohammedan visited Mecca."

"Good-bye, then," she said, hurriedly, as she extended her hand.

He held it for a moment, while his speaking glance sought her own, and then he bent his head and pressed his lips upon it. Was he mistaken? He thought the soft, white, little hand trembled.

He assisted her into the carriage, and declining the invitation of the earl to return with them, he re-entered the hut as they drove away. His heart beat tumultuously, and hope awakened new aspirations in his proud heart—Hope, that often creates, that despair may destroy.

CHAPTER XVI.

"What constitutes man's chief enjoyment here?
What forms his greatest antidote to sorrow?
Is't wealth? Wealth can at last but gild his bier,
Or buy the pall that poverty must borrow."—CLASON.

A LONG, anxious hour passed, and still Henry did not return. The wind swept through the streets, and made the old building shake as with the tremulousness of age. There came gusts of rain pattering against the glass, and that was followed by the rattling sound of sleet. The night was black and piercingly cold. Mrs. Kane pressed the two infants in her arms, and Dolly rested her cheek, wet with tears, upon her mother's knee. The two men contemplated her misery; the officer with emotions that a familiarity with suffering could not altogether deaden, and Hurdy with a savage expression of triumph upon his repulsive countenance.

"Why don't he come back? he will die in the street, I know he will," said Mary Kane, as the hail beat against the window.

"You'll be there soon yourself, only fifteen minutes of the hour now remain," said Hurdy.

She made no reply, but moved backward and forward in her chair, moaning piteously.

"The hour has expired, do your duty."

"Can't they remain here to-night, Hurdy?"

"Let them, at your peril."

"It's an awful night."

"And Mr. Greasebeans' business is worth something."

The officer had a large family to support, and necessity will not admit of either kindness or generosity in the estimation of some persons.

"If I must, I must, but it is hard. You hear what he says, madam."

"I do. There is no hope for me. I would go to little William's father, but alas! he is absent from London, and Philip Hogan too. I do not know where he lives now."

"You will go out quietly?"

"It is useless to resist; my hour has come. Better perhaps to die now, than to suffer longer," she replied calmly.

"I am sorry for you, upon my soul I am," said the officer.

"My husband is torn from me. My little boy, dear, noble, little Henry, is frozen to death. We have nothing to live for. I am willing to die."

With despair riveted upon her countenance, she took a child upon each arm, and with Dolly clinging to her dress, descended the staircase, and walked out into the night.

"Ma, what you take me out this dark night for? I'm cold, and the rain hurts my face. Let us go back, ma, and walk to-morrow, when it's warm and light."

"We can never go there again, my child."

"Then where shall we sleep? It's time for me to go to bed now. Im' so sleepy and cold. Frank Tot wants to go home too; hear how he cries."

The rain fell fast, and its icy drops pierced through their slight covering. She wrapped the clothing around them, as well as she could, to protect their tender bodies from the storm, and in doing so exposed herself to its fury. But a mother's devotion kept her warm. Turning down an alley she sought shelter from an overhanging roof, which protected her from the rain. Clasping all three of the children in her arms, she tried to keep them warm with the heat from her own body. Benumbed with the cold, they all slept.

Hurdy stealthily followed her footsteps, after separating from the officer. He aroused her from the torpor into which she was fast sinking. He seated himself beside her and took her hand in his own. She shrank from his touch as from an adder's.

"Monster! why do you pursue me?"

"Because you are too handsome for my peace."

"Let go my hand, or I will scream for assistance."

"You'll get none. It is not a night the police love to be out in."

"For mercy sake leave me—leave me to die in peace."

"Not yet, not quite yet, sweetest," replied the brute as he encircled her waist, and pressed his vulgar mouth to her own.

She shrieked, but he pressed one hand upon her throat; in the struggle the helpless infants fell upon the frozen earth, and their cries mingled with the imprecations of Hurdy, the faint moans of the wretched woman, and the howling of the storm.

"Robert! Robert! Robert!"

But her husband could not defend her. His services were required to enable Britannia to "rule the waves."

She struggled until her strength was completely exhausted, and at last overcome, she fell upon the ground and blood gushed in torrents from her mouth. She had ruptured a blood vessel. But the purposes of the fiend were not arrested.

She remained insensible for some time after the monster stole away. At length recalled to consciousness by the cries of her children she rose from the ground. She felt that death was laying his icy grasp upon her.

"I have no other recourse now but to die. I may never see Robert again on earth. But oh! God of Justice! let me meet him in heaven!"

She employed her remaining strength in taking off her outside garments and in wrapping the children carefully up in them. She smiled tranquilly as she felt their warm limbs and saw them sleeping calmly; and then with a prayer for their safety, she reclined upon the pavement until her flickering light should go out. The hemorrhage continued; she became weaker and weaker; her limbs seemed turned to ice.

"Robert—I—I—love—you—oh—so—so much. Meet—me—in—heav———" A fresh gush of blood choked her utterance, and her heart ceased to beat.

The sleet and rain turned to snow, as if to make a winding sheet worthy of the spotless purity and devotion of her character. The children slumbered, and the snow fell, lightly, as if it would not disturb their rest, but only spread over them a white mantle, to keep out the cold.

Henry lay some time upon the ground before recovering from the effects of the blow. When he regained his feet, it was with a confused idea of what brought him out that stormy night; but when he looked up to the blaze of light that burst from the windows, as if it was ambitious of dispelling the darkness that hovered upon its outposts, he remembered everything—the reason why he was in the street, his mission to Mr. Greasebeans and its results. The forms of dancers, decked with all the extravagant ornaments that wealth could purchase, or that vulgar taste coveted, were seen within, moving to the voluptuous notes of the Redowa; without, the storm howled through the street, as if in anger at the presence of enjoyment.

Henry, now very nearly exhausted, for the want of food and rest, dragged his weary limbs towards home: no,—towards the place that was once his home, for now he was houseless and homeless. The buildings seemed to reel as if they were on a spree, and the creaking of blinds resembled the sound of maniacal laughter. Still he toiled onward, braving the wind and breasting the snow, that now descended in large flakes, after the manner of the "devil whipping his wife." He thought he heard the wailing of a child; yet it came so indistinctly to his ears that he was left in doubt. He listened anxiously. Perhaps it was Frank Tot. Again he heard it; it *was* the cry of a child, and down that alley. With the quickness of thought he flew onwards. A small drift of snow was lying under the projecting eaves of a house. In the centre of it was Dolly.

"Ma! ma! Oh, Ise so cold. Why do'nt you wake up?"

"Dolly, dear Dolly, how came you here?"

"It's Henry! it's Henry!!" And the child wept afresh—but from joy, now.

"Where is mother? I do'nt see her, Dolly."

"She is laying there asleep, under the snow; and she won't wake up, for I've tried ever so hard to make her."

Henry turned in the direction that she pointed. A white hand was all he could see. It was stretched forth as if imploring that aid which the suppliant might never receive. With a cry of anguish, he knelt beside it. It answered not to his touch: it was cold as marble. He brushed away the snow. The face of his mother which had dwelt so tenderly upon him at the moment of their separation, when she wrapped the handkerchief around his neck, and kissed his cheek—was now white—white as its winding sheet. He called, softly at first, so as not to rouse her too suddenly. No voice answered, no smile played upon her lips. He laid his hand upon her face, and a shudder passed through his frame; for the touch chilled his blood.

"No! Oh no, not that; for God's sake, not that—not dead! Dead? Why, she will never kiss me again; never kiss Frank Tot, nor Dolly, if she is dead. Never talk to us, pray for us. Come ma, wake up; say you are *very* cold, but that fire will warm you. Won't you, dear ma?" He laid his cheek to her mouth; he placed his hand upon her heart; all was still as the grave. "Then she *is* dead, and we have no parents, no protectors—alone, all alone!" He threw himself upon the body, and clasping it in his arms, wept as if his heart would break.

Voices were heard approaching.

"It was down here."

"No, not in that alley—it was further down the street."

"Hark! Yes, it *is* down there."

Philip Hogan and his companion stood by the snow-drift. Their strong natures were subdued by the spectacle. Silently they lifted the child from his mother's corpse. He did not resist, because, overcome by long-sustained toil and anxiety, he had fainted.

"Frank Tot and William's here, too," said Dolly.

"Where, my child?"

"In the snow, to keep 'em warm. The snow kept me warm, while I lay quietly. But now the wind hurts me. Won't you take us to the fire?

"That I will," said Hogan.

They raised the two infants from the snow-drift. The stranger, little William, was cold: death had claimed him as a victim. Frank yet breathed; his extremities were chilled, but the pulsations of his heart, like the signal given at sea, spoke of life and hope. They wrapped the clothing round those who "still lived," and Hogan threw off his thick coat and added it to what already protected them from the storm.

"Now let us carry Robert's children to my house. His wife and the baby can remain for the present; no one will molest them now." Hogan's good wife manifested all the interest of a mother for the sufferers. She placed them in bed and gave them warm drink to stimulate vitality, and in a few minutes she had the satisfaction of witnessing a change in their appearance. The warm blood revisited their purple lips, and the pale hue of their cheeks receded before the tide of life that was now upon its flood.

Frank Tot opened his eyes and smiled, unconscious of the irreparable loss he had sustained.

"Where is my ma?" asked Dolly.

"They're gone to bring her here," replied Mrs. Hogan sadly.

"Oh! I'm so glad, I shall see my ma again; and she'll talk to me now, won't she?"

The kind woman turned away her head, and a groan burst from Henry's bosom.

"What ails oo, Henry? Why don't *oo* be happy? They're goin' to bring ma here, where she will be nice and warm. I told her not to go out walking such a dark, cold night. She won't do so any more, will she?"

"Alas! no, poor child."

"But what makes oo look so? Don't oo want my ma to come here. Isn't there nuff fire to keep us all warm?"

"Not enough to warm her again," said Mrs. Hogan, as the big tears rolled down her cheeks.

"Then let me put some more coal on, for ma will be *very* cold, I know she will, for her hand was just as hard as ice. My pa will pay you some day."

And Dolly got out of the bed and put some coal in the grate with her little hands. Mrs. Hogan did not know how to undeceive her as to the fate of her mother, and she waited for circumstances to do it.

"Don't oo think it looks more cheerful now?"

"Yes."

"Will ma think so too? Oh! here she comes! here she—"

Dolly paused abruptly when she saw her mother brought in, pale and cold as when she last saw her. They laid the corpse upon a bed in the inner room. Henry and his sister stood beside it. The boy gazed steadfastly through his tears upon the face of the dead, wringing his hands, but uttering no sound except occasionally an agonizing sob, that expressed the desolation of his heart. Dolly was at first awed by the solemn appearance of the corpse; it could not be that mother whose face always wore a loving expression. She surveyed the features critically, and to solve her doubts she pushed a chair to the side of the bed, and getting upon it, tried, with gentle touch, to raise the lids of the eyes. The orb that met her view *was* her mother's, but so fixed and glassy, it appalled her. She looked long and anxiously upon the corpse; she traced each line, examined each feature; she pressed her lips upon the cold cheek, and perceiving no motion, receiving no caress, her lips quivered, and then the foundation of her grief gave way. She threw her arms around her brother's neck, and together they mourned over the pulseless form of the unsympathising dead.

Preparations were being made for the humble funeral. A plain coffin was all that could be afforded, and into that the body was placed, clothed in the scanty livery of the tomb. England required the services of her husband to make heroes with, whom she could worship in their life-time and embalm with her tears after death. Heroes, who would strengthen her power, and visit with injustice and contempt, the country of their birth. England, overburthened with philanthropic love for the human race, claimed the services of Robert Kane, but she neither cared for his helpless wife while living, nor buried her remains after death. How could it be expected, in the great struggle for national supremacy and renown, that the happiness of *her own* people should arrest the attention of the government. The eyes of her statesmen were raised to such a height in order to ascertain what particular corner of the world most needed the delicate and persuasive diplomacy of their cannon, that it would really be asking too much to require them to listen to the hopes and fears of the vulgar instruments of their wills. What had they to do with the *feelings* of the common herd? Was it not enough that they were to be offered up as a sacrifice upon the altar of British ambition? Did not their rotting carcasses and bleached bones increase the renown of their country? What happier fate *could* ambition desire? And so onward rolled the government like a vast Juggernaut, crushing and mangling the helpless victims of its power. Still forward it rolled through domestic altars, across sacred hearth-stones; the fell precursor of ruined hopes, blasted happiness, sickness, suffering and death.

The hour had arrived when the body was to be consigned to its final resting-place.

"Henry, *must* they put ma in the ground?"

"Yes, Dolly."

"In the *frozen* ground?"

"Yes."

"Won't she be cold there?"

"No."

"Why not? I should be."

"Not if you were dead, Dolly."

"Can't people feel when they are dead?"

"No."

"How long will ma stay there, Henry?"

"For a long, long time; after you and I grow up and die, long after that."

Dolly sadly reflected upon his words.

"But won't ma be hungry in——No, she can't if she don't feel. Poor ma, she'll never take me on her knee again, never put me asleep, never kiss me, never pet me any more. Dolly got no ma now. Dolly wants to die too."

They gently forced the child, frantic with grief, from the coffin. The lid was closed, the screws driven home, and the body was borne away.

"Father! father! why don't you come and keep them from carrying ma away. Come quick, or we shall never see her again, never see her again!" shrieked the child as she caught a last glimpse of the coffin.

Henry's grief was more subdued, but it was not less intense. For several days he could not leave the house, and remained in the corner a picture of mute despair. He began, however, to rally his energies, for he felt that greater responsibilities now rested upon him. His sister and brother had no other protector, and with the impulses of a noble boy he prepared to discharge what he believed to be his duty to them. Mrs. Hogan insisted that they should remain with her, although they could not well afford to make an addition to their family.

One week after the funeral Henry asked Mr. Hogan what he should do.

"Do, my young friend? Why remain here with Dolly and Frank Tot."

"I can't remain here in idleness; I should not be happy, Mr. Hogan."

"Then why don't you return to your post at Mr. Greasebean's?"

"Never, sir! I will never put my foot within the walls of his factory again."

"Then we must see what else can be thought of, if you insist upon doing something."

"Thank you, Mr. Hogan; if you please. I know I shall be happier if I can work for Dolly and Frank Tot, for they have no one to do it now."

A situation was obtained in another manufacturing establishment, where, for the same number of hours' labor, he obtained the same compensation which he had received from Mr. Greasebeans. Faithfully did Henry perform his task. His head often ached and his limbs throbbed with pain, but true to his purposes he was at his wheel every morning at five o'clock. It was necessary, in order to do that, to rise from his bed long before daylight, now the days were so short. Frank Tot was not awake when he left in the morning, and he was nicely tucked up in bed before he returned at night, so that Henry could only pet him on Sundays. But Dolly never would go to bed until he returned; because she wanted to kiss him and thank him for all he was doing for her. On his way to the factory he passed by a toy shop, and he often paused for a moment to look at a nice little doll that was hanging invitingly at the window, to excite the slumbering desires for maternity in the bosoms of all little girls who passed that way. Henry thought how happy the possession of that doll would make his sister, and once he walked into the store and asked the price. "One and sixpence." His heart sunk at the magnitude of the sum. The fruits of three days' labor could not be spared from the necessities of life; still, as he walked by the shop the doll hung temptingly there. Dolly had nothing to amuse her all day, she must be so lonely without him. He reflected upon the subject long and painfully. What would Mr. Hogan say, if, while indebted to his roof for shelter, he should be guilty of such extravagance. And yet it would make Dolly *so* happy, the possession of that doll. The temptation was too great, and he finally entered the shop. The doll had been sold. Now that it was beyond his reach, he was *certain* the purchase would have been altogether right, and he was very sorry it was sold. The woman observing his chagrin, said she could make him another just like it. Was she sure it would be exactly like it? She answered in the affirmative. And then he timidly asked her if she would receive instalments of one penny a day. The honest face of the boy interested her, and she replied that she would. As evidence of his sincerity, and to bind the bargain, he paid down the first instalment of one penny. Every night as he returned home he deposited a like sum. He worked more cheerfully at his task after the bargain was made, for he thought of the happiness the present would give Dolly. At length the sixteen instalments were all "paid in," and the doll was delivered to him.

"Have you no brother?" asked the woman.

"Oh yes, a dear little fellow."

"Don't you want to buy this horse and wagon for him?"

"I should like to very much if I had money to spare," he replied, with a wistful countenance.

"The price is one shilling, but you are such a good boy you may have it for eight pence."

"How it would amuse Frank Tot," thought Henry.

"You may take it now, and pay me one penny a-day for it."

The temptation was too much for his prudence, and he bought it. It was Saturday night, and taking his gifts home he laid them carefully away until morning, so he might witness the pleasure with which they were received.

After breakfast he gave the doll to his sister. And he was compensated for all his toil by the joy with which she received it. Alternately throwing her arms around his neck and pressing the doll to her bosom, she gave way to lively demonstrations of pleasure. When the first emotions of delight were over she looked from Henry to Frank Tot, as if she thought he too ought to have a present. Frank's lips began to quiver, for his young ideas managed to give shape to a charge of partiality. When Henry placed upon the floor the horse and wagon, Frank Tot looked first at the wagon, and then at Henry, and then at Dolly, with a half-wise, half-pleased expression upon his features, as if the judgment he was making up upon the merits of the horse and wagon was incompatible with anything like merriment. But when he had arrived at his own diminutive conclusions upon the articles in question, he proclaimed his satisfaction by vociferous cooings and energetic clapping of hands.

It was apparent to Mr. Hogan and his wife that Henry Kane was overtasking his strength. His form was emaciated; his cheeks became pale and his eyes sunken, while there was a listlessness in his movements which betokened great physical lassitude. He would not listen to their persuasions to discontinue his daily task, until his strength entirely gave way. One morning he essayed to rise from his bed; but his head swam round, and he could not stand. Three times he made the attempt in the belief that it was only imagination; finally he was obliged to yield, and daylight found him still in bed. A long and wasting disease now preyed upon his frame, and at last there seemed to be no hope of his recovery. To Hogan this was a severe blow, as it required the greatest industry and economy to provide for his own family. When he began to despair of Henry's life, the thought occurred to him that Mr. Greasebeans, whose philanthropic efforts in the cause of foreign missions was the theme of universal praise, might not think the helpless children of Robert Kane altogether beneath his charities. He had been told it was necessary for such good men as Mr. Greasebeans, in order to behold suffering and oppression in far off countries, to elevate their eyes at an angle which carried their vision altogether above the lowly mendicant at their own doors. Nevertheless, he was not without hopes of being able, by a fervent appeal to the sympathies of that gentleman, to induce him to withdraw his gaze from foreign amelioration and emancipation long enough to observe the distressing situation of the motherless children. To accomplish that object he started for the counting-house of Greasebeans, Snodgrass & Co.

Mr. Greasebeans was engaged in conversation with the Rev. Ebenezer Rumfelt, and Hogan seated himself in the corner until the conference was over. As usual they were devising means for carrying on a vigorous assault against oppression in all its strongholds, provided it was entrenched upon any portion of the globe except that from whence their charities issued. According to their definition of charity, it did not apply, in the remotest degree, to the subjects of Great Britain. It was enough that they could boast "I am an Englishman;" and it made not the slightest difference whether the annunciation came from a full stomach, or was the scarcely perceptible echo of famine in its appeal for bread. It could not be expected that charity, *English* charity, would grapple with facts, stern, unyielding facts, *vulgar* facts of every day occurrence, when there was so much pleasure to be obtained in a free indulgence in the romance of imagination, and, what it would be so unchristianly to overlook, so much *notoriety* also.

It was apparent that the discourse of the Rev. Ebenezer Rumfelt had been more than ordinarily unctuous, for the sympathetic face of Mr. Greasebeans was very perceptibly elongated. The corners of the mouth were piously drawn down, while the eyes were sanctimoniously elevated. The senior member of the well known house of Greasebeans, Snodgrass & Co. was seldom more aroused, than by the information communicated by Parson Rumfelt.

"Do you say they actually roasted—"

"Baked."

"Baked a victim, under the very drippings of the Lord's sanctuary?"

"Verily, in the presence of the servant of the Lord; and, not satisfied with such an *awful* exhibition of profanity, they asked him, wouldent he—the Rev. Nicodemus Straitjacket—take a slice!"

"Of the victim's body?"

"Cut from the loins, which they assured him, with significant gesticulations, was considered a tit bit."

"Well, what of it?" said Dykeman, who had just entered. "Don't you partake of the body of the Savior a dozen times a year; and not only that, but drink of his blood, and pretty deeply, too, some of you, when it is of good quality? Why, you are worse cannibals than the Hottentots; for you *pretend* to eat and drink of that which, in fact, you never touch, while they 'go the entire swine,' with the utmost simplicity, and an entire absence of any thing like deception or humbug."

"Mr. Dykeman, you have such strange thoughts," observed Mr. Greasebeans, with strong marks of commiseration upon his pious countenance.

The Rev. Ebenezer Rumfelt shot a glance of indignation at the blasphemer, which was intended to overcome him as effectually, though not after the manner, that Goliath was vanquished by David. But Dykeman was proof against the assaults of Mr. Rumfelt's florid countenance; much more so, indeed, than the latter was suspected of being in the matter of either rum, brandy, or gin. This opinion, however, was based more upon the hue of his complexion, than upon any facts admitted by the reverend gentleman, or elicited in the "course of human events:" a condition of affairs, nevertheless, that warranted one of the clergy in hinting to Mr. Rumfelt that, if he had not been justly accused in regard to complexion, he had *better take in his sign.* A solemn joke, which severed, for all time, the amicable relations which had existed between the two reverend ambassadors.

"And they persisted in their disgusting repast, notwithstanding the protestations of the clergyman?" asked Mr. Greasebeans.

"Not only that, but by divers flourishes they manifested the greatest satisfaction, during the operation, and even went so far, by way of showing their appreciation of the person of Mr. Strait-jacket, as to signify that they had dined on far less acceptable carcasses than his own would make, if it was duly cooked, and properly seasoned."

"Profanation! What! boil a sacred ambassador, like a saddle of mutton? Mr. Rumfelt, they would find you in such excellent condition that you could be *done* without the aid of brandy sauce, even. I'm not sure but they'd find you well *pickled* now," said Dykeman, most unfeelingly.

"*Mr.* Dykeman, I wish you to understand that I consider your remarks personal—*vulgarly* so, sir"—exclaimed Mr. Rumfelt, as he adjusted his wig after the approved mode, though rather more fiercely than was altogether consistent with the divine sanctity which he scrupulously affected. This wig deserves a passing notice. It was not a wig of a decided character, with straight hair, and unmistakable part, which says "I am a wig, and I don't care who knows it." On the contrary, it was one of those wigs that are intended to deceive the unsuspecting, by its air of negligence; strongly resembling an uncombed head, which the owner had forgotten to adjust before leaving his room, and was, therefore, compelled ever and anon to push up and down, to puff out and in, as a proper regard for appearances seemed to justify. In short, it was a wig that might have been indicted and found guilty, under the code of morals which condemns false pretences.

"If such frightful crimes are perpetrated, it is evident our exertions must be redoubled in the glorious cause of humanity," observed Mr. Greasebeans. "A greater supply of money should be despatched at an early day."

"I have now on hand fifteen hundred pounds for such purposes, besides a special fund of nineteen hundred pounds, for the abolition of slavery in the United States. Do you learn, Mr. Rumfelt, that there have been any recent atrocities in the slaveholding states calculated to arouse the indignation of the virtuous, and make them contribute liberally? You know all such cases should be duly proclaimed, so that the good movement may not be arrested."

"Recent advices from the unimpeachable Mr. Roorback, state that four cases have come to his knowledge, where the owners of slaves, in the heat of passion, actually buried them alive."

"Horrible! That intelligence, if we make what we ought out

of it, cannot fail of adding two thousand pounds to the special fund."

"If it is properly advertised, by fitting wood-cuts, with coffins, hammer and nails, &c. &c. &c., I think you might *reasonably* count upon two thousand pounds, and that sum will enable you to set apart quite an item for incidental expenses," said Dykeman.

Mr. Rumfelt answered this opinion by casting a furtive glance at Mr. Dykeman before he continued his remarks.

"Mr. Roorback also informs us, that one week before he wrote, two children were starved to death by their unfeeling masters."

"Come now, that is really too frightful," ejaculated Mr. Greasebeans, with strong marks of indignation upon his usually benign features.

"A fate that is constantly witnessed in Ireland, in the mining districts of England, and in London, too," replied Dykeman. "But that's nothing, for it has been demonstrated, not only by anatomists, but by the society which has the honor, Mr. Greasebeans, of claiming you as its president, that it is much more painful for a negro to die of starvation than for a white man ; which may be accounted for upon the hypothesis that the slave, being ordinarily well fed, finds it a more disagreeable operation to have his food suddenly stopped, than the free-born Englishman, who, from subsisting, any number of years, upon just enough to keep body and soul from dissolving partnership, gets accustomed to his fate by the time the supply ceases altogether. And this I assume to be much more consistent with the Christian religion, than the barbarous practices of our transatlantic brethren."

The only response vouchsafed by Mr. Rumfelt was a look of withering contempt, designed to make Dykeman understand that he, Dykeman, occupied at that moment a position infinitely beneath the notice of Ebenezer Rumfelt.

"Does Mr. Roorback make mention of any *cash transactions* in human flesh ?" asked Mr. Greasebeans, without indicating whether he did or did not coincide in opinion with his reverend visitor, as to the precise locality then and there occupied by Mr. Dykeman, in his estimation.

"He informs me that sales frequently take place by which relations are separated from each other."

"An example we are daily setting them by the operations of our press-gangs ; with this slight difference, that with them those who are taken away, and those who remain, are well fed and clothed, while with us the family of the victim, as in the case of Robert Kane, are delivered over to suffering and death. These things, however, can all be reconciled by the aforesaid hypothesis, that white folks can and ought to suffer more than black."

"He states further," continued Mr. Rumfelt, without even deigning a glance at Mr. Dykeman, "that these sales, in separating man from wife, and resulting in second marriages, beget a disregard for the nuptial tie, and consequently a corruption of morals, the bare contemplation of which is truly appalling."

"*Dreadful !*" uttered Mr. Greasebeans.

"There is," observed Mr. Dykeman, who would take part in the conversation, notwithstanding the evident disgust with which his remarks were listened to by Ebenezer Rumfelt, "a manifest reason why Englishmen should be permitted to indulge in the severest animadversions upon the absence of nuptial fidelity among the 'rest of mankind;' a license which we have purchased by the correctness of our own deportment in that regard, as a nation and as individuals. It is true, some of our monarchs have not been shining lights for the guidance of the faithful. It was shrewdly suspected that the wife of Richard the Second was no better than she should be. The consort of one of the Edwards was also accused of being rather too unmanageable and hard to satisfy. Queen Bess, too, was not above suspicion, and George the Fourth, the most accomplished gentleman in all England, did not render that fealty to the matrimonial tie which is indispensably necessary in order to enable every well-regulated family to enjoy the full fruition of connubial bliss. It has also been intimated that licentiousness and debauchery prevailed, to an extent unparalleled in the history of any other nation on earth, during the reign of Charles the Second, but that was only the natural effervescence which might reasonably have been expected after the round-headed, crop-haired rule of Oliver Cromwell. And even now, the fashionables of England do not set a very commendable example, in the matter of conjugal fidelity, if we are to credit the portraitures (so much lauded by the press of London,) drawn by G. W. X. Y. Z. Reynolds. On the other hand, we can boast of one *striking* example of loyalty to the marriage knot. Henry the Eighth will, for all time, stand out prominently as the exponent of connubial faithfulness, in this, that he adhered to one wife until he had murdered her, before he would yield his royal hand to another. Probably the world will never know another such a beast as he proved himself in connection with his half dozen wives. We can pardon him, though; of course we can, because he was sometimes deceived, and also because he was the head and front of the reformation in England. In consideration of those facts, we can overlook a world of rascality. We also have this additional consolation, for whicn I trust we shall be duly grateful. It is not half so wicked for white people to indulge in such sinfulness, (which I regret to say has been too prevalent ever since David cast liquorice eyes upon Uriah's wife,) as it is for negroes; an exemption from culpability which must be traced to the fact, that, being the descendents of Ham, they are the especial favorites of the Almighty."

"And he finally says," inquired the impenetrable Ebenezer Rumfelt, "that the planters are turning their attention to the raiseing of children for the slave market."

"As they would cattle?" remarked the senior member of the house of Greasebeans, Snodgrass and Company, with his sanctimonious face greatly elongated.

"Precisely so."

"Which I assume to be an excellent improvement; for to propagate the human species faster than the old fogy laws of nature would permit, cannot be otherwise than an amendment highly acceptable to the divine founder of those laws," observed Mr. Dykeman. "We had better introduce the system into Great Britain, if it has not been patented in the United States, for the purpose of increasing our own population; as the amazing numbers, who, strange to say, prefer barbarous, half-civilized, slavery-accursed America to their native country, is sadly interfering with the population of the British Empire. There is one powerful argument in favor of this valuable amendment of the laws of nature, as applied to this country, Mr. Greasebeans, which will not fail to present itself to you in a business point of view. The wealth of the house of Greasebeans, Snodgrass, and Co., will be increased in proportion to the decrease of the wages of labor, caused by a surplus of operatives. Do you take, Mr. Greasebeans? It is true that result will multiply the distress among the poor, but we are not supposed to be affected by such consideration, provided the distress and suffering only exists in Great Britain."

"Mr. Greasebeans, it is useless to conclude the interesting statement made by Mr. Roorback this morning," said Mr. Rumfelt. "I will avail myself of another opportunity when we shall not be subjected to impertinent interruption." And adjusting his wig with a delicate touch, Mr. Rumfelt left the office with a stateliness of bearing, that indicated an ability to sustain all the religion and morals of the United Kingdom upon his own shoulders.

"Mr. Greasebeans," said Hogan timidly, "I called this morning to see if you would contribute something for the support of the children of Robert Kane, who was seized a few months ago by the press-gang."

"Really now, Mr.; what's your name?"

"Hogan."

"Hogan, I don't see in what way I can assist you."

"His wife perished on the night you turned her from your house ——"

"Allow me to interrupt you, Mr. Hogan," said Mr. Greasebeans, as he smoothed his white neck-cloth; "on the night she was ejected by virtue of legal process. You should pay a proper regard to terms, Mr. Hogan."

"At all events, she was turned into the street that fatal night, notwithstanding the earnest supplications of her son."

"You could not, of course, expect me to attend to business on the night a party was given at my house."

"Not if it was to save the life of a human being?"

"Of course not. The house of Greasebeans, Snodgrass & Co. have established certain inflexible rules, which are not departed from under any circumstances. The senior member of that house, discovering how admirably they worked, adopted similar rules for the government of his household."

"Well, Mrs. Kane died that night—"

"You have mentioned that fact once before," remarked the imperturbable Mr. Greasebeans.

"And her three young and helpless children are now at my house," continued Hogan.

"I trust you take excellent care of them, Mr. Hogan."

"I do, to the extent of my ability ; but having a large family of my own to support, I find it impossible to do justice to them all."

"Ah!"

"I hope, therefore, you will give a small portion of the large sum you are devoting to the abolition cause, for the temporary support of those poor orphans."

"*Mr.* Hogan are you aware of what you ask?" replied Mr. Greasebeans, with unusual vivacity. "Do you know that *that* fund is to be sacredly devoted to the righteous cause for which it was raised, and that it would be worse than profanity to divert it to any other purpose? Get thee behind me, tempter! I am proof against your seductions."

"I am sorry if I have made an improper request, Mr. Greasebeans."

"You ought to be, for there is no higher crime known to morals than seeking to undermine the charitable resolves of the virtuous and good."

Mr. Greasebeans wiped the tears from his spectacles, which the consciousness of an assault upon his rectitude had gathered there; for his feelings were very much hurt. Hogan did not exactly comprehend the offence he had committed, but he had no doubt it was of a very heinous character, or it would not have drawn tears from Mr. Greasebeans' spectacles. Still the condition of the helpless children was uppermost in his mind, and he ventured hesitatingly to remark—

"Perhaps you may not consider it wrong to contribute something out of your private funds for those unfortunate orphans, who—"

"Mr. Hogan, you will please excuse me from listening further to your requests. My nerves have really been so much shocked by your unfeeling, I may say, *cruel* assault, upon my virtue, that I am quite incapacitated from attending to any business to-day. You will excuse me, Mr. Hogan, I know you will, after having so unkindly assailed my nervous system. Good morning, Mr. Hogan. Dykeman, show the gentleman the door."

"You see," observed Dykeman, as he bowed Hogan into the street, "all the philanthropy of Mr. Greasebeans is awakened by foreign missions. It cannot be expected, therefore, that he should interest himself in the cause of domestic suffering. You will appreciate the purity of his motives Mr. Hogan, and make mention of it wheresoever you may have an opportunity. Good morning, Mr. Hogan; I hope you may have a nice time with Robert Kane's children."

Hogan turned gloomily away, for he had a half-formed idea that unutterable meanness was at the bottom of these hypocritical protestations.

CHAPTER XVII.

"I think of thee;—that eye of flame,
Those tresses, falling bright and free,
That brow, where 'Beauty writes her name:'
I think of thee—I think of thee."—PRENTICE.

ELLEN KNOWLES, confident that she had entrapped the affections of her cousin, impatiently awaited the hour when he should make a declaration of love. She was apprehensive that Lord Melville might disclose the part she had taken in his arrest; and, therefore, she often threw herself in the way of Christie, to give him opportunities of declaring his passion. For that purpose she walked over to her aunt's several days after he rescued Lady Katharine from the river. Her heart beat triumphantly when she saw him seated in the cozy little parlor before a cozy fire. The aspect of the room spoke of love and marriage. And now, she thought, was the favorable hour for a disclosure of his passion.

"Ah, Ellen, you are welcome. Take this chair by the fire; the keen air has given your cheeks a rosy hue, which, by the way, is not a stranger to them."

"Are you so observing? I was not aware you ever noted such trifles. I thought, so far as you are concerned, a lady might be white, green, or blue, without attracting attention."

"It would not be considered a matter of very great importance provided her heart was not *black*, cousin Ellen."

The girl winced.

"And do you estimate the moral qualities so highly?"

"Far above either personal beauty, rank, or wealth."

She paused. Could it be possible he had obtained a knowledge of her character. If so, her aspirations were hopeless, and her scheming vain. But no, her dissimulation had been too profound.

"I am exceedingly happy, cousin Christie, that our opinions agree upon this subject, for I prize purity of thought and purpose above all other gifts."

"These sentiments do you honor."

"Yes. Although I have worldly expectations something more than moderate, in prospective wealth to be derived from my father, still that is the least of the attractions which, I trust, I possess. I speak to you thus frankly, Christie, because I have felt for you the affection of a sister——"

"For the last twelve months?"

"What do you mean?"

"That your conduct towards me before that time savored more of contempt then affection."

"Ah, Christie, believe me, it was the bearing of a petted, wayward child, who took that way of showing her regard."

"I am glad to hear it, because appearances pointed in another direction, cousin Ellen."

"Thank you, Christie, for your generous confidence in my protestations."

"And you have always entertained for me sentiments of the kindest regard?"

"Always; how can you ask the question?" she said, fixing her large, brilliant eyes upon him for a moment, with something very like brazen effrontery, and then they melted into a look of love and devotion.

There could be no mistaking their appeal. But Christie generously resolved not to unmask her. Voices were now heard in the yard in loud conversation. They both recognized the imperious tone of Lord Melville. Christie started to his feet.

"Do not go out; you must not, indeed you must not," said Ellen, with passionate earnestness.

Before he could release himself, Melville stalked into the hall.

"You thought to escape me, did you, fool that you are. Why, Satan may as well attempt to fly from damnation."

"What want you here, my lord?"

"Your body—aye, your body."

"You have no claim upon me."

"Have I not? Did not yourself and mother become security for a neighbor, Richard Burnham, some fourteen months ago?"

"Yes."

"Has the debt been paid?"

"I do not know."

"Well, I do. It has not; I have purchased it, and am your creditor again, aye, and of that old woman who dared to threaten my mother a few weeks ago."

"I did not threaten her without a cause, braggart. Beware, sir!" replied Mrs. Kane, fiercely.

"Fool! fool! to think of aweing *me* thus."

"Scoundrel! dare you use such language to my mother," exclaimed Christie Kane, as he violently seized Melville by the throat, and shook him until he was black in the face.

The officers rescued the nobleman from the grasp of his assailant, when he staggered to a seat.

"*Won't* you suffer for this?"

"Doubtless; but not longer than you will remember it."

"Officer, arrest both those persons."

They were both seized.

"And now I have a word to say about you, my fair but treacherous dame," he said, addressing Ellen Knowles.

"For God's sake! spare me," she said, imploringly.

"Did you spare my great aunt?"

"Oh, forget that—forget that."

"What do you mean by such conduct, Ellen?" asked Mrs. Kane.

"She is afraid I will tell——"

"Don't, for mercy's sake, don't tell it."

"How urgently she requested me to cast her affectionate cousin, Mr. Christie Kane, into prison."

Ellen staggered to a chair.

"It's a lie—a base, malicious lie," she screamed.

No, Ellen, your conduct is evidence of its truth," said Christie. calmly.

"And you believe the accusation?"

"I do."

"Ah! ha! my young lass, your hopes are destroyed, and by me, by *me*, Lord Melville!"

"*Lord Melville no longer!*" said Mrs. Kane, in a deep, hollow voice.

All eyes were turned upon her. They were appalled by the ghastly paleness of her countenance, and the diabolical expression which was stamped upon every lineament of her face.

"What do you mean, woman?" said Melville, with a look of awe.

"I mean—"

"Don't, aunty; there may yet be hope," said Ellen imploringly.

Mrs. Kane paused; she was evidently deeply troubled, for there was a gurgling in her throat that sounded like the death-rattle. The spectators were motionless, as they observed her working countenance. At length, with a violent effort, she spoke.

"No, Ellen, there is no hope. Our expectations have been destroyed by this brute. He has availed himself of his position, not only to thwart the hope that I have cherished for more than twenty years, but he has been guilty of the most fiendish cruelty to one who has always treated me with kindness, notwithstanding my neglect and abuse."

"What does all this mean, old woman?" exclaimed Melville, who had rallied from the stupor into which he had been thrown by her language and manner.

"I'll tell you what it means," she cried fiercely. "It means that you are not Lord Melville! It means that you are *my* son! It means that Christie Kane is Lord Melville, the son of the Duchess of Sunderland, and the heir to a dukedom!"

The bystanders heard the annunciation with amazement. The officers released their hold upon Christie Kane as though the information had invested his person with a sanctity not hitherto possessed. Melville sank back in his chair. His jaw dropped, and his face was as pale as if stamped by the ineffaceable characters of death.

"Gentlemen, I have spoken the truth," said Mrs. Kane, addressing the officers. "It shall all be explained before the proper tribunal, but I will remark here that a friend of mine was wet-nurse to that young man," pointing to Christie Kane, "who was of the same age as my own son," and she nodded to Lord Melville. "The infants were exchanged. The Duchess was not the wiser, for she never visited the nursery. My object was to procure a marriage between Ellen Knowles and the heir of a dukedom; unless my son proved to be a man who would adorn the position which he occupied. In that case, I resolved to let the secret die with me. But I learned at an early day, that he would disgrace the rank into which he had been foisted, by his unsufferable bearing and inhuman conduct. I then resolved to carry out my original scheme. But my designs have been thwarted; thwarted, too, by the agency of my own son; and it is, therefore, without one throb of pity that I consign him to the position for which he was destined by nature."

"What proof have you of your assertion, bold, bad woman?" said Melville, who rallied again.

"Proof that is overwhelmingly conclusive. The evidence of the wet nurse, who is still living, and of the attending physician."

"As for the wet-nurse I fancy her testimony will be considered of little value, having been, as you admit, a party to the crime. And as for the physician, it would be a difficult thing for him to swear that in the robust form of yonder boor could be traced the features of the babe of twenty-two years ago. Bah! you must exercise your ingenuity with greater skill to manufacture a respectable falsehood."

"Christie Kane, have you a mole upon your arm half the size of a blackberry?" asked Mrs. Kane.

"I have."

"Will you let us see it?"

"Certainly."

He removed his coat, and rolling up his sleeve disclosed a mark upon the arm near the shoulder, resembling the half of a blackberry.

"That mark will explain all, for it was commented upon at the hour of his birth by the physician, the monthly nurse, and the Duke of Sunderland himself. What say you now, sirrah?"

Melville rose from his seat pale as a corpse, and left the house.

"I always thought he was a flunkey," said one of the officers.

"Yeas, it wer always apperent he didn't belong to our class, he was so demned vulgwar," replied the other, as he indulged in the refined habit of picking his nose.

"Gentlemen, you may withdraw," said Mrs. Kane, pointing to the door.

"I spose we may," said the officer hesitatingly.

"Go!" said Christie sternly.

"Certainly, my lord, if you desire it," said the officer obsequiously.

"Your *lord!* does desire it," said the young man contemptuously, accenting the word.

"And now," said Christie, taking Mrs. Kane by the hand, and conducting her to the sofa, "all I require of you, as a slight return for the years of wrong you have made me suffer, is to keep secret for ten days the knowledge of my birth."

"I will," replied Mrs. Kane.

"I thank you; and now let me assure you that for the many

acts of kindness I have received at your hands, I shall always be grateful, and it shall be manifested in a more substantial manner than by woods, merely."

Christie Kane retired to his chamber, and reflected long upon the intelligence he had received. Could it be possible that he, the humble farmer, was heir to the wide domains of the Duke of Sunderland? Was the haughty Duchess his mother? Was that proud Duke his father? How would they receive the intelligence? All these questions forced themselves upon him, until his brain whirled with excitement. It was stepping into a new world. To leave the humble dwelling where he thought he was born, for the castle of Mornlow, and the splendid residence in town. To control the destinies of men, instead of having his controlled by them. To be elevated to the level of that class he had so often and so freely denounced. It is not strange that to have his existence thus changed should produce a state of strong and irrepressible excitement. And what were his plans for the future? He could not arrange them in that moment of agitation, but one important step he resolved to take at once, and that was, to solicit the hand of Katharine Montague in marriage. It was a bold step, and one which, if it failed, would cause him much unhappiness. A less scrupulous lover would have waited until his suit was sustained by the powerful auxiliary of rank. Not so Christie Kane. He could not accept as the noble what would be denied as a man. There was something in the bearing of the maiden which bade him hope, notwithstanding the hereditary pride of the family. But did he not hope rashly, to suppose the daughter of that illustrious house could stoop from her lofty position and ally herself with a peasant? He resolved to incur the risk, and as there was no time to be lost, he started at once for the castle of Montague. Arriving there, he informed the liveried waiting-man that he came to inquire of Lady Katharine Montague's health.

The servant, less mannerly than most of the Earl's retainers, gave him a supercilious glance that measured his dimensions from head to foot.

"Do you hear me, sirrah?"

"Yeas, but I doubt if her ladyship will feel herself honored by inquiries from such as you."

"Insolence!"

"Ah! Maister Christie, it's mesell is glad to say yez. Come in. Her ladyship left orders for yez to be admitted, if yez called."

With a throbbing heart, Christie Kane followed Phelim Savor into the drawing room.

"Mr. Christie Kane," he announced at the door.

Katharine Montague was seated upon a luxurious sofa near the fire. She arose as he entered.

"I am glad to see you, Mr. Kane. You have delayed a long time, before calling to ascertain whether my health suffered from that night of exposure."

He thought her voice trembled as she spoke, and he knew the color deepened upon her cheek.

"If I had supposed my absence would be noted, I certainly should have paid my respects earlier," he replied, as he pressed the hand she had extended towards him.

"Pray take a seat;" and she made room for him beside her, by removing the piece of embroidery that lay upon the sofa. "So you see you are of more consideration than you thought."

"And the assurance makes me the happiest of men," he responded warmly.

"As happy as if it came from your fair cousin Ellen?" she said archly.

"Far more so—oh, *indeed* far more so. If you only knew, Lady Katharine," he continued impetuously, "how often my mind has dwelt upon your person, since the first hour I saw you beneath the oak; with what fondness memory has lingered upon the few words of interest that have fallen from your lips; with what anguish I have heard the slighting taunt, and witnessed the look of contempt, you would partly comprehend the absorbing, overwhelming love with which you have inspired me."

"Mr. Kane!" she exclaimed, starting up; but meeting an appealing glance from his eloquent eyes, she sank upon the ottoman again.

"I know the distance which separates us, for it has often appalled me. I have tried to control my affections—with what intensity nights of silent anguish could prove. It was unavailing; and now, impelled by a resistless impulse, I came to lay my affections at your feet. I pledge to you the pure and unalterable affections of a man who would not, if he could, boast of higher rank than that to which every man of honor may claim. Reject me—trample upon the sacred impulses of that heart which beats only for you, and it will stlll, like the bruised flower, yield its purest offering to thee."

"Mr. Kane, I may not listen to you," she said—while the hand he had taken, trembled, but was not withdrawn. "I appreciate the offer you have made me. I will even confess it has gratified my feelings; but I cannot—nay, I *must* not accept it."

"And I am rejected because I am a peasant?" he said, as he rose to his feet.

"No, no—I—I—yes; I will frankly tell you, that if my feelings were permitted to dec ide, I might—that is—oh! what shall I say?"

"You love me, then—say, dearest Lady Katharine, that you love me," said Christie, as he encircled her waist with his arm, and pressed his lips to her own, in a long, lingering kiss, while her head rested upon his shoulder, during a moment of fond abandonment.

"This interview must end. You have no right to wring my heart with anguish," said the maiden, as she released herself from his arms.

"And I am hopelessly rejected? It is well; I have been justly punished, for daring to hope that a *parvenue* might ally himself to the daughter of an illustrious house."

"Do not let us part in anger. But for the prejudices of caste, I might perhaps, reward your devotion. I cannot say more."

"And you, Lady Katharine Montague, with your brilliant intellect and just contempt for the hollow distinctions of society, still yield to its prejudices. Then farewell, forever; your affection is not worth the seeking."

"Go, sir," she replied indignantly, as she pointed to the door. "You do not know what is due to a lady of rank."

With a low bow, he withdrew.

"Thus ends my boastful opinion of the power of love. Wealth and rank are henceforth nothing to me but instruments with which to relieve that class of society, in whose cause my feelings will always be interested," muttered Christie Kane, as he turned his back upon the castle of Montague. As he emerged into the highway, he met Phelim Savor.

"Phelim, you expressed an anxious desire to return to my service a short time since?"

"Yez."

"Are you still desirous of doing so?"

"Yez may well say that same, Maister Christie. Lady Katharine is an illegant and well-spoken lady, and I'm grateful for her kindness, but I love no one as well as yersel', Maister Christie. Indade I do not," he said earnestly.

"Well, in a week I will take you into my service again."

"I'm thankful to yez. I've no objection to the Montague living, or to any other, bekaze we are servants, and it's an honorable badge of servitude. Yez say, I'm not like to some poor divils, who perform the work of servants, but object to wearing the emblim. Now that's what I calls a carrying two faces under one hat—a most riprehinsible prosading."

"Very well, Phelim, call at Mornlow Castle in a week, and inquire for me."

"Yez. At Mornlow Castle," repeated Phelim, wonderingly.

The duchess was seated in an elegant arm-chair. Breakfast was over, and she was yawning through the London daily papers; because she thought the wife of a duke ought, at least, to have a superficial knowledge of passing events—at least of all the murders and other heinous offences; which her grace loved to dwell upon, as they exemplified the rascalities of the substratum. She had gone through the intellectual column headed "Crimes and Casualties," when Katharine Montague was announced.

"My dear Kate, I have been *dying* to see you; indeed, my anxiety had risen to such a height, that but for the damp atmosphere, I should have gone over to the castle. Do tell me all about your escape. Were you not shocked at having the vulgar arm of that plebeian around you? Any one can tell he is a fellow of low blood by his features. How different from the aristocratic lineaments of Lord Melville; upon every feature of which is stamped the evidence of noble birth. It is the easiest thing in the world, Kate, to point out the cream of our aristocracy. No one could doubt for a moment that Melville belongs to that exclusive class."

"I presume even your grace would have thought little of vulgar arms, at such a moment," said Katharine, with a smile.

"Oh! my dear Kate, you can't comprehend the unutterable loathing with which I regard the horrid creatures. I really believe I should rather die, if it was not for having the nasty water in my eyes and nose. Water, too, that is mixed with dirt; faugh!"

"And then to be covered up with dirt after your death."

"No, Kate, no; nothing but the purest Italian marble, carved at dear delightful Florenee, will hold the remains of Adelaide, Duchess of Sunderland."

"One looks so disagreeable after being drowned," remarked Katharine Montague, gravely.

"Yes; I do not know, upon reflection, but I should have preferred a rescue by even such a low bred fellow as—as—what is his name?"

"Kane, Christie Kane," replied the maiden, with a blush.

"The one who had the impertinence to contend with my son for the prize at the steeple-chase!"

"And had the audacity to win it," replied Katharine, as her eyes flashed.

"May I ask your Grace what is the news in London."

"Her Majesty has returned from the Highlands."

"Then we shall soon depart for London."

"We go the beginning of next week."

"Who are to be the lions of the season?"

"A charming negro girl from the United States will be one of them."

"A negro girl! your Grace is merry."

"Not at all. We have found it necessary to elevate the negro standard, in order to accomplish our designs upon American Slavery. With all their devotion to the cause of the negro, the trans-atlantic abolitionists do not regard him as their equal, and it is true, as Charles Dickens says in his 'household words,' that the slaves are prevented from escaping in greater numbers, because their condition, when free, in the Northern States, is more degrading than in a state of bondage."

"And you, the celebrated and accomplished Duchess of Sunderland, the favorite of her Majesty, intend to patronize a negress!"

"Of course I do. All that is necessary to elevate the negroes in the United States, is to patronize them here. Once let the Americans see the English nobility and the London aristocracy patronizing a negro wench, and believe me, two months will not elapse before those servile imitators will conceive a wonderful respect for their sable brethren."

"And has she no claims upon your attention except her color?"

"Yes, she sings well, and that is the reason we assign for manifesting so much interest in her. The effect, however, will be the same in the United States."

"What is the cause of the intense interest which you take in the affairs of the great republic?"

"To witness its overthrow, and thus destroy the fruitful cause of rebellion and anarchy in Europe."

"I supposed it could not be traced to charitable impulses, for there are objects enough in Great Britain to awaken its slumbering energies."

"No doubt of it, my dear Kate, and the only apprehension we have is that the American abolitionists, stupid creatures, will discover it."

Voices were now heard in loud altercation at the door.

"I tell you I will see her."

"Indeed you cannot, I have received positive orders to exclude you."

A sound that resembled very much a boxed ear, was succeeded by the noise of a body falling upon the floor, and the next moment the exquisitely dressed body servant of the Duchess of Sunderland rushed into the room, with the blood streaming from his nose. Close upon his footsteps strode the tall figure of Mrs. Kane.

"Here is that horrid creature again, and I'll be blessed if she has not hurt Frederick Augustus."

"Yes, and I'll hurt your feelings, if I do not you body, before I leave this room."

"Frederic Augustus, call the porter, this woman's presence is disagreeable."

"Stay; I have but a brief explanation to make. Adelaide, Duchess of Sunderland, you must hear it."

The solemnity of her manner awed the Duchess.

"Two months ago, I—*I*, Margaret Kane, prostrated myself at your feet; I implored you to save me from want, and suffering. You spurned me from your presence! You! Aye, you, who thought yourself beyond the reach of unhappiness; *you*, who are bending all the energies of your feeble intellect to bring revolution, wretchedness and woe upon a people who have committed no other crime but to save and protect English subjects, whom English philanthropy surrenders to the tender mercies of starvation. I told you then, that I would humble your pride, and I'll do it even at the hazard of ruin to myself. Duchess of Sunderland! you have a son whom you idolize, notwithstanding his faults?"

"I have, I have; what danger threatens him?" exclaimed the Duchess, in an agony of apprehension.

"Upon whom rests the hopes of your house?"

"Woman, why do you harrow my feelings? Tell me, Oh! tell me, Melville is not dead, and I will grant all you ask." And the proud woman clasped her hands in mortal fear.

"Ah! ha! you love him then? Now will I wring your heart-strings, as you have wrung mine."

"My God, Kate, what does the woman mean?"

"That Lord Charles Melville is not your son!"

The Duchess sprang to her feet. Her limbs were rigid, the blood receded from her cheeks, and her lips were drawn back from her teeth.

"Now the iron enters your soul. Ha! ha! ha! Now, woman, you are mortal! *He is not your son!* He is mine, the son of the poor thing whose prayers you scorned; and your son, *your* son is—is—the poor despised plebeian, *Christie Kane!*"

"Christie Kane?" said you Christie Kane?" demanded Katharine, eagerly.

"I did, but that annunciation carries with it woe to you, also, imperious maiden. You rejected the offer of Christie Kane; do not flatter yourself that they will be renewed by Charles, Lord Melville."

Scowling upon her victims, the savage woman stalked from the room.

With a low moan the Duchess sank upon the floor.

He who supposes that unalloyed happiness finds a resting place in the abode of rank and wealth, has never witnessed the splendid misery that interposes itself as remorselessly between the favored classes and uninterrupted felicity, as between the humble laborer and domestic bliss.

CHAPTER XVIII.

"The constitution of this country has always been in a moving state, either gaining or losing something."—Lord Mansfield.

The truth of Mrs. Kane's assertion was verified by the family physician and the Duke of Sunderland. From that hour nothing was seen or heard of Mrs. Kane's son. It was supposed his pride could not brook the taunts he would be subjected to from those whose ill-will had been aroused by insufferable insolence, and that he had left the kingdom; but whither he had fled no one could conjecture. Christie Kane, or Lord Melville, as he will now be designated, took up his abode at Mornlow Castle. He was graciously received by the Duke, and the Duchess confessed to Katharine Montague that his face, now that she minutely examined it, had an aristocratic, rather than a plebeian cast. Indeed she thought it blended the features of the Duke and herself; an expression of opinion which was intended to be highly complimentary to the young man. Lady Katharine suggested that her grace might not hesitate to be saved from a watery grave by his "vulgar arm." The Duchess shook her head reprovingly as though she suspected there was a little bit of malice in the allusion.

"If you do not feel such an aversion for him as you did for Chărles—poor boy, I love him yet—I should still cherish the hope that our houses might be united by a marriage between you."

Lady Katharine's face was crimsoned in a moment.

Lord Melville did not exhibit any decided marks of affection for his parents. The character of neither were to his liking. They were too selfish, too fond of notoriety. Besides, that want of care during his infancy which courted his unhappy fate, was not calculated to awaken any lively manifestation of filial attachment. To both his bearing was respectful and courteous; nothing more. It was soon apparent to the Duke that his son was quite as determined in carrying out his purposes as the real Christie Kane, though the efforts of the former were mainly directed to ameliorating the condition of his tenants, instead of tormenting them. His quiet energy and scrupulous justice soon made itself felt, and the Duke surrendered the management of his estate almost entirely to him. Its vast concerns took him from the castle nearly all day, and he returned at night with the consciousness of having performed his duty. In two days the establishment would break up, and the family would return to town; still Melville had not called at the Castle of Montague. So carefully had he avoided the usual haunts of Katharine, that he had not even seen her since the fatal occasion that witnessed the destruction of his hopes. The day preceding their departure, Lord Rossmore and his family were to dine at Mornlow. For the first time Katharine was to meet her lover as Lord Melville. As she stood before the mirror she examined her face and figure with a judgment more than usually critical. She thought the mercury gave back an image of unsurpassed loveliness.

She was examining the paintings and statuary in the gallery at Mornlow Castle when she heard footsteps approaching. Her form was concealed by a marble figure, and without being observed she saw Lord Melville enter the gallery. A melancholy expression was stamped upon his features, and he examined the family portraits with a listless air. At length his attention was arrested by the portrait of his great-grandfather, the founder of his house. The artist had succeeded in delineating the stern and energetic lineaments of the first Duke of Sunderland, who, scorning the humble avocation of a shoemaker, had abandoned it for the more congenial occupation of a soldier.

"There was a man," soliloquised Melville, "worth half the effeminate nobility of the present day. A man whose vigorous intellect and determined courage made him the artificer of his own fortune. And his descendants, the further they are removed from him, will boast more and more extravagantly of a long line of illustrious ancestors, all, all sprung from a highly respectable shoemaker! Rank! what art thou worth?" and he laughed bitterly.

Katharine wished to escape unobserved from the gallery, but she could not.

He paused before the portrait of his grandfather.

"And this man, who, but for the resolute daring of his father, would have been a shoemaker, as well as the son of a shoemaker, could not so far *degrade* himself as to marry the accomplished daughter of a baronet, whose affections he had won, notwithstanding he saw her sinking into the grave broken-hearted. Rank! what art thou worth?" and again the bitter laugh rang through the gallery.

A cold sweat gathered upon the forehead of the maiden.

"Ah! here is a noble, true-hearted Englishman; my great-uncle, Sir Marmaduke Drakeman, whose fascinating manners and splendid person made him a universal favorite. But he would not, no, he would not marry the haughty damsel who had rejected his hand before he was knighted! Old fellow, you possess that true pride which is worthy of admiration, and I honor you for it," and he affectionately tapped the cheek of the baronet with the gold head of his cane.

Turning to the opposite side of the gallery, he beheld the form of Katharine Montague. She resembled, in the paleness of her complexion and the rigidity of her form, one of the statues by which she was surrounded. Raising his hat he bowed profoundly and withdrew without uttering a word. As they were seated at the dining-table, the chairs were all occupied but one. Melville did not return to Mornlow until the Earl of Rossmore and his party had left Montague castle.

The following day both Montague and Mornlow castles were deserted by their occupants, with the exception of Melville, who remained at Mornlow for several weeks to protect the tenants upon the estate as much as possible from the severity of winter. He retained only the housekeeper, a chambermaid, and Phelim Savor. When the weather would permit, he rode over the wide domain of the Mornlow estate, accompanied by Phelim. The former steward had been discharged, and one with a moderate amount of soul was engaged. When the weather was stormy, Melville caused a fire to be built in the library, where thousands of books were piled upon each other, covered with dust almost as old as themselves. He was seated there, pouring over one of Gibbons' pompous and resounding pages, and listening to the pattering rain, when Phelim Savor entered the library.

"If yez lordship plazes, Sir William Belthoven is in the drawing-room, and says he would like to see yez."

"Sir William Belthoven, the politician?"

"No, yer lordship, the mimber of Parliament."

"The words are synonymous."

"I know that, yer lordship; and he is such an intilligent gintleman, who niver carries two faces under one hat. He'll tell yer lordship all about the sacred rights of the fraymen. Shall I tell Sir William yer will coome down?"

"Do you think I shall be entertained?"

"Be intertained is it? Why the bayronet is the most illigent spaker in all this part of England. He manages to plaze ivery body, and that shows a great dale of ability, don't yez think it does?"

"Tact, Phelim, nothing more."

"Well, of koorse that means the same thing."

"Conduct Sir William Belthoven hither."

"Yez."

"Sir William Belthoven, you are welcome to Mornlow."

That gentleman responded with a soft and winning smile. It was charged by his enemies, that Sir William had triumphed in no less than eight canvasses by the assistance of that smile. In fact, they were so unkind as to insist upon it, that *that* smile, his low, confidential tone, deferential manners, and unsurpassed abilities as a listener, had been the foundation of his popularity with his constituents. His most unfaltering opponent, Sir Pertinax McFlummux, had been often heard to declare that he should have defeated Sir William three times out of the five canvasses he had stood against him for parliament, if it had not been for the patience with which that accomplished politician could listen to everything that was said to him. He had been known to sit upon a very hard board for no less than two hours, while a poor voter poured a melancholy tale of suffering into his ear, which found an appropriate response in the long and sympathetic countenance of Sir William; a correct representation of which said countenance would have immortalized Hogarth. His features had an elasticity which any politician might envy, for upon divers occasions, Sir Pertinax Mc Flummux had, with spiteful eyes, seen him mounted upon a sharp rock, which Sir Pertinax had no doubt was hurting him considerably, while he listened with smiling visage to the dull wit of a horse-jockey, who was known to possess considerable influence with the blacksmith and inn-keeper. Sir Pertinax was wont to exclaim—

"Damn it! who can expect to triumph in a canvass against an opponent who can listen to everybody and everything."

Sir Petinax McFlummux was right, for popularity won by a *good listener* will maintaini ts power when principles lose their hold upon the masses.

"I am fortunate in catching you at home. This is the second time I have called, but I never have laid eyes upon you since your splendid success as a horseman against the supposed heir of Sunderland. Having, by the favor of the Duke, your father, been honored with a seat in parliament for many years, I deem it my duty, as it certainly is my pleasure, to cultivate the good opinion, and obey the wishes, of himself and son." And the baronet gave a popularity-seeking bow.

Sir William made the same speech at least three hundred and sixty-five times a year to at least three hundred and sixty-five different individuals, whose position ranged from the Duke of Sunderland, the most illustrious of his constituents, to the humblest squire; indeed, he had been heard to intimate something very much like it, to his country tailor; for Sir William had two tailors, one for the city and one for the country, in the same way that Solomon Greasebeans had two consciences, one for American slavery, and the other for English serfdom.

"You honor me by your deference to our house."

"It is only a just compliment to those upon whom rests the dignity and power of England. For what are the opinions of the scum of the earth, who delve in its bosom, worth, compared to the wishes of our aristocracy?"

"A compliment I must place to the credit of Lord Melville, at the expense of Christie Kane," said the young man sarcastically.

"Oh no," said the baronet, with an unmoved countenance; "any one could have seen upon the occasion of your triumph at the steeple-chase, that in your veins flowed the blood of the gentry, if not of the noble."

"It is strange that no one ever intimated as much to me."

"Pardon me, no. It would have been an unauthorized interference in your affairs. But pray, are you much of a student since your restoration, if I may so term it; for I presume in your more humble sphere you had not much time to devote to literature?" said the baronet, anxious to change a subject which was becoming disagreeable, notwithstanding his tact.

"I managed to obtain a knowledge of standard works, historical as well as fictitious."

"And what do you think of the writers of the nineteenth century, for we have a double interest in our own times?"

"I think most of them are as much inflated with vanity, as their talents are overrated by the public. In the estimation of some of our authors, the world never produced such geniuses as we have the privilege of worshiping, in their persons; and they require us to mourn over the dearth which their conceptions and productions inflicted upon exhausted nature."

"Ha! ha! good, upon my word; but bilious, though. Well, the world does flatter them."

"So it does; and we are *bound* to admire, as the creation of almost superhuman power, James' 'solitary horseman,' Bulwer's resounding periods, Scott's rhymes, and Dickens' ghosts."

"By the virtues of our amiable queen, but you wield a trenchant blade. I would not like to have you for a competitor in a canvass!"

"Have no fears of that, good Sir William. As long as bribery and corruption, trickery and meanness are the principal levers to turn elections; while Parliament but echoes the wishes of the government and the will of the queen; so long as representation is a mockery, so long will I scorn a seat in the Parliament of Great Britain."

The baronet smiled complacently.

"A little experience in these matters would smooth down your prejudices amazingly. Familiarity with such matters destroys their repulsiveness."

"Precisely so, and that is the reason why it is so much to be apprehended; for it undermines and destroys the purity of the elective franchise, and courts favor with the crown, by practicing disloyalty to the people."

"Disloyalty to the people? Is not that a *new* phrase, my lord, for one of the hereditary nobility to utter?"

"Undoubtedly, Sir William; but I trust that with my accession to these poor honors, I have not lost my right to call things by their proper names. Yes, sir, disloyalty to the people! By what authority do we make one half the population of England perform the duties of slaves? Who constituted us their masters?"

"Why, they have the right to leave our service if they will," said the baronet.

"The mendacious argument that has been used to humbug and deceive for the last one hundred years. An argument true in form, but false in substance, and known to be such by those who shelter themselves beneath it. They have the *right* to leave our service, say you; but *can* they? *That's the question!* Are we destitute of coachmen? Do we black our own boots? Do we perform menial service as degrading as that rendered by the darkest son of Africa? Cast your eyes over the landed estates of our most celebrated proprietors, and tell me if you do not see disease, hunger, and death! Walk through our manufacturing establishments, and deny, if you can, that overtasked frames are hurrying rapidly to the tomb! Traverse the mines, and note the terrible suffering of those whose hearts never rejoice in the light of day! Witness the collier riots, instigated by starvation alone! and tell me, not that they have the *right* to leave our service, but *can* they? *That*, I repeat, *is the question;* and until you can answer it in the affirmative, prate to me no more of their right to leave our service. A subterfuge like that from Sir William Belthoven? Sir, it is unworthy of you. Do you suppose, with that glorious land of refuge, the United States, before them; with its genial climate, fertile soil, and republican government, they would hesitate between it and want, servitude, and the dread realities of early graves? No! sir, no. We have reduced them to such abject poverty that they *cannot* escape. We have mercilessly robbed them of money, of physical and mental energy; and there is no fear but that a sufficient number will always remain in bondage, to supply us with servants, and fill our coffers."

"Your language is pointed, my lord," said the baronet, half seriously.

"Because I have tasted the bitter cup of oppression, and I *feel* that the language of truth should alone be used in discussing it."

"I am fearful your opinions would not be popular with your class."

"What care I for the good will of my *class*, if it is to be obtained by a sacrifice of honest convictions? For what am I indebted to my class? Not for support, not for education, but for a recognition of my rank when it was forced upon them."

"If you do not speak less cautiously, my lord, they will make you out a republican."

"I care not if they do," he replied, sternly; "they will only declare the truth—a truth they had best not probe too deeply, or it may flash upon the awakened understanding of the masses, that queenly powers are exercised by her majesty only by sufferance, and that they have only to assume the rights which God gave them, and has never withdrawn to this hour, to divest her of all semblance of authority."

"You forget, my Lord Melville, that the prerogatives of the queen are guaranteed by the glorious and unchangeable constitution of England."

"You must allow me to say, Sir William Belthoven, that, for an *enlightened* legislator, you confound terms more frequently than I could have supposed it possible. You ought to know that your glorious constitution is not unchangeable. Let me show you what Lord Mansfield, the most profoundly imbued of all our judges with legal knowledge, said of your unchangeable constitution."

Melville rose from his seat, and took from the book-case an ancient-looking volume.

"Here is what that distinguished jurist said in 1766, five centuries after the Magna-Charta was forced from King John by the English Barons, many years after William and Mary ascended the throne, and long after the nobility had limited the power of the throne to its present sphere.

"'The constitution of this country has always been in a moving state, either gaining or losing something.'

"'The constitution is nothing more than a combination of laws, which can be diminished, enlarged, or repealed, like any other statute, as the caprices of parliament and the humor of the sovereign may dictate.'"

"You are better versed, my Lord, in the science of government than I supposed. You will be my most influential constituent; if I can do anything for you, command my services, either in or out of parliament."

"Thank you, Sir William. Phelim, show this gentleman the door."

"And now Phelim," he said, after that individual had returned, "the clouds have disappeared, order our horses, and we will visit some of the tenants."

"Yez." And Mr. Savor disappeared with becoming alacrity.

In a few minutes they were mounted, and riding through the lofty gate that spanned the entrance to the private grounds of Mornlow.

"Did yez not find Sir William Belthoven an illegent gentleman, as I told yez?" said Phelim, confidentially, as he smoothed down his top-knot.

"Do you think him such?"

"How can your lordship ax the question?"

"Because I have some doubts myself upon that subject."

Phelim was silent, while the pretensions of Sir William passed under a thorough revision; for if there was any one thing of which Mr. Savor was proud, it was that his master had the right to think for him. They jogged on in silence for some time, but it was apparent to Melville that Phelim was laboring in the production of an idea. He twisted himself around in the saddle until his weight rested upon one thigh, and opening his mouth, proceeded to scratch that portion of his face contiguous thereto, while the neighboring eye was modestly closed, as if it was unwilling to observe the satisfaction with which the cheek enjoyed the operation—very much after the manner we have seen a dog scraping his neck with his hind foot, while seated on the ground, with his head turned away, his mouth drawn upon one side, and his eye shut.

"Ain't yez considered much more respectable, now yez is a lord?" he at length managed to ejaculate.

"Perhaps so, by some persons."

"And it's mesel' thinks that same; for ba ma sowl, what's fine clothes worth, if they do'nt make you more ov a gentleman?"

"Would you place a higher estimate upon your claim to that title if I should give you a suit of my clothes?"

"Thry ma, and say. Hoot ma lord, do yez think I'd be after koorting Suzy McGowrie ony more if yez made ma a gentleman in that way?"

"It will not be well for you, Phelim, if ever I find you guilty of any rascality."

"And sure yez woulddent call it rascality if I wer to become a gintleman, and shoulddent kape ony more Sunday evenings wid Suzy? Why the nobility do that same, when they are eleviated, an it would ba a bold man who'd call them unjintlemanly."

"Phelim Savor, your opinions are all wrong. Is it possible you can think rank makes a man honorable, or respected?"

"Yez. Ain't yez a *lord?* And would yez hev that heavenly title, until yez wer better than common men?"

"Man! man! how degraded have you become, to be controlled by a phrase, and awed by a title. Phelim, you suppose a *lord* must be something more than human, because he possesses a "heavenly title?"

"Yez."

"Now let me undeceive you. The word *lord* is derived from two Saxon words, half-*loaf*, and ford—to *give*—and therefore he was styled a *bread-giver*. He was originally a miller, or a charitable person. If the former, Dick Sykes, who grinds wheat for the neighborhood, is a lord; if the latter, the class have strangely degenerated, and I fear but a small number at the present day could rightfully claim the title, if it depended upon the quantity of bread they give."

"Ba ma sowl, no. Especially yez predecessor; for bee the holy Saint Pathrick, he wanted to take bread out of our mouths, instead of giving it tul us."

"Square the conduct of the English nobility with that charity and good fellowship which originally gave the title, and there must be few, very few, in the British empire with whom to dishonor our heavenly father, by prefixing a divine appellation to the name of a human being.

"Begorra! I niver thought of that. If the giving ov bread entitles us to be called lords, it's yez and meself ought to be mighty fine lords; for little we ate, sometimes, when we had to give all to the stewart, at the castle beyant, to pay the rint. Bad luck tul the nobility. We'll vindicate our right—will the poor divils throughout Angland, Scotland, and Ireland—to the title of lords, bekase all the bread that's given coomes from us. Be the holy Saint Pathrick, it will not sound so bad nayther. *Lord* Phelim Savor; *Lord* Dick Sykes; *Lord* Simon Spew. *Begorra*, I like it."

Lord Melville dismounted before a small cabin, the door of which was opened by a tall and venerable-looking old man. His white hair, stooping form, and tremulous voice, betokened great age. He extended his shrivelled hand and welcomed Melville with a glad smile.

"My lord, I looked for you to-day. I have not much longer to live, and I knew you would make me happy as often as you could, with your presence."

"Thank you, Mr. Sherman. How do you feel to-day?"

"Much the same. My constitution has been too much shattered in the service of your father and grandfather for me to pass a day without pain. But, thank God, it will soon be over, for every time I look in the glass I think my hair is becoming whiter, and the wrinkles upon my forehead are deepening."

"You have seen hard times, my poor old friend."

"You may well say that," he replied, nodding his head. "And yet what hopes I had when a young man! I was a favorite of your grandfather's steward, and held the farm now occupied by Henderson. I had won the affections of a neighbor's daughter, a guileless, beautiful girl. We were married; five years of wedded bliss and two boys and a girl rewarded our union. The evil times came. The steward died: he was succeeded by a villain, who sought to corrupt the fidelity of my wife, and being indignantly repulsed told your grandfather I was exciting disloyalty among his tenants. Our crop was unfortunately cut off that year. We could not pay the rent. He made the Duke believe I could pay it, but would not. We were turned from our home. I sought employment elsewhere; and in my absence the steward—my God! why didst thou suffer it? visited the hovel where my wife was, and by force, brute force, accomplished her ruin."

The tears trickled down the cheeks of the old man; his bosom heaved, and he struggled violently for breath. Melville sprang to his side for he thought the moment of death had arrived. But he rallied, and continued his story in a low, tremulous voice.

"She died that night upon my bosom, and we buried her upon the slope of the hill yonder. Fifty years have elapsed since they heaped the earth upon her bosom, but the anguish I now feel for her loss is as keen as it was then. So lovely, so pure, so affectionate, and to be murdered by a brute!"

Deep sobs burst from the bosom of the old man.

Melville did not interrupt his grief.

"Broken-hearted, I had nothing to struggle for, to hope for; but my children cried for bread. Long years of suffering ensued. Money and food was required by the government to subsidize the enemies of the tyrant Napoleon, and to feed our soldiers who were endeavoring to arrest his blood-thirsty career. Food was scarce; one of my sons died from starvation. I saw him dwindling away, but I could not help it, for toil as I did for fifteen hours a-day I could not obtain sufficient food to keep them all alive. To save them, I eat scarcely half enough myself. All would not do. He died in my arms, and I never shall forget that last terrible struggle with the fell monster. His starting eyeballs, his limbs racked with agony, his loud, piercing shrieks, becoming fainter and fainter until he expired with a faint moan. Oh! how I rejoiced when I laid his unconscious form upon the mattrass, and knew he was beyond the reach of suffering. I had the satisfaction of knowing during the long years that succeeded, that our sufferings purchased the liberty of Europe, for Bonaparte was overthrown."

"How have you been deceived by a crafty government," said Melville, in a low tone, "as to the designs of the *Republican* Emperor?"

"My children never married because they would not bring innocent beings into a world of woe and misery, and so we have lived together until we are all old people."

"Why did you not apply to my grandfather?"

"I did, but he always referred me to his steward. After the death of that wicked man I went to him again, but he told me he was too old to listen to the complaints of his tenants. He, too, died shortly after, and then we suffered more than ever."

"From my father?"

"Yes, he was young and extravagant, and required more money than his father. Rents were increased, and you may well believe they were collected. When he had sown his wild oats, his son, or the person every one supposed was his son, tyrannized over us most shamefully, and our condition was wretched indeed."

"But why did you not emigrate to the United States?"

"Ah! that is what we often hoped for, and prayed for, but we could not raise sufficient money to pay the passage. You must think, my dear Lord Melville, how destitute we were. No friends who had the ability to aid us, and every penny we could earn was only enough to keep us from hunger."

"I know, I know."

"Some of our friends would occasionally receive a few pounds; enough to pay their passage to that land of promise. How happy they were, and how we envied their blessed lot. My son said if he could once get to America, he would earn money and send it to me and Sarah, but he was never able to go."

"Would you like to go now: if so, I will pay the passage of all three?"

"Will you?" said the old man eagerly.

"Yes."

He paused in deep thought.

"If any one but you were our master, I would so gladly accept your offer. But now I am satisfied to remain, for I wish my body to repose beside that of my wife. After I am gone will you assist John and Sarah to reach the United States?"

"I will, if they wish to go."

"They are as happy here as they could desire, and if your counsels were always to prevail, they would rather live and die here. But life is uncertain, and I should quit this world much happier if I knew they had the power to leave England if they desired."

"To place the matter beyond doubt, here is a hundred pound note, which you may keep for them."

"Many, *many* thanks for your kindness, my dear young sir; the Lord will bless you for your kindness to us, and all your father's tenants. If you only knew, Lord Melville, how widely different is the condition of affairs now and before you were sent to bless us! Then, nothing was heard from one end of the estate to the other but lamentations and curses. Now, smiling faces are everywhere seen, and the praises of their young lord are heard upon every lip."

"I am very glad to hear my father's tenants are happy. It shall always be my duty, as it is my pleasure, to make them so, for they have as much right to enjoy the happiness which this poor world can bestow, as the Duke of Sunderland."

"May heaven shower its richest blessings upon your head for those words. Not because I shall live long enough to witness your kindness, but I have seen so much unhappiness in my long life, that I am overjoyed to think there are better days in store for those who are younger than myself."

"Good bye, my venerable friend. I believe you have made me as happy as you are yourself."

And with a countenance beaming with satisfaction, Lord Melville mounted his horse and returned to Mornlow.

CHAPTER XIX.

> "Bright flag at yonder tapering mast,
> Fling out your field of azure blue;
> Let star and stripe be westward cast,
> And point as Freedom's eagle flew!
> Strain home! O lithe and quivering spars!
> Point home my country's flag of stars!"—WILLIS.

ROBERT KANE was taken on board a government vessel, anchored in the Thames, and heavily ironed, a precaution that, for the hour, was unnecessary. The blows that he had received on his head, in the struggle with the kidnappers, produced insensibility, and he lay for a long time unconscious of his fate, as he was of the manacles upon his limbs. At length reason recovered her throne, and he awoke to a full knowledge of his situation. His wounds were painful, especially the one that had scarcely healed, and was now cut still deeper than before. Raising his head with great difficulty, he glanced around the hold, which was faintly lighted by a lamp that obstinately refused to give out its rays upon such a dismal scene with any degree of cheerfulness. Now and then it flashed up, but it was more in spite than a settled determination to discharge the functions of a serviceable lamp. By the aid of its dim light, Robert Kane counted thirteen men manacled like himself. They all belonged to the lower classes, a fact that in no small degree illustrated the shrewdness of the English government. In the first place, their forms were inured to toil, and to short rations likewise; and in case of a paucity of stores, they could be taught to fast, as the Dutchman made his horse, with the soothing observation that he "would tink not'ing of it when hes got used toot." And in the second place, it was found much easier to kidnap a poor man, who had no friends, than one whose disappearance would cause at least a temporary excitement. The argument was decidedly in favor of the poor man, and, therefore, the government claimed his services. A difference which was, no doubt, exceedingly gratifying to that chosen class.

It must not be inferred that all who occupied that small hold were as deserving of a better fate as Robert Kane. Some of them had drunk deeply of what, in polite circles, would be called "dissipation," but which, in the present case, could be termed nothing less than a fondness for the meanest kind of Scotch whiskey, and an exceptionable quantity of black strap. Their features were bloated as much from the excessive consumption of bad liquor, as from the blows that had been freely dealt about their ears, for the purpose of beating it into their dull comprehension that the government was desirous of bestowing upon them the honorable rank of high private in the regular service; a distinguished mark of favor which it was supposed they would acknowledge by at least three years service, provided the balance-sheet of life was not struck during that time; and provided, farther, that their services were no longer required.

There were others who bore their sufferings with far less indifference. Upon their gloomy countenances was set the unmistakable seal of despair, which spoke of severed domestic ties and ruined hopes.

While Kane was contemplating this spectacle of horrible suffering, another victim was rudely thrust into the hold.

"Ha! ha! here coomes another unwolluntary pathreot to defind his koontry and make her an hexemple for all ambitious nations. It's mesell that hopes he'll hev a nice time for the next tree years."

A groan was the only response of the new comer. Robert turned his head and encountered the half-averted eyes of Riley. The eyes of the villain could not meet those of the man whom he had so grievously wronged, and he cowed before his gaze with the sneaking look of a person conscious of his immeasurable rascality.

Day, shorn of its brightness, found its way into the hold, and soon after, one of the subordinate officers entering, removed the fetters from the limbs of the prisoners, with the exception of the handcuffs. They were then ordered upon deck. If they had just emerged from the dust and smoke of battle they could not have presented a more wretched appearance. Their heads were terribly cut; their clothes were nearly all torn off, revealing broken arms, and bodies awfully bruised and lacerated. They were wounds that are more frequently given by enemies than by friends. But who can take such liberties with our persons if our *friends* cannot? To the deck, then, staggered these wretched creatures. The officer in command inspected them.

"This lot is rather badly bruised, Hurdy; how comes that?"

"Why, you see, they are obstinate devils——"

"Hoot! No swearing on the quarter-deck."

"Beg pardon, but they fought like mad. They will make all the better soldiers when they get broken in, though."

"A process which, it seems, you undertook yourself, if we may judge from the number of broken heads visible this morning."

"Well, as I told you, they were more than ordinarily pugnacious. One fellow will make a capital sailor or soldier, for he is as strong as a lion, and as quick in his motions as a cat."

"Which one?"

"That one with the sullen countenance," he said, pointing to Robert Kane.

"Step forward, fellow."

Robert moved with great difficulty in front of his companions.

"What are you best fitted for, sailor, marine, infantry, cavalry, or artillery?"

"Neither," replied Robert, firmly.

"Your modesty is worthy of the highest commendation, and it shall be rewarded," said the officer.

"You either do not, or will not understand me," said Kane.

"What may your meaning be, then, my fine gentleman?"

"That I will neither act as a sailor or marine, or serve in the infantry, cavalry, or artillery."

The officer winked at his companion, and a coarse laugh was heard from the main-deck.

"You won't?" said the officer.

"No."

"And what may be your reason for so sapient a conclusion?"

"I have never received a solitary favor from the government, except the privilege of contributing my aid to support its extravagances. I have been torn from my family, who are left to starvation. I will not assist that government to gratify an insane ambition, or redden my hands with the blood of its victims."

"He has the ring of good metal, and will prove a valuable acquisition. In his case you have earned your bounty."

"But can you conquer him," asked a gentleman, who seemed, from the cut of his dress, white neckcloth, and nasal pronunciation, to belong to the clerical fraternity.

"If you doubt it, you scarcely comprehend the efficient training the service has adopted for the proper discipline of such customers. We don't exalt the national character for them, and then tolerate disobedience of orders, when we think proper to claim their grateful acknowledgments."

"No; that would be expecting too much forbearance from even the benign and merciful government of Great Britain," responded the clergyman.

"Well, sirrah! are we to expect a mutinous spirit in you?"

"A mutinous spirit can only be shown by one who has, in some way, admitted the right of the service to control his actions."

"Upon my word, a special pleader. A parliamentary reformer could not have defined the *supposed* rights of an Englishman with greater precision."

"He's a terrible obstinate fellow," interposed Riley, "and has often threatened me, her majesty's most——"

"Silence!" thundered the officer.

"Yes, sir," replied Riley, shrinking into his accustomed insignificance.

"I have your answer?"

"You have."

"Boatswain, bring the cat."

"Aye, aye, sir," replied the boatswain, in as cheerful a voice as if he was about to perform the most grateful duty that could be asked of a sympathizing mortal.

It was a brawny arm he disclosed as Kane's hands were elevated above his head. The old salts looked on with stoical indifference; the officers as if they duly appreciated the scientific results of the lash; the clergyman with a devout conviction that wholesome discipline was truly beneficial in controlling the lusts of the flesh, and also with a distinct idea that the government of Great Britain, whose power it was necessary the contumacious individual should sustain, upheld the Church of England. The knot of mangled human beings witnessed the preparations with different emotions. Riley rubbed his hands gleefully. Some regarded the resistance of Kane as worse than foolish, and others sought to learn in his fate the result of obstinacy.

"Now, boatswain, see what effect fifty lashes will have upon this person."

The brawny arm of the boatswain swung round his head, and down fell the cat upon the quivering flesh of Robert Kane. Nine red stripes were left upon the back of the victim. Again and again the merciless cat descended, until ninety stripes had furrowed his shoulders and loins.

"Now, Boatswain, rest a few minutes, and give him a chance to reflect while his back smarts. I have known miraculous changes of opinion under such circumstances."

Robert's countenance was a shade paler, but the same determination was still stamped upon his forehead.

"You can proceed, Boatswain; our merciful intentions are not duly appreciated."

"Rebellious flesh deserveth chastisement, yea, verily, for its own good," ejaculated the divine.

The blood now followed each sweep of the lash, and the suffering flesh was grooved into waves. The blows fell downwards, then upwards, and then crosswise, as the ingenuity of the boatswain prompted their direction. Cold drops of sweat stood out upon the forehead of the wretched man, and from the reopened wound upon his brow the dark blood slowly trickled away. The muscles of the lower part of his face trembled, but resolution still flashed from his eyes.

"Your arm is weaker than usual, boatswain," observed the officer, sarcastically.

"The rod well administered chastiseth the disobedient," said the clergyman, who saw in the obstinacy of the victim an assault upon the stability of the government, and consequently upon the church of England.

"You wouldn't think so, if the application was made to your own back," replied the boatswain, who nevertheless redoubled his exertions as he dashed the cat into the quivering body of the poor fellow.

"Fifty!" shouted the boatswain, as he separated the cats with his fingers. They were cemented with blood.

"It can never be sufficiently deplored that our slaveholding brethren in America have not the same excuse for using the lash," said the clergyman mournfully.

"I must confess an inability to discover the difference," replied the officer. "The lash in either case is only required to enforce obedience."

"But here the application is made by the supreme power."

"Upon the bodies of free-born Britons, who boast of the gentle laws of *merry England*," said the officer; "while in the United States the lash is wielded by those who derive the right from the constitution, the supreme law of the land."

"But herein consists the difference," said the clergyman. "The slave—that is to say, the Englishman—if—"

"Which lucid explanation means, when rightly understood, that the slave is black, and the Englishman is white, a consideration of no small importance at a time when the descendents of Ham, that especial favorite of the Lord, are winning the sympathies and seducing the affections of half the beautiful aristocracy of England, with their ebon skins and irresistible attractions. Boatswain, put double irons upon that fellow; place him in solitary confinement, and feed him upon bread and water till to-morrow morning. If he is still obstinate he shall receive fifty lashes more. Begone, sir."

Kane withdrew from the deck with great difficulty.

"And now who else refuses to obey orders?" he exclaimed, fiercely.

No rebellious glance met his own; they had been subdued by the terrible punishment inflicted upon Robert Kane.

"It is well," said the officer, "you know what to expect if you display a mutinous disposition. Boatswain, let the handcuffs remain upon these fellows for the present."

Robert Kane maintained a firm, unflinching countenance until he was alone, and then the big tears that anguish forced from him coursed down his manly cheeks. It was not physical suffering that shook his frame and made his heart throb almost to bursting. No, he could endure that without a murmur. But the deep humiliation of having the lash applied to his back. *His* back. The husband of Mary Kane, the father of three lovely children, all, all dishonored by the awful scourging he had received. A free-born Englishman, with rights, *apparently*, as sacred as those which guarded the person of a belted earl, publicly to receive fifty lashes, and for no other offence than a determination not to recognize the right to drag him from the bosom of a helpless family, who had no other earthly protector but himself. His feelings were crushed, and he looked upon himself as the most abject of human beings. Still he had one duty to perform, from which disgrace could not release him. He must return to his family or perish in the attempt. He could not endure the thought that those dear creatures—dear to him in spite of his dishonor—should suffer for the want of bread. It was a determination to avail himself of every opportunity to escape, that had induced him to set at defiance the authority of the kidnappers, for a performance of duty, he supposed, would be regarded as a recognition of their right to claim his services for an indefinite period of time: and consequently the power to arrest him as a deserter should he succeed in effecting his escape. But could he endure the terrible punishment they would certainly inflict upon him? He would rely upon God and his own resolution. The next morning he was again brought forth; again refused to yield; and again the scourge was applied to his lacerated back. The wounds of yesterday, from which the blood was still oozing, were reopened by the remorseless cat. The pain was intolerable, the form of the sufferer quivered at every blow, and from the mangled flesh the blood, (only a *white* man's blood, however,) ran in streams to his feet. Before the fifty lashes were inflicted Robert Kane fainted. He was borne to the place of solitary confinement, and left with a supply of bread and water.

A raging fever now attacked his frame, followed by delirium. He imagined a thousand devils had formed a league to torment him. All the ingenuity that is usually ascribed to that inventive fraternity seemed to be exhausted, in discovering means to rack his frame. At one moment they contrived, with the assistance of hellish machinery, to roll mountains upon his head. The weight ought to crush him—and he tried, *so hard* to die—but there the mountain rested ; and although it was slowly compressing his skull upon the brain, it appeared as though ages would elapse, before dissolution could take place. At last he experienced all the agony of death—the gasp—the death-rattle—and he smiled, that all was over ; when the mountain was removed, consciousness returned, and a chorus of satanic laughter rang in his ears. He was then placed in an immense cauldron. It was filled with water to his throat, and then a continuous stream of hell-fire, with the traditional bluish tint, was poured under it. The water became warmer ; it began to simmer around the edges ; the heat was insufferable ; and then the horrible thought flashed upon him, that when it boiled, the water would mount to his lips ; his breath would stop. He tried to spring to the surface, but his feet were rivetted to the bottom. Slowly the waves rolled towards him, each larger than the one which preceded it. The boiling foam touched his lips. He raised himself to his utmost height ; it entered his nostrils, and with its fierce heat burnt his vitals ; his blood rushed madly through his veins. Thank God ! a few more struggles—but oh ! so frightful—and all would be over. Death would *not* relieve him. The water receded, to his shoulders ; it became colder ; it congealed, and he was in the centre of a solid mass of ice. Death clutched his limbs, his pulse beat feebly ; the grim monster seized his heart, and it became as solid as a rock. He ceased to breathe, and the anomaly was presented to his startled fancy, of a man living without respiration. He tried to conjecture how long it would last, but his ideas became confused ; they, too, seemed to be frozen ; and at last he sunk, for a moment, into a state of insensibility. It was not death, though, for his tormentors returned with redoubled vigor to the assault. He was horror-stricken, when he beheld among the foremost the features of his wife—but so changed ! No flickering ray of affection lingered upon her features. They were sharpened and twisted into the direst representation of malicious hate. He shouted her name in tones of affection and entreaty ; still onward she led the ferocious band, stimulating their passions by appealing to them in the language of the infernal regions. Seizing him by the hair, he was borne aloft—up, up—he thought she would pierce the sky. His head whirled as he gazed downward into the void beneath. With a loud burst of hellish laughter, she released her hold, and he shot through the realms of space. Beneath he could see a vast sheet of liquid fire ; the waves of that ocean which rolled onward, driven by no cooling breeze, but borne along by the shoals of damned spirits, who restlessly moved from one shore to the other, in the vain hope that a way was to be opened for their exodus, during some one of the revolutions of an endless eternity.

Into this lake of fire he plunged headlong.

The boiling liquid penetrated the marrow of his bones; still he sank deeper and deeper, until he saw nothing but fire; breathed nothing but fire; felt nothing but fire. A spirit more gentle than the rest came to his relief. It laid its hand upon his arm, to bear him aloft. The touch was grateful. He opened his eyes, and saw the physician of the ship bending over him.

"You are very ill."

Robert nodded his head.

"Water"—he whispered.

It was placed to his lips, and he drank it eagerly.

"You may remove these irons; it will be a long time before he can escape, without them," he said, to a person who stood behind him.

They were taken off.

"Now bear him amidships; he must have light and air."

The violent attack of brain fever yielded slowly to the efforts of skill. They did not intend to kill the body; they only wished to destroy every manly sentiment that elevates him who walks the earth in God's image, above the brute. Blind obedience must control his mechanical power, and to accomplish that object, the government of England, the humanizing, civilizing, slavery-hating government of England, adopted the benevolent and christian-like practice of *brutalizing* her subjects. The process, however, was so strictly in accordance with the divine teachings of the Redeemer, the professed morality of the Church of England, and the reported sanctity of the British character, that no voice was heard to denounce it. Parliamentary reformers, eminent divines, the nobility, gentry, farmers, all, exhibited their appreciation of the system by a silent and complacent acquiescence.

Slowly Robert Kane's strength returned, and with it a determination to effect his escape, if possible. The vigilance of the officers had been relaxed during his illness, but he now anticipated another resort to severe measures. His only chance of escape was to let himself down into the Thames, and swim ashore. This must be attempted on a dark night, when his movements could not be observed from the ship or the shore. He had many doubts as to whether he had sufficient strength to swim to the shore, especially as the water was now exceedingly cold. He resolved, nevertheless, to make the attempt, and he only waited for the moon to rise later. At least two days more must elapse. They slowly dragged their length along. He was agitated by a feverish solicitude. At last the day arrived. The sky was overcast with clouds, and a cold, drizzling rain was falling, calculated to make the unhappy indulge in that luxury—which would be more prevalent, if the English had not made it so vulgar—throat-cutting. The raw wind thrust its rude breath into every nook and corner pervious to its assault; the signs upon the stores seemed to have a threatening scowl, and the huge fish that was suspended from the awning-post, as a significant adjunct to the name of Brad*brook*, over the door, appeared to have a larger mouth than usual, as if the unlucky wight who entered the store that day would incur the risk of being "taken in" as summarily as Jonah was disposed of in the whale's belly. A warning that the cash-box and acquisitiveness of Brad*brook* were quite equal to the capacity of the fish that took such a fancy to Jonah's person; with this material difference, however, that whereas the whale conscientiously "gave up" Jonah, after reflecting for three days upon the gross impropriety of his conduct; a strict regard for justice and the proprieties of life which Bradbrooks never thought of imitating. A condition of things that might have been expected in a house where losses and gains meant losses by the customer and gains by Bradbrooks.

It was upon the night of such a day as this, that Kane resolved to stake his hopes of freedom. He was anxiously counting the hours, when he saw the officer in command enter that part of the ship, followed by Riley. The officer cast a momentary glance at Robert, and was passing on, when Riley said in a fawning tone—

"If your honor pleases, is it not time for that person to be ironed again? I think he intends to escape."

"Who?"

"Him," pointing at Kane.

"Pooh! he can scarcely walk."

"He's agoing to give you the slip, I'm sure on't."

The officer cast a searching look upon Robert Kane.

"Well, tell the boatswain to iron him before he turns in to-night."

"Couldn't he do it now, to prevent accidents?"

"No, he is on shore."

"I think I could do it myself," said the considerate individual.

"Could you? Will you be kind enough to inform me who commands this vessel, you or me?"

Riley cast his eyes to the floor.

"Have the goodness to withdraw, for I think I never saw so mean a looking person as yourself."

Riley slunk away; but before he mounted the ladder, he scowled upon Robert and shook his finger at him menacingly. To add to the dangers that gathered round him, he heard the officer issue orders for the vessel to be got under weigh for the Downs that night. Daylight—if that could be called light which was merely the haze of a London atmosphere—had disappeared, and darkness shut in, like an impenetrable wall. The clock struck nine—ten—eleven. Still Riley hung, like an evil genius, about that part of the vessel occupied by Kane. Robert was unable to conceal his uneasiness. Riley observed it, and it afforded him intense satisfaction.

"I know you want to escape, but you *shan't*," he said, approaching Kane and scowling into his face.

"Why do you annoy me with your presence? Have you not already persecuted me enough?" said the other, imploringly.

"No! I'll stick to you like a leech. The boatswain will soon be here; I think I hear him coming now. Until he places the handcuffs upon you, I shall favor you with my company," replied Riley with a ferocious grin.

The clock struck twelve. The sound of oars was heard approaching; it was the boatswain. Riley laughed sardonically. There was something insufferably aggravating in his looks.

Robert Kane suddenly sprang upon him. He attempted to scream, but Kane's hand grasped his throat with such violence that his tongue protruded from his morth.

"Now, what prevents me from slaying you like a dog?"

But he did not. Cramming a handkerchief into Riley's mouth, he bound his hands behind him, and then pitching him into a corner, he sprang up the hatchway, and cautiously approached one of the port-holes. It was the wrong part of the ship The boatswain was mounting the side, and his lantern flashed full upon Kane's person. Fortunately, he was not observed, and concealing himself beneath the cannon, he waited until his movements could not be observed. Then darting to the other side he dropped into the Thames. The cold water chilled his blood, and he thought he should sink. But the recollection of his wife and children nerved his arm, and gave new vigor to his frame. Striking boldly out for the shore, he soon placed several rods between him and pursuit. Hope grew brighter, when he heard the voice of Riley proclaiming his escape. Lights were visible in the ship. Orders were rapidly given, and several boats started in pursuit. Turning down the stream, he managed to elude the party sent towards that shore which he was endeavoring to gain. He now slowly approached the vast forest of masts that lined the bank. His strength was fast deserting him. For every yard he advanced he was borne down two. Yet manfully he struggled on. Voices were heard descending the river; they approached nearer and nearer. Then lights danced upon the water, and played, as if in mockery of his suffering, almost upon his person, when he glided behind the stern of a merchantman. The boat swept past, and for the moment he was safe. Making his tedious way between the vessels that lined the shore, he at length reached the wharf. And now the difficult task remained of ascending to the street. Thrice he attempted it without success. Aware that he was only exhausting his powers, he nerved his limbs for one vigorous trial. His hands clutched the top of the dock, but it was covered with ice; desperately he held to it; his fingers yielded, and he sunk with a faint cry into the water. He had scarcely reached it, when the powerful form of a sailor plunged in. The exhausted sufferer was seized as he sank, and borne to the side of a ship. A voice answered the call of the deliverer, and they were both raised to the deck of the vessel. Robert could not stand, and they laid him in a hammock. He expressed his gratitude by pressing the hand of the sailor.

"I'll be darned tew darnation if I woulddent eneemost jump intew the Connecticut, when it war half friz over, if a feller bein' was a trien so alfired hard tew keep his smellers above high-water mark, as you war. I guess yeou'd feel a *leetle* more comfortable if them clothes of yourn were off. Here's a *sweet*, as the Kennucks say, when they want more'n one room in a tavern. They're mine—Ezekiel Belknap, at your service—yeou can hev them jist as long as yeou please; allers, if yeou like."

Robert Kane said he would avail himself of the offer.

"That's jist exactly right. Let me help you off with your'n."

"But you are wet yourself," said Robert, faintly.

"A sailor is accustomed to that. I guess yeou giv somebody the slip to-night."

Robert did not know whether to confide in the sailor or not. The latter observed his hesitation,

"You needdent be afeard I'll blab. We Yankees hevent the almightiest love for your government, any way you can fix it. The pesky critters are a conjering and a tryin' all the *hull* time to upset us. They do'nt want us—now put on the jacket—to get no more sile, when the hull world knows we can't giv hums to them as hazzent any here, and never can hev, unless we set our stakes over agin. We must hev Mexico; and them Canadas of hern won't be worth a cuss, until we hev 'em, which we're bound to dew.—Now slip on my shoes.—So yeou may tell me the whole story."

It was so grateful to his feelings to meet one human being who was not his foe, and that person not an Englishman! And he confided his story to the sailor.

"I'll be crucified heels upward, on a tamarack or moosemissy, either one or t'other, if that ain't eneemost the hardest case I ever herne tell of. But you diddent list, though?"

"No, I would have died first."

"That's the right grit. Neow I can tell yeou the best thing to be done. Dooze your wife know what has become of yeou."

"I think she does."

"Wall, this ship—the Nancy Ann—sails for New York in one week. She won't carry many passengers. Yeou must bring yeour family on board the night afore."

"A thousand thanks, my kind friend, but the kidnappers robbed me of the last penny I had on earth."

"Wall, want of money sha'nt prevent yeou from reaching a land of liberty, anyhow yeou can fix it. I'll pay your passage myself fust. But no fear of that. Captain Chauncey Smith goes the *hull* hog when his dander's riz. Besides, there's scarcity of hands, and bein' a stout chap, you can work your passage, after you get more strength."

And so it was arranged that Kane should bring his family on board the "Nancy Ann" the evening before she sailed. To avoid the danger of being seized again, it was agreed that Ezekiel Belknap should communicate the joyful intelligence to the wife of Kane on the following day. Their plans being all arranged, Robert partook of a warm supper, prepared by his new friend, and then, with a heart overflowing with happiness, he fell asleep, to dream of the rescue of his wife and his little ones from worse than African bondage.

The next morning Ezekiel Belknap started for the home of Robert Kane. His heart was light, for he was conscious of doing a kind act; and, regardless of the attention he attracted, he whistled yankee doodle with the utmost vigor, now and then accompanying it with a *rub-a-dub* upon an imaginary drum.

CHAPTER XX.

"I did but prompt the age to quit their clogs,
By the known rules of ancient liberty,
When straight a barbarous noise environs me,
Of owls and cuckoos, asses, apes, and dogs."—MILTON.

LORD MELVILLE was seated in the dressing room of his mother, at the paternal mansion, in London. He had been in the city only a week, and the Duchess availed herself of the earliest opportunity to make some suggestions as to his conduct for the season. That estimable female did not regard it as indispensable to prescribe a plan of operations for more than one season.

"Charles," she softly uttered.

"Madam."

"Don't be so formal, Charles. I can hardly reconcile it to my painfully severe sense of propriety, to admit a person into my dressing-room whom but a few weeks ago I regarded as a stranger. I can never hear the duke approach this secluded apartment without a thrill of fear, unless you take more pains to make me feel he is your father, and that I am your mother."

Melville smiled.

"Charles, you are in a new world; and it cannot be supposed you are familiar with its regulations; you will, therefore, listen to one whe has seen much of society."

He bowed.

"You will prepare yourself for all sorts of advances, from all kinds of people. The Jeremy Diddlers will have designs upon your purse; the politicians upon your influence; and mammas, who have marriageable daughters, upon your person. You will, of course, disregard them all. The Diddlers always; the politicians until you enter parliament, and the mammas for this season. You are too young to marry. Early marriages have a tendency to destroy those remarkably fine proportions for which the nobility are celebrated. Besides, you will require one season to make a choice. Now there is Kate Montague, a remarkably fine girl, only she is too charitable. She was good enough for the young man I thought my son (poor fellow, I wonder where he is)."

"She is good enough for the best man in all England," said Melville, enthusiastically.

"I will not deny that she is an excellent girl. Her form is exquisite, as I have reason to know; her health is perfect, though she was rather pale when I saw her last. But she is not the daughter of a peer of the highest rank, nor does the blood of royalty flow in her veins. She will do, if nothing *better* can be accomplished; you understand, Charles."

"I do."

"Now for this season you must only study the chances, notwithstanding the attentions with which you will be favored. Do not suffer your affections to be entrapped. I must impress this matter upon your attention with greater pertinacity, because young men who have not been accustomed to the language of flattery, yield a willing ear to its seductions. And especially beware of beautiful, but *poor* girls, whose only attractions are fine complexions, beautiful eyes, and well-developed busts, which they disclose with great liberality. You must have a wealthy bride, for the revenues of our estate are scarcely sufficient for our own wants; and although you are not so extravagant as that young man was, still you expend more in charities, and I do not know which is the most reprehensible. You must marry a wealthy girl; and here I wish to impress a fact upon your mind so forcibly that you will never forget it. I know twenty young ladies who can not only boast of fine complexions, beautiful eyes, and well-developed busts, which, by the way, they do not disclose, but of enormous wealth and high rank."

"If they do not disclose their busts, am I to ascertain whether they are well-developed, or made up of cotton after the plan adopted by Lord Macdonald in the case of Lady Templeton?"

"How was that?"

"By thrusting a pin into the cotton, its full length, without causing pain."

"Fie! for shame, Charles: he slandered Lady Templeton."

"Perhaps so."

"I believe I have said all I desired," replied her grace, leaning back in her chair, very much exhausted by her speech, and excessively thankful that her maternal duties were discharged.

"Am I to understand that my too susceptible affections are to be overpowered by none other than a lady who possesses wealth, rank, health, and beauty?"

"Of course," replied the duchess, languidly.

"Will my conduct be considered reprehensible if I fall in love with a maiden who does not possess rank?"

"Can you doubt it, my son?"

"What does this thing called *rank* amount to?"

"Every thing, except health, beauty, and wealth."

"Now let us see if it is not the most worthless trifle that ever deluded poor, weak human nature. The baronet is proud, yet he is inferior in rank to the earl; the earl is haughty, yet he looks up to the marquis; the marquis bears himself loftily, still he must yield precedence to the duke; the duke looks down upon the earl, yet bows most humbly to royalty. And what is *royalty* but frail, perishable humanity, that trembles at the approach of death, and whose spirit will be awed in the presence of angels! Travel along the avenue of social life until you reach that class, who, destitute of rank, make an idol of fashion. What do all their heart-burnings and struggles for pre-eminence amount to? In the effort to *outshine* each other (for at best it is but a show of tinsel) in the purchase of gaudy equipages, and flashy dresses and furniture, fortunes as well as reputations are often squandered. An energetic woman forces her way along the high road of fashion (fashion! how have they disgraced you!), yearly dropping off the least fashionable, as she designates those who are often the most *respectable* of her acquaintances; and whom, by the way, she fawned upon and *begged* to return her calls one year ago. At last she sees but two sets ahead of her; the Jimses, who are avowedly at the head of London fashion, and the Prowties, who take position next to them. She strives *desperately* to eclipse the Jimses and the Prowties, but unavailingly. And who are the Jimses, who stand, like Banquo's ghost, in her path? Some thirteen years ago they disgraced themselves by harrassing the dying moments of their father, in order to make him disinherit a brother and sister that their own coffers might be replenished. They propped the old man up in bed, with a board in front and pillows behind, while the son-in-law '*took a race with death*,' as it was judicially termed, for the purpose of seeing whether the grim monster could enfold the dying man in his grasp before he could prepare a will which was to put money in his pockets, and those of other leaders of *fashionable* society, by the cheating process of swindling the blood relations of the poor, harrassed, and dying old man! Then, too, was presented the painful spectacle of the lawyer '*running up the steps*;' not to alleviate pain—not to prolong life, but to have the '*unconscious signature*' of the dying man affixed to the fraudulent instrument: thus disgracing, while it put money in the pockets of the leaders of *fashionable society!* Then was the rapid reading of that same instrument more rapidly concluded when the *conscientious* lawyer saw that the features of the victim were distorted with pain! Then the death-rattle mingled with smothered exultations, when that deed of unmitigated rascality was consummated, which dishonored while it enriched the leaders of *fashionable* society! Notwithstanding the ineffaceable stamp of infamy was affixed by that transaction to the characters of the Jimses, still the ambitious Mrs. Woodle is dying of envy because she cannot rival them. What a pitiful ambition!"

"My dear son," interrupted the Duchess with a yawn, "what can tempt you to devote so much time to trades-people, retired grocers, and the descendants of coopers and shoemakers? What have I to do with such scurf? The most fashionable—fashionable? faugh!—among them are not the equals (socially) of our *commonest* baronets. Don't suffer your thoughts to dwell upon the *scum* of earth. Their claim to pre-eminence is illustrated by an anecdote, which is related of the wife of a retired tradesman. Her mind had been absorbed by religious subjects for fifteen years, when her daughter was old enough to 'bring out,' as they call it. She issued cards for a large party and placed them in the hands of a fellow named Brown, who, I have been told, buries dead people and makes the reputations of the living; that is, among the common people. The next day this fellow, Brown, returned the cards with the remark that more than half the persons she wanted him to invite were dead and buried a dozen years before, and that he ought to know, as burying people was in his line of business. Think only of an alliance with the noblest in the land, my dear Charles."

"High or low, rich or poor, it is all vanity and vexation of spirit, for as Sir Charles Coldstream is made to say, '*there's nothing in it.*' My determination is immovable. I shall never marry."

"Wait till Katharine Montague has brought her fascinations to bear upon you, before you express yourself too confidently."

Melville shrugged his shoulders.

"You don't know her. She has rejected half the desirable beaux in London."

The servant here announced Sir William Belthoven.

"You must entertain him, Charles; he is only a member of parliament, but he is a politician. Beware of him."

"Never fear but I will be upon my guard."

Melville welcomed Sir William with something more than his usual cordiality. Perhaps it was owing to the fact that the Baronet had more of the countryman in his appearance than he had seen since his arrival in the metropolis.

"I called with the hope that you are disengaged to-night," said the Baronet.

"I am at your service."

"Well, I have secured seats at St. James' theatre."

"I will gladly accompany you."

"Then we will proceed at once. My carriage is at the door."

"If it is not too far, I should prefer walking."

"No; we can arrive there in time."

And descending into the street, Sir William ordered his coachman to meet him at the theatre at the termination of the performance, and the two gentlemen proceeded thither.

The streets were brilliantly lighted, and Melville observed the shops and the crowd with much interest. At length his attention was arrested by an individual who stalked before them. His weather-beaten hat had received all the polish of which it was capable, but owing to divers bruises it had manifestly encountered in the course of a protracted existence, it hung down with a disconsolate churlishness. To obviate this defect, it was cocked jauntily upon one side of his head, so that a person, inclined to scrutinize that once respectable beaver, would be at a loss to determine whether the crown occupied a horizontal position, or whether the rim was made to assume at attitude at once fierce and facetious. His brown coat had apparently done its owner "some service," for the warp and filling could be easily seen by the gas-light, while the obtrusive elbows had succeeded in obtaining, at first, faint glimpses of surrounding objects—as a school-girl peeps through her lattice—and then an uninterrupted view of all sublunary things. A white collar, that had the appearance of sustaining his ears, was confined to his neck by a somewhat faded plaid handkerchief; but it is with sincere regret we are forced to express the opinion that said collar had no connection whatever with either cotton or linen, as the double-breasted vest was buttoned with scrupulous care from his waist to his chin. The blue pants had hitherto resisted every attempt made by his enterprising knees to acquire a more familiar knowledge of the outer world. He had recently examined that portion of his nether garments with an anxious eye, and the truth flashed upon him with an unpleasant distinctness, that the conflict between cloth and bone would soon disastrously terminate. He had formerly indulged in the luxury of straps to his pantaloons, but they had been thrown aside the moment the idea occurred to his mind that they increased the friction upon his knees, and consequently would accelerate the catastrophe which he so much dreaded. The walk of Mr. Theophilus Ruxton—for by that name was this individual known—was stately and self-possessed. He considered it eminently undignified to hasten along the street with the speed of a lawyer or a shop-keeper. It pleased him to cast courteous glances at the aristocratic beauties who promenaded the street, and if a carriage of more than ordinary splendor dashed along, he surveyed the establishment with a critical, yet patronizing look. One hand rested contentedly in a pocket of his coat, while the other was gloved with kid, the original color of which could only, by a violent resort to supposition, be determined. Thus attired, Mr. Theophilus Ruxton slowly preceded Melville and his companion. The nobleman called Sir William's attention to the singular figure, whose movements never failed to produce a smile upon the features of the most gloomy.

Mr. Ruxton arrested his steps in front of St. James' theatre, and drawing forth a hand-glass, the highly-polished brass rims of which were made to resemble gold, he proceeded to examine the bill, casting, at the same time, side-long glances at each person who entered the theatre. Melville and the Baronet remained upon the side-walk, scrutinizing the appearance of the stranger. Mr. Ruxton observed them, and raising his beaver, he bowed gracefully as he advanced towards them.

"A charming bill to-night, gentlemen; the benefit of an excellent manager and a worthy gentleman; one who is contributing in no small degree to our amusement."

The gentlemen advanced towards the door.

"Am I deceived in supposing you extended to myself an invitation to witness the performance?" said Mr. Ruxton, with a bland smile.

"Ha! ha! He is an original, Melville. I am not aware that any invitation of the kind was extended. If you are desirous, however, of witnessing the play, here are two shillings. I presume you have no objection to entering the family circle."

"I have a most decided objection," said Mr. Ruxton, with an offended air. "I never make my appearance anywhere else than in the dress circle;" and he surveyed his well-brushed coat with a glance of the utmost complacency.

"Oh, very well, here is a crown; you shall not be disappointed."

"Thank you, sir. I will accept the *loan* of this sum, because I have no small bills with me; but with the distinct understanding that it must be returned. I cannot receive it upon any other condition."

"Certainly, Mr.—Mr.—"

"Mr. Theopholus Ruxton, I shall consider it a favor if you will receive my card—but—really—I am so unfortunate as not to have one with me—singular—but I hope you will excuse me?"

"Those little mistakes will occur with the most aristocratic."

"Ah, I see you can appreciate the embarrassment of a gentleman, Mr.—Mr.—"

"Sir William Belthoven."

"Have I the inexpressible felicity of addressing that illustrious gentleman; nay more, the happiness to receive a temporary loan from him. Theopholus Ruxton, you are more than ordinarily fortunate! Sir William, if I can assist you, either in your contests before the people, or in carrying any favorite measure through the house, I trust you will not hesitate to command my services."

"I shall avail myself of your generous offer with the warmest gratitude," replied the baronet.

"Sir William Belthoven, good night."

"Good night, Mr. Ruxton."

And that individual succeeded, with some difficulty, in raising his beaver without betraying its dilapidated condition.

"The good opinion of a dog is preferable to his ill-will, you know," observed Sir William Belthoven, as he conducted Lord Melville into the theatre.

The proceeds were for the "benefit of the manager." The propriety of which annunciation cannot be easily discovered, as the net proceeds generally find their way into his pockets, though it was rather more consistent with common sense than the bills of a juggler, the sole performer at his entertainments, which invited the community to attend his benefit.

St. James's Theatre was crowded to excess. There were many representatives of the English nobility present, and as the baronet directed the attention of his companion to them, Melville was fain to admit that his mother had not over-estimated the physical attractions of the aristocracy.

"In the box to the extreme left sits George of Cambridge, who aspired to the hand of her Majesty, until her affections were won by the portly figure of the German prince. By his side is the relict of Earl Moncton. You perceive, by her frisky actions, that she has not been a widow long enough to feel comfortable. In the adjoining box is the Duke of Bomford, renowned for his magnificent parties and—nothing else. He believes that the intellect and social standing of a person are measured by the length of his moustache."

"Then the keeper of a gambling-house I met to-day ought to be a prodigy of wisdom and fashion, for he wore the longest moustache I ever saw," said Lord Melville.

"Ah! yonder is an acquaintance of ours."

"Where?"

"In the box opposite to the one occupied by George of Cambridge."

Melville's glance followed the direction indicated by the baronet, and his eyes met Katharine Montague. Her look was frigid, as they exchanged formal bows, while her recognition of the baronet was exceedingly gracious.

"There now is the most fascinating lady in the English peerage. Witty, well-informed, lovely, and charitable. With a wife like that I would defy competition upon the hustings."

"Why do you not make the attempt to win her?" asked Melville in a hoarse voice.

"The truth is, I am not a marrying man!"

The truth was, he had been rejected by the maiden twice.

The young Duke of Gildermear entered the box where Katharine Montague was seated. He was received by the lady with marked affability. Melville could not withdraw his glance from her animated countenance. She saw his eyes were riveted upon her, and she redoubled her efforts to fascinate the Duke. She evidently succeeded, for he did not leave the box during the performance.

When the curtain fell upon the last scene, Melville and the baronet emerged from the theatre into the vestibule. They encountered there Katharine Montague and the Duke of Gildermear, who was still by her side.

"Sir William Belthoven, I am glad to see you," she said, cordially extending her hand. "What news do you bring from the country?"

"Lamentations at your absence," said the baronet.

"Always prepared with a delicate compliment."

"Only when some extraordinary occasion like the present inspires it. But, I beg your pardon, you do not recognize an old acquaintance;" and stepping aside, Melville and the lady stood face to face.

No passing emotion was observable on the countenance of the maiden, as she said—

"Lord Melville, late Christie Kane, I believe; I think I have met your lordship before?" she said, taking the Duke's arm.

"Madam, I am highly flattered by the unexpected and *unsought* recognition of a lady celebrated as you are *reputed to be* for refined manners, candor, and *truth.*"

With a haughty inclination of his head, Lord Melville mingled with the crowd who were leaving the theatre. The adieus of Belthoven were spoken with his accustomed blandness, and then they entered the baronet's carriage. As the door closed, Belthoven saw an acquaintance approaching.

"My Lord, you must let me introduce that person to you. He is an American member of congress. You will like him."

"Gentlemen, you must sup with me to-night," said Melville, after he was introduced to the American.

They protested it was too late.

"Both politicians, and make that answer," said Melville. "As you will. To the residence of the Duchess of Sunderland, James."

"Yes, sir."

After they had supped, they entered the library.

"I suppose you smoke, Mr. Jones; Sir William, I know, does."

"Yes, in the city," said the baronet.

"And why not in the country?"

"Policy forbids. Some of my influential constituents do not like it. They say it is a wasteful extravagance; and one of them hinted that my principles might evaporate as easily as the smoke of my cigar, if I had no more regard for public than I had for private economy."

"What is to be the prominent question before parliament this winter?" asked Mr. Jones.

"We hope to make the subject of American slavery the great question."

"What folly."

"How so?"

"You ought to direct your attention to the wants of your own people first."

"And desert the cause of the poor slave?"

"Gentlemen, as it is only midnight," said Lord Melville, "let us devote a few minutes to the absorbing question of American slavery. It would give me much pleasure to hear the opinions of an American senator upon the subject."

"There is a great deal said about the horrible condition of American slaves," replied Mr. Jones. "Evils that are necessarily connected with slavery, here and in the United States, must be examined by comparison. Applying to them that test, let us see if there are not strong grounds for palliating African slavery, if we cannot justify it, notwithstanding the anathemas that are launched against the institution by the liberty-loving aristocracy of the British empire. Now then for the comparison; for I repeat it is by this rule, alone, that the relative merits and demerits of the two systems can be ascertained. There are no people so clamorous in the cause of the slaves as yourselves, and I shall compare their condition with that of your peasantry. I believe the facts will sustain me in the assertion, that the former are happier than an equal number of the latter—especially your parish apprentices."

"You are surely jesting," said Belthoven.

"I was never more serious. The African adapts himself with greater readiness to circumstances than the white man; is naturally more cheerful; and you may say his happiness is traceable to those causes—and it is so to a certain degree—but it is also attributable to an abundant supply of wholesome food, the absence of care, and an easy life."

"An easy life! Come now, I like that," replied the baronet.

"I know it is difficult for an Englishman, accustomed to witness suffering in its most revolting aspects, to believe that slaves are a happy and contented race. It is not necessary to examine their condition to be assured of the fact. Indeed, it is demonstrated in Dickens' Household Words."

"In *Charles Dickens'* Household Words?" exclaimed Sir William.

"Precisely so; and I presume you will hardly accuse him of being a defender of slavery. Here is what he said, among other things, in an elaborate review of the slavery question, in a number of that interesting periodical, which I have in my pocket.

"'It is pleasanter to think of slaves in Cuba flying before bloodhounds, than to know that the slaves of North America learn to identify themselves with their masters, and to lie down contented with their place among farm animals, because they are well fed; and that in the year 1850, out of three million slaves only a thousand fled away in search of liberty; the greater part even of that thousand seeking not liberty for its own sake, but as a means of escape from the punishments incurred by theft and other crime.'

"He also states in the review that there were in the parish of St. James

"'Ten or fifteen negroes who had laid by more than enough to purchase freedom, but who would not purchase it. One of them, when questioned on the subject, answered: I am well-treated and not over-worked; if I am sick, I am attended to. If my wife bring me a child, they rear it. When I become old, I shall be allowed to rest—and would you have me quit all this for an uncertain future.'

"Further on, he says:

"'It is the greatest horror of the slave system to our minds, when men can live contented under so complete an abnegation of their manhood. Born to the system, bred to the system; degraded, by being set to labor in sight of a whip, like brutes; so working on a motive against which a well-bred brute comes to rebel—thousands of negroes are content to be well fed and housed, occasionally patted on the head or played with, and when their master finds it needful to reduce his stock, part, with a mere transitory brutish pang, from a contented wife in Maryland, perhaps, to lie down content, with a new wife, in a new stall, in Tennessee.'

"One more paragraph, and I have done with Dickens' article.

"'In truth, it must be acknowledged that the free Americans, the very abolitionists themselves, are stout supporters of the slave system, in act, whatever they may be in theory. In the free states of America, the negro is no less forced down out of his just position as a man than where he works under the planter's whip. Even in an English drawing-room, the American who meets by chance a guest with negro blood marked in his forehead, feels like a cat upon whose domain some strange dog has intruded, and is not easily restrained, by the rules of English courtesy, from spitting.'

"Now, Sir William, from the facts here stated by Dickens, I shall draw some conclusions, and

First. That the condition of a free negro is quite as degraded as that of a slave, because he is 'forced down out of his just position as a man,' which I assume to be about as cutting an allusion to abolition hypocrisy as the English language is capable of expressing.

"The fair inference can be drawn from this statement, that the American abolitionists must elevate the negro so far in the social scale as to meet him in a drawing-room without feeling inclined to spit.

"*Second.* That they would not, in the cases mentioned by him, purchase their liberty, although they possessed the power; conclusive evidence that they prefer bondage to the state of social outlawry which they are required to submit to in the free states.

"*Third.* That they are so well satisfied with their condition, notwithstanding the quantity of tears—crocadile as well as pearly—which are shed over it annually; that out of the one thousand who effected their escape in 1850, the '*greater part*' sought liberty '*not for its own sake*,' but as a '*means of escape from the punishment incurred by theft and other crimes*.'

"*Fourth.* He is so well satisfied with slavery, that he parts with a mere transitory, brutish pang, from a contented wife in Maryland, perhaps, to lie down content with a new wife, in a new stall in Tennessee."

An unanswerable refutation of the popular fallacy, that those separations occasion grief and despair, for it seems that the wife is "*contented*" with the separation, and the husband is "*content*" with a new wife; so they are both satisfied. There is nothing in the antecedents of the slave at all inconsistent with this statement of Dickens; for in Africa he is a cannibal, and in the northern states his presence creates an irresistible desire to spit.

"*Fifth.* That out of three millions slaves, only one thousand fled in 1850; not in search of 'liberty for its own sake, but as a means of escape from the punishments incurred by theft and other crimes.' Now then, if the greater part of the one thousand made their escape to avoid the punishment due to crime, there were very few who fled in search of '*liberty, for its own sake*.'

What a commentary upon the sickly philanthropy of abolitionism! Nearly a thousand slaves running away to avoid the punishment of their offences. *The road along which they fled still open*, and the remainder of the three millions yet in bondage! It must be exceedingly gratifying to abolitionists who have been expending their sympathy upon runaway slaves, to be assured that they have mingled their tears with those of burglars, thieves, and murderers! One thousand scamps could hardly supply the sympathetic demand. The country sprinkled over by that intermeddling and officious class known as abolitionists, extends from Maine to Oregon. It is true they are found in *darker* clusters in some localities than in others. If each spot favored with their presence is to be blessed by a runaway thief, the supply must be largely increased.

"Take another cigar, Belthoven," said Melville, as he readjusted his person upon the sofa.

"I repeat," continued Mr. Jones, "the road open to the fugitive from justice is not closed to the fugitive from labor, and I appeal to common sense when I ask, if the yoke upon the slave is so heavy as it is represented by the abolitionists, would the *greater part* of those who escape, flee from justice instead of from insupportable cruelties. Dickens assails the American abolitionists because the free black 'is not less forced down outof his just position as a man than when he works under the planter's whip.' He has not stated the case with sufficient force. In every essential characteristic which elevates the negro above the brute, the slave is the superior of the free black. In the south it is amusing to witness the efforts of the slave to imitate the chivalrous bearing of his master. They have constantly presented for their imitation the manly conduct of southern gentlemen; they are associated with them from infancy to old age; in childhood, upon the play-ground, and by a daily contact amid the business and pleasures of manhood. Thus they acquire a moral tone, which is rarely seen among the negroes of the north. They despise a mean action, and when giving evidence in court, their truthfulness is the theme of universal admiration. They must radically change the political and social condition of the free black population; they must extend universal suffrage, instead of having a property qualification of two hundred and fifty dollars, as they have in what they call the Empire State; they must suffer them to occupy seats beside them in the house of God, where there should, if anywhere, be equality; they must be allowed to take front sofas at the opera; they must have places assigned them, with white guests, at the dining-table, in warm weather as well as cold; they must admit them to social and political equality without feeling inclined 'to spit,' before they can compare the mental condition of the free black with that of the slave."

"But the sinfulness of holding human beings in bondage! To buy and sell the immortal mind! Why, Mr. Jones, the bare contemplation of the monstrous wrong is enough to make a sensitive man shudder!"

"Especially if his sensibilities have been softened by political manœuvering for twenty-five years," said Lord Melville.

The American continued—

"This affectation of horror sits quite as ungracefully upon you, Sir William, as it does upon the mawkish society of Dexeter Hall, whose sympathies are exclusively enlisted in foreign missions."

"I really cannot reconcile it to my conscience to palliate slavery," said the Baronet, as he gave utterance to a pious sigh.

"There are many individuals at the present day," said Mr. Jones, "who are wise above what it written. They affect greater sanctity than the Almighty ever required. Let us see how the protestations of these Pharisees compare with the word of God. In the olden time, slavery was not only tolerated, but the 'peculiar institution' was expressly established. The thirteenth and fourteenth verses of the twentieth chapter of Deuteronomy reads thus—

"'13. And when the Lord thy God hath delivered it into thine hands, thou shalt smite every male thereof with the edge of the sword.

"'14. But the women, and the little ones, and the cattle, and all that is in the city, even all the spoil thereof, shalt thou take unto thyself; and thou shalt eat the spoils of thine enemies, which the Lord thy God hath given thee.'

"Now here is not only a divine recognition of the popular doctrine that 'to the victor belongs the spoils,' but there is an intimation that women are more desirable captives than men, for they were to be retained, while the sterner sex were to taste the edge of the sword. What would your abolition friends think of such sanguinary and wholesale slaughter at the present day?

"Again slavery is authorized in the 25th chapter of Leviticus:

"'44. Both thy bondmen, and thy bondmaids, which thou shalt have, shall be of the heathen that are round about you; of them shall ye buy bondmen and bondmaids.

'45. Moreover, of the children of the strangers that do sojourn among you, of them shall ye buy, and of their families that are with you, which they begat in your land: and they shall be your possession.

'46. And ye shall take them as an inheritance for your children after you, to inherit them for a possession, they shall be your bondmen forever: but over your brethren, the children of Israel, ye shall not rule one over another with rigor.'

"Such were some of the commandments of the Almighty. But modern sanctity is shocked at the idea of buying and selling human beings, when Omnipotence placed the bondsmen and cattle of the Israelites upon the same footing."

"That was under the law of Moses," said Belthoven, promptly.

"Very well, was God not quite as incapable of committing sin then as now? or is he a changeable being, advising iniquity and oppression during one century and condemning it in another? Are his precepts of to-day worthy of obedience? And was the morality of the morning of our earth too barbarous for the enlightened understandings of modern philanthropists? Are they purer now than God was then? Has Omnipotence been gradually undergoing a transition until he is almost as holy as modern abolitionism?"

"You are too severe. We claim that a more charitable system was proclaimed by our Savior."

"So the Almighty is not an unchangeable God? Proceeding from frail mortality, and applied to Jehovah, it is a modest assertion. But I will not suffer you thus to assail the conduct and motives of Jehovah. I deny that either Christ or his apostles ever uttered one solitary word against the institution of slavery; and yet they were surrounded by bondmen and bondmaids."

"But did he not issue the command to 'Do unto others as ye would that they should do unto you?'"

"Yes; but was that any thing more than a general precept which was not intended to abrogate the full force of a positive injunction? What were the *positive requirements* of the apostles? Here are some of them. The First General Epistle of Peter, chapter 2:

'18. Servants, be subject to your masters with all fear; not only to the good and gentle, but also to the froward.'

"First Epistle of Paul the Apostle to Timothy, chapter 6:

'1. Let as many servants as are under the yoke count their own masters worthy of all honor, that the name of God and his doctrine be not blasphemed.'

'2. And they that have believing masters, let them not despise them, because they are brethren; but rather do them service, because they are faithful and beloved partakers of the benefit. *These things teach and exhort.*'

"Here are express commands which cannot be affected by general principles. But there is a case which will illustrate this point. A rich young man once came to the Redeemer to inquire what he should do to gain eternal life. Jesus replied:

'Go sell all thou hast, and give to the poor, and come and follow me.'

"The term, 'all thou hast,' undoubtedly included slaves, for all rich men of that day owned them. The command, then, was not to free his slaves, but to *sell* all he possessed. Not only was slavery recognized in this way, but St. Paul sent back a runaway slave to his master; a proceeding in striking contrast with the *foraging* propensities of abolitionism. Sir William, you are, or to speak more correctly, you would have us believe you are too good, much holier than Jesus professed or taught. You should abandon the pious and purifying schemes of a politician, and seek some portion of the earth where a more charitable religion is taught than that expounded by our Savior."

"I can only repeat," replied Belthoven, with unmoved countenance, "that I am satisfied with the heavenly mandate, 'Do unto others as ye would that they should do unto you.'"

"Which I have shown was announced as a general principle, and not intended to conflict with positive requirements. But if that is the only argument you can adduce to justify a crusade against slavery, let me show you how it can be obeyed in letter and spirit."

"How?" asked the baronet.

"By doing to your starving peasantry as you would that they should do unto you; and as our slaves are as much ours as your horses are yours, do not steal them from us, unless you would have us do unto you likewise by committing a foray upon your possessions. You are fond of quoting that portion of scripture, and yet you are not willing to make it the rule for the government of your own actions. Suppose you were a slaveholder, and all you possessed on earth consisted of slaves which you had derived by will from your father—a species of property that you were justified in holding by the laws of God and the constitution of your country, would it please you to have them stolen by a set of thieving, *mousing* abolitionists? Do you think they would be doing unto others as they would that others should do unto them, when they piratically engaged in the nefarious business of running your negroes into Canada?"

The baronet moved uneasily in his chair.

"I have been interested by your facts and arguments," said Lord Melville; "will you favor us with an enumeration of the evils that prevail here, which you were desirous of comparing with the objectionable features of African slavery?"

"Really, my lord, it is too late."

"It is never too late to learn."

"Briefly, then," said the senator, "I will draw the comparison between your slaves and our own. We have seen, according to the admission of Mr. Dickens, that very few slaves escape from labor *per se*. How is it with the subjects of Great Britain? Not only are we yearly deriving large accessions to our numbers from England and Scotland, but the stampede from Ireland is so great, that it threatens to depopulate that portion of the English empire. Now, sir, what causes the emigrant to abandon home, friends, relations, and the groves of his ancestors? Suffering—*suffering* unto death. Starvation constantly assails him, enters his miserable dwelling, and seizes upon his miserable wife and helpless children, and that, too, under the eyes of his unfeeling landlord. I have examined the condition of your peasantry, and I can conceive of nothing more horrible than their condition. I have the report of a commissioner who was appointed to examine into the condition of hand-loom weavers, made to the parliament of Great Britain in 1840. With your permission I will read an extract from it, to prove that the slave is never reduced to such a horrible state :—

'Children of seven years old can begin to turn the wheel to spin flax, which is very hard work, and they are kept at work from five in the morning till nine at night.'

"Now, operatives and mechanics in New York city have adopted a rule (which very generally prevails elsewhere,) not to work more than ten hours a-day, and yet a child of seven years of age is kept at hard work *sixteen* hours! Your parliament receive a report stating that fact, and then, with sanctimonious countenances, lament that their 'cousins across the ocean' can be *so* sinful as to hold human beings in bondage! Why, sir, a negro slave, long after he is seven years old, is master of his own time, and labors not at all. English pauperism in 1840 was too horrible, yet it was not improved in 1846, if we may judge by the following article in the Liverpool Times :—

"In many places there are no potatoes left: in none will the perishing root be found after May. . . Even at Turlough many families are at this moment, we learn, without food, and the wretched sufferers are in vain endeavoring to get provision in time, that their children may not die.'

"Still there is no diminution of extravagance among the aristocracy. You may travel throughout the southern states and you will find nothing that approaches in the remotest degree these frightful pictures of destitution."

"But then," said Belthoven, "families of negroes are sometimes forcably separated."

"I admit it," responded the senator, "but not so frequently as your own countrymen are sundered by a necessity quite as irresistible. If starvation threatens them, how long will they refuse to divide families in order to preserve life? This is no mere supposition. That it is a stern reality is proved by the destitution which is visible around your manufactories in your cities, and even in the agricultural districts. It is demonstrated by the thousands who throng to our shores, as to a place of refuge. It is illustrated by the presence of disease, when men and children are not supplied with 'proper nourishment.' It is exemplified as death advances towards the spot where famine has long rioted. As painful as it may be for the slave to be torn from his relations, it is not so frightful as that mental and physical agony which forces its victim to rejoice at the death of her offspring, or compels the strong man to watch his wasting energies, his fleshless limbs, his feeble pulse, —to note the departure of strength—to count the hours that must elapse before he will stand upon the verge of the grave—to wrestle with death, again and again, and still know that the destroyer will soon obtain the victory! And in the midst of his own agony, to turn his aching eyes upon his patient wife—his weeping babes—to observe their emaciated forms, pale cheeks, and sunken eyes! He knows, too, that of the wealth—boundless wealth, which is wrung from the poor only to be thoughtlessly squandered, such a small portion would save those quivering frames from torture and death! I *do* think," continued the American rising, and speaking with more than his accustomed energy, "that when Great Britain looks at this picture, and then assumes, with the cant of a hypocrite, to lecture us about the sinfulness of holding mankind in bondage, she deserves the execrations of men and the vengeance of heaven."

A pause ensued. The baronet's countenance was thoughtful.

Jones took half-a-dozen turns through the room, and lighting another cigar, threw himself again upon the sofa. His features had acquired their usual tranquillity, and he resumed the conversation in a tone of voice more than ordinarily low and musical.

"Now turn from that picture, and examine the condition of the slave. His childhood is devoted to recreation; in manhood his powers are not overtasked: and in old age he is provided with a home. In sickness he is tenderly nursed, from the hour that his helpless form occupies the cradle, until he is gathered to the grave. I may hereafter show that whatever debasement is exhibited by the black is owing to *race* not *servitude*. The fact is now all I have to do with."

Belthoven turned uneasily in his chair.

"You made rather a severe allusion to my country, a moment ago. You surely would not charge the imperial government with the suffering that is produced by famine?"

"At all events the imperial government should not assume the duty of a censor, while its own subjects are dying for want of food. You should take the beam out of your own eye, before you try to remove the mote from your neighbor's. But I do *distinctly* charge the negro-loving government of the British empire with the crime of *wilfully* murdering her people. What reduces them to starvation? It is primogeniture, the national debt, her system of rents, and the wretched policy of inclosing vast tracts of fertile land in parks. The national debt was incurred to gratify an officious inclination to engage in continental wars. The lower classes are crushed to the earth, for the purpose of gratifying the vanity and strengthening the authority of their oppressors. A beautiful system, is it not? Not satisfied with levying taxes for national purposes, they authorize the nobility to divide up the kingdom, and then subdivide it among their tenantry. The nobility will, of course, sustain a government that gives them such extraordinary privileges; and in order to surround it with that splendor which is supposed to dazzle the vulgar, they must have money, and they wring it from the scanty earnings of the lower classes. Whatever suffering it may produce, the *rent* must be paid! If it takes the last morsel of bread from the hand of infancy, the *rent* must be paid! The *rent* must be paid, because, without it, the nobleman could not arrest the attention of foreign courts. The *rent* must be paid, or the gigantic system of fraud which enables the British aristocracy to trample on the life-blood of the masses, would be overthrown. Not satisfied with extorting money from the lower classes, to pander to the ambition of the government, and feed the vanity of the nobility, you have crowded your ragged population into farms that are not large enough for an American grave-yard. The nobles have the power to underlet their possessions to knights and squires, who in turn underlet to farmers, who underlet to the serfs. They are all interested in pressing down the latter class, because upon their shoulders rests the vast fabric of British despotism. Not only must they be dazzled by an exhibition of splendor, but, as if to confound them by the exercise of useless power, whole tracts of country are devoted to the chase. Each nobleman must have his park, his trained pack, and neighing steeds. The fairest portion of God's earth, which might yield food for a starving people, ministers to the pride of your aristocracy."

"But what can we do?" inquired Belthoven.

"What can you do? Atone for your sins, before you lecture us! What can you do? Diminish your taxes. Reduce the salaries of your officers. Do not be guilty of the folly of bestowing millions upon military chieftains. Curtail the benefices of your clergy. Cut up your parks into farms. Feed your people instead of stag-hounds. Reduce your rents, and consider a pompous exhibition of splendor of less importance than the lives of your lower classes—*and finally emancipate your parish apprentices.*"

"You are altogether too great a leveller," said Lord Melville, bitterly. "You do not know our people; the fact is they were destined for hewers of wood and drawers of water. You can't imagine how they like it, and how obedient they are. A kind word, a gentle pat on the shoulder, satisfies them for a world of labor. One thing is certain, they will not bear prosperity. We address them as imperiously as a southerner does his slave. If we admitted them to equality of rights, they would soon become free. No, sir, they require hard treatment. It is necesary to break their stubborn spirits. When that is done, it only requires an occasional steeple-chase, a procession now and then, and a fair once a year, to give them something to talk about, and they are satisfied."

"I am glad you are frank enough to admit the truth. You *have* broken the stubborn spirit of the English peasantry. That spirit which, inspired by Wat Tyler, threatened the British throne—that spirit which brought the head of Charles the First to the block, and elevated one of the people to supreme authority. It is as effectually broken as the most violent enemy of the chartist demonstration could wish it, after its failure to march on London. The spirit of the slave is not more crushed than that which feebly throbs in the breasts of the English peasantry. And yet Charles Dickens mourns over the loss of spirit in the slave! Believe me, gentlemen," said the American, rising to take his leave, "you are guilty of injustice, in warring upon our institutions. Your blood flows in our veins; we speak the same language; we seek not to assail your rights. Both nations have a common interest; and surely, when we are annually affording an asylum for thousands of your paupers, who would starve under your present system, it is unkind to bring the power of wealth—wealth wrung from honesty—to bear upon our institutions, for the purpose of destroying them. If you must intermeddle in the affairs of others, turn your strength upon Russian despotism. Relieve your own continent from tyranny and misrule before you cross the ocean, to make war upon your best friends."

CHAPTER XXI.

" Again thy winds are pealing in mine ears!
Again thy waves are flashing in my sight!
Thy memory-haunting tones again I hear,
As through the spray our vessel wings her flight."—SARGENT.

EZEKIEL BELKNAP, with a cheerful countenance, threaded the streets of London in search of Kane's family. There was an easy self-possession in his awkward gait, while he soliloquized—" I'm a sovereign, bona-fide, of the everlastin and etarnal United States *ov* Amariky, and I calkerlate that's a leetle ahead of the nobility *any how you can fix it.* How them nobles *dew* put it on! and taint cause they've any right tew, for the whole world knows they ain't the upper crust, any how you can fix it. They're no better than second-rate furniter. It's the Americans who're the rael simon-pure. And the best of the hull thing, they don't know their infe-raority. Now jist twig that aer feller. He's one on 'em; I can tell by his walk, which says it as plainly as all outer doors. *Jist* twig him, neow. Haw! haw! haw!" roared Ezekiel, as the head of the individual whose motions he was watching, came rudely in contact with the hod of a mortar-carrier. The concussion not only shook the body of the gentleman, but left a plentiful supply of mortar upon his elegant coat. " Haw! haw! I guess you won't be gazin' at the next pair of pooty legs, if they are only kivered by nice white stockings. Skin me alive if they *ain't* pooty though; they're as taperin' as the masts of the Nancy Ann. An' don't she show 'em kinder modest-like, as if she only thought how she should git over the mud without lettin a mossel of dirt sile her petticoats. I'll be etarnally exflunctified if she *dooze* hev any idee that a single pair of men's eyes is admirin them pooty legs of hern. Though I dare say she would calkerlate that the mud wasn't half so deep if them thar war spindle-shanks. Come neow, Ezekiel Belknap, yeou hev little to dew tew make sich sarned observations when yeou are out on the sarvice of a friend.

Yankee doodle come tew town,
Tew buy a stick of candy—"

The rest of the stanzas was never to be heard by that part of London, for Ezekiel's attention was attracted by two persons, who stood upon the corner of a cross-street. One of them beckoned to an omnibus driver to " hold up." It was evident they were engaged in that branch of trade known as the itinerant tinning business, for they bore in their hands a soldering-iron, some lead, and a pail of rosin. One of them was very filthy; he was evidently the junior, and, therefore, the working member of the firm. The dress of the other was plentifully smeared with grease and rosin, and he smelt strongly of his occupation. The latter personage called, in a tone of voice intended to impress upon the driver the vast difference in the relative claims to respectability of self and partner—

"Driver, let this fellow get up there with you;" saying which he ensconced himself in the stage with an air that a cockney nobleman might have envied.

"*Dew* look at that skunk! Wall, its jist exactly like the hull proceedins in this country. There's nary ragamuffin in this leetle island—woouldn't make a respectable koenty in York state—but fancies himself a darnation sight better than some other ragamuffin. Why I wouldn't squat deown here if they'd make me noble by ever so many paytents. En passent, as the Frenchmen say. I never could tell heow they can *paytent* a feller so as to make him a nobleman. But I spose, as necessity is the mother of invention, they've kinder found out some way. They must be an all-fired mean set of skunks, to require a paytent to make them noble, fur in America we are all noblemen by *nature's* paytent; which I take to be e'en abeout as good as ary paytent her majesty can git up, though they tell she dooze manufacture children fast, and pooty good ones at that."

Ezekiel Belknap now proceeded with all due activity to the house where Kane resided. He enquired for Mrs. Kane. The occupants of the two lower stories never heard of such a person.

"Wall, I kinder think they don't cozzin much hereabouts, any way you can fix it. I guess if aunt Jerusha lived in this old rookery, there would be precious few men, women *and* children, whose hull history she couldn't repeat, from the moment of thar birth, includin the midwifes', and the doctors' fees. Say, can *yeow* tell whether ary person by the name of Mary Kane lives hereabouts?"

"No," gruffly replied a humpbacked, one eyed man.

"Wal, yeou needn't be so tarnation sassy if yeou don't. I calkerlate politeness must be a dear article in these parts, judgin from the stingy way yeou deal it out."

The sailor continued to mount the staircase. "They're stuck in around here jist as thick as pismires. We must hev the hull of Mexico, and them Canadas tew, or we can never giv hums to all these critters. An it must be done before you can say Jack Robinson, for they'll swarm arter a while wus than uncle Solomon's bees. Can *yeou* tell whether or no Mary Kane, relict of Robert Kane, defunct, is a livin in this building?"

With wonderful sagacity, Mr. Belknap declined admitting the mortal existence of his friend, for fear he might jeopardize his safety thereby.

"I think there was a person of that name living in this room a few months ago."

"Peers tew me yeou arn't overly neighborly in London."

"Our miseries will not let us."

"Then you'd better emigrate to Ameriky."

"America, where's that?"

"*Jeru*salem! what ignorance! Don't know the almightiest country on airth? Look-a-heah, stranger, yeou otter die, yeou otter. We've been a kickin and a poundin of John Bull's carcass enough tew make him allers recollect his younger brother Jonathan, any way you can fix it. Dooze Mary Kane stay here neow?"

"No."

"I guess yeou otter know where she is."

"I don't though; nor I don't care!"

"It's no wonder yeou can't keep up with the smartest nation on airth. I wouldn't give a continental dam for as many spews as yeou are as I could stack on uncle Solomon's turnip-patch. Not know America! Old Pittis has forgot more than yeou ever knew, and he never was allowed to be half-witted."

"Did you ask for Mary Kane?" inquired a boy some dozen years of age.

"Wal, I did."

"She's dead!'

"Dead! impossible."

"I seed here put in the ground."

"My God! that is tew hard; tew hard!"

"Are you her brother?"

"No, but if I was, I couldn't feel wus. Poor Kane."

"She froze to death in the street."

"Boy, I b'lieve you're lyin'."

"No I aint."

"In the streets of London? Why what in tarnation did she leave her hum fur?"

"She was turned into the street by the direction of her landlord."

A prolonged whistle was the immediate response to this intelligence.

"Wall, if I didn't kinder hope, for the sake of relationship, that the charitable people of this country war sometimes slandered, but neow I blieve the hull truth was never told on e'en. May the pesky critters allers live under a monarchy, and never know the blessings of a free government, fur they don't desarve it, and that's the wust punishment I can wish the unfeelin skunks."

"Would you like to see Mr. Kane's children?"

"Whar are they?"

"At Philip Hogan's."

"Well?"

"No, they expect his oldest son will die."

"Yeou needn't tell me any more. My heart is already too heavy. I'm sorry some other person can't tell this news tew Robert Kane. Good bye."

And the honest fellow started upon his return.

"Yankee doodle came tew town,

Tew——It's no kinder use; I *can't* sing; I can't even whistle. My feelins are rael bad; yes, any way you can fix it."

With a heavy heart Ezekiel Belknap returned to the "Nancy

Ann." Robert saw in a moment that some great misfortune had occurred, as the sailor stood awkwardly twisting his hat.

"You bring bad news?"

"I dew, and I'm sorry for't."

Kane's face became paler.

"Tell me the worst," he said, with a painful effort.

The sailor hesitated.

"A man who has been publickly whipped can bear anything," said Robert, and his lip quivered.

"It's very bad; I'm *so* sorry to say it's *very* bad."

"My wife is ill?"

"She is dead; and neow you know the wust," replied the sailor as he precipitately left that part of the ship, for he could not witness the burst of grief that he was certain would follow the announcement.

The form of the unhappy man seemed frozen. For several minutes he remained stationary, and then rising, without speaking to any one, he left the ship.

He was not apprehensive of another assault from the kidnappers; he did not even think of them, but straightway went to the house where he left his family. He was told they were at Hogan's. With uncertain steps he entered the room. His features were so haggard that Mrs. Hogan did not at first recognize him.

"She is gone, yes, kind, faithful, gentle Mary is not here; she is dead."

"Father," uttered a weak voice.

He turned to the little bed in the corner of the room. A thin, emaciated arm was extended towards him, from which the bones protruded through the skin.

"My God! can this be Henry?"

"Yes, father, it's me."

Gazing upon the form of the sufferer, the muscles of his face contracted, and then the tears started to his eyes, while deep convulsive sobs escaped from his bosom.

"Don't weep, dear father; it's better I should die. I've suffered so much, and I want to be with mother in heaven, where there is no pain."

"Have I deserved this?" said Kane, as he knelt by the bedside, and kissed the wan cheek again and again.

"Pa, is it oo?" said a little voice at his side.

"Dolly, at least you are spared to me!" he exclaimed, clasping her in his arms.

"And here's Frank Tot, too. Don't oo want to see Frank Tot?"

He took Frank upon his knee. The child looked at him earnestly for a moment, and screamed.

"My own child don't know me!"

"Oo looks so strange, pa. What makes oo so pale? Haven't oo had enough to eat, pa?"

He pressed her silently to his bosom.

"Say, pa, is oo hungry; if zoo are, Mrs. Hogan will give oo something to eat, for she is a good ooman."

"She *is* a good woman, and heaven will reward her."

"Do not think of it, Mr. Kane. I have done no more than Mrs. Kane would if she had been——"

"Living! But she is not, and I shall never see her again. Never more hear her gentle voice, never more see her sweet smile. All is over. She was, too, such an affectionate wife, such a devoted mother. Ah me! ah me!"

"And poor ma froze to death," said Henry faintly.

"What is that?" exclaimed Kane, starting to his feet.

Henry was awed by his manner.

Mrs. Hogan did not speak.

"What did he say, Mrs. Hogan: Mary frozen to death?"

"Alas! it is too true."

"How?" he inquired with terrible distinctness.

"She was driven into the street, with her children, by Solomon Greasebeans."

"And that bad man, Hurdy," said Henry.

"Monster! Vengeance will yet be appeased. It is too much for human endurance."

The strong man was prostrated by grief. He rallied again, and all that night he watched over Henry. The time for taking nourishment was passed. He could only moisten his lips occasionally with water.

"Father!"

"What, my child?"

"You must not mourn for me after I am dead."

"You must not die, Henry."

He shook his head mournfully.

"I can't live many hours. father. See, the bones are already through the skin. I shall die, but I shall be happy, far happier in heaven."

A groan was the only reply.

"And it will be better for you, father. Two children are as many as you can take care of, and I had rather die than see Dolly and Frank Tot suffer. But you must promise me one thing, father."

"Anything you may ask, Henry."

"Take Dolly and brother with you to America. Don't keep them here where they steal fathers and leave their wives and children to starve."

"And leave forever the grave of your mother?"

"We shan't always be separated, dear father. We shall all meet again in heaven if we die happy; and I am certain we shall, for we have nothing to make us wicked."

"Yes, Henry, we shall meet in heaven."

"But you will promise to take Dolly and Frank Tot to America, won't you?"

"I will, if God spares my life."

"Thank you, father; I shall now die a great deal happier. I want you all to have a home that nobody can turn you away from, where kidnappers never knock people down and beat them.'"

Kane startled as though an adder had stung him.

It was evident Henry was fast sinking. His breathing was more rapid, and the clammy sweat of death stood upon his forehead. His limbs were rigid, and his fingers were pressed into the palms of his hands. A calm smile lit up his features as his eyes turned to his father's face. Their language was expressive though voiceless.

"You see how bravely I can meet death," he whispered.

But death was not a foe to be encountered without dread, and the emaciated form shook convulsively; the body struggled long for life, but at length the throes became less and less violent, the muscles of the mouth relaxed, a shudder ran through the frame, and the spirit of the noble boy was taking its flight towards heaven.

With a cry of anguish the father pressed the soulless clay to his bosom. No smile, no motion responded to the caress, and with a thrill of agony he laid upon the bed all of mortality that remained of the first-born child, who had been watched with so much fondness by the doating father from the hour he was first placed, a very little thing, in his arms. The body was committed to its mother earth.

Two days must elapse, and then the "Nancy Ann" would sail for the New World—a *new world* to all who have never tasted the sweets of liberty and the blessings that flow from the principle of equality—a *new world* to the victim whose spirit has been broken, and whose body has been lacerated by the rod of tyranny—a *new world* to the humbled subjects who flee with horror and dismay from the hypocritical, festering, and savage governments of the old —the *new world* of hope, and freedom, and happiness for the millions of human beings whose hearts never before throbbed but with a consciousness of suffering wrongs; wrongs that a despotic power not only thinks itself justified in committing, but without the aid of which its infamous usurpation of inalienable prerogatives would be summarily avenged. To this *new world* Robert Kane now directed his attention; not, it is true, with the same hopefulness as when his wife was to have been the partner of his flight. Still his promise to Henry, and a desire to place his surviving children where they would not be subjected to the brutalities that had been inflicted upon their parents, stimulated him to take efficient measures for their escape. He had no doubt but that the press-gang would seize his person again if they had an opportunity. The danger was also to be apprehended that search would be instituted by the officer in command of the ship for his arrest as a deserter. Thus surrounded by perils, he had to act with the utmost prudence. Fortunately, Hurdy was not apprised of his place of concealment at Hogan's. It, therefore, only remained for him to exercise proper caution in getting his children and his little store on board the "Nancy Ann," to warrant the conclusion that his escape would be effected.

His friends assisted him with all the cheerfulness that his unhappy situation commanded. They were fearful the strong arm of power would arrest him before he went on board the "Nancy Ann;" and even when once there, he necessarily incurred the hazard of running the gauntlet of the English fleet, which not only clouded the Atlantic Ocean with its canvass, but, hovering around the channel, guarded the prerogatives of the British throne, with the sleepless vigilance of Juno's Argus.

At a late hour on the night preceding the day the "Nancy Ann" was to sail, Robert Kane, in spite of the remonstrances of Hogan, started to bid a last adieu to the graves of his wife and child. The cold wind swept through the streets of London. The clouds hung upon the city, and the tops of the houses appeared to be blended with their dark outlines. The police, wrapped in the livery of authority, gloomily "beat their rounds," benevolently cursing their fate because there was nothing *else to beat.* Robert Kane silently threaded his way, intent only upon his mission of grief; for there are moments when the mind is so occupied with its own suffering, that it has no thought for aught else. A few persons were still abroad, but they passed unnoticed as he sped onwards. One man cast a searching look at the bent and humbled form of Kane, and turning, with exultation gleaming upon his savage features, dogged the steps of the mourner. Hurdy followed him with the stealthy fidelity of a cat even into the sacred resting-place of the dead. With the fell determination and disgusting appetite of the hyæna, he would have preyed upon the form no longer animated by vitality. Robert knelt by the grave of his wife. The frozen earth was melted by his tears. The human fiend, who stood with folded arms, smiled scornfully.

"Faithful, devoted Mary; I thought we might, together, enjoy the blessings of a happier home. But fate has decreed otherwise. And now I must part with all that remains of your dear form, Mary. An ocean will soon roll between us. Never more may I kiss the earth that covers you; and, until the archangel's trump awakens the slumbering dead, may it rest lightly upon your bosom. Farewell, dear Mary; farewell, dear Henry—we shall meet in heaven.'

"Ha! ha! a pathetic scene."

"Monster! dare you pollute this sacred spot with your presence?"

"You see I am here."

"Then begone, and leave one who has so much cause for hating you, alone with the dead."

"He! he! he!" laughed the other gleefully. "You want to get rid of me, now, do'nt you? But you wont, though, until I have placed you in a situation to receive punishment as a deserter. Aye, as a *deserter;* do you hear?"

"If you will not go, I must bid adieu to her grave."

With eyes rivetted to the mound of earth, Robert Kane was slowly leaving the spot.

"Not so fast, my good fellow; you will please accept my company"—and Hurdy laid his powerful grasp upon Kane's shoulder.

"Hurdy, you have placed yourself in the path of a desperate man. I would not take the life God gave, notwithstanding the provocation you have given me; but I warn you to beware! Take your hand from my shoulder."

"Boy; for you are nothing but a boy in my grasp, even if you had not been weakened by the cat——"

He did not finish the sentence, for he was startled for a moment, by the glance of fire that shot from the eyes of Kane. It was for a moment, however, and then he shook the form of his prisoner with the utmost violence. Robert saw by the aid of the faint gas-light that penetrated to the spot, that there was no hope of a rescue, even had it been prudent to claim it.

"Mr. Hurdy, before you interfered with my happiness, I was a hard-working, honest man, the husband of a lovely and affectionate wife, and the father of three beautiful children, whom I managed to support, with considerable difficulty it is true—but still, with rigid economy, and by denying myself every luxury, I *did* support them. Without any provocation upon my part, except poverty, you seized my person; you saw me brutally scourged—yes, *brutally* scourged——"

"I did, I did," interrupted Hurdy, rubbing his hands.

"You assisted in turning my wife into the street, from whence she never returned alive."

"I did, I did," said the monster, still joyously.

"And you brought my noble Henry to that gloomy spot."

"I did, I did."

"Now, do you not think there is enough for your soul to answer for, if you let me go, heart-broken as I am, to the only asylum for a defenceless mortal, on earth?"

"Not half, not half. I expect to see you whipped to death; to see both your children starve—*starve!*"

"Abandoned villain! What provoked such fiendish hate?"

"I'll tell you," he replied, hissing the words into Kane's ears. "Your wife preferred you to me. But I have been terribly revenged. In addition to all the accusations you have cast upon me, there is one more you might add to the rest."

"What is it? I thought you had exhausted the catalogue of human atrocities."

"Oh dear, no! Let me tell you." And again his words were hissed forth, as if by the tongue of a serpent. "I kidnapped you, because I could not otherwise accomplish my designs upon your wife——"

"Hold!" shouted Kane.

"On the night she was turned into the street I forced her—aye, *forced* her to submit to my embraces. Ha! ha! ha!"

"Then, villain, you shall die."

The struggle was long and desperate. The one contended for life—for Hurdy saw gleams of insanity in the eyes of Kane—the other for vengeance. They were both men of powerful frames. Robert's, it is true, was weakened by sickness, but it was now nerved by the wildest fury. Hurdy would have shouted for assistance, but the hands of the assailant were clutched upon his throat. They reeled backwards over graves and against tomb-stones, in that fierce conflict. Twice they fell upon the frozen ground, and each time they rose—Kane still clinging to the throat of his foe, with the remorseless hold of a tiger. Hurdy exerted all the powers of his vast strength to shake him off, but unsuccessfully, and at length he grew black under the eyes, his tongue protruded from between teeth that grinned like a fleshless skull. Reeling to the earth, he fell upon the grave of Mary Kane.

"Not there—you shall not die there, remorseless villain," shouted Kane, as he fiercely hurled the body away. Hurdy recovered his breath; he gasped faintly, and tried to regain his feet. Kane witnessed his exertions, and again that terrible gleam shot from his eyes. Hurdy saw it.

"Mercy"—he faintly articulated.

"Mercy! Have you ever shown it? No—it is an act of *mercy* to rid the world of such a monster. Prepare to die."

"One hour—only one hour!"

"Not one minute."

"Do not—oh! as you hope for mercy hereafter, do not kill me."

"Have mercy!" seemed to come from Mary's grave. Robert started; was it reality, or the false-whispering of his brain.

"No, no—it is the warning of some fiend, who would save the life of this monster, for the service he will render in the cause of Satan."

"Have mercy!" the soft voice seemed to say.

"Gentle Mary, I will obey you. Wretch, begone! But hark you: if ever you cross my path again, you shall die. Away!"

Hurdy staggered from the spot, feeling his throat as he went, and turning his head first to one side and then to the other, to see if it was not dislocated. He did not proceed far, however; but having ascertained that his neck was all right, with the exception of being considerably bruised and feeling decidedly uncomfortable, he halted behind a pretentious tomb-stone, which announced the important fact that the dust slumbering beneath it was much more honorable than the ashes that reposed under the adjoining mounds.

Protected from observation, Hurdy watched the movements of Kane. A scowl of ungratified malice wrinkled his savage features.

"*Won't* I be revenged!" he muttered between his gnashing teeth.

Robert Kane arose from the grave of his wife and slowly left the spot. Hurdy followed him as steadfastly as Satan tracks the footsteps of the sinner. Arriving at Hogan's, Robert entered the house, while Hurdy hastened with all possible speed to collect his band.

Time pressed: the small hours of the morning were rapidly increasing, when Kane, accompanied by Hogan, Dolly, and Frank Tot, started for the "Nancy Ann." Dolly's eyes opened with timid surprise, at first, and then observing her father with the baby in his arms, she nestled to the bosom of Hogan, and soothed by the motion, fell asleep. Frank cried when the cold night-air penetrated his lungs, but he, too, was soon pacified by the gentle words of his father. Kane cast eager glances up and down each street, but no one pursued them. The river was not far distant; he thought he could see the tapering spars of the "Nancy Ann." He breathed more freely; already he tasted the sweets of liberty; his heart bounded with a strange, happy delight.

"What is that?" he inquired.

"Footsteps," rejoined Hogan.

"And in pursuit. Faster! faster!"

They increased their pace to a run. The pursuers were unincumbered, and rapidly gained upon them.

"*Now* I have you," exclaimed Hurdy, exultingly, as, accompanied by three confederates, he rushed upon the fugitives.

"Off! off!" shouted Kane.

"By the eternal God, *no!*" replied Hurdy, as his grasp was once more laid upon Kane's shoulder.

"Then take the death that is a thousand times too merciful for such a monster."

Thought is not quicker than the long blade of Kane's knife pierced the heart of his foe. With curses upon his lips, Hurdy fell to the earth.

They were still three to one. Robert had thrown away his knife; he would not shed more blood. They were overpowered, for the motions of each were embarrassed by a child. Suddenly another combatant appeared.

"I kinder guess three to *tew* ain't the clean thing, no heow yeou can fix it, so yeou may see heow that are feels in your paunch." Saying which, Ezekiel Belknap sent a tremendous blow into the abdomen of the most powerful of the kidnappers, and as it was an upward blow, his head struck the pavement first.

"I calkerlate yeou never tasted a ginewine Varmont Sockdolager afore. Well neow my hand is in, I might jist as well spile the pro*fyles* of the hull crobboodle, so here's at yeou jist as slick as flap-jacks buttered on both sides tasted on a airish mornin."

The Englishman squared himself after the most approved method of the ring.

"Yeou don't calkerlate, I gues, to come it over Ezekiel Belknap with that are slighter-hand business, dew yeou? Wall, I'll give yeou the allfiredest hug *yeou* ever had, unless yeou've been squizzed by a grizzly bar."

In a moment the sailor was within the guard of the other, and encircling him in his arms, pressed him with such violence that he screamed with pain.

"I knowed it; I jist knowed it. Whenever a feller begins to dance abeout like like a pea in a hot skillet, a flourishin his fists this way and that way, yeou may be *sure* he'll flummux. I'll gin yeou one more jist by way of a clincher. He! oh! he!"

The kidnapper groaned with agony.

"I persume you'll stay tew hum another night, instead of skylarkin abeout. Pesky critters, *leave!*"

They did not require a second invitation, but moved hastily away.

But although they had escaped these foes, the police were aroused. Rattles were heard in every direction. The light of day having appeared, the gas was turned off in the streets. As they freed themselves from the kidnappers, however, a thick fog-shut down upon them.

"Follow me," said the sailor. They clustered together and hurried towards the ship. Their movements were arrested by a dozen rattles in front.

"This way," whispered the sailor.

Having once departed from a direct line, it was difficult to strike the right course again. The fog became still more dense, but while it prevented the police from seeing them, it also rendered the attempt to find the ship exceedingly dangerous. Thrice had they turned their course without success. The police, as if aware they had enclosed them, now narrowed their circle. Turning in that direction which seemed the least guarded, they found themselves at the point anxiously sought for. With the exception of Hogan, who had succeeded in effecting his escape, the fugitives entered the ship, and were secreted in the hold by Ezekiel. No sooner had he accomplished that feat, than he returned to the deck, and reclining against a mast affected to be asleep. The fog now lifted and through his half-closed eyes, Mr. Belknap saw a group of police officers approaching the "Nancy Ann." Two of them stepped upon the deck.

"Who commands here," said one of them.

"I swow, if I han't been caught a nappin," said Ezekiel, rubbing his eyes. "Captain Smith commands the Nancy Ann."

"Have any persons entered the ship during the last fifteen minutes?"

"Nary livin critter, I'm sartain, for I'm dreadful wakeful."

"So it would seem," replied the other sarcastically.

"Sartain; when it's necessary."

"Bill, you were mistaken, they can't have entered here."

"Perhaps I was; let's look further and then return here if we are unsuccessful elsewhere."

As they left the ship Ezekiel's fingers cut certain fantastical flourishes in front of his nose, which, to the well informed in such matters, is understood to express the idea that the operator entertains the liveliest contempt for the individual who has elicited the aforesaid digital flourishes.

Orders were now issued to cast off the fastenings that secured the ship to the dock. With more than ordinary speed the "Nancy Ann" was extricated from the shipping that surrounded her and stood out into the Thames. It was an anxious moment for Robert Kane, for, to be seized now, when he had incurred so many difficulties, would be doubly painful.

The police having prosecuted their search without effect were now returning to examine the "Nancy Ann." When they reached her berth she was in the middle of the stream. With earnest gesticulation they beckoned for her to "heave to." Their orders were answered by a second edition of those digital flourishes, enacted by Ezekiel Belknap, which, judging by the effect produced upon the police, had a language that the conservators of the peace were not wholly unfamiliar with, though it is not to be supposed they ever required their own fingers to perform such fanciful convolutions and spasmodic jerks.

A consultation seemed to be held by the police. Apparently they had decided on a pursuit, for two of them entered a boat and pulled vigorously towards the receding ship. So rapid, however, was the motion of the " Nancy Ann," as she was driven down the river by the wind and tide, that unless they obtained more speed, the pursuit would be hopeless. They seemed to be assured of the fact, for they pulled in the direction of a revenue cutter. Robert Kane stepped upon the deck to watch his pursuers. By the time the cutter was "under weigh" the "Nancy Ann" was a mile ahead, and going through the water at a rapid rate of speed. At length Kane lost sight of his pursuers altogether.

While the good ship was passing the English fleet Kane involuntarily trembled. He was still within the grasp of remorseless power. Each moment the " Nancy Ann" glided away from those bristling cannon he breathed more freely, and when at length he was beyond their reach he uttered an involuntary shout of gladness.

After a long rest the good ship snuffed the breezes of the Atlantic, as she laved her sides in the green waves, or plunged her prow into the rolling billows. Laden with the hopes of liberty, she started for the shores of America, the " land of the free and the home of the brave."

CHAPTER XXII.

" For all the rest,
They'll take suggestions as a cat laps milk ;
They'll tell the clock to any business that
We say befits the hour."—SHAKESPEARE.

MRS. SOLOMON GREASEBEANS, although she would doubtless scorn the imputation, was a *sponge*. She could have been indicted and found guilty as such any week day of the whole year. And it was intimated upon the strength of opinions, known to have been entertained by her most intimate friends, that she was not entirely guiltless of the charge on that day more particularly set apart for divine service. And yet, strange to say, some of her friends rather liked the operation of being sponged, as it was performed by Mrs. Solomon Greasebeans. She did not assail them as though *all* their good nature, as well as their favors, were to be absorbed. She had too much tact to be guilty of such coarseness. It was accomplished by a delicate process so well understood by the sagacious sponge. The reputation of Mrs. Greasebeans, nevertheless, was that of a lickspittle and toady, though her most devoted friends, only, took the liberty of saying that such was the fact. And herein consisted the superior adroitness of Mrs. Greasebeans' tactics. She never was known to make a direct application for favors, like Mrs. Furnlace, for instance, who was guilty of the bad taste of urging specific requests; as, "May I have your carriage to make calls in; I have such a horrid dread of the small-pox whenever I enter a hackney-coach." Or, "Will you lend me five pounds until my husband arrives," or, "Can I wear your elegant scarf, unless you intend to wear it for the *third* time this season." Mrs. G. beans, (for she was recognized by the different appellations of Grease-beans, G. beans, and Grease b.) was never known to be guilty of such flagrant indiscretions. The principal weapon employed by the lady for the purpose of accomplishing her object was flattery; though as a formidable auxiliary thereto, she most effectually sustained the character of a newsmonger, a very desirable character, indeed, if you wish to amuse a portion of the feminine gender; *what* proportion of that indispensable sex shall be left for them to decide. If Mrs. Greasebeans did not anticipate a very comfortable dinner at home, owing to a scarcity of game at her market; or, because she sent too late, or did not take the trouble to send at all, it is a reasonable supposition that Mrs. Greasebeans intended to dine somewhere else. Where can she pay for a good dinner with flattery and news? Why at Mrs. Flukins, to be sure. Flukins always sets a good table. Flukins' parlors are elegantly furnished. and Mrs. Flukins is never tired of hearing them praised. There were two subjects of conversation which Mrs. Flukins could dwell upon from morning till night, without the slightest evidence of fatigue. They were as inexhaustible as that unusual theme, the weather, is to a bashful man or a saphead. Her *parlors* and Henrietta Maria *Flukins*. In her mind's eye, Mrs. Greasebeans saw the complacent features of Mrs. Flukins, while she, Mrs. G'beans, was pointing out the beauty of the rosewood furniture, the gorgeousness of the carpet—roast goose and boiled turkey just placed upon the table—the magnificence of the statuary—baked duck, her favorite dish—the splendor of the mirrors—grouse—the richness of the curtains—champagne, Heidsick, at that. If all this failed to elicit an invitation to dine, the grace, bearing, and accomplishments of her charming young friend, Henrietta Maria, freely dwelt upon, was certain to procure for the goose, turkey, grouse, and baked duck—especially the *baked duck*—the honor of being consumed by Mrs. Solomon Greasebeans, consort of Mr. Solomon Greasebeans, senior member of the great house of Greasebeans, Snodgrass & Co. An honor rarely conferred upon dead animals. In the parlor of Mrs. Flukins, and the beauty of Miss Flukins, Mrs. G'beans saw dinners *ad infinitum*, and she always thought there was no more appropriate time than the present for enjoying one of them. She could not reflect upon the subject with placid indifference, or without a certain nervousness in the region of the stomach, and she therefore rung the bell.

"Bridget, what's for dinner?"

"The remains of last week's ham."

"That ham is getting quite too ancient; it possesses as few attractions, calculated to tempt one's appetite, as Mr. Greasebeans does, since he turned grey, and wears spectacles. What else?"

"Some corned beef."

"I shall not dine at home to-day. I think, as the weather is gloomy, Mrs. Flukins would like to be entertained. Get my second hat."

Mrs. Flukins not being an admirer of light or substantial literature, and possessing no taste for needlework—which, in her estimation, poor people made decidedly vulgar—was yawning away the hours until dinner; repining, because the weather was not pleasant enough for her to shop, or to make calls. It was a matter of perfect indifference to Mrs. Flukins if James could not get along without the aid of his "Solitary Horseman," Dickens without his ghosts; Thackeray, without proving himself a greater snob than he could delineate. So far as she was concerned, the "solitary horseman" might have been kept upon his steed until both had petrified, or "putrified," as Mrs. Partington would have it. Dickens might have written himself out a dozen times instead of twice, and Thackeray might have proved himself a more finished snob than he has ever described.

The door-bell summoned Sally. She escorted an itinerant merchant into the parlor. Probably his net receipts were not large, for his dress had a decidedly Jeremy Diddler appearance. With an air calculated to propitiate the rich lady, he displayed his wares.

Mrs. Flukins examined him through her eye-glass (she used an eye-glass instead of spectacles, so that people might attribute it to shortness of vision, instead of age,) for a few moments, and then said languidly—

"Go away, dirty man; you make me nervous."

"I beg your pardon, madam, but I assure you my poverty is not in the slightest degree of my own choosing."

"What a horrid creature. *Dirty* man *do* go away."

"Is there nothing I can show you?" persisted the travelling merchant, with characteristic importunity.

"Nothing."

"Thread?"

"Never sew—vulgar."

"Lace?"

"No'"

"Silks?"

"Sally!"

"Handkerchiefs!"

"Show this man to the door."

"Gloves?"

"Sally, call the police."

"Yes, mem, going; another time I hope——"

"Dirty man——"

"Gone!"

Mrs. Flukins applied her perfumed handkerchief to her cultivated nose, while she cast a look of disgust at the spot recently occupied by the merchant. She then rose from her luxurious chair, and, with studied grace, walked to the mirror. Grace—*languid* grace, was Mrs. Flukins' interesting weakness. She could not spend more time attitudinizing, if she expected to become a model for Hiram Powers, in the conception of another Greek Slave.

Every position the human form could be made to assume, gracefully, was known to Mrs. Flukins. She devoted at least one hour each day to "*mirror practice*," as she facetiously called it. She rested the weight of her form upon one foot, and then upon the other, and contrasted the effect produced by each position. She confessed to a partiality for the "left leg position," as she styled it, in the privacy of her own parlor. Though she was not positively certain, but that the other was almost as much admired by the men. Her lovely hand—for even Mrs. Flukins' rivals were forced to admit that her hands did stand age remarkably well—gracefully rested upon her forehead, with the thumb placed upon the temple, and the fingers slightly bent, so as to display their curving outlines. Another favorite attitude of Mrs. Flukins—and what she did to perfection—was to rest her elbow upon the back of a chair, with the fore-finger of her left hand—because that hand was the smallest—resting upon her cheek, within easy-travelling distance from her mouth, whither her little finger made frequent excursions, for the benefit of its health. Lip dew being considered, in the estimation of many ladies, an admirable medicine for sick fingers, which any one can discover, by observing how often applications are made thereto—especially by maidens who have beautiful hands, red lips, and pearly teeth; it being a curious fact, that the fingers of all such are much oftener indisposed than those who have big hands, thin, pale lips, and scraggy teeth.

Mrs. Flukins would then run the extremities of her taper fingers through the mass of curls (carefully dyed, for Mrs. Flukins, in anticipation of the final end of all flesh, considered it her duty to dye twice a week, at least, by way of familiarizing herself with the grim monster) that clustered upon her cheek. But that attraction, which Mrs. Flukins most prided herself upon, was the skillful management of her large black eyes. They were made to roll in every conceivable manner, from the devotional gaze at the ceiling, which was the chef-d'œuvre, to the side-long, half-timid, half-furtive glance, that could not brook the thorough examination she was conscious of eliciting; the full and melting lustre, that betrayed the whole ocean of trusting confidence with which she was inspired, were all displayed with a matchless art, that awakened the liveliest enthusiasm in the bosom of the no longer youthful Mumford Flukins.

Again Sally was summoned.

"What o'clock is't?" said Mrs. Flukins, with an attitude, for she even practiced on the waiter.

"Three."

"One hour before dinner. I wish somebody would call; even that dear, agreeable sponge, Sol. Greasebeans' wife, would be a God-send. That's her ring now; I can tell it, for it's a *hungry* ring. Well, she can earn a dinner in an hour any day. Tell her I am at home, Sally. How different she is from some of my friends, who, most inconsiderately, drop in as the dinner is being dished. I would not care if they did not eat so much as to become stupid, thereby depriving me of the scandal which is my due after feeding them. I must change my dinner-hour occas—"

"Ah, my *dear* Mrs. Greasebeans, how kind of you to call such a nasty day. I am *so* glad to see you."

"Thank you, Mrs. Flukins. You are well, I hope? and dear Henrietta Maria?"

"She is still poring over Dickens' last, though how she can laugh and cry over his endless twaddle I never could tell, unless it is because he clatters on, like the old water-wheel at my father's in the country. It's well enough, you know, to glance over them, because it's fashionable to say you have read his works. But she, foolish child, takes pleasure in their perusal. Well, what's the news? I have been crazy to see you. I know you have heard a world of pleasant scandal to tell me since you dined here day before yesterday."

Mrs. Greasebeans indulged in a small deprecatory laugh.

"It is too kind of you to welcome me so cordially. I should not call here so often if it were not for your agreeable manners, and to enjoy a sight of charming Henrietta Maria, as well as to take another peep at your elegant furniture, which I can never sufficiently admire."

Mrs. Greasebeans had made this speech at least forty times; but she counted largely upon the ability of Mrs. Flukins to digest it twice a week throughout the year.

The large black eyes of Mrs. Flukins cast a gratified glance around the parlor.

"I have a little bit of news to tell you."

"I knew it."

"You may recollect Lord Snizzle?"

"Ah, yes; he calls here constantly since the night of your party. To tell you the truth, he is dying for Henrietta Maria."

"She is too good for him. He don't pay his tailor's bills!"

"Is it possible?"

Rich plebeians think nothing so reprehensible as the non-payment of bills.

"Yes. Mr. Presshard trusted him until the prospect of having his accounts liquidated became gloomy; and at length he took legal steps to obtain his dues. The officer found Lord Snizzle in a lofty mood. 'Your lordship,' said the officer, 'has suffered these small items to accumulate, until, in the aggregate, they amount to a very considerable sum. Mr. Presshard would consider it a great favor if your lordship will favor him with your check for the aforesaid sum of sixty-seven pounds, nineteen shillings, eleven pence half-penny.'

"'Certainly,' replied his lordship, seizing his pen and a blank check.

"'But has your lorship any funds in bank to meet the check?'

"'Not that I am aware of; but being of a very prying disposition, I did not know but that you could find what I have sought for in vain.'

"'Come now, Lord Snizzle, this won't answer the contract. I must have the money.'

"'Base is the slave who pays!' ejaculated his lordship, theatrically.

"'Lord Snizzle! I must inform your lordship that a knowledge of Shakespeare won't save you the next time I call. Good morning, your lordship.'

"Mr. Presshard has not received the amount of his bill to this day."

"Scandalous! But he dresses well."

"For the very best reason in the world; he never pays for his clothes. I should like to know if a person under such circumstances ought not to dress well? The truth is, his lordship is no better than a genteel 'Jeremy Diddler;' and avowedly so, too, for he does not hesitate to ask his friends to patronize such and such establishments, because, to bring customers to them is all the compensation he ever expects to make. It is so even at watering-places. He is a favorite with landlords, because he gets up hops, and supper-parties, and balls, all of which help to swell the profits of the hotel-keepers. They can afford to board him for nothing, as he makes others pay his bills ten times over. His own being settled after the manner of Wilkins Micawber. Such I understand to be the prominent trait in his lordship's character."

"This is all news to me. I never knew before why Lord Snizzle happened in so often about dinner-time. The mystery is now explained. He is a regular sponge."

Mrs. Greasebeans cast a quick glance at her friend to see if there was a sarcasm in her meaning, personal to herself. The countenance of Mrs. Flukins was impassive.

The dinner bell rung.

"That's for your dinner. I will bid you good morning," and Mrs. Greasebeans rose apparently to take her leave, without intending to do anything of the kind.

"Oh no; dine with us."

"Not to-day, dear Mrs. Flukins. I have some amusing things to tell you, but they will keep until I can call again."

"I can't hear of a refusal. Come, Henrietta Maria will be offended if you go before dining."

"The mention of that dear name proves too powerful for my resolution. (She had seen the baked duck go up.) For this once I will accept."

This was at least the five hundredth time the inflexible resolution of Mrs. Greasebeans had been overcome in the same manner. In fact the resolution of that estimable lady melted away like wax before heat, in the presence of a good dinner. All the time she was protesting so decidedly against dining, she was just as certain of being helped to a leg and thigh, (and eating it, too) her favorite part, of that baked duck, as if it was then and there invitingly reclining upon her plate. Mrs. Flukins so understood it, for the solemn protestation of Mrs. Greasebeans that she had an excellent dinner at home—a fabulous statement—or that Mr. Greasebeans could not dine without her, never ended by a reservation of her appetite for the supposed dinner, or in enabling Mr. Greasebeans to dine that day. She was invariably found at the close of the dining hour comfortably seated in the back parlor of Mrs. Flukins, red with a satisfied appetite and plenty of champagne, and quite as regardless of the excellent dinner at home as she was indifferent to the unfilled stomach of Mr. Solomon Greasebeans. It was impossible to conceive a more grateful person than Mrs. Greasebeans, when she had dined heartily, especially on baked duck; and that she *had* dined well on the day in question, was verified by an entire skeleton of that animal, which was lying upon and around her plate at the time preparations were made for the fifth course.

For half an hour, therefore, Mrs. Greasebeans continued to retail the news which had accumulated on her hands, much to her inconvenience, during the last two days. The mottos of Mrs. Greasebeans, in the news line, were, "quick sales" and a "rapid turning over of my stock in trade." This she was in the habit of designating as a comfortable arrangement for herself, and doing justice to the community at large. This manifestation of a disposition to "keep the thing moving" was duly appreciated by all the parties interested: and, consequently, Mrs. Greasebeans was enabled to sleep with a conscience which is only vouchsafed to those who are blessed with a *realizing* sense of having performed their duty to themselves and to society.

After Mrs. Greasebeans had eased her mind in that regard, she felt so much better that she concluded an airing in the elegant carriage (damask lining) of Mrs. Flukins would not be injurious to her health. She had a *penchant* for that carriage—had Mrs. Greasebeans, it was so stylish; and the horses were so beautiful, and the driver and footman looked so aristocratic and distingué-like. Mrs. Greasebeans entertained not the slightest doubt that an airing in such an establishment was more conducive to satisfactory digestion, than one of less pretensions could possibly afford. Hence she was often seen in fashionable thoroughfares with Mrs. Flukins, whenever the nobility were out in force. Upon such occasions Mrs. Greasebeans only recognized her most distinguished acquaintances, which she did with a marked flourish, in some cases extending out of the window, when it was bestowed upon a person *enormously* rich, or who had an entrée to the saloons of the minor nobility: those friends who *rode their legs*, not being observed upon such occasions. After they had returned, Mrs. Greasebeans mentally discussed the propriety of going home before tea. Mrs. Flukins was noted for delightful teas; and she seemed in such excellent spirits, that Mrs. Greasebeans thought there was no danger of boring her: a result which she had sufficient tact to foresee would occasion the loss of any number of valuable dinners. Nevertheless, the ham and corned-beef would give Mr. Solomon Greasebeans an excellent appetite for a substantial tea. After weighing the matter, she thought it was worth the risk, and she issued the six hundred and fifty-ninth edition of her eulogies upon the splendid furniture of the parlor, and the fascinating accomplishments of Miss Henrietta Maria Flukins, which met with a ready demand. The cost was very trifling, because the conscience of Mrs. Greasebeans was a merchantable article; and the trouble was a matter of quite as little consideration, for she had long since stereotyped the plates.

As she expected, Mr. Solomon Greasebeans was announced, and simultaneously with his arrival, entered Mumford Flukins, Esq.

The greeting between the two gentlemen was cordial; but the mental reservation of Mumford Flukins, Esq., was any thing but complimentary to his visitor, being nothing less than a voiceless opinion that "them Greasebeans are the *damdest* sponges in her majesty's dominions:" a highly reprehensible suggestion, which it is not to be supposed Mr. Solomon Greasebeans or his estimable sleeping partner had the slightest notion could be entertained by the smiling Flukins—an instance of misplaced confidence, which undoubtedly has its parallel in more cases than a confiding public would cheerfully admit.

"Well, Mr. Greasebeans," said the insinuating voice of Mr. Flukins, "how goes on the glorious work of emancipation in America?"

"Much better than we expected. The American abolitionists are falling into the trap we set for them, with a stupidity which is amazing in a people so shrewd upon all other questions."

"I have often thought," replied Mr. Flukins, adjusting his elegant cravat, "that they must be demented not to discover the transparent object we have in view while we are stimulating their fanaticism, which we know, if they do not, must end in the dissolution of their boasted confederacy."

"Yes; and what renders the whole subject a matter of bewilderment to me, is the fact that they are so very dull of comprehension as not even to *suspect* our motive. If fanaticism had not blinded the reason of the ignorant asses, they would perceive that the motives of the Duchess of Sunderland and her associates cannot be prompted by a passion for liberty, for the suffering and despotism that exist upon their estates, never were equalled upon the plantations of the southern states."

Mr. Greasebeans carefully adjusted his wig after this conscientious admission, and smiled complacently upon his wife and Mrs. Flukins, its influence even extending to Henrietta Maria, who had just entered the room.

"There is another consideration that ought to awaken their suspicions. If we are so absorbed with the grand idea of abolishing slavery, why not—I speak it, of course, ironically, and with all deference for her majesty—establish a republic here; or, at all events, raise the masses from the worse than African bondage that prevails under the pleasing rule of a *limited* monarchy? which, I take it, means a monarchy whose favors are limited to half its subjects."

And Mr. Flukins indulged in a sly smile.

"I have had occasion, as you well know, Mr. Flukins," observed Mr. Greasebeans, confidentially, "as the president of the association for the abolition of slavery in the United States, to weigh carefully every act of our society, so as not to awaken distrust in the minds of our American co-laborers, for it is only through them that we can accomplish any thing, as George Thompson, M.P., found to his cost. I have been the more particular in the management of our affairs, because I assume it to be the duty of the humblest of her majesty's subjects to contribute his aid for the maintenance of the present order of things."

Mr. Greasebeans, after this annunciation, thought it would not be unbecoming to indulge in a small and modest cachinnation, which he proceeded to do. After having refreshed himself in this innocent way, he proceeded :

"I have not only dreaded that their suspicions might be aroused in the matter to which you have, with so much sagacity, alluded (Mr. Greasebeans was unconscious of praising himself.) but I have also apprehended that they might in some unlucky moment think of the way we are treating Ireland—perfectly justifiable of course, though difficult of explanation—and also question the purity of our motives in laying waste the garden of Asia with fire and sword. A proceeding also excusable upon the authority of the Bible, and the rules of international law, though quite as difficult to explain. And finally, I have been in constant dread that they might inquire the reason why we overlook the abject condition, not only of our own people, but more particularly the awful spectacle presented by Russia, where even the semblance of liberty is excluded, where the white man's life is at the disposal of his master; where there is no law but his untrammelled will; where they are bought and sold with the soil; where despotism has no check and justice no balance; where the knout, the halter, and the knife are wielded at pleasure; and where the subject has no choice between the joys of his fireside, the snows of Siberia, and death. A condition of things a hundred times worse than has ever been pictured by even Mr. Roorback. Why do we desert our own continent to meddle with the affairs of another? Why are not our sympathies aroused for Russian serfs as well as for African slaves? Why do we pass by a greater, in order to lament over a lesser evil? Why are we so mute when observing the terrible condition of the poor Russian, who is protected by no law, and sheltered by no public opinion? and so clamorous while pitying the slave over whose master both law and public opinion exercise a legitimate control? If I was an American I should propound these questions to her grace the Duchess of Sunderland, and to every abolition society in England. And what reply, my dear Mr. Flukins, would truth force from us? Why, that we have every thing to hope, and nothing to fear, from the example of Russia, while we have everything to fear, and nothing to hope, from the example of the great western Republic! Do you not think the American abolitionists ought to reflect upon these things?"

"Indeed I do," replied Mr. Flukins, with increased respect for the acumen of Mr. Solomon Greasebeans.

"So do I, but they don't though," said Mr. Greasebeans, rubbing his hands. "They are our tools, our blind, idiotic tools, who only have sufficient sense to do our bidding, and madly destroy the only model (between us) government on earth. We have completely hoodwinked them; they are as blind as bats, as stupid as apes, and as full of malignant hatred towards their glorious constitution as the most inveterate monarchists could wish."

"You have hopes of dissolving the union?"

"Not a doubt of it; how could it be otherwise with a band of abolitionists, now swelled into the imposing appearance of a powerful faction, whose support the unscrupulous will always try to win by making concessions to their peculiar opinions? A faction that already possesses sufficient influence to corrupt and disorganize the old parties. Dissolve the union? Why it is as good as dissolved already, and only requires a few more years of silent assault by British philanthropists to be utterly and irremediably overthrown."

CHAPTER XXIII.

"A woman moved is like a fountain troubled,
Muddy, ill-seeming, thick, bereft of beauty;
And, while it is so, none so dry or thirsty,
Will deign to dip or touch one drop of it."—SHAKESPEARE.

THE attentions that were now bestowed upon Lord Melville would have turned the head of a man less scornful of protestations. He did not fail to observe that the most decided exhibitions of partiality came from mothers who had daughters to dispose of, and younger sons, who were engaged in the interesting occupation of "raising the wind." The former invited him to their houses and the latter invited him to the gambling-table. The first he disposed of by informing them he was not a marrying man, and the last by loaning them divers sums varying from ten to one hundred pounds, according to the position they occupied in society. He turned with loathing and disgust from flattery and dissipation, while his heart bled at the misery which prevailed among the poor, that fashionable extravagance might receive no check.

The season was at its height. Parties, balls, theatres, operas, and concerts, succeeded each other in rapid succession, as if those who so eagerly run after pleasure were exempt from the inexorable doom which cut others down at their side, and shut them out for ever from the bright earth which they worshipped. They were blind to the sword suspended over their heads by a single hair. Others died, were buried beneath the cold, damp earth, to fester and to rot; no more to hear the voice of affection, never again to meet the look of love; chained to one gloomy spot, with no fellowship but corruption, no touch, but its remorseless grasp; no voice but the rattling coffin, as it and the remnant of mortality crumbled into dust. Still onward pressed the thoughtless crowd, as if they, *they* were never to *die!*

The Duchess of Sunderland was the sagacious counsellor of her son, as the opinion of the world goes. She suffered his health and his morals to take care of themselves, while she watched over his *settlement* in life. It was more important, in her opinion, that Melville should marry well, than to live long, or conduct himself as a man of honor. The anxiety of her grace was by no means singular. Society rather likes it than otherwise; it finds favor with most ambitious mothers, and what mother is not ambitious for her son?

The Duchess ascertained that Melville did not fall in love with the first pretty face that had a smile for him; on the contrary, she imagined he was more than ordinarily averse to anything like a closer union than a daily intercourse with his female acquaintances. She threw him constantly in the way of "good matches," but some how or other, with the obstinacy of a bad "lucifer," he would not "take." (Upon reflection, a *diabolical* pun.)

He often met Sir William Belthoven, who amused him by his frank admission of the humbug which was practiced by politicians and fashionables. He often called at the residence of the Duke of Sunderland, and took Melville in his carriage to places he thought would interest him.

As the young nobleman was seated in the library, a few weeks after they attended the theatre together, Belthoven was announced. He desired the company of Lord Melville for a few hours.

"I do not promise you much pleasure during this call."

"Then why do you take me there?" asked Melville.

"To make you acquainted with some ladies, who are highly gratified at being called blues; and with others, who are so much dissatisfied with the sphere in which society requires them to move, that they wish to encroach upon ours."

"Shall we meet an advocate of woman's rights?" inquired Melville, with a degree of interest that surprised Belthoven.

"Yes, one of the most formidable of their lecturers."

"What manner of woman is she?"

"She is not only a stout supporter of what she calls the "right" of her sex to practice law and medicine, but she is supposed to have a decided predilection for certain garments that have hitherto belonged to the male sex."

"What can induce them to put forth such extraordinary pretensions?"

"Some persons are ungracious enough to declare that it is owing to the hermaphroditish nature of those individuals; and they even go so far as to insist, that, from their proclivities, and the masculine direction of their thoughts, they are not proper associates for the female sex, but should be required to organize a community apart from those whose *oneness* is unmistakable."

"A shrewd idea," said Melville, as he ejected the stump of a cigar from the window.

"Indeed, so confident are they of the correctness of their opinions, that they do not hesitate to assign reasons therefor, the most cogent of which are the coarseness of feature, strength of form, roughness of manner, and absence of that sensitiveness and delicacy which characterize a lady, and distinguish her from an hermaphrodite and a man."

"Very possible," said the nobleman, sententiously.

"Not satisfied with this charge against persons whom they accuse of having mixed natures, they specify the causes which produce this vehement desire for woman's rights. They say it is attributable to the vulgar natures and peculiar temperaments of the different individuals, and to the want of attention, not to say admiration, with which the sterner sex never fail to honor beauty, especially when it is adorned with modesty."

"But the lecturer—does she grace the hustings?" asked Melville.

"I cannot say I admire her; she has a disagreeable expression about the mouth when she speaks—what a young lady called a *floppy* expression, when saying she always felt inclined to strike the said mouth with the back of her hand, whenever that feature was more than ordinarily loquacious. This she declared to be a great temptation, even in the social circle. But when its contortions were brought into full play, upon the hustings, the impulse became almost irresistible, and would positively require gratification, but for a decent respect for the feelings of the auditory, and a proper regard for the garments of the *hateful* individual."

"Personal ugliness is certainly a decided objection in a declaimer. But this Mis.—Mrs.—"

"Mrs. Duke."

"This Mrs. Duke itinerates, I presume, for the purpose of *gratuitously* instructing her sex?"

"Not at all, my dear fellow; she charges as much for an admission to her lectures as they are worth."

"Then, her efforts are not entirely disinterested."

"Come, now, Melville, do not be guilty of injustice. There is very little disinterested philanthropy manifested in this world by men or women."

"I believe not."

"Mrs. Duke does not despise money, and she is fond of applause."

"There are a sufficient number of slang allusions interspersed throughout her lectures to enable the hi! hi! boys to express their approbation. But this is the house."

A dozen persons were assembled in the drawing-room when Belthoven and his companion entered, and beside the sagacious countenances of some elderly ladies, they beheld the sweet faces of several maidens. They imagined that being seen in the company of literary females would induce the belief that their own hours were surrendered to the acquisition of classic lore. Belthoven remembered that they had resorted to several other expedients to obtain husbands. These, he presumed, had proved abortive, as they were staking their last chance upon blue stockingism.

Melville engaged a beautiful girl in conversation. She had just stepped from childhood into society, and her charming *naivete* amused him exceedingly.

Belthoven was not so fortunate. He had almost succeeded in passing the knot of blues, who, with a consciousness of possessing masculine qualities, boldly occupied the centre of the room, when the veritable Mrs. Duke addressed him—

"What did you think of my last lecture, Sir William?"

"I had a strong inclination during its delivery, to propound certain interrogatories."

"Let me hear them now," replied Mrs. Duke, as she squared herself, like a boxer; though with both toes turned in, and form erect. When she had thus assumed position, and cast a triumphant glance around the room, she inclined her head with an affectation of modesty a little upon one side, while her somewhat extensive foot caressed the carpet.

The Baronet looked about him as though he would gladly effect a retreat; but all eyes were riveted upon them. Cursing the folly which prompted him to rush into a discussion, he raised his eyes to the countenance of his formidable opponent. Hers were fixed with a remorseless and taunting expression upon him, and the floppy movement of her lips became more than ordinarily disagreeable as she inquired—

"Shall we not be favored with your inquiries now, Sir William?"

"Yes, Madame, to your heart's content," he mentally exclaimed, as, with a powerful exertion, he controlled his rage and contempt.

"I felt strongly tempted to ask you, Mrs. Duke, why you inflicted upon your audience such vague generalities and unmeaning words, when you were pretending to communicate information, and inculcate new ideas?"

For a few moments Mrs. Duke was confounded by the audacity of the Baronet.

"I was not aware, sir, that my language was either vague or obscure."

"Then, madam, while you are not only asserting the rights of your sex, but assuming the position of a teacher, you have failed to arrange your ideas, or to acquire a terse, compact, or even intelligible style."

A flush of indignation overspread the countenance of Mrs. Duke as she replied—"Your criticism is frank, to use no harsher phrase."

"It can be understood, at all events. If, following your advice, the softer sex throw themselves into the busy scenes of life, they will be fortunate enough if they receive no rougher treatment than is implied in the word *frankness*. But to convince you that I am not guilty of injustice, I have merely to say that I passed several knots of your auditors, who differed in opinion as to the *points* you were endeavoring to establish. Now it has been the aim of all men who have sought renown as writers or orators, to make themselves understood. It was the terse, pointed, compact language of Junius and Calhoun, that gave them a world-wide celebrity—a celebrity that could never have been obtained by stringing together unmeaning words and thoughtless phrases, which tickle the fancy without approaching the judgment."

"Am I to infer from your language that you think me disqualified for the duties of a lecturer?" inquired Mrs. Duke with a supercilious look.

"Far be it from me to take upon myself the character of a judge—"

"I thought it would be rather presumptuous!" exclaimed Mrs. Duke, who was evidently moved.

"I will remark, however, since I have been dragged into this discussion, that the most celebrated orators and reformers studied, with a painful devotion, the best models. The structure of language, the arrangement of thought, the modes of expression, were examined and compared for months and years before an attempt was made to enlighten others. They were never guilty of the arrogance of becoming teachers before they were themselves informed."

Mrs. Duke was petrified at such boldness; and yielding the prominent position which she had hitherto occupied, she seated herself upon a sofa, and glared at him as if she would learn the extent of his presumption.

"Although your language was obscure, I think you intended to be understood as claiming for your sex the right to practice law, to vote, to heal the sick, and to mingle more freely with men in the transactions of life."

Mrs. Duke bowed.

"And you assign as a reason for demanding such an extraordinary enlargement of your sphere, that the tender natures of women will mitigate the cruelties of which men are guilty, by acquiring more influences with, and obtaining greater power over our sex, than you now exercise?"

Mrs. Duke bowed again.

"Now, madam, the reverse of these propositions I will take upon myself to maintain."

"Impossible."

"I assure you my opinions are capable of demonstration. If your programme is adopted, the result will be, *first*, the loss of that tenderness, sensibility, and modesty, which constitute the foundation of your power; and *second*, shorn of these attractions, you can no longer fascinate and control us by the magical influence of love and admiration."

"I shall consider you a wonderful reasoner, if you can satisfy me of the truth of your assertions," said Mrs. Duke, sarcastically.

"If I can, it will relieve you from the trouble of redressing the supposed wrongs of half the human race. I would be called a cruel, not to say *wicked* man, if, having the power, I should obstinately refuse to exercise it, for the purpose of removing from your path this mighty responsibility. In making the effort, my remarks shall be intelligible.

"*First*—The career which you propose for the adoption of your sex, would occasion the loss of that tenderness, sensibility, and modesty which constitute the foundation of your power.

"I need not remind you how inexpressibly dear to infancy is female tenderness. It soothes the wounded spirit, banishes weariness, alleviates pain, guides the tottering steps, and encourages the lisping voice. As childhood struggles up into manhood, female sensibilities are its strongest support—with whatever opinions others may regard our emotions, we are certain to find sympathizers in mothers and sisters. Their hearts beat responsively to our own, and while turning aside the heaviest blows of fortune, we are ever cheered on by their approbation. They become at once our counsellors and our friends, and to them we confide hopes and fears that are proudly withheld from the sterner sex.

"And when man seeks a helpmate, he remembers that 'modesty' is the highest quality which adorns a woman; and, passing by the female who, assuming a brazen face, *demands* the admiration of men, he seeks one whose aspirations, like the fragrance of a delicate flower, lingers around its own beautiful form; revealing her power, as it does its sweetness, within the sacred precincts of home.

"If these arrest affection and elicit love, what must be the influence of adverse qualities? Fatal, indeed!

"I believe it is not denied that woman can reach a lower depth of mental degradation than man. If this is a correct assumption, it may be interesting to examine the causes which precipitate her from the realm of purity and virtue, where she commands our respect, to the slough of infamy, where contempt cannot reach her. Their downward tendency is accelerated by the manners of the age—by local conventionalities—or by the folly of classes. During the reigns of Charles the Second of England and Louis the Fifteenth of France, there was a frightful prostitution of morals, and virtue unavailingly resisted the progress of corruption. Sometimes the moral blight was confined to localities, and elsewhere goodness maintained its power. The vices of Paris were unknown in the Provinces, and they only were liable to imbibe the venomous exhalations from a diseased society, who came within its influence. That one class may become noted for a shameless disregard of the proprieties of life, is proved by the description given of Sarah, Duchess of Marlborough, who made her appearance at the chambers of Lord Mansfield, before he was elevated to the bench.

"'I could not make out, sir, who she was,' said the clerk, 'for she would not tell me her name; but she *swore* so dreadfully that she must have been a lady of quality.'"

The conversation was hushed throughout the room, and the company listened to the remarks of Sir William.

"You have described the influence of tenderness, sensibility, and modesty as elements in the female character," said Melville; "I should be pleased to hear your reasons for supposing that the career assigned them by the advocates of woman's rights, would destroy or impair those estimable qualities."

"Yes, that is precisely what we are anxious to hear," said Mrs. Duke, as she rewarded Melville with a gracious smile.

"And that is precisely what I am ready to communicate. I announce, as a proposition which cannot be denied, that character is essentially moulded by prevailing customs.

"To illustrate:—Cannibals serve up human beings with as much nonchalance as an American housewife would a pig. Indians torture their prisoners. A Pagan bows to his idol; Mahommedans believe in one God, and one Prophet; Catholics reverence the Pope; while Protestants ridicule his pretensions. A nun shrinks from the gaze of the world; an Amazon mounts her steed and goes forth to battle. The man of God teaches mercy; the warrior immolates his foe. The modest girl keeps her person covered; the belle traverses the muddy street to reveal it. A sensitive woman robes her form; a ballet-dancer studies how much she may disclose. The conscious blood mounts to the cheek of a modest female, at an indelicate allusion; habit causes her to applaud vulgarity when it does not even possess the poor merit of a *double entendre.*

"Now, madam, if the human mind is so flexible, what must be the result, if woman assumes the hardening, nay, corrupting duties of our sex? If she practices law, how long will the impatient blood mantle her cheek, as vulgar testimony is given to the jury? When will the shrinking modesty which lights up her countenance like a ray from heaven yield to brazen effrontery? If she studies physic and surgery, how soon will she acquire that insensibility to suffering which enables the practitioner to amputate a limb with cool indifference, or to witness dying throes without emotion? If she mounts the hustings, how indispensable will become the "hi! hi! hi!" of the populace. All these things will produce a roughness of manner, an obtuseness of feeling, a violence of temper, totally inconsistent with our opinions of female excellence. If such must be the effect of your system, women will be rendered incompetent to perform the duties which you are anxious to assign them."

"How is that possible?" asked Mrs. Duke, in a querulous tone.

"She cannot temper the passions of men with justice, because her own do not slumber; she becomes indifferent to the sufferings of others, for her sensibilities are destroyed; she cannot uphold the barrier which mercy has erected to stay the wickedness of men, because that which a benign Providence gave her for her own protection is broken down and destroyed."

"I should like to hear something else beside mere assertion," said Mrs. Duke, tartly.

"You have studied history to little purpose, madam, if illustration is necessary. Nay, you are chargeable with positive indiscretion, in assuming the right to lecture others, without having been impressed with these facts, while observing the ordinary transactions of life."

"Indeed!" exclaimed Mrs. Duke, as she vigorously fanned herself.

"Unquestionably. You would have women exercise the function of men, for the purpose of softening their natures? Well, some of your sex have been intrusted with power. Catharine, Empress of Russia, was celebrated alike for her unpitying cruelty and unblushing profligacy. Maria Theresa exulted over the carnage of battle-fields. Elizabeth was an unfeeling monarch, whose jealousy compelled her to sacrifice friends and foes. Cleopatra possessed beauty and fascination, but they were at the services of the lover who could bid the highest for them. Lady Macbeth contemplated murder without remorse. Isabella obtained a notoriety quite as infamous as her favorite Mortimer, by the terrible death of Edward the Second. Mary Queen of Scots, by uniting herself to the murderer of her husband, justified the charge that she connived at his assassination. And 'bloody Mary,' the most vindictive and remorseless tyrant who ever disgraced the throne of England, was followed to the 'portals of the tomb,' by the execrations of outraged humanity. The disgraceful conduct of these women fiends, illustrates the fact that an habitual contemplation of suffering and crime, instead of sharpening our sensibilities, as you believe, has the effect of first paralyzing and then destroying them."

"It is singular you did not mention the name of Queen Anne," said Mrs. Duke, tauntingly.

"I did not allude to Queen Anne because her memory is below criticism. You have not forgotten the reply of Lady Churchill when accused of employing supernatural influences, in her interview with the Queen, that she controlled her Majesty not by witchcraft, but by the magic of superior intellect. Look at the French, Scotch, Irish, German ; aye, and American women, too, who labor beneath roofs, or, what is still worse, in the field. What has toil and exposure effected? It has deadened their sensibilities, bronzed their complexions, wrinkled their foreheads, bent their forms, soured their tempers, and placed them beyond the influence of romance."

"But we do not intend to labor," exclaimed Mrs. Duke.

"Why then do you claim the privilege, if you do not expect to perform the duties of men? If you would become merchants, you must visit the docks. If you practice law, the drudgery of the office and the court room cannot be transferred to another. One whose office it is to heal the sick, must not shrink from exposure to cold and heat. If your ambition points to the cultivation of the earth, your field operations will require unremitting attention. Absorbed by such duties, what time will you have for the adornment of your person, or the cultivation and refinement of your intellect? Your 'rights' are acknowledged, but in the loss of tenderness, sensibility, and modesty, your legitimate control over our sex is gone for ever. That which we cheerfully accorded to graceful weakness, we withhold when claimed by coat and boots. In ceasing to rely upon our protection, you forfeit that watchful care which is your surest and safest defence."

"There is another decided objection to the doctrine advocated by Mrs. Duke. We have duties at home which nobody else can or will perform," said a lady, whose son had that day astonished the court and jury by a brilliant forensic effort.

"I was about to allude to that subject," replied Belthoven, as he gracefully bowed to the matron. "Look at our weekly bills of mortality! How many of those who are daily deposited in their silent homes, have not passed the boundaries of childhood? What is the cause of this fearful mortality? It must be traced to ignorance or neglect. And what excuse is there for such culpability, not to say wickedness? If the mother suffers her offspring to perish because she is unacquainted with her duties, she ought to qualify herself to save the being intrusted to her charge instead of clamoring for woman's rights! If she wilfully neglects the helpless infant and suffers its little form to struggle unavailingly with diseases, until the feeble body can no longer resist the embrace of death, she should implore divine mercy to sharpen her moral perceptions, instead of engaging in a conflict for woman's rights? With the attention bestowed, even now, to the nursery, thousands are cut off in childhood ; but if you obtain additional cares and new responsibilities, there will be a serious interference with the population of the earth."

"You think, then, that women are fitted for drudgery alone, and that they should be satisfied with rocking cradles, making shirts, and sewing on buttons!" said Mrs. Duke, scornfully.

"If such conclusions are drawn from my argument I have spoken to little purpose. No, madam; I would relieve her from drudgery, by intrusting to man's stronger frame and sterner will, the rougher duties of life. The sphere retained by woman is large enough. Society has claims upon her which she cannot meet, if her time is devoted to the realities of the outer world. She must qualify herself to become the companion and counsellor of her husband, and the moulder of destinies, which Providence, in giving her children, has committed to her charge. There is no cause for the restlessness which pervades your little circle. The female sex are almost unanimous in their approval of our social regulation. They do not demand an extension of their privileges or their responsibilities, and I venture the assertion, that the popular movement which places the estate of the wife at her own disposal, can be traced to the justice and affection of our sex, and not to the clamor of yours.

"And why should they not be satisfied? Have not the men whose deeds occupy the largest space in the compilation of the historian, admitted that the foundation of their fortunes was laid by female hands? Are not the praises of your children constantly elevating a monument more enduring than the baseless fabric of a vision, upon which you would rest your hopes? Cannot the chivalrous tenderness and gallantry with which you are treated satisfy your ambition? Or will you cast aside that confidence in our sex which has rarely been betrayed—throw off that gentleness which is your safest protection—disrobe yourself of that modesty which the basis of your power, and thus shorn of your strength, commence a warfare upon public opinion, to be succeeded, if that prove unavailing, by the sterner conflict of arms?"

As Belthoven concluded, decided marks of approbation were heard throughout the room.

"I thank you, on behalf of my sex, for the ability which you have displayed in assailing some of the fallacies of the present day," said the lady who had once before addressed him.

"I must apologize for occupying so much time, but that was partly owing to an imprudent denial that the lecture of my fair antagonist was the perfection of oratory. I shall be more cautious in future."

Refreshments were now brought in, and the conversation became general.

"Belthoven, who are those persons occupying the sofa yonder? While listening to you they were, nevertheless, strongly attracted towards each other."

"I will tell you, Melville. The man belongs to that class of persons who are so intensely desirous of *mourning* for somebody, that they occasionally put crape upon their hats when their relations are all in the enjoyment of lamentably good health. The female belongs to another class, who wish to compromise with the Almighty by inducing him to pardon their insatiable avarice, as a reward for ostentatious charity. The individual who has joined them, is known as the person who carries two faces under one hat. They are a charming trio."

"Ah! ah! you are i' the mood for criticism to-night," said Melville, as he resumed his seat by the side of the girl who had captivated his fancy.

With what eagerness these men of the world turn aside from the current, down which fashionable women are crowding and jostling each other, in the struggle for admiration, to the tranquil bay, in whose untroubled waters the barge of innocence is still moored, while its happy owner is gathering flowers upon the bank, or reposing beneath the foliage whose blossoms perfume the air.

The saloons of the Countess of Memberton were crowded by the rank, beauty, fashion, and intellect of London. It was *the* party of the season. Not only were all the lions of English society present, but foreign countries were represented by diplomatists and persons occupying high public stations; for *wealth*, alone, found much difficulty in foisting its possessor into the exclusive circles of London.

Lord Melville entered with Sir William Belthoven. Both were graciously received by the Countess—the first for his rank, and the last for his agreeable manners. They passed through the rooms.

"Yonder stands the French Ambassador, decked out in a court dress, which indicates the fondness of his nation for gaudy trappings," said Belthoven. "Still further on is the American Minister."

"The one with the tall form, venerable appearance, and plain attire?"

"The same."

"The Americans may well be proud of such a representation. What are his antecedents?"

"Minister to Russia, an American Senator, Secretary of State, and an aspirant for the office of President of the United States."

"Unsuccessful, of course, or he would not be here?"

"Yes, he was too well known."

"Surely, that was not considered an objection."

"Undoubtedly, during his long political career he has made too many enemies, awakened the envy of too many rivals. Egad! Lord Memberton has presented Lady Katharine Montague to him. With what a complaisant air he inclines his head upon one side. She is evidently pleased with the conversation of the old bachelor."

"Let us proceed," said Melville.

"Ah! Snizzle, how are you?" said the baronet, unctiously.

"Well's could be expected. Rooms too demm'd quowded."

"Your lordship is jostled."

"Yes, by quitters who have not been noble more than ten or fifteen years."

"Did it ever occur to your lordship, that there are some human beings who have not been ennobled by the decrees either of nature or royalty?" said Melville.

"No! are they? I thought majesty could make any person a nobleman," replied Timothy, Lord Snizzle.

"Majesty can confer the title, but your lordship is a standing illustration of the fact, that nature is the only skillful artificer of true nobility of soul."

Lord Snizzle pondered upon these words after Melville and the baronet had resumed their walk.

I'm demmed if his language wasn't insulting. I'll call him out, *dem* me if I don't; that is, if Sir Pertinax McFlummux advises it," muttered Snizzle, as he thrust his glass into the socket of his eye, and proceeded to inspect the company with the orb thus fortified, while the other maintained a vague expression, as if the responsibility of a faithful performance of duties, that usually devolved upon both, now rested upon the glassed one alone.

Who is that splendid-looking woman, who manages to retain a circle of admiring gentlemen around her?"

"That is the Marchioness of Berkley, widow of the late Marquis of Berkley."

"What! the lady who created so great a sensation in Paris last winter?"

"Yes. She laid aside her grief and her weeds at the same time, and it was a remarkable coincidence that the auspicious event occurred at the commencement of the fashionable season. I have often observed, that grief, which appeared to every one inconsolable, miraculously takes its departure just before a ball at Windsor Castle, or a magnificent soiree at Almacks."

"Was there not a little bit of scandal connected with the illustrious name of the marchioness, before she was called upon to mourn the death of her husband."

"Oh yes; just enough to gratify her dearest friends. No positive proofs were discovered; you know there never are, unless the injured party applies for a divorce. You see the malicious, who are probably no purer themselves, like to turn over frailty, and hence it is generally better to hush up any little foibles. Besides the exposure makes the relations feel so uncomfortable."

"Who was the gay Lothario?"

"It has never been deemed safe to mention his name, as royal blood flows in his veins."

"She is a magnificent-looking creature."

"Not twenty-five, yet, either. She classes you among her admirers," said Belthoven, as he returned the graceful bow of the marchioness.

"How so? I have never spoken to her."

"But your eyes have expressed your admiration. Come, will you be presented?"

A negative response was upon his lips, when he saw Katharine Montague pass, leaning upon the arm of the young Duke of Gildermier, and listening to his low voice, as if she was fascinated by his words.

"Certainly."

The knot of gentlemen who surrounded the marchioness gave way, as the baronet and Lord Melville advanced.

The former exchanged salutations with the lady.

"Will you allow me to present to your ladyship my particular friend, Lord Melville?"

"Willingly," said the marchioness, frankly extending her hand, and suffering it to remain a few moments within his own.

"I have long desired an introduction to the son of my dearest friend."

"I thank your ladyship for such flattering words."

"And how is your mother?"

"Quite well, I thank you."

"Is she here to-night?"

"I saw her in yonder saloon a few moments ago."

"Come: I am sure you will conduct me to her."

Bowing to the circle that yet surrounded her, the marchioness confidingly took Melville's arm.

It was doubtless by the merest accident that she proceeded in the opposite direction to the one indicated by him as the spot where the Duchess of Sunderland was to be found.

The pressure of lace, brocades, and diamonds increased, as they proceeded; and the soft, warm, form of the lovely marchioness rested against his own, as if she felt the most trusting confidence in his willingness to protect her from a contact with any one else.

"I heard of your singular history while I was in Paris," she remarked.

"Turning the heads of half the Parisian courtiers," he replied gayly.

"Ah! my lord, I have been unjustly accused," she observed, sadly. "Entering society for the purpose of allaying the grief occasioned by the loss of an excellent husband, I could not avoid attention without positive rudeness. Those attentions were construed into admiration; for you know, Lord Melville, how the world is given to exaggeration."

Her voice was low and musical; her fragrant breath played upon his cheek, and the bust of dazzling whiteness was temptingly revealed, as she bent towards him, so that her words could not be heard by others.

"Your ladyship speaks truly," said Melville.

"Amid all my engagements," she continued, flatteringly returning to his early history, "I was absorbed by the account of your hard fate, prior to the discovery of your birth."

"And yet it was no worse than what thousands of our peasantry are constantly suffering."

"Alas! your words are too true. I have always mourned over the melancholy condition of the laboring classes."

Her voice trembled as she spoke. Can this be *acting*, thought Melville.

"I am delighted to breathe the fresh air. Those rooms are so crowded. How balmy is the atmosphere. It seems like spring."

They walked to the further end of the balcony, and the Marchioness seated herself upon the steps leading to the conservatoire. The music floated upon the night air with soothing sweetness. The mild rays of the moon lit up the fair complexion of the lady, as half reclining, she assumed a posture calculated to make an impression upon the young and inexperienced—though of this she seemed to be unconscious—as it was only in their presence that she ventured to indulge in graceful abandonment.

"It is a dangerous path you have to tread, and one calculated to test the experience of a gentleman so young and confiding," observed the Marchioness, as her lustrous eyes met his own.

"Why so?"

"Young, titled, rich, and—and—may I add—without transcending the modesty of my sex—gifted with a person and an address that will make an impression upon the female heart. Can you ask me 'why so?'"

Voices in low conversation fell upon the ear of Lord Melville, and turning his glance upward to the casement which overlooked the balcony, he met the riveted glance of Katharine Montague. When she observed that his eyes were fixed upon her, she turned away, and with her companion, the Duke of Gildermier, proceeded to the more thronged saloons. An hour later, Melville was sauntering through the rooms devoted to the fine arts. But few occupied them, and he examined, at his leisure, the gems with which the walls of several apartments were ornamented. He had passed through all the rooms but one, and into this he now entered. No other guest was there. His attention was arrested by a painting of the Madonna. Never had the lineaments of the mother of Christ been more exquisitely drawn upon canvas. He was absorbed by the artist's skill, when he heard a sigh. Turning his head he saw an alcove connected with the apartment. He could not be mistaken; it was the figure of Katharine Montague, seated upon a sofa, with her eyes fixed, but with a vague look, upon a painting. He folded his arms and contemplated the maiden. She sighed again, and pressed her forehead with her ungloved hand, and then rising, encountered the glance of the young nobleman.

"Lord Melville?" she said, faintly.

"Yes, *Lord!* Melville," he replied with intense scorn.

"Do you come here to insult me?" she exclaimed, raising her form to its full height.

"I was ignorant of your presence in that alcove. I supposed you were more agreeably occupied with his *Grace*, the *Duke* of Gildermier."

Her eyes were fixed sorrowfully upon him. "Lord Melville; nay, *Christie Kane*, how have you altered since the hour you periled your life to rescue me from death! Why, oh *why*, have you so strangely changed?" said the maiden passionately, as her graceful form inclined towards him.

"Dear Katharine—for dear you will ever be to me until this heart ceases to beat—from the moment I first beheld you, I have lived only in your presence. God only knows *what* I have suffered. I dared to hope—rash fool that I was—a peasant, upon whose brow the Almighty had stamped his image—but still a peasant; whose heart never throbbed but with honorable emotions—but a peasant still. I was rightly served. I was ignominiously rejected."

"No! no! no! Christie, you cannot, you must not say that," she said eagerly.

"If your decision had been otherwise, I could have worked for you, suffered for you, *died* for you. How bright was the future!" he continued, sadly. "With what a halo of joy was every object gilded by hope. How I *prayed* that your love might be won; and when hope was utterly destroyed, what nights of sleepless agony I suffered. You had no right, dear, *dear* Lady Katharine, to crush the feelings of one whose love for you bordered on idolatry."

The maiden could not restrain her tears, as she observed the seal of woe which was stamped upon every lineament of his working countenance.

"I will explain all to him," she said vehemently. "Christie, *dear* Christie, I loved you then, and I love you still. *Can* I say more?"

"Why, then, did you announce our separation forever?" he replied sternly.

"A union between us was then impossible. My father would have refused his consent—the prejudices of class would have forbidden it. But now—"

"*Now* it is too late!" replied Lord Melville, gloomily. "You refused the man; you may not wed his title."

"But surely you understand the decrees of society."

"I understand that Lord Melville is not as worthy of your love as was Christie Kane, and yet you rejected the latter, and would accept the former! '*What a deformed thief this fashion is!*' No! Lady Katharine Montague, the dream is over. I have loved you passionately, *madly*. I shall do so until my pulseless form finds its last resting-place. There is nothing now to hope for—to live for—and a heart-broken man, I shall only find peace at the threshhold of the tomb. Farewell, Lady Katharine, we shall never meet again but as strangers."

Lord Melville reached the door, and turned his head to obtain one last look of the maiden. She stood in the position she occupied when he turned from her. Her hands clasped upon her bosom, her eyes eagerly watched his movements, and scalding tears coursed each other down her cheeks.

"Dear Katharine!"

"Dear Christie!"

And they were locked in each other's arms.

CHAPTER XXIV.

" Afar from thee ! the morning breaks,
But morning brings no joy to me ;
Alas ! my spirit only wakes
To know I am afar from thee."—BETHUNE.

ROBERT KANE felt like another being as the " Nancy Ann" glided through the channel fleet, and bounded over the blue waves of the Atlantic Ocean. If the vessel was not " searched" before she landed in New York his escape was certain. How he longed for the moment to arrive when his feet would press *freedom's* soil ! and, beneath the stars and stripes, he could walk the earth the slave of oppression no more! If he should again fall under the jurisdiction of that power, from whose grasp he fondly hoped he had forever escaped !

" I kinder guess yer glad tew see them are pocket pieces of the queen grow smaller and smaller in the distance ?" said Ezekiel Belknap.

" You say truly, my friend ; I never wish to see them again !"

" They wanted tew make yew serve a prenticeship at that are bisness ?"

" Yes ; but, thank God ! who made you my friend, I have escaped them."

" Neow, dew yeow know, the tarnal critters would jist as soon pick yeow up for a desarter as they'd eat a piece of roast-beef."

" But I never enlisted."

" Law ! what do they keer about that ? Diddent they enlist for yer ? Why, the greedy skunks say that an Englishman once, always an Englishman ; and that a man with a red head might as well expect it to turn black, as for a Britisher to expatriate himself. They'il lie, tew, like Sam Hyde, about it."

" But your constitution gives me the privilege of acquiring the rights of a citizen by naturalization. I cannot serve two masters."

" The very question that's bound tew kick up the alfiredest rumpus some of these ere times ever yeow seed. When John Bull and Brother Jon'than makes up their minds tew claim the sarvices of one critter, yeow may expect some profiles to be spiled on both sides, for the'il hurt each other considerable ; but if the old gentleman thinks we will flummax when we've made up our minds tew dew the clean thing by any of his cast-off folks, he'll bark up the wrong tree any way you can fix it."

" But your government may not protect her adopted citizens ?"

Ezekiel Belknap did not reply verbally for several minutes ; but removing his tarpaulin from his head, he tendered it for Kane's acceptance. Not content, however, with this response to what he regarded as a *monstrous* proposition, he said,

"I calkerlate yeow don't intend that for a *sassy* speech, dew yeow?"

"Of course not."

"Wall, I spose so; but it's enough to raise the Ebeenezer of them as are not very gritty, any heow yeow can fix it. What! give up a man arter we've presented on him a paytent, a makin on him one of nater's noblemen? I calkerlate yeow don't understand the feelins of the rael Simon Pure republican. Let Britannia rile our tempers a small smidgen, and see if we'll cave in?"

"Would you risk a war first?"

Mr. Belknap placed his tarpaulin on one side of his head, changed his tobacco from his left to his right cheek, walked to the side of the "Nancy Ann," and squirted a quantity of juice into the sea that would have excited the indignation of William Moon, who was so devoted to the weed, and so excessively economical, that he always swallowed the tobacco, juice and all. He then proceeded to roll up his sleeves, displaying thereby an arm of the most formidable proportions.

"Thar are them among us, Mr. Kane, who think we shall spile for the want of a fight unless we have it soon. Why, there was skersely a day while 'Nance' — the familiar name of the ship — was lying in the harbor of New York that we diddent see sich a musterin of soldiers in the streets."

"I was not aware that you had a large standing army in the United States."

"Havent! They wer citizen soldiers a goin out to prac*tyse* on thar own hook; and I swan if their targets diddent allers come in perfectly riddled. Some on em, tew, were byes skersely in their teens. No, sir, we must have a fight soon, if we can find a reasonable excuse, or we shall spile."

"Many citizen soldiers in New York city?"

"Morner an our whole standin army. Yes, we're itching fur a fight with somebody; we don't keer whether it's with England, or Spain, or Mexico. If with the first, we shall relieve her of all further trouble about Canada. Them French Canadians don't hanker after the English government any way you can fix it. If we have to lick Spain, we shall annex Cuba; and if them Mexicans rile us agin, we shan't leave them a patch of airth large enough for a buryin-yard. We otter kept the hull country when we tuk it afore, by good rights."

"And so you have universal suffrage in the United States?"

"I spose it could hardly be called sich," replied the sailor, as he deposited a formidable piece of tobacco between his teeth.

"Dissipate?" he inquired, tendering the knife and plug to Robert Kane.

"No, I thank you."

"Not ben able to indulge in such luxuries. Them tarnal skunks, I spose, thought all the nice delicacies were intended for their own guzzles. Wall, I guess, it's a fine thing in Ameriky, whar a man can chew as much tobacco as he wants tew, and squirt the ambier all abeout the sile of freedom! No, I can't say as how we have univarsal suffrage in America; for, you see, the slaves, bein no betterer than cattle, ain't allowed to vote; and the free niggers in the Empire State, bein human only to a partial extent, arn't suffered to vote neither, unless they have proved their humanity by scraping together two hundred and fifty dollars."

"Does that qualify them?"

"It dooze. You see the niggers are a raggamuffin set. It's doubtful whether they are intirely human beins, any way you can fix it, and they only prove themselves sich, by a haggling and a scrapin', until they are enemost tuckered out, in getting them two hundred and fifty dollars."

"All the white population are considered capable of self-government, I suppose?"

Mr. Belknap's bosom heaved with smothered indignation at the question, but pity for the ignorance of the other controlled his feelings.

"I can pardon sich questions in a furrenner, cause they ain't sposed to understand our system, Mr. Kane. But in America, we coulddent overlook insults implied in such interregatories. *Dooze* any American ever ask *if* Queen Victoria abundantly fulfills the requirements of scripture, to multiply and replenish the earth? You may jist as well inquire if free-born white men are capable of self-government. *Ax* them that question, and see what they'll say."

"It's a glorious system," said Kane, thoughtfully. "And I see no reason why it should not work well, if the representative obeys the will of his constituents. Tell me, Mr. Belknap, do your public officers never violate pledges given before election?"

The sailor removed his tarpaulin.

"Why you see, Mr. Kane, there *is* some skunks, that have the meanness tew set up fur theirsels arter election is over. Their as perlite as a basket of chips while they are asking the people for their votes; but, once elected, and the horse is another color. Now, there is the president; he don't let on much during the contest, when everybody else is a ripping and tearing the hull time; but his silence is amazin' discreet, for he says jist nothing, calkerlated to spile the exertions of his friends and his own chances. When he gits elected, he holds his head jist as high as ary king in all Christendom. He takes the executive bit atween his teeth, and goes it rough-shod straight over democrats, whigs, abolitionists, secessionists, and the whole cobboodle, until the people git riled, and then they jerk him back upon his hanches in a little less than no time. They are amazin' good-natured, are the Americans, when they have their own way, but once get their dander up, by a tryin' tew dew as yer please, and they will yank yer up, standing, in a brace of shakes. Tain't no use tew try to ride them folks booted and spurred, no how you can fix it. It ain't to be did. They think no more of leading an unruly president out of the white house by the ears, and a kickin' on him all the way down Pennsylvany Aveny, as far as the De Pot, than they would of pitching into a skunk, that was a ciferin abeout a hen-roost. There was John Tyler, a good enough president—in fact, a fust-rate man—for he did enebeout right in a ve*toe*ing them bank bills; for I guess they desarved no better than to *toe* the mark, and the people woulddent a cared if he had kicked them as try'd so pesky hard to force 'em through. But because they thought they had a right tew call him a whig, they sposed he was bound to approbate the hull set of whig measures; that is, them as was whig measures, *then*. And when Captain Tyler wan't to be druv, and was bound to set up fur hisself, they commenced abusin' on him, and a cussen on him, until arter awhile no one thought it was respectable to speak well of Captain Tyler."

"But that was a case where principle was involved, Mr. Belknap," said Kane.

"Not a smidgen; dew you spose they would pass one of the measures they abused Captain Tyler for ve*toe*ing ten years ago?"

"I presume so."

"Not a darned one on 'em. You see they argufied the passage of them measures to save the country from ruin; but the country escaped ruin without them, so now they ain't any use, no how you can fix it."

"But the President must have a great many difficulties to encounter."

"He dooze. A pesky sight on 'em. His temper is continually riled by them office-seekers, who, with great patriotism, insist that their services are indispensable; that the wheels of government are bound to grow rusty unless they grease them. Why the skunks are the most brazen-faced critters in the unevarse. Tough, tew. And unfeelin'. They killed two presidents. Thems as the British, Injins, and Mexicans coulddent hold a candle tew, the office-seekers cut right down, like grass afore the scythe of the young man whose untimely fate is recorded as having transp*yr*ed on Springfield mountain, when the pysen sarpent bit him on the heel. The truth is, Mr. Kane, the profession of office-seeking is eneabeout the most skulduddery bisness on airth; not half so respectable as

"'A life on the ocean wave.'"

"Have you followed the sea from boyhood?" asked Robert Kane.

"Only a dozen years. Afore that, I made a small experiment at in-door service, in the city of Bosting. But it diddent suit my turn of mind, any how you could fix. They axed me tew dew ever so many nasty things, which turned my free-born stomach. I went to service; so I thought I would tucker it eout. But I coulddent dew it, no how you could fix it. The hull thing went right straight agin my notions of equal rights and no monopoly. The hull consarn was a monopoly from A to izzard. The best things went up stairs, and skersely the least mossel came down except the bones. They done nothing, and we did everything, from rocking the cradle to blacking boots. One day the cook said we wer tew haive abeout the finest turkey as ever gobbled. The news made a flustrification; what could a got into 'em up stairs? The turkey was put down tew roast, until it was done—was that turkey. But we diskivered he was *done afore!* The fact was that gobbler had deceased so many days anterior tew the period when he was tew haive the honor of bein' gobbled by us, that a skunk was a nosegay compared tew his dead body. All our danders was riz, and we were enemost up to the bili'n heat, when the chambermaid, an impertinent hussey, (in love *out* of the house, tew,) came down, and told me to black my master's boots. That was the cap-sheaf. 'Yeou swingecat,' said I, 'I'll haiv yeou to understand that I'm a free-born native American citizen, and the servant of no man, except as a matter of courtesy at the end of a letter. And I'll have yeou tew understand, *tew*, that it was a darned mean trick tew send a dead gobbler here, who's been defunct, I'll bet my gizzard on't, not a minit less than five days—and the weather warmish, at that!"

"'You had better shut up, Mr. Belknap,' said she, 'for I heard master say you was the most impertinent servant he had.'

"Servant! I exclaimed. A free born native American citizen, *a servant!* Take them ar boots back tew your *master*, and tell him I guess they'll spile afore Ezekiel Belknap blacks em. *Master* indeed! *Servant*, indeed? I jist walked off, and I've never bin in sarvice since."

For a week the Nancy Ann encountered strong head winds. Instead of abating, the storm increased in violence. Robert Kane saw, from the anxious face of the captain, and the serious bearing of the crew, that danger was apprehended. He was told the ship had sprung a leak, that she must soon go down. They had but one serviceable boat, and that could not live in such a sea. The hold began to fill with water; all hands were called to the pumps; it gained upon them slowly in spite of their exertions. The storm abated, but it was impossible to close the aperture in the keel of the ship. Kane pressed his children to his heart. Death stared them in the face. Hope was in the act of expiring when a joyful shout was heard at the masthead of the Nancy Ann. A ship had been signaled. She was bearing down towards them. She was an English merchantman. Even that was better than sudden death. A few hours of terrible suspense, and the passengers and crew were taken on board the "English Queen," bound from Liverpool to Quebec. In an hour the "Nancy Ann" careened upon one side and went down.

There was a company of British Grenadiers on board the "English Queen." Kane was once more within the grasp of his direst foes. He involuntarily trembled as each one of them passed him. It was horrible to stand in such dread of human beings, but he could not help it. What was this power of England, that it hemmed him in on every side, and from whose grasp it appeared almost impossible to escape? He could hardly repress his feelings, so irritating were the bondman's chains that encompassed his limbs.

The commander of the grenadiers frequently examined the manly figure of Robert Kane with a professional eye. But he had no authority to steal him, and he was not aware that he had been in the clutches of the press-gang.

Favorable winds now wafted them rapidly towards Quebec. Hope again revived in the heart of the fugitive. If he could succeed in reaching the open country beyond Montreal, he might pass unobserved among the crowd of emigrants, to the United States. Ezekiel Belknap promised to accompany him through Canada, and to do all he could to assist him. Between the two men a strong affection had been awakened—in the heart of Kane by a sense of deep obligations to the sailor; and in that of the latter by a consciousness of having conferred them. Little Dolly, too, loved the sailor, and often sat upon his knee, watching his countenance, and listening to his yarns.

"It's amazin strange, when these lords and ladies of your'n so pertiklerly interests theirsels abeout the southern niggers, that they don't shed a tear neow and then at the misfortins of their own poor folks."

"I have often thought of that, Mr. Belknap. Perhaps they want to draw attention from our condition by riveting it upon the slaves."

"I spose so. Not a bad idee nuther, for it's fust rate tew make people talk abeout our neighbors instead of oursels. I heered them say in Lundon that they are a goin to send over a special agint tew excite the abolitionists. It won't dew no good no heow yeou can fix it. They made Mr. Thompson, M. P. exercise shankes' mare in Bosting a few years since, and that city ain't overly fond of slavery nuther. Why can't them pesky critters mind their own bizness. We don't stick our fingers in their roast beef. I'll be darned tew darnation if they hadn't better let us alone, or we'll pitch intew Ireland with a few thousand short boys."

"Short boys? what are they?"

"A set of scamps, who don't know when they're whipped. It will be a doin the community a sarvace to git them killed off. We are a spilin for an opportunity to make use on em, and if Great Britain don't keep her eyes skinned, we'll giv her such a lambastin as she never had. The hypocritical old sinner! She opposes everything—but her own interests. She's a preaching all the hull time agin slavery, when her own subjects are any number of times wuss off than our niggers. She kicks up a rumpus every time we take a slice of territory from our neighbors, jist tew straighten out our legs on, while she is a rollin over and a turnin over herself, until she's got the better part of Ashee. Don't she boast that the sun never sets upon her possessions? and that the tap of her drums follows the light of day as the sun crosses each degree of longitude? Arter a while she'll exhaust our patience, and then look out for squalls."

The "English Queen," beat up the St. Lawrence, and at length anchored beneath the frowning walls of Quebec. There the crew of the "Nancy Ann" separated, and Kane, after expressing his gratitude to Captain Smith, started with his children and Ezekiel Belknap for Montreal, thankful for his safe exit from the "Gibraltar of America." Crossing the St. Lawrence at Montreal, they commenced their journey on foot for the Canada line, bearing the children in sacks upon their shoulders. Here again they were doomed to disappointment and delay. Frank Tot took a violent cold: and they were forced to remain for several weeks in the French country, until his recovery. The sailor would not desert his friends, and after a long delay, they again started together for the United States. Robert Kane's hopes beat high as each league of Canadian territory was traversed. The sailor enlivened the way with anecdotes of land and sea.

"Yer can't tell heow tender the home government is of her Canada subjects. They touch them as gently as if they were wax figures. The French tuk it inter their heads a few years ago, to set up fur themselves. But the English population stuck to the hum government, and the rebellion was crushed Arterwards, the hum government thought they'd conciliate the French, and so they refunded the money lost by the rebels in a quarrel they had provoked themselves. The English and American tories were awfully riled, and they fell tew cussin and a swearin, and neow they would jump at the chance of annexation. So would the French tew, for that matter, and the Queen knows it, and hence her gracious and affable treatment of them. You see the example of Brother Jonathan is sposed to have a wonderful effect on them Canadians. But I calkerlate if—"

"My God! we are lost," exclaimed Kane.

"What on airth is the matter?"

"My evil genius," replied Kane, pointing at the slight figure and fiendish countenance of Riley.

"Fool, to think you could escape me!" exclaimed the miscreant, shaking his clenched hand at Kane. Placing Frank Tot in the arms of the sailor, Robert sprang towards Riley. Leaping over the fence, the latter disappeared in the grove of dark timber which fringed the road. In a few minutes Kane returned from the pursuit pale and agitated.

"Wall, may I flummux tetotally in the face of an inemy, if I understand what this all means," said Ezekiel Belknap.

"I will tell you. That villain is my irreconcilable enemy. He was impressed at the same time I was, and has made his escape or been placed upon my track. In either case he will compass heaven and earth to ensure my capture."

"Whew! Wall, we musent let the grass grow under our feet now, any way you can fix it. There is a custom-house officer and a sheriff in the next village who would jist as soon lay their paws on yeow, as if yeow were smuggled goods, or personal property not exempt from execution sale. We mast tek tew the woods. Here, follow me on this are hard-pan for awhile," saying which, the sailor stepped upon that portion of the road where the clay had been trodden to almost the consistency of a rock. They proceeded in this way until they came to a bend in the road.

"Neow let us divarge upon them are rocks. Tuther side of them woods is another road leading to the Varmount line. Unless he gets the sheriff to raise a posse come-it-at-us, as the lawyers say, it'll be hard if we can't escape. I wouldn't be at all surprised if he should dew it, for the darned skunk teks purticular pleasure in a showin his zeal for the queen since his appointment."

As the sun approached the western horizon, they arrived upon the bank of a river, the outlet of Lake Memphremagog.

"Here we will camp for the night," said the sailor.

"Where, Mr. Belknap, I don't see any house," said Dolly.

"I spose you will jist exactly think arter a while, my little darling, that I'll fix yeou eneabeout the nicest place tew sleep in ever yeou seed."

"In the dark woods? Won't the bears come and eat up you, and me, and pa, and Frank Tot?"

"I rayther guess not. Ketch them aputting their noses again them pistils and this are knife."

Saying which, Ezekiel Belknap took a formidable brace of pistols and a long, dangerous-looking knife, from his bosom.

The sailor verified his word. He drove two poles into the earth, and placing a cross piece in the forks, and two more extending slantingly from that to the ground, proceeded to attach poles to the rafters thus constituted. These he covered with spruce, hemlock, and cedar boughs to a sufficient depth to shed rain. Then making a thick bed out of hemlock bows, he declared the tent fit for a princess.

"It's a fortunit circumstance that I laid in plenty of provender this morning, as we should have found it cold comfort bein here without a mossel to eat. Bread, cheese, butter, salt, cold ham—I guess it will dew."

"Never fear but we shall find it a feast. Many is the time I have had food not half so good to eat."

'But this is not all. We'll help ourselves to some of her Majesty's fish."

"I don't see any," said Dolly.

"Jist come down to the bank and I'll show yeou."

The air was balmy for it was now the month of June. The light of day softly faded away, leaving an unclouded sky. A gentle breeze agitated the foliage and sighed through the leaves of a tall pine which erected its towering form upon the bank of the stream. The air was laden with forest odors, the sweetest of all perfumes. Here and there a twinkling star, no longer rivalled by the sun, sent its rays of light into the forest, where they peeped through the trees or danced in the stream.

Arranging his hook and line and attaching them to a long pole which he cut from a thicket of larches, the sailor walked out upon a moss-covered log that spanned the river. It was at the foot of the rapids, and the water there formed an eddy. Into that he cast his line. The hook had scarcely descended a foot beneath the surface of the stream when the line was straightened. The rod bent in the hand of the sailor as he raised it, the water was agitated for a few moments, and then a large trout dangled in the air. They returned to the camp in half an hour with a plentiful supply of fish. A fire was kindled in front of the camp, and upon the coals Ezekiel Belknap broiled his trout.

Dolly watched the sparks as they soared upward, and tried how many she could count before they went out. Some were lost among the tree tops, and she wondered if they helped to make up the "starry host" that now gathered in the sky.

Frank Tot sat upon his father's knee with his round black eyes fixed upon the sailor as he broiled the fish. After he had eaten his supper he looked at the light and at the darkness as he nestled in Robert Kane's bosom, and wondered himself to sleep.

They all laid their weary limbs upon the grateful bed at an early hour. After breakfast the next morning they started on their journey again, and soon emerged from the intricacies of the forest into the road.

"Yonder is the outlet of Magog Lake. And see, the Mountain Maid is about starting. If we can get on that are craft we shall be in Varmount in less than two hours."

"Heaven grant that we may," said Robert Kane, as his glance ranged along the shore of the beautiful sheet of water.

"I'll be darned tew darnation if that are pesky critter ain't after us with a sharp stick."

"Where?" inquired Kane, anxiously.

"In tother road. Don't you see him and the sheriff with a possey?"

"All is lost; I knew I should never reach a land of liberty. Accursed government, how am I followed by your vengeance, and for what?"

"Never give it up so. Time enough to cave in when the sheriff has hold of you."

"Well, then, what is to be done?—return upon our footsteps?"

"Never. Ezekiel Belknap don't craw fish arter that sort, no way you can fix it. I calkerlate we can reach that are boat afore the '*posse-come-il-at-us.*'"

"They are mounted while we are on foot."

"But they've got twice as far tew go as us. So come on."

They ran with all speed towards the dock where the Mountain Maid was trembling with the respiration of her steam. Their flight was witnessed by Riley and his party, who urged their horses to their utmost speed. The fugitives were in the centre of the little village which surrounds the outlet; the sheriff and his band were upon its borders. The steam-boat was in the act of leaving the wharf. At this critical moment Kane stumbled and fell. In the effort to save Frank Tot from injury, he wrenched his arm violently. The sailor did not pause in his flight, but leaping upon the boat, he addressed a few earnest words to the captain, and, leaving Dolly in his charge, bounded upon the shore again. The escape of Kane now seemed hopeless. He ran since his fall with far less speed than before, while the horsemen were dashing rapidly through the village. The sailor was by his side.

"Give me the boy. Neow, if you place any valley upon liberty, buckle to it!"

The savage laugh of Riley was heard. It gave Kane fresh strength. He bounded forward; and as the steam-boat was leaving the dock, both Kane and the sailor leaped on board.

"Stop the boat! stop the boat!" shouted the sheriff. "I command you in the queen's name." The cry was echoed by Riley;

but the Mountain Maid moved rapidly from the shore. *They were free!*

It was a lovely morning; not a cloud could be seen along the vast expanse of azure; not a breath of air ruffled the glossy bosom of the beautiful lake; for a beautiful lake it is, the enchanting Memphremagog! Poets have written of Loch Lomond and of Como, but no lovelier expanse of water can be seen on the surface of this earth than the romantic and beautiful Memphremagog.

The Mountain Maid stopped a few moments at the base of the "Owl's Head," whose frowning summit is now often visited by the tourist. As the boat was passing an island in the middle of the lake, Ezekiel Belknap said,

"Neow, Mr. Kane, dew yeow see any particular difference between the tew ends of that are island?"

"No; except some few inequalities."

"One looks as fair as t'other, don't it?"

"Precisely."

"Wall, one end is in her majesty's province, and t'other is in the state of Vermont."

Kane was speechless.

"Yes, yeow are in Canada neow. Neow, yeow are in Vermont. Your hand; welcome—welcome tew the

'Land of the free and the home of the brave.'"

Robert Kane fell upon his knees, and, with uplifted eyes, returned thanks to Heaven for his escape.

The farms upon the shore of the lake presented a lovelier appearance; the rays of the sun shone more brightly: and the mountain summits were shaded with a softer and more dream-like atmosphere than he had ever seen before.

As the boat landed at the dock in Newport, he sprang upon the shore, and pressed his lips upon the soil of freedom.

"Thank Heaven, we are at last free! One half my dear family have been murdered by the bloody laws and government of England, yet I am thankful that two dear children are spared to me. Happy country! henceforth you shall be my home; and, protected by your constitution, I will try and win that peace which was denied me in my own land."

CHAPTER XXV.

"Flag of the free heart's hope and home!
By angel hands to valor given:
The stars have lit the welkin dome,
And all thy hues were born in heaven.
Forever float that standard sheet!
Where breathes the foe but falls before us,
With Freedom's soil beneath our feet,
And Freedom's banner streaming o'er us."
DRAKE.

SIX years have elapsed since the events occurred which were narrated in the last chapter. In a comfortable dwelling, situated on the border of a prairie, sheltered by a grove, and overlooking Michigan, the most lovely of the western lakes, sat two children, one ten and the other seven years of age. The oldest had apparently been reading the Bible, for it still lay open on her lap. An expression of happiness was visible upon her features, while the boy looked thoughtful and troubled.

"I have read these commandments so often to you Frank, that you ought to know them by heart."

"I do," he replied, shortly.

"Then why, my dear brother, don't you obey them?"

"Cause other boys swear, and fight, and steal birds' eggs, and why shoulddent I?"

"Because it is wicked, Frank; and you have no right to act wickedly if all the boys in the United States should. Now, Frank, do you think father loves you?"

"Oh yes, that I do."

"Is he kind to you?"

"That he is."

"Would you do anything to offend him?"

"Not if I was to die first."

"Well, your heavenly father created you, he watches over you, loves you better, even, than your earthly father does, for he sent his own son, whom he loved better than you do me and father both, to die that you might be saved. Now, Frank, when he has done so much for you, and is yet watching over you, and keeping you from sickness and danger, do you think it is *generous* to offend and grieve him?"

"No, I'll be damned—Oh! Dolly, I didn't mean to say that."

"Frank, I am afraid you are a very thoughtless, wicked boy," said Dolly, as a tear stole down her cheek.

"Dolly, dear Dolly, don't say that. I'm thoughtless, but I ain't wicked, for I love everybody—except—except Jim Lee, who licked me last week. I can't love him until I lick him back, and then I will."

"But you don't love everything, Frank, for you rob birds' nests."

"Do you think that is wrong, Dolly?"

"Certainly it is; and it is very sinful to throw stones at frogs, as you were doing last spring. You have no right to make dumb things suffer unnecessarily. They were created by God, as well as ourselves, and are entitled to protection against cruelty. It is just as sinful, Frank, to torture a dumb beast, as it is a human being, and I think, *more* so, because the flesh of both can feel pain, while one can proclaim its wrongs, aud the other cannot."

"I won't hurt dumb animals any more, Dolly, indeed I won't; only if you'll just let me give Jim Lee one good licking, to pay off old scores."

"No, Frank, it is very sinful to fight and quarrel; your heavenly Father will be offended with you, if you do so."

"But you read in the bible the other day where he commanded the Israelites, I believe it was, to make war upon their neighbors, and kill and capture them, and burn their cities."

"That was in the old testament, Frank."

"But izzent he an unchangeable God?"

"Yes."

"Well, would he tell the Israelites, to do anything sinful in the old testament."

Dolly was puzzled a moment, and then she said—

"I suppose he told them to punish his enemies because they were so wicked."

"They couldn't a been wickeder than Jim Lee, and I reckon God would like it if I should rout him and put him to the sword, just like the Israelites did."

"Frank! Frank! how unhappy you make me," said Dolly, weeping bitterly. "I have done all I could to make you a good boy. I've prayed twenty times a day to God to give me knowledge; for, Frank, you have got no mother to watch over you. I feel such a weight *here*, when I think of my responsibility, for that was what the minister called it," and the little girl pressed her hand upon her heart. "I fear I am but a poor weak child myself, for I can't make any impression on him. Would that poor dear mother had lived," and she wept more bitterly.

"Don't cry, pray don't cry, dear Dolly. I can't bear to see you. I will do any thing for you, if you will *only* just not cry. There, that is a good girl. Now I am happy, for I won't vex you any more. Now, Dolly, tell me more about my mother."

"Frank, she was the kindest and most affectionate mother ever was; and she was so fond of you! She petted you morning, noon, and night. And poor *dear* Henry! She loved him *so* well, too: and me, too. We were all her favorites."

"You never told me what made her die, Dolly."

"Because I can never bear to think of it," said the child, wiping her eyes with her apron.

"But do tell me now, Dolly! I should so like to know."

With a powerful effort, and with a voice broken with sobs, Dolly said:

"We were all turned into the street one cold night, and mother froze to death."

For some moments Frank tried to think whether he understood her.

"Froze to death! Did you say *froze* to death, Dolly?"

"Yes."

"Was she so cold that her hands, and feet, and arms, and face, were hard—hard as ice? Don't say that for *pity* sake!" he said, imploringly.

"Yes, Frank, it is true," said the weeping girl.

"Who turned her into the street?" he inquired, as he doubled up his hand.

"The landlord."

"And did the government let him do so?"

"Yes, and a great many worse things than that."

"Where was my father, then?"

"He had been knocked down, and taken on board a ship, to fight for the government that suffered his wife to die in the street!"

Frank paused a few moments, and then he said, as if his mind was unalterably made up—

"Dolly, I hate the government of England worse than I do Jim Lee, and if I can get an opportunity, I will fight the British to the last moment of my life—*that* I will."

"It is thus that England makes irreconcilable foes," said Robert Kane, pointing to the form of his son.

"And it is thus that Ameriky knows how tew reward good citizens," replied Ezekiel Belknap.

"How so, my worthy friend?"

"You've been elected a member of the legislature, by a large majority. I calkerlate that would go agin the grain of them buggers who thought you wa'nt good enough to black their boots, in the old country."

"I am grateful to my fellow citizens for their partiality, and I hope my acts will not disappoint them."

"It would be difficult to dew so, for your principles were well known afore the election. My stars and garters! What a change has come over yeou since I fust kneouwed yeou, Robert Kane. Then yeou were a poor fugitive, a tryin' to escape from persecution; now, the owner of a fine farm, a comfortable house, and a member elect tew the legislature. Darn it, heouw much better off you are than me."

"But what I have you shall always enjoy, Ezekiel. I am too much indebted to you ever to be ungrateful. You have now been here a year, and you are happy, ain't you?"

"Very. Ony sometimes I long for the sea agin. I should spile altogether if it wan't for this lake, which kinder satisfies the "cravins of the spirit," as Parson Remsen says. And when I see you so well tew dew in the world, I'm content tew stay here awhile longer."

"I hope you may never leave me. I have enough for all of us, and I don't know what Frank would do, if he did not have you to learn him how to sail his little ship."

"You mussent leave us, Mr. Belknap," said Frank; "for I want you to learn me how to be a sailor, so I can fight the British, when there's another war. I want to revenge the death of my poor mother, and the wrongs of my father."

"How her loss weighs upon us all. Hard fate! Incurable injury! With Mary and Henry, I should have nothing to wish for," said Kane, sadly.

"Wall neow that are is a figger for a scare-crow, any way yeou can fix it," said Ezekiel Belknap, pointing to a man who was approaching the house from the road.

It was the figure of a person still young, but so emaciated! His countenance was pale and haggard, and upon every lineament was written suffering and disappointment. His dress was ragged and filthy, and altogether he verified the fidelity of Ezekiel's comparison.

Robert Kane courteously invited him to enter the house; but he had no sooner crossed its threshold, than Kane started back. His glance was rivetted upon the countenance of the stranger, while his features alternately assumed an expression of severity and compassion.

"Lord Melville! Can it be possible that Lord Melville stands before me?"

"If it is, there must be a new paytent of nobility," said Ezekiel Belknap; "for I never seed sich a figger as that anywhere but in a cornfield."

"You see before you one who thought himself Lord Melville, but who was not," replied the stranger, in a hollow voice.

"And who are you, then?"

"Your brother."

"My brother? And who was he whom we all thought Christie Kane?"

"Lord Melville."

"Brother in misfortune, as well as by blood, you are welcome," said Robert Kane, as he embraced him.

"I do not deserve this kindness," replied Christie Kane, as he wiped the tears from his eyes; those tears, the first he had shed since childhood.

"Why not, my brother?"

"Have you forgotten my brutal conduct the night you were in the hands of the press-gang?"

"Oh never think of that; it is all forgiven."

"But I cannot forget it. I have tried, but it is ineffaceably impressed upon my mind. I have wandered over the United States to find you, for I heard of your escape. Miserably clad, often nearly starved, I wandered on in hopes of meeting you at last that I might have the privilege of asking your forgiveness before I died. And whenever my heart failed me, and I was ready to despair, I thought of your bleeding face and stiffened form, and as I beheld them that night, and then I pressed onward once more. And now I have found you ; can you forgive—?"

"All! everything is forgiven, dear brother," said Robert, throwing his arms around his neck.

"Then for the first time in six years, I am happy—*so* happy," said Christie Kane, as he sunk upon a sofa.

"But you are hungry, Christie, I am sure, for you look so pale."

"I have eaten nothing for twenty-four hours, and I have walked since yesterday morning fifty miles."

"Why did you not eat? Thereis not a house within fifty miles of this place that a hungry person could not have obtained food."

"I know it; but I could not eat. I ascertained yesterday morning that you resided here, and I thought of nothing but of seeing you."

"Poor uncle," said Dolly, as she ran to the kitchen, to tell the housekeeper to set the table instantly, for her uncle was *very* hungry.

"And now your wanderings are over, for you will always remain with us."

"This is indeed a lovely spot, and one calculated to make me forget what I have lost, if anything could," replied Christie Kane, despondingly.

"Your loss is comparatively trifling, my dear brother," replied Robert Kane. "You have lost wealth, but what is that, compared to the healthful mind and frame of the man who complies with the eternal decree, to earn his bread by the sweat of his brow? You are removed from the circle where dissipation corrupts the young and prostrates the old, but you will gain the sweet rest of contentment and peace. You have lost rank, but sti'l there is within your grasp that inestimable jewel, in the presence of which pales the unsubstantial privileges of created rank—the patent of nobility upon which nature affixes its seal, and which, guarded by honor, bears the indestructible stamp of divine approbation."

THE END.

www.ingramcontent.com/pod-product-compliance
Lightning Source LLC
LaVergne TN
LVHW010241110826
845151LV00004B/1352